# Soulmates

by

## Nadine Nightingale

*Drag.Me.To.Hell. Series, Book Two*

**Soulmates**

Cover Art by *Debbie Taylor*

The Wild Rose Press, Inc.
PO Box 708
Adams Basin, NY 14410-0708
Visit us at www.thewildrosepress.com

Publishing History
First Black Rose Edition, 2017
Print ISBN 978-1-5092-1352-8
Digital ISBN 978-1-5092-1353-5

*Drag.Me.To.Hell. Series, Book Two*
Published in the United States of America

**When I wake up, I don't smell coffee,**
scrambled eggs, or bacon. I inhale the unmistakable
scent of regret. I want to stay in bed, keep my eyes
closed, and forget last night ever happened. I learned a
long time ago to face my mistakes. To never run from
what I did, 'cause at some point—when you least
expect it—shit comes back, biting you in the ass. It's
better to deal with whatever crap you've produced
*before* it turns into karma.

I slowly blink my eyes open. The space next to me
is empty. Alex sits at the small kitchen table, nose
buried in the files he got from JJ. "Morning," he says as
I throw the blankets away and sit up. "Sleep well?"

"Yeah," I murmur, totally aware he's staring at my
back. "You?"

Alex's footsteps echo through the room. Moments
later, he presses his full lips against my alerted skin.
"Better than in a very long time."

He trails kisses down my neck. My heart skips
several beats. Geez, what's with him? Shouldn't he be
all what-the-fuck-did-I-do, rather than can-we-pick-up-
where-we-left-off?

I lean down and grab my clothes from the floor.
The ones I can find. "I need a shower," I choke out,
walking to the bathroom.

## Praise for Nadine Nightingale's *Karma*, Book One of the Drag.Me.To.Hell. Series

"*KARMA* is probably my favorite paranormal book that I have reviewed in a very long time."

*~SBR Blogs*

~*~

"Nadine Nightingale has nailed this one dead on with pure entertainment, action and attitude throughout!"

*~Tome Tender Book Blog*

~*~

"This is the first book in the Drag. Me. To. Hell. Series and I was blown away by how much I freaking loved this book!"

*~Reviews From The Heart*

~*~

"*KARMA* is a fun, exciting, and phenomenal story that I can't get enough of! I definitely can't wait until the next installment."

*~Bookalicious Babes Blog*

## Dedication

Mom, you're the toughest woman I know.
When I grow up, I want to be just like you.
Love you to the moon and back.

"Love is composed of a single soul inhabiting two bodies."

~*Aristotle*

## Chapter 1

Jerking my eyes open, I'm blinded by the bright sunlight creeping through my chiffon curtains. "Knockin' on Heaven's Door," Alex's favorite Guns N' Roses song, blares through the speakers of my digital radio alarm clock. *Awesome.* As if jerk-face haunting me in my dreams isn't bad enough. The universe seems to give a shit about the deal I'd made with my ex-lover. Or why else would it torture me with those fucking nightmares?

"You're such a slut!" Chelsea, aka the Nun, aka roommate from church-hell, yells from the living room. The walls of our three-bedroom apartment at Green House are too fucking thin.

"Oh yeah? And what are you, Jesus with boobs?" Bonnie, my best and only friend, barks.

Pressing a pillow over my head, I try to block their voices out. This isn't how I pictured my new life at NYU, and it sure as hell isn't what I had in mind when I'd given up my old, carefree life as a witch. I'm so over their senseless fights. They've been living together for a while now. They still can't ignore each other. Granted, it's hard to turn a blind eye to the Nun. If she isn't demonstrating against abortion, or writing a blog post about Evil Women Who Scream Rape When They Practically Asked For It Because They Wore A Too-Short Skirt, she's determined to make Bonnie's life a

1

living hell.

"That's blasphemy, Bonnie!"

"Sue me." The fighting continues.

*That's it! I'm going to kill 'em.* With a headache from hell and still half asleep, I stumble to my door and yank it open. They're standing in the common room, which consists of an open kitchen and a small living room. "Shut up! Both of you!"

Bonnie's eyes almost pop out. "Did you hear what she just said?" She sounds offended.

"The whole freakin' floor heard you guys," I snap.

They shoot daggers at me. I don't care. Running a hand through my disheveled hair, I walk to the fresh brewed coffee and pour some into a dirty cup. Why can't these girls wash up?

Chelsea glares at me with an I'm-so-much-better-than-you expression, rolls her eyes, and heads to her room. The girl knows what's good for her. Have to give her that much.

"I want her out!"

*Jesus!* "And I want you to stop yelling, Bonnie. I'm not deaf."

She lowers her voice. "I'm serious. I can't live with her."

*You don't say?* I take a drink of the black gold and pull myself onto the kitchen counter. "We've already tried to get rid of her, remember? But like it or not, all residence halls are full."

Bonnie puts a hand on her hip. It's paradoxical. Usually, I'm the one with temper issues. Lately, I couldn't care less about bitch fights. "Did you have a good night?" I ask, trying to take her mind off the Nun.Bonnie's pained expression fades, and she flashes me a bright smile. "I had a date with Cappuccino Guy. He was…" She pauses. "Wow. Just wow. I can totally set you up with one of his buddies. Just say the word."

I knit my brows. "Nah. If I need a date doctor, I'll call *Hitch*." Downing the rest of the coffee, I get on my feet. "I need a shower."

Bonnie throws her cute curls over her shoulder. Her shiny cognac eyes fill with concern. "Did you have another nightmare?"

I lean my hip against the counter and close my eyes. The vicious dream pushes through my subconscious. The images are so fucking vivid, it's as if I'm still trapped in it.

****

*The wind rattled the leaves of the massive trees as plants wove around my ankles like poisonous snakes. I looked up. The sky closed in on me. Black wings beat the chilly air. Ravens owned the firmament. Hundreds of them blocked the faint light from the crescent moon.*

*Quickening my pace, I reached an old, savaged cemetery. My pulse jackknifed in my neck as I stared at an inverted cross leaning against the king-sized iron gates. I moved closer and read the inscription carved into the black wood:* Lasciate ogne speranza, voi ch'intrate. *My Italian was rusty, but I knew Dante by heart. "Abandon all hope, ye who enter here." With a jarring sound, the gates opened.*

Don't do this.

*Too late. It felt as if a magnetic pull lured me into the cemetery. I passed through the gates of hell.*

*Ravens perched on crooked gravestones, throwing spooky shadows on the burned grass. The tang of sulfur engulfed me, stinging my nostrils.*

*This was insane.* Turn the fuck around and walk away.

*Every cell in my body wanted to listen to the voice in my head. I couldn't. The place had me under its spell.*

"Amanda!"

*Bonnie? I turned, trying to locate her.*

"Amanda."

*Hysteria tinged my voice.* "Bonnie, where the fuck are you?" *Desperate, I faced one of the ravens.* "Where is she?"

*The bird's charcoal eyes pierced me. Then it spread its wings and flew toward a shabby mausoleum. A single black candle burned on the steps. There it was again, the magnetic pull. In a trance-like state, I stumbled toward the old tomb and the door swung open.*

"In here." *Bonnie's honey-colored skin was wrapped in a white toga. She looked like a Greek goddess, but her beautiful cognac eyes were white and empty.*

*I blinked.* "What the hell is going on?"

*A crooked smile on her lips, she yanked the door open farther.* "Come and see for yourself."

"What the—" *Peeking over her shoulder, words stuck in my throat. My heart stopped.* "Alex?" *He laid on a mortuary table.*

*Was he—*

*No! I tried to push past my best friend, but inhuman and terrifying laughter pulsated through the eerie night.*

"He's gone, Amanda," *a dark voice whispered.*

*An ocean of black feathers covered the ground.*

4

*Ravens croaked in agony as a shadowy figure in a dark cloak crushed them with its boots.*

*Dread infected my system and I had trouble breathing. I wanted to run, but the black feathers turned into rattling snakes. The creatures hissed, and I knew they'd attack if I made a wrong move. "W-who the hell are you?"*

*The demon laughed. "Ah, love. 'What is in a name?'" The snakes crawled left and right, opening a path for the cloaked creature. "'That which we call a rose by any other word would smell as sweet,'" the black shadow said, advancing toward me.*

*I should have been shocked by the fact a demon quoted Shakespeare, but my gaze drifted back to Alex. "What did you do to him?"*

*The shadow figure stopped inches in front of me and ran its blazing hand over my cheeks. "All in good time, love." Then Bonnie slammed the mausoleum door shut, trapping Alex's lifeless body inside.*

\*\*\*\*

"Amanda?" Bonnie's voice draws me back to the present. "Did you have another nightmare?"

I run an index finger over the dark circles beneath my eyes and nod. "They're getting worse."

"Worse how?"

I trace the scar Walter's bullet left on my chest, not sure how to describe the uncanny feeling. "They're way too real. I've slept eight hours, yet I feel like I was up all night, running a triathlon."

Bonnie grabs the coffee pot and pours me another cup. "Did you call Alex?"

Did Cappuccino Guy screw her brains out? Alex, aka jerk-face, is the last person I'd give a buzz. Twenty-one months ago, hunter-heroic barged into my life and made me believe we had a chance at happiness. For the first time, I indulged in the fantasy love wasn't just an illusion. When the witch hunter learned I was his favorite kind of prey, things turned ugly fast. He threatened to kill me, and if it wasn't for his brother Jesse, he would have gone through with his threat. Then, three months ago, he walked back in my life with a proposal I couldn't pass up. His brother had gone missing, and if I helped him, he would never bother me again. We found Jesse and saved a bunch of kids abducted by a bokor and his pedophile asshole friend, Walter. Alex honored his promise and didn't contact me again.

"Why would I call him? Jesse is safe, I paid my dues, and he hasn't bothered me again. Everything is perfect."

Bonnie arches a brow. "You don't look so perfect, Amanda."

"Really?" I grin, or at least I try. "I thought I totally rocked this American Apparel underwear."

"Amanda." She folds her hands over my shoulders. "We both know he isn't just any guy. He's the f—"

Anger rises through me like toxic smoke. "Don't you dare," I warn her. "You promised you'd never bring this up."

She plays with a strand of her rebellious curls. "I'm sorry. It's just... I'm worried. Ever since you went on that stupid road trip, you don't date, don't screw." She draws a deep breath. "Fuck. You don't even live."

I'm so not up for this conversation. I put the cup in the sink and stalk to our tiny bathroom next to my room. "Don't wait on me," I hiss, slamming the door shut.

"You're such a bitch," she barks.

I couldn't agree more.

**\*\*\*\***

Working the dayshift at Lindy's Diner, I refill the sticky sugar bowls. It's been three months since I said goodbye to my past. Two months without reading cards. One month of respectable work as a waitress, and two fucking weeks of nightmares. Goddammit, I feel like a freaking member of AA.

"Amanda!" Lindy calls from the kitchen.

Hands shaking, head thumping, I put the sugar down and turn around. "Yeah?"

Deep lines on her forehead, she raises a brow at me. "New customer. Table two."

God, I miss my old life. I straighten my apron and grab a menu. Approaching table two with a half-hearted smile, I put the menu down. "Welcome to Lindy's Diner." I point to my tag. "My name is Amanda. What can I get ya?" The sentence is branded into my brain. You wanted this, I remind myself. Yeah, but back then I hadn't known a normal life was equivalent with becoming suicidal.

"What would you suggest?" my new customer asks. He's about twenty-five, wears a fancy black suit and expensive leather shoes. Not exactly a typical Lindy's Diner customer.

I pull the pen out of my ponytail and reach for my notepad. "Pancakes are nice. Apple pie is great. Everything else pretty much sucks." Joe, our Italian chef, is freakin' amazing, but Lindy likes to keep her costs low. Even Joe can't turn shit into gold.

The dude leans back, and his lips curve up at the

corners. "Pancakes and pie it is, then."

I jot down his order and walk to the kitchen. After handing the paper to Joe, I nibble on cookies until my phone vibrates in the back pocket of my jeans. Peeking through the kitchen door, I check if Lindy is nearby before pulling it out.

Bonnie's name flickers across the screen. I hadn't expected to hear from her after our little argument that morning, but the girl doesn't just love me at my best. She also accepts me at my worst. And in the last couple of weeks, I've been nothing but at my worst.

*Still mad?* she texted.

*Maybe*, I sent back, not ready to let her off the hook so easily.

*Suck it up. Double-date tonight nine. Dress up, he's hot!*

Has she lost her mind? I look like one of the zombie strippers. Hot on the outside, rotten and dead within. *No!*

*Yes!*

Bonnie had made up her mind, and the girl is like a pit bull when she wants something. I'm bound to lose a WhatsApp argument with her, so I decide to talk her out of it later. *We'll see.*

*See you in Penrose's class?*

*Yes.* I hit the send button and put the phone away before Lindy catches me texting.

I return to the counter and see the guy with the fancy leather shoes holding up his cup. "Table two," Lindy snaps.

"I'm not blind."

"Then move your lazy ass. The coffee ain't serving itself."

Grabbing the pot, I stalk toward him. "Anything else?" I ask, filling his cup. I don't mean to sound like a bitch, but I just can't help it.

He studies me with big, arctic-blue eyes. There's something about them that gives me the creeps. I just can't put my finger on what it is. I try to read his aura, but the colors are blurred. I haven't had a clear reading since the damn nightmares started. I've tried, God knows I have, but it's like I'm constantly glaring at a fucking rainbow. What good is it to be a witch if you can't use your gifts?

"I'm Legend, by the way."

*Sure, and I'm Jada Pinkett Smith.*

"Would you, maybe, care to join me?" He sounds casual, not pushy.

"Sorry. Can't," I grumble.

He holds my gaze. Chills ripple through me.

Oh no. Not here. Not now.

\*\*\*\*

*The way too familiar scent of rusty iron and death hung in the air as Legend stood in the living room of the comfy family home. He'd been told by the first responding officers the scene was barbaric, but the word couldn't adequately describe what he saw. Vicious crimson stains covered the walls, part of a liver lay on a white leather sofa, and a bloody hand print decorated the large flat-screen TV.*

*Legend drew a deep breath and focused on the disfigured corpse. The weird symbol carved into his head bugged Legend a lot. Four people slaughtered, and all wearing the same mark.*

*"Sir," a young officer said to him. "The coroner is here."*

*"Give me a sec," he ordered, scanning the crime scene. No sign of forced entry, no murder weapon, and he'd bet his ass there'd be no DNA or fingerprints.*

*The young officer glared at the corpse. His face slightly green, he looked sick to his stomach. "What animal would do something like that?"*

*Animal was the keyword. The rib cage of the poor bastard was torn into pieces, most of his organs removed, the body had been twisted in an unnatural way, and the victim's face unrecognizable. "I don't know," Legend said. "But whatever killed him won't stop."*

*"Whatever? You mean whoever, right?"*

*Legend pulled a pack of cigarettes out of his jacket and went to the door. "No. I meant whatever."*

****

My knees are like jelly as the sickening vision fades. The symbol carved into the man's head had been a sigil. In other words, a demon's calling card. Every demon has its own. But this one, I had seen before. It had been carved into the chest of Mister Sinister, the guy who'd attacked me in an alley. The dude Alex thought I'd iced.

"Are you all right?" Legend sounds genuinely concerned.

My hands tremble. "Just a little dizzy."

He loosens the collar of his shirt. A weird tattoo crawls over his neck. Looks like some sort of symbol. "Sure you don't want to join me, Amanda?"

Before I can answer, Lindy shouts, "Amanda!"

For once, I'm glad my boss is a freaking tyrant. "Sorry. Gotta go."

Chapter 2

I'm late. Again. It's quarter past four when I sprint up the stairs to Professor Penrose's philosophy class. I used to be reliable, but between the diner, my busy class schedule, and the goddamn nightmares, I had to scratch punctuality from my resume. Damn, how I miss the good old days. Sleeping till noon, reading cards till midnight, and partying with the owls—all a distant memory.

*Told ya normal is overrated.* I should have listened to the censorious voice in my head.

Loaded with a stack of books and coffee, I barge through the door of the packed auditorium, searching for Bonnie. Easy peasy. The girl is an eye-catcher. Her tight, ivory lace shirt accentuates warm honey-colored skin. Mesmerizing curls cascade down her back, almost reaching her butt, and her charisma lights up the auditorium like a Fourth of July firework. She's playing with a pen, pretending to listen to Penrose. The girl hates philosophy, but today, of all days, she chose a spot in the freaking front row.

I proceed down the stairs. Like the mess I am, I trip over my own feet, spill my triple-shot espresso in the process, and burn my goddamn hand. "Fuck!"

Heads turn and whispers echo round the room. Great. Now I'm not just late but also the center of attention. *Gotta love being a student.*

"The girl is unbelievable," Little Miss Sunshine, next to me, says to her pearl-necklace-wearing BFF.

Bitch and Bitchier, as I like to call them, are both friends of Chelsea. They've hung out at the diner a couple of times, glaring at me as if I bathed in virgin blood in my free time.

"What do you expect from a devil worshipper?" Bitchier asks quietly.

I'm no stranger to the rumors my lovely, catholic roommate spread after she'd seen my tarot cards. Yet it blows my mind that in the twenty-first century, reading cards is still associated with Satanism.

Bitch shifts closer to her friend and grins. "I bet it's why she gets good grades all the time."

"Must be," Bitchier says. "Look at her. She doesn't exactly scream intelligence. Slut? Yeah. Einstein? Not so much." They both giggle.

I can live with a label like slut, but insulting my intelligence never ends well. Wiping my coffee-soaked hand on my jeans, I face the stupid-ass bitches and smile. "You've got it all wrong. I don't get good grades because I'm tight with Lucifer. I get 'em 'cause I screw the profs." I give their virtuous clothes a lingering once-over. "You should try it sometime. Sex, I mean. It could pull those sticks out of your asses."

The looks on their faces are priceless, but my little stunt attracted a far greater evil. "Ah, Miss Bishop," Professor Penrose says. His Welsh accent is thick. "It's nice you finally grace us with your presence." He's the most popular professor on campus, but the Welshman, as he refers to himself, still holds a grudge against me for calling him a Brit.

*I gotta learn to keep my goddamn mouth shut.* In

another life. Maybe.

Securing my books under my arm, I beam at the lean giant. "What can I say? The best always comes last." "She's got a point," second-row, Yankee-baseball-cap dude says, loud enough for the whole auditorium to hear. The idiot gives me a creepy stare right under Penrose's nose.

Penrose shoots him a narrow-eyed look. "Is there anything you would like to share with us, Mr. DeLuca?"

He grins from ear to ear and turns his baseball cap around. "Nope."

"Good," Penrose utters, focusing on his notes. "Then let's—"

"But plenty I'd like to share with her."

The students burst into laughter, and DeLuca and his DUFF (Designated Ugly Fat Friend) fist-bump each other like stupid teenagers.

Did the state declare this the Piss Amanda Bishop Off holiday, or am I just surrounded by morons?

Penrose's mouth slips into a frown. "Ms. Bishop, I think you should take a seat before Mr. DeLuca loses his last ounce of dignity."

The other students laugh harder, but DeLuca blushes and shuts up. *Well done, Welshman.* I begin to understand why students adore him.

A grateful smile on my lips, I move down the aisle to the front row and fling myself into the empty seat next to Bonnie. "Where the hell have you been?" she whispers while Penrose tries to calm down his audience. "I texted you twice."

I yank the MacBook out of my bag. "What do you think?"

She cuts her eyes to me. "Lindy?"

Turning my laptop on, I nod. "Bitch hates me, B." Lindy hates everyone, but for some reason, I occupy a special place in her black heart.

Bonnie raises her thick brows. "Just quit the damn job already. You know my mom's offer still stands."

Bonnie's mom isn't just one helluva mambo, she's also richer than Richie Rich. The second she heard I went straight, she offered to pay my tuition and whatever else I needed. No way in hell I'd accept money from her or anyone else for that matter. "Drop it, B. I wanted a normal life. Last time I checked, having a fuckin' job was part of the deal."

"Maybe, but being bullied isn't," she snaps, raising her voice.

Penrose shoots us a warning glance. "I would certainly appreciate if we could focus on what's really important—"

"The Giants game on Saturday?" George, the wannabe quarterback, asks. The guy lives in Green House, like we do, and is the definition of a jock—good looks, no brain.

"No, Mr. Blackwell. I was talking about souls." Penrose sounds annoyed.

George straightens his team jacket. "That's hardly more important than the game."

I doubt there's anything more important to George.

"I believe Dr. Duncan MacDougall would disagree," Penrose objects. Facing the rest of the bored students, he clears his throat. "Can anyone tell me what Dr. MacDougall's take on the human soul was?"

Most students hang their heads. Bonnie ignores Penrose and shifts closer. "About tonight," she says, excitement gleaming in her eyes. "I was thinking The Bitter End. Sound good?"

Nothing sounds good when it's paired with the words: double, blind, and date. "Look, B, I know you're trying to cheer me up, but—"

"Ms. Bishop." Penrose's voice is sharp, his eyes narrowed to two slits.

I keep my gaze glued to the laptop screen. "Yes?"

"You seem to know an awful lot about MacDougall's take on human souls. Why don't you share your knowledge with the rest of us?"

*Thanks, B.*

Reluctantly, I meet Penrose's gaze. "The guy spent most of his life trying to prove souls exist."

Fiddling with his gold Oxford cufflinks, he smiles with approval. "Excellent, Ms. Bishop." His gaze shifts to the other students. "Dr. MacDougall's determination on the subject became legendary." He pushes a button on his laptop, projecting a slide on the wall. It's an old newspaper article that reads: *Soul Has Weight, Physician Thinks.* "In 1901, MacDougall initiated an experiment in which he weighed six patients while they were dying from tuberculosis."

"The whole thing was a hoax," DeLuca mutters behind me.

Bonnie nudges me in the ribs. "He's your date."

I stare at her. "Penrose?"

Bonnie laughs. "No, dumbass. *DeLuca.*"

My jaw drops, and I forget we're in the middle of a freaking philosophy class. "Are you fuckin' crazy?"

Penrose pulls one side of his mouth up. "I take it by your choice of language, you don't agree with Mr. DeLuca, Ms. Bishop?"

More like his existence doesn't agree with me, but let's not split hairs. I give Bonnie my best death glare and clear my throat. "No, Professor Penrose, I don't. As far as I know, MacDougall was able to measure the souls of four patients."

A twinkle in his eyes, he nods. "Correct. Four of his patients had lost three-fourths of an ounce."

"Doesn't prove a thing," Blind Date from Hell barks. "He had six patients, not four. It's hardly scientific proof he delivered." His arrogance annoys the hell outta me.

"Hot and smart," Bonnie says to justify her choice.

I pay no attention to her. The only other option would result in a blood bath and prove the rumors I'm the incarnation of serial killer Elizabeth Báthory true.

Professor Penrose stretches his lean frame and moves toward his desk. "It pains me greatly to admit Mr. DeLuca has a point. Scientifically speaking, MacDougall's experiment failed." He pauses a moment to adjust his glasses before addressing the class again. "We're not here to discuss success or failure, though. Instead, we will focus on the reasons behind MacDougall's obsession." He changes the slide to a painting of a dying man whose soul levitates above him. "Why would an educated man like MacDougall risk his reputation to prove humans are more than just cells?"

I half expect Bitch and Bitchier to recite every paragraph of the Bible addressing souls, but they keep as quiet as the rest of us.

Frustration seeps into Penrose's features. "No one?"

Silence.

His eyes find mine. "Ms. Bishop." Everyone looks at me. "Since you seem somewhat of an expert on the subject, would you tell us if you believe in the existence of a soul?"

"Yes," I murmur. "I believe souls exist." *Because when I don't suffer from demonic nightmares, I happen to be able to read 'em.*

DeLuca's laughter rings in my ears. "Sure." He fights for composure. "And Earth is the center of the universe, right?"

I want to strangle the idiot, cut the arrogant smile right out of his face, but there'd be too many witnesses. So I keep my gaze on Penrose, who's obviously amused, instead. If DeLuca wants to throw curve balls, I'm game. "Exactly my point," I say matter-of-factly.

"Please tell me you're not serious."

I rotate a hundred and eighty degrees and face the arrogant idiot. "Six hundred years ago, humanity threw a fit when scientists suggested the sun was the center of the universe. Hell, it resulted in full-blown riots. Yet, there were men like Galileo trying to prove the unthinkable."

DeLuca cocks a brow. "Yeah, and Galileo was right, wasn't he?"

I hoped he'd say that. "He was. But that didn't stop people from declaring him crazy or putting him on trial for heresy, did it?"

DeLuca leans forward, and for a moment I wonder if he's going to jump at my throat. "You can't compare Galileo to MacDougall."

"Oh, really? Well, let's see. Both educated? Check. Scientists? Check. Opposing other scientists? Check. Trying to prove the unthinkable? Double check."

DeLuca takes his cap off and runs a hand through his golden fringe. "Still not the same."

"Why?" Penrose interjects, reminding me we're still in the auditorium.

DeLuca purses his lips and gives Penrose the what-kind-of-a-question-is-that look. "For starters, souls are invisible."

"So is the air you breathe," I counter. "Just because *you* can't see it, doesn't mean it's not there."

"You're right." DeLuca's lips curve into a mischievous grin. "But air isn't something the church invented to scare the crap out of people. I mean, this whole soul idea comes with baggage. Think heaven and hell, sin and morality."

I see where the idiot is coming from. But just because some assholes use the concept of the soul to force a certain kind of behavior on humanity, doesn't mean the idea itself is wrong.

"Speechless?" he asks.

I gaze into his big amber eyes and sigh. "Wanna know what your problem is?"

He shifts to the edge of his seat. Curiosity flickers across his handsome face. "Please, do tell."

"You think of a soul as something supernatural or divine. But what if it's really just the energy that keeps us together? Our life essence."

"Life essence?" He laughs. "Do you listen to yourself, sugar? Next thing you're going to tell me is aliens walk among us, and vampires glitter in the sun."

I swallow laughter and give him a look. "A word of advice?"

"I'm all ears."

"You should cut back on the paranormal romance

books. They're obviously messing with your head."

The whole auditorium bursts into laughter. Even DeLuca's DUFF can't keep a straight face.

"Amanda." Bonnie pinches my arm so hard, I bet it'll bruise.

Penrose looks from DeLuca to me. "Apart from the reference to Mr. DeLuca's taste in books, you made a few valid points, Ms. Bishop. It's a real shame the lecture is drawing to a close." He faces his other students. "I'm looking forward to next week. Have a good day, ladies and gentleman. And remember," he says as the first students leave. "Don't do anything you can't justify through rational argument."

*Like going on a date with DeLuca?* No shit.

I shove the MacBook in my bag, and Bonnie slams her book onto my table. "Why do you have to be such a bitch all the time?"

I throw my backpack over my shoulder and grin. "Because it's in my fuckin' nature, B. You, of all people, should know that."

She crosses her arms. "I know what you're trying to do, and it's *not* working. Tonight is happening. Like it or not."

The idea of going on a date with DeLuca gives me the willies, but my argument with him had nothing to do with tonight. He's an ignorant idiot who needed a lesson. Too bad Bonnie is gone before I get a chance to explain.

Pissed off, I trudge up the stairs, checking mail on the phone, and bump into a rock-hard chest. *Nice abs.* Real shame I can't say the same about the personality that goes with it. "Get outta my way," I snap.

DeLuca straightens, showing off his strong arms

and broad shoulders. Most likely there's a hidden eight-pack beneath his tight blue thermal shirt. Shame, none of it can atone for his crappy personality. "Bonnie didn't exaggerate," he says, grinning wickedly. "You really are one of a kind."

I let out a sharp breath. "I am. Unfortunately, I can't say the same about you, DeLuca."

He turns his cap around, the crown facing the back, and tilts his head to the side. "My friends call me Bridge."

I focus on the hundred unread emails and frown. "Do I look like I give a fuck?"

I step aside to walk away, but DeLuca reaches for my backpack. "Wait. I have a feeling we got off on the wrong foot."

I yank free of his grip. "Gee, you think?"

"I was—"

"An idiot? Moron? Douchebag?"

He bites his lip. "Trying to impress you."

I raise my brows. "By hitting on me in front of Professor Penrose?"

He shrugs. "You accused me of reading chick lit in front of our classmates. Guess we're even, huh?"

Why the hell am I even talking to him? I shove my phone in my jacket and run my fingers through my knotted hair. "Look." I try hard to sound nice. "I have no idea what Bonnie was thinking when she arranged our date, but we're clearly from two different planets, and I doubt we'd have much fun. So why don't we—"

"Whoa." He holds up a hand. "Are you trying to brush me off?"

I grin. "So you do have a brain after all?"

His amber eyes pierce mine. "You really shouldn't

do that."

I place a hand on my hip and glare at him. "Yeah? And why's that?"

DeLuca's lips curl into a half-smile. "Because"—he leans closer—"you'd regret it."

His fucking confidence annoys the hell outta me. "I doubt that."

"C'mon, Amanda. Give me a shot. I'm hot, smart, and lots of fun."

*Hot? Yeah. Smart? Arguable. Fun? Definitely not.* "I'm not your type."

He gives me the are-you-fucking-serious look. "Sexy, intelligent, and fierce? Sorry, sugar, but you're exactly my type."

*Persistent and unable to take a hint. Say hello to a stalker in the making.* "Still not interested."

A devilish smile tugs at DeLuca's lips. "Soon you will be, sugar."

"That would be on the seventh of never or the eighteenth of ain't gonna happen, DeLuca."

"We'll see," he says and walks away.

*Cocky son of a bitch.*

Chapter 3

Blowing hot air into my icy hands, I turn left onto Third Avenue. It's freezing, and I regret wearing a mini-dress. Scratch that. What I really regret is leaving my room. It's not like I haven't tried to escape this ordeal. Hell, I'd spent the rest of the afternoon trying to talk Bonnie out of this stupid idea. Arguing with her is as fruitful as teaching a snail to walk on two feet. Sure she means well and all, but Bridge DeLuca? Really? He's an annoying know-it-all. Even Alex "jerk-face" Remington would be more fun to go on a freaking date with.

*Suck it up. One drink and you're outta there.* It's not like I have much of a choice.

I hug my brand new fit-and-flare coat closer when I realize how empty the streets are. Odd. NYC never sleeps. It's always crowded and busy, which is why I fell in love with it in the first place. Tonight, though, it almost seems as if the fog-covered streets are part of a ghost town.

The theme song of *Once Upon a Time in the West* comes to mind, and I hurry on with a creepy feeling in my stomach. I should take a cab. Problem is there are none. I continue down the silent street, my skin crawling. *Something ain't right.*

I stop dead in my tracks and scan my surroundings. No one in sight, yet I can't shake the sneaking suspicion someone's watching me. I blame the fucking nightmares for messing with my head, but when the streetlight next to me flickers, I wonder if there's more to it than paranoia. Quickening my pace, I hurry past dim buildings.

A blood-curling howl echoes through the hazy streets. The smell of sulfur crawls up my nose. A fraction of a second later, I see a weird shadow from the corner of my eye. It kinda looks like a dog. Except dogs don't have fiery red eyes.

I stop again and slowly face the *thing.*

It's gone. Or, maybe, it was never there.

*Jesus, I think I need a shrink.*

\*\*\*\*

The queue leading to The Bitter End is endless. I can already tell half the crowd will have to spend their evening elsewhere. The small club with the wooden façade is famous for its live acts and packed most nights. Bob Dylan, Taylor Swift, and Lady Gaga— they've all performed here.

Tiptoeing, I'm trying to get a glimpse of the door when Billy the Bouncer, one of Bonnie's one-night stands, waves me over. Screwing a security guy certainly has its perks.

Most of the dressed-to-kill chicks give me the evil-eye as I pass them on my way to the door. I couldn't care less. It's their fault they don't have an awesome best friend.Billy plants a kiss on my numb cheek. "Looking good, Amanda."

I point at his *Men in Black* outfit. "You too, Billy."

He smiles at me. "Who's the lucky bastard that gets to date my favorite customer?" I wave airily. "Blind date with a moron."

He throws his head back and breaks into a lusty laugh. "Blind date sorta implies you haven't met the guy before, so why are you calling the poor bastard a moron?"

I draw a sharp breath. "Long story."

He tilts his chin at the queue. "I've got nothing but time, honey."

Spending the rest of the night with Billy sounds better than meeting up with DeLuca, but I promised Bonnie I'd show. "Tempting. But B will raise hell if I don't get in there soon." She'd already sent me a couple of furious texts.

Billy sighs. "You'd better hurry then." He nods at the entrance. "Bonnie and a boy toy named Troy are already inside." Jealousy thickens his voice.

I can't hide a smile. "So, you're still secretly in love with my best friend, huh?"

The heavily muscled beast of a man averts his gaze and blushes like a little kid. "The one that got away," he mutters. I've heard that line from several ex-lovers of Bonnie, and I don't blame them—she *is* one of a kind. Unfortunately, she's also the female version of Jesse, Alex's little brother, and sometimes I wonder if breaking hearts is some kind of sport for her. I point to the mostly female audience. "Who's playing?" I'd bet my money on some teen star, but I doubt The Bitter End's standard has dropped so low.

"The Neighbourhood," Billy replies. "Club's packed already."

I breathe a sigh of relief. At least the music will be good. "All right." I give him a genuine smile. "I better get going."

Billy nods. "See you later, honey."

"Rather sooner," I assure him before I stagger into the club.

In and out in a heartbeat is what I keep telling myself as I push through the horde. The band isn't on stage yet, but the crowd is already going crazy.

I find Bonnie, Cappuccino Guy, and DeLuca at the front-row table with the best stage view. Didn't expect less from my best friend.

"Hey," I mutter as I reach them.

DeLuca jumps up to get the chair for me. I deliberately pick another one. I hate gentlemen.

He drinks me in. "Wow, you look great, sugar."

"Thanks." The tight red mini-dress I bought last week fits me perfectly. Paired with a hint of red lipstick and my blonde curls, I look like a modern-day Marilyn Monroe.

Bonnie's hand is dangerously close to Cappuccino Guy's crotch. "Thought you'd stand us up."

Boy toy named Troy never once takes his eyes off my best friend. "Yeah," he murmurs. "We were about to come and get you."

I pull a face. "Sure you were." *Right after you screwed Bonnie in the car.*

Ignoring my comment, he grabs Bonnie's hair, pulls her closer, and shoves his freaking tongue down her throat. *Gross.* Cappuccino Guy is handsome and all, but there's something about him I just can't stand. Since I can't read auras, anymore, I don't even know what it is.

DeLuca might be an idiot, but he senses I'm about to puke my guts out if I have to bear witness to these obnoxious tongue-acrobatics any longer. "Can I get you a drink?" he asks, drawing my attention away from the kiss.

"Bourbon," I choke out. *Lots of bourbon.*

He jumps to his feet. "Coming right up."

Sitting there like the fifth wheel, I wonder why the fuck I didn't stay home. I'm tired, grumpy, and not in the mood to watch live porn. My so-called best friend obviously doesn't care. She's too busy sucking the life out of her date.

A middle-aged woman appears on the stage. "Are you ready to rock?" she yells into the mic. The crowd answers with loud whistling and frantic clapping. "Then give it up for…" She pauses for dramatic effect. "The Neighbourhood."

The second Jesse Rutherford sets foot on the stage, the crowd screams and shouts like fucking lunatics. Guys clap. Girls fan themselves as they drink in the hotness of the rock star.

I scowl. *Why the fuck are people so crazy about rock stars?* Granted, the dude is sexy, but I'll never get the whole fan-girl hype that turns ordinary chicks into mad sirens.

Just when Brandon Fried sets the rhythm for "Sweater Weather" on his drums, DeLuca slams a bottle of bourbon on the table and grins. "You looked like you could use more than just a glass."

I gawk at Bonnie and Cappuccino Guy. "If he keeps that freak show going, I'll need another bottle just to sanitize my eyes."

DeLuca laughs. "Can you blame him?"

"I blame her," I say.

The first song is almost over when the dude finally pulls his tongue out of Bonnie's mouth. "You guys having fun?" She's completely out of breath.

I give her a look. "Hell, yeah. I mean, what could be more fun than watching you guys make out to the tunes of The Neighbourhood, right?"

Bonnie furrows her brow. "Drop the bitch act, Amanda."

Elbows on the table, I smirk. "It's either the bitch act or vomiting on the table. Your choice."

Bonnie's lips part, but before a single word leaves her mouth, Cappuccino Guy leans over the table and whispers something in her ear. Whatever he says lights up her face, and a second later she's on her feet. "Jason left his phone in the car," she says, cheeks flushed.

I love Bonnie. God knows I do, but if looks could kill, she'd drop dead right about now. "Couldn't you at least have the decency to come up with a better excuse, B?"

She shrugs. "Leave some bourbon for us?"

I can't even say "fuck you," because Cappuccino Guy pulls her toward the exit.

*I'm going to kill her for this.*

I let out a long, pained breath as my favorite Neighbourhood song, "West Coast," starts.

DeLuca's gaze is glued to the lead singer. "Damn, I love this song."

"Me too," I admit.

His soft amber eyes lock on mine. "We do have something in common, huh?"

I manage a weak smile. "Stranger things have happened."

DeLuca hands me a squat glass of bourbon and lifts his in a toast. "Here's to music."

I down the shot. Leaning back in my chair, I relax a bit.

"The dude's voice is dope," DeLuca says, drooling.

I laugh. "You from the 80s or something?" Seriously, who uses the word dope to mean good anymore? Last time I heard it was in *Straight Outta Compton*.

He beams at me. "What's wrong with the 80s?"

I raise a brow. "Other than scrunchies, shoulder pads, and leggings?"

"C'mon, leggings are luscious."

I give him a look. "Yeah, no. No, they're not."

We listen to a few songs in silence before DeLuca opens his mouth again. "Ms. Bishop," he says as the audience applauds. "Do you live by that rule?"

"What rule?"

He brushes his angled fringe out of his face and grins. "The best always comes last?"

I trace the edge of my glass and nod. "What about you? Any rules you live by?"

He props his elbows on the table and leans in. "Only one."

"Always annoy your date before the date?"

He grins sheepishly. "All right. Two."

I shift the glass from one hand to the other, waiting, knowing he'll tell me without me asking.

He downs his bourbon and slams the empty glass on the table. "The other is rules are meant to be broken," he says, wiping moisture off his lips.

I knit my brows. "Is that so?"

"Why so surprised?"

I look him over—black button-up shirt, hipster hairstyle, and dimples. "You don't exactly come across as a rule breaker."

He circles my wrist. "And what's dating the girl

who humiliated me in front of a whole auditorium?"

I bat my lashes at him. "Playing hard to get?"

DeLuca runs a hand over his face and sighs. "I'm that transparent, huh?"

"Nope. I'm just that good."

Despite my initial doubts, we spend the rest of the night listening to The Neighbourhood and discussing MacDougall's experiment. I can't believe I'm saying this, but DeLuca isn't as bad as I thought. Sure, the guy is a total non-believer. Atheist. Scientist. Stubbornist. *That's not even a word.* Who cares? It describes him perfectly. But beneath all the skepticism hides a decent human being who's pretty funny.

DeLuca's gaze locks with mine as the band bows for an enthusiastic audience. "Wanna check your calendar again?"

"Why?"

He cups my elbow. A spark of electricity jolts through me. "Because I have a feeling tonight has turned into the seventh of never and the eighteenth of ain't gonna happen, sugar."

I pull back. "I don't do relationships," I warn.

His gaze glides from my cleavage to my eyes. "But I'm pretty sure you want to do me, Amanda."

Chapter 4

The smile turning up the corners of my mouth as I blink my eyes open feels unnatural. Not that I've never woken up with a grin plastered on my face, but it's been so long, I can't remember the last time.

Stretching my sore muscles, I listen to Bonnie singing in the kitchen. Any other day it would bug me, but after sleeping through the night without demonic interference, I kinda enjoy the sound of her voice.

Hugging my pillow, I grab my phone from the nightstand. Six missed calls from an unknown number. In the last two weeks, I've had several such calls. When I pick them up, no one says a word. Either someone constantly rings the wrong number, or I'm being stalked. I ignore them and open the text from DeLuca.

*Wouldn't it be nice if we made it to a room on the second date?* he wrote.

My fingers fly over the keyboard. *I sorta liked Washington Square Park.* If I had a conscience, I'd feel bad about screwing him. Especially after I'd judged him so harshly. But, hey, I slept through the night. That's all that matters.

*Up for round two?* he texts back.

More sleep and fewer nightmares? *Eleven pm. My place. No sleepover!*

*Later, sugar. ;)*

I put my phone on the nightstand, push the blankets

away, and get on my wobbly feet. My muscles feel like Jimi Hendrix's guitar strings: all worked up and still on fire. Having lived like the Virgin Mary for the last few months has taken its toll on me. I almost forgot sex is a lot like yoga—stop practicing and you lose flexibility.

"Amanda?" Bonnie knocks on my door as I gather my toiletries to hit the shower. "You up?"

"Yeah, come in." I don't usually sound so cheerful in the morning. I bet Bonnie will see right through me, but it's not like I plan on keeping DeLuca a secret.

The door cracks open, and my crazy best friend sticks her head in. The girl is a miracle. I might be every guy's wet dream, but she's a flawless beauty, and even at seven in the morning, she looks like a cover model of *Sports Illustrated*. She covers her eyes with both hands. "You alone?"

I laugh. "Unlike you, I don't spend the night with my one-night stands."

Bonnie barges in. She flashes me a smug smile. "So, it's true, huh? Amanda Bishop screwed Magic Bridge. And here I thought you'd joined Chelsea the Nun in celibacy."

I throw my toiletries on my chair. "What's with you and all those stupid nicknames? Cappuccino Guy, Billy Bouncer, Magic Bridge—you make 'em sound like villains in a DC comic."

She throws herself onto my freshly-made bed. "I met Jason at a coffee shop when he ordered an extra hot cappuccino. Billy *is* a bouncer, and Bridge?" Her eyes widen. "Well, from what I've heard, his moves are like Channing Tatum's."

She's not exaggerating. The boy could get a role in *Magic Mike XXXL*. I stumble to my closet, reach for my favorite black sweater, and shrug. "Can't argue with that."

"I'm happy you finally got laid. Really am." She narrows her eyes at me. "But what happened to, 'he's a moron, and I'd rather date Lucifer'?"

DeLuca *is* a moron. He's also funny and easy to be with. "Let's just say, I reconsidered after sleeping through the night." I'm not in the mood to admit I've been a prejudiced bitch.

"No nightmares?"

"Better. No dreams whatsoever. At least none I can remember."

She breathes a sigh of relief. "That's good, right?"

I thrust my fingers through my wild hair. "Good? It's freakin' awesome, B. Had I known sex would ease my nightmares, I would have slept with the whole football team by now." Okay, maybe not the whole team, but I wouldn't have lived like a virgin either.

Her cognac eyes sparkle. "So you'll see him again?"

I pull ripped skinny jeans out of my closet. "Don't get too excited. I'm not in it for the guy, only the unbroken sleep." DeLuca is a nice distraction. The thing is, there are no butterflies or fireworks in my belly when I'm with him. Judging by the way she looks at me, she's about to give me her no-one-will-ever-live-up-to-Alex-but-you-need-to-try sermon. My ringing phone saves me just in time. "Unknown," Bonnie says, passing it to me.

*Again?* I push the accept button. "Hello?"
Silence.
Bonnie leans back on her elbows, watching me with eagle eyes. "Who is it?"

I shrug. "Helloooo?"

Someone's breathing at the other end.

"All right, douchebag. Talk or I'll hang up."

Jerk cuts the line first.

"I'm guessing that wasn't Bridge, huh?"

I glare at my phone, overcome by the same sick feeling I had last night when I saw the *thing* with the red eyes.

"Amanda?"

"Nope," I say, throwing the phone on my bed. "Wrong number."

She has that look on her face, a cross between worry and frustration. "There's something I have to tell you," she admits after a long pause.

My mood barometer drops to happy with a hint of irritation. "Shoot."

Bonnie taps her foot. She does that a lot when she's nervous. "Do you promise not to go all bitch-witch on my ass?"

I've had some sleep. I assume I can keep my aggression under control. "I'll do my best."

Tapping her foot a little harder, she stares at my bookshelf. Bonnie struggles to find the right words, and if I could read her aura, it would most definitely be light gray, indicating fear.

I start to freak a bit. "What could be so bad that you, of all people, are rendered speechless?"

She plays with a loose curl. "Melinda?" she whispers, voice cracked.My stomach dips. "Melinda, as in my sister Melinda?" I haven't heard from Perfect Housewitch since Alex told her I'd been shot.

Bonnie bites on her lower lip. "That's the one."

I stalk toward her, fear in my heart. "Something

wrong with—"

"No. He's fine."

About two hundred pounds lift off my chest before irritation bleeds into my system. "Then what is it? Did her Women's Committee cut the budget for the next garden party?"

Bonnie jumps up. "Damn, Amanda, why is it so difficult to talk to you about your sister?" Bonnie doesn't get pissed off easily. Right now, she looks like she's about to wrap her small hands around my neck to choke the life out of me.

"Because she's a red flag?"

Bonnie crosses her arms and gives me a killer look. "It shouldn't be like this. You guys are family. So why don't you *both* get a fucking grip and act like it for a change?"

I saunter to the desk and unplug my MacBook. "Blood doesn't make you family." Just thinking of Melinda sharpens my tone and tenses every muscle DeLuca worked so hard to relax.

Bonnie wants to defend my sister. I see it in her eyes. Since she's not suicidal, she doesn't.

Swallowing the hatred for Melinda, I shove the laptop in my bag. "All right, I'll bite. What does the Queen of Good Behavior want?" Not that I care, but for Bonnie, I play along.

Anger hardens her soft face. "Know what? I've been your messenger for ages, Amanda. But I'm done playing the peacemaker." Like a fury on crack, she staggers to the door.

Her melodramatic tendencies get worse by the day. "Just tell me what she wants, B."

Fingers clenched around the doorknob, she looks

over her shoulder. "You really want to know?" Her voice is calm. A little too calm, maybe.

*No, I don't.* I nod anyway."Then you better call her," Bonnie says before slamming the door behind her.

I fall onto my bed and glare at the ceiling. How the fuck did this morning go from I-want-to-kiss-the-world-because-I-had-no-nightmares to I'm-a-dumb-bitch-who-pissed-off-my-only-friend? Damn, Melinda really does bring out the worst in me.Exasperated with myself, I snatch my towel from the thrift-store chair I bought last week and head to the bathroom.

When I get out of the shower, Bonnie is long gone. The nagging guilt in the pit of my stomach, however, is still very present. Normally, I don't give a fuck about other people's feelings, but I do care about Bonnie's. An apology is needed. The girl has put up with my family shit for way too long. If I'm not careful, she'll soon realize what a fucked-up friend I really am and, eventually, walk away. Just like Mother Dearest predicted.

Getting ready for my lectures, I pour a cup of coffee. Chelsea looks up from her newspaper. "Where have you been all night?"

I fling myself onto the sofa. "What are you? My mother?" *There's definitely some resemblance between the two.*

She fiddles with the sleeves of her silk blouse. "Of course not. My children would never be so godless."

*Godless? Ha!* I'm not the one who threw a fit when gay marriage was legalized. "Why don't you go seduce a priest or terrorize some poor gay bastard, Nun?"

She neatly folds her paper. "I don't get it, Amanda."

There are a lot of things she doesn't get. Unlike Bonnie, I refuse to play her games.

I go through my emails and sip my coffee. "You seem to be a smart girl."

*Bitch and Bitchier would disagree.*

"Why would you follow Bonnie's example and become a sinner?" she continues.

What she's really trying to say is why does a white girl act like a black slut, and for that I want to fucking kill her. Bonnie and I argue a lot, and I don't always agree with her choices, but I'll be damned if a bitch like Chelsea talks crap about her in my presence.

Murder on my face, I meet her gaze. "Know what, Chelsea? You pretend to be all righteous and good, but you're really just a racist bigot who doesn't know the first thing about Christian love."

Her mouth forms a shocked O. "What did—"

Rising from the sofa in slow motion, I get in her face. "You heard me, bitch. And if you know what's good for you, you'll never talk about my best friend again. If you do, so help me God, I will make sure you get firsthand experience of the viciousness of hell." A wicked smile curls my lips. "Got it?"

Distress creeps into her sturdy features. "You are so—""Ready to kill you? Boy, you're quick."

Stumbling backward, she grabs her paper and disappears inside her room.

*Good choice.*

Chapter 5

I walk out of class with a headache from freaking hell. Majoring in psychology seemed like a good idea, considering how well I can read people. Sometimes, though, the purely scientific approach to people's behavior bugs me. The brain has a great impact on attitudes, aggression, and moral thought and action, but so does the soul.

Hoping lunch with Bonnie will be more rewarding, I stroll down the long hallway. I'd texted her earlier and asked her to meet me at the coffee shop on campus for a quick lunch before my shift at Lindy's starts. She wasn't really up for it, but having had the most convincing argument—which may or may not have involved a free latte, sandwiches, and as much dessert as she wants—she agreed. Thank God. Almost thought I'd have to do a naked I'm-sorry-your-friend-is-such-a-failure dance in front of the whole campus.

I'm about to head down the stairs when two hands blind me. "Hey, sugar," DeLuca whispers.

Pulling his hands off my eyes, I spin. "Stop calling me that." I hate nicknames.

He brushes golden hair out of his face. "Can't help it. You're just too damn sweet."

I cross my arms. The guy is already starting to piss me off a little. "What do you want? And don't tell me you missed me." I have a feeling the warning is needed.

A boyish smile tugs at his lips. "Would I lose points on the screw-buddy scale if I said I did?"

*Jesus, he acts like he wants to be your freakin' boyfriend.* Doesn't matter. He helps me sleep. That's all I care about. For now. "Kinda," I answer honestly. My gaze drops to his crotch. "But you can always make up for it."

His rich laughter echoes through the hallway. "That's reassuring."

I sigh. "Care to tell me why you're stalking me?"

He raises his brows. "I was going to ask if you wanted to join me for a bite."

*Don't say I didn't warn ya!* Sometimes, I wish there was a fucking kill-switch for the damn voice in my head. I hold two fingers up. "A: I already have a lunch date, and B: I don't eat with my sparring partners."

He tries his puppy look on me. "Shame. I happen to know the best burger place in town."

"I'm vegetarian," I murmur, suddenly thinking of Alex. He figured that out all by himself. No explanation needed.

DeLuca shrugs it off. "You can always just sit there and appreciate the company."

I throw my hair over one shoulder. "Or I could walk away and pretend this never happened. Spare you the embarrassment and ignore the fact you're acting like a lovesick puppy."

He closes the gap between us and leans in. "You're a lot more fun when you're pushed against a tree, moaning my name."

DeLuca holds my gaze when I get the feeling we're being watched. I press my hand against his well-defined chest and shove him away. That's when I see them—Bitch and Bitchier. They stand two feet away, staring at us as if we're the new Tarantino flick.

"What's up?" DeLuca asks, peeking over his shoulder.

"I think we have an audience."

He winks at the girls. "You know they think you're a devil-worshipping witch, right?"

I glare at the gossip-spreading bitches. "So they know my secret, huh? I should probably whack them."

The fact there's not the slightest trace of humor in my voice draws DeLuca's attention back to me. "Are you saying the rumors about you are true?"

His shocked expression is mesmerizing. I bite my lip to keep from bursting into uncontrollable laughter. "Not the bathing in virgin blood part, but other than that?" I shrug. "They're not that far off the grid."

For a moment, there's fear in DeLuca's eyes. Then, as if someone hits him with a baseball bat, he snaps out of his delirium and laughs. "Damn, you're good."

I squint. *At what? Scaring the shit outta people?*

"You should major in drama, not psychology."

Why is it when I try to tell the truth everyone thinks I'm joking? I'm close to asking DeLuca just that when Bitch walks toward us. "Bridge?"

He turns around. "Hey, Jules."

Bitch's gaze locks with mine, but she quickly looks away. "Can I talk to you?"

DeLuca nods. "Sure. What's up?"

"Alone," she emphasizes.

I can take a hint. "I better get going. Virgins don't bleed out by themselves."

Her jaw drops.

I walk away.

\*\*\*\*

When I get to the coffee shop, Bonnie is waiting for me at the entrance. "You're late," she murmurs, pointing at her watch.

I tilt my head to the side and smile. "And you look like someone just ruined your new Louis Vuitton bag."

She refuses to cut me slack. "Keep up the attitude, and I'll order the whole menu."

I throw my arm around her shoulders and grin. "Anything to make my grumpy best friend happy."

"You're unbelievable, Amanda."

I pull her through the door. "You still love me, don't ya?"

She sighs heavily. "Get me a double-shot latte, a mozzarella panini, two cookies, and a brownie. *Then* we're talking."

"Your wish is my command, Your Majesty." She lets me off the hook too easily. That's Bonnie. The girl can never stay mad at me for long. Even when we were kids, and I got her into all sorts of trouble, she had that forgiving streak.

I'm still nibbling on a lemon cupcake when Bonnie is on her second cookie. She's so freaking delicate no one would believe she eats like the big green guy who smashes everything coming his way.

"I know I'm sexy like that. Devouring cookies and all. But something tells me it's not the reason you're staring at me, is it?"

Poking at the icing on my cupcake, I blow out a long breath. "You know how I don't apologize. Like ever. Right?"

She takes another bite. "Yeah, so?"

My belly cramps. "Let's assume I wasn't such a selfish bitch, and I actually apologize for my mistakes."

"Okay," she says, wiping her mouth with a napkin. "I'm assuming."*Jesus, why the fuck is it so hard for me to say sorry?* Keeping my gaze on the table, I dig my nails into my palm. "Well, if that were the case, I'd probably tell you I was a bitch this morning while you were trying to be a friend."

A half-smile curves up her lips. "Is that so?"

I shrug. "I would also tell you the reason I believe blood doesn't equal family is you."

Confusion paints her face. "What?"

"Remember Grams's funeral?"

She tosses the last piece of her cookie. "Which part?"

"The part where my mom threw me out of the house in the middle of the funeral party?" Bonnie's uneasy. She starts bouncing her leg. "It's not like anyone there could ever forget that. She called you Satan's bride, Amanda." Her voice is a mixture of sadness and resentment.

I look around the coffee shop. "She did, didn't she?"

Bonnie rests her hand on mine and squeezes it gently. "Your mom is a real piece of work."

Pushing the memory to the darkest part of my soul, I nod. "But that's not the point.""Then what is?" Leaning back, I focus on George, the wannabe quarterback hitting on the poor barista. *That girl is so out of his league.*

"Amanda?" Bonnie's voice is soft.

*Damn, why the fuck did I start this conversation?* Doesn't matter. I did. Now I gotta pull my head out of my ass and finish it. "Remember what you said when she dragged me out of the house by my hair?"

Bonnie blushes. "That it takes evil to recognize it?"

The look on Mother Dearest's face is branded into my brain. Thought she'd have a stroke or something. "Those were your exact words, B. What about Melinda? Do you remember what she said?"

Bonnie props her elbows on the table. "No, not really. Why?"

I force a weak smile. "Because Melinda never said a word. She just stood there, watching her haul me out of the house and... Didn't. Say. A thing." I draw a deep breath. "You were the one who stood up for me. The one who tried to protect me. You always have, Bonnie."

Her eyes glaze. She's close to bursting into tears. "Your mom had no right to talk to you like that. And Melinda...well, she was too scared to do what was right. So, I took a stand and told her off. It's not a big deal."

*Not a big deal? She's big on modesty these days.* "You fought for me like a sister would, like a sister should. That's what makes *you* the only family I have."

Bonnie's gaze drops to her half-eaten cookie. "If that was an apology," she says, shoving her plate away, "which clearly it wasn't, I would totally accept it. But you shouldn't be too hard on Melinda. She's been through a lot, and she's still the one who takes care of—"

"I know, and I'm grateful for what she does..." I wrap my fingers around the takeaway cup. "But it doesn't change how she treated me."

Bonnie plays with her cookie. "She's worried about you."

I'd laugh, but I'd have to apologize again. "That would be a first, B."

Bonnie pulls her curls into a high bun. "Trust me, Amanda. Melinda sounded terrified when she called me. Never heard so much fear in her voice."

"What, does she worry I'll set the campus on fire?"

"No." Her voice turns dead serious. "She thinks you're in danger."

I almost stab my eyes out with the plastic fork. "What?"

Bonnie traces her eyebrows with her index fingers. "She said something about your grams having warned her."

"Grams?" My voice turns sour. "That's bull. Why the fuck should Grams come to her and not me?" When we were kids, Melinda and Grams were like one, but at some point their relationship went downhill. I blamed my mother for it but came to understand there was more to the story than I'd thought.

Bonnie shoves a piece of cookie into her mouth. "I don't know why your grams came to Melinda— probably because she's the medium. Anyways, when I told her about your nightmares, she—"

"You what?" I yell, lava flooding my veins.

She makes a face. "Calm down. I didn't mean to. It kinda…it just came out, all right?"

*Calm down?* The girl never told on me. Not when I set fire to my mother's beloved rose tree or when I took my dad's car for a joyride. Now she throws her loyalty out the window over nightmares? "Since when are you such a snitch?"

She holds her hand up B-style. "Would you stop it already? We both know something is wrong with you,

Amanda." Her gaze burns through mine. "Sure, you slept through the night after screwing DeLuca, but what about the fact you can't read auras? Hell, you don't even get visions anymore."

"I *do* get visions," I say, defending myself.

"Yeah?" She ogles me suspiciously. "When was the last time you had one?"

I cross my arms. "Not that it's any of your business, but I had one just yesterday."

"What?"

I lean back. "I had this weird customer. Name's Legend—"

She bursts into laughter. "Let me guess; his best friend is a German shepherd?"

The name really is weird. "No," I moan. "But the guy had a weird tattoo, and when I looked into his eyes..." The picture flickers across my mind, and I shiver. "I saw him standing over a dead man."

She shifts closer. "Why didn't you tell me?"

I shake my head. "When, B? In Penrose's lecture or at The Bitter End, when you walked out on me to get lucky with Cappuccino Douchebag?"

Guilt washes over her face, turning her soft features into hard granite. "One word. Just one word, Amanda, and I would have ditched Jason."

I never questioned that. Bonnie loves sex as much as life itself, but she'd send every guy to hell if I needed her. "It wasn't a big thing," I say, trying to ease her conscience. "The guy is probably a cop or something, and the vision was random." I don't tell her about the sigil carved into the dead man's forehead or that Legend thought "whatever" killed him and not "whoever." She's freaked out enough as it is. No need to make things worse.

"Random vision?" She runs a hand over her face, smearing her mascara in the process. "You never have a random vision. Besides, don't you think it's sorta weird the guy shows up just when you're going through a magic crisis?"

She has a point. The nightmares, my fucked-up abilities, Melinda's warning, and Legend—all happening at once—is strange. Yet, I don't see how any of it can be connected.

"Amanda." She waits till I look at her. "I know you don't want to hear this, but you need to call Alex."

"No." Even if I was surrounded by a horde of demons, I wouldn't call jerk-face.

"What if that Legend dude is a hunter?"

"He's not." Am I trying to convince her or me?

Bonnie gives me a look. "One day that stubbornness will get you killed."

A half-hearted smile spreads across my face. "We all have to die one day."

She stirs her latte. "Yeah, but I'd rather go to your funeral later than sooner."

I've survived my mother, a psycho bokor, a freaking pedophile, and hunter-heroic. I doubt nightmares or a guy named Legend can kill me. "Don't worry, B. Bad weeds grow tall."

She silently stares at her coffee for a while. When she looks up, there's a flash of excitement in her eyes. "Hey," she says, grinning from ear to ear. "I have an idea."

*I'm in deep shit.*

Chapter 6

I glare at the depressing snow clouds dimming the afternoon sky. "I can't believe you talked me into getting a tarot reading over cookies and latte," I snarl, fighting the urge to pick another fight with Bonnie.

"I'm convincing like that." She flashes me a brilliant smile. My face stays frozen, and she adds, "It'll be fun. I promise."

I'm a witch. Walking into a fortuneteller's place to ask about my future is as bad—maybe even worse— than doing the walk of shame in front of a whole frat house.

Bonnie's hand lands on my shoulder. "It's just a reading, not the end of the world."

"Says the mambo who refuses to practice magic."

Bonnie's gaze drops to her new Prada boots. "This isn't about me. We need to figure out what's going on with *you*, Manda."

*Manda?* I stop dead in my tracks. "Don't call me that."

She pulls her brows together. "Call you what?" I'd say she's messing with me, but she looks genuinely confused.

"Manda," I say, hugging my winter coat closer to my chest.

"I didn't."

I give her the don't-mess-with-me-'cause-I'm-crazy look. "Stop fooling around, B."

Bonnie narrows her eyes. "I've known you for ages. Never called you Manda, did I?"

I'm not deaf. I heard her. "Whatever," I snap as we turn into a dark alley. "Where the hell are we, B?" I scan the surroundings, wondering if the fortuneteller has chosen this fucked-up area for a reason. I would have. It adds to the mystery. Plus, people love to be scared.

She hauls me past the waste of a Chinese restaurant and several fire exit stairs. "Almost there," she promises seconds before we reach a rusty iron door. "See?" She points to a small neon sign. It reads Madame Josephine. Palmist, Tarot Reader, and Healer.

I'm staring at the green, blinking letters when a distant memory pushes through my consciousness.

****

*A date. Why in God's name did I agree to go on a date with Alexander Remington? Sure, he'd made it sound like it wasn't a big deal when he tried to convince me it was just dinner between two friends, but I knew better.*

*Threading his fingers through mine, he pulled me toward a small Indian restaurant. "Damn, I'm starving." He sounded so happy and carefree, it scared the crap outta me.*

*I jerked my hand out of his and faced him. "I can't do this." Alex and I weren't friends, and we never would be. He just didn't know it yet.*

*Bending down, he smiled. "Can't do what, Manda? Have dinner?"*

*I shook my head. "You know exactly what I'm talking about."*

47

*He squinted. "No, I don't."*

*I was frustrated. "Us, going on a freakin' date, Alex. I mean, we don't even like each other." That sounded stupid even to my own ears. It was the truth, though. Yeah, we couldn't take our hands off each other, and lately we'd spent more time kissing than fighting, but Alex was still the kinda guy who thought he was meant to save the world while I would only ever try to save myself.*

*For the longest time, he just stared at me, his malachite eyes eager to read me. "It's just a meal, Manda."*

*My brows rose. "Is it?" I asked, annoyed he not only lied to me but also himself. "Curry turns into pasta, and before we know it, we're all dressed up in some fancy restaurant and you're trying to put a ring on my finger."*

*"Wow." He laughed. "Easy, there. In case you haven't noticed, I'm not the marrying type."*

He isn't the type who dates a selfish bitch either. *"Then why the fuck are we doing this?" In a couple of days, our little road trip would draw to an end, and if God was as merciful as he'd been painted, we'd never see each other again.*

*"Amanda." He reached for my hand, but I pulled away.*

*"No," I said. "This is crazy and stupid. We should head back to the motel and do what we do best."*

*With one long stride, he closed the distance between us. "Tempting." His lips brushed the edge of my mouth. "But…" He trailed kisses down my neck, and I instinctively dropped my head back, giving him more access. "I need some real food for a change."*

*I shied away. "You're a jerk, Alex."*

*"It's what you like about me." The wicked grin and the confidence in his voice irritated me like hell. When I didn't say anything, he rested his hands on each side of my shoulders and sighed. "Relax, Manda. We're on the same page. Friends with benefits, right?"*

*When our little affair had started, those words pushed the fear and doubt I had about us into oblivion. Now they sounded like a bad excuse. "Because that worked so well for Justin Timberlake and Mila Kunis?" I shot back, hoping he'd see how absurd this all was.*

*Alex's beautiful eyes darkened. "Life isn't a movie," he countered. "There ain't no happily ever after in real life."*

*I felt defeated and didn't even know why. The right thing to do was to tell him what I really was, to turn the fuck around and walk away. Instead, I let him drag me across the street without further resistance.* One pathetic witch I am.

*Soft autumn rain dropped down on us as he led me past a shop window decorated with dream catchers, a golden Hand of Fatima, and Ra's All-Seeing-Eye. A small sign leaned against the door: Palm Reading. Money Back Guarantee. I hadn't touched my cards in weeks and felt like a meth addict going cold turkey.*

*Only when Alex stood in front of me, did I realize I had stopped walking. "Want to get your palms read?" There wasn't a pinch of salt in his voice.*

*Nervous laughter escaped me. "Don't tell me you believe in this stuff." I hated to sound like a skeptic, but playing the game was essential for survival.*

*He scrubbed his fingers through his thick dark brown hair. "I kinda do."*

*Alex was a hunter who worked for the Paranormal Analysis Unit of the FBI—of course he believed in palm reading. He had firsthand experience of what the supernatural could do. Hearing him say it out loud, though, warmed my heart. Back in the day, before I learned love was an illusion, I'd dreamed of being with someone who accepted magic exists. Someone who wouldn't think I was nuts when I told him the truth about me. Now I stood next to a guy like that and had to act like it was all bullshit.* How ironic is that?

*"So, you're into new age crap?" I asked, keeping up the façade.*

*Disappointment skated over his remarkable features. "I don't burn incense or pray to Ganesha, if that's what you mean." He glared at the Eye of Providence in the shop window. "But I do believe there's more between heaven and earth than* most *of us know."*

*"But palm reading?" I forced a half-hearted smile. "Do you honestly believe someone can see the future in the palm of your hand?"*

*Alex wiped a few raindrops off his face and frowned. "Doesn't matter what I believe," he said, his aura changing into a dark, sad blue. "You obviously think I'm nuts." Alex wasn't naïve. He knew he had to pay a high price for hunting evil. Settling down, or being completely honest with a girl, just wasn't in the cards for him. He had accepted his fate a long time ago. Yet it hurt him I was just another chick who'd laugh at him if he told me the truth.*

****

Bonnie bangs against the iron door like a lunatic. "Where the hell is she?"

I forget about Alex and reach for her hand. "Let's just go. My shift starts in an hour, and Lindy is gonna kill me if I'm late." That isn't the only reason I want to get the hell away from here, but it's the most convincing.

Bonnie pulls her phone out of her coat and shakes her head. "Give me a minute."

*If you love me, God, you'll let that door stay closed.* I have no intention of learning about my future. A part of me—a very big part—is terrified of what the fortuneteller might see. The nightmares are all about Alex. What if he's in trouble? Or worse, what if those dreams are death omens? Could I stand back and do nothing if I knew what was coming for him? Would I be dumb enough to break the deal we'd made and let him back in my life? I lean against the cold brick wall, realizing I never want an answer to any of those questions.

The heavy door swings open and a bald dude in his early forties walks out. "She's expecting you," he mumbles before rushing down the alley.

*So much for your unconditional love, God.*

My muscles stiffen. "Any chance I can bribe you into leaving?"

She grabs my wrist and hauls me inside. Guess that means no.

We head down the narrow hallway. The walls are covered in red paint and ornaments of golden glitter. Rose incense sticks burn on a small cabinet. The scent is a welcoming change from the Chinese waste outside.

Bonnie's fingers are wrapped around a black velvet curtain."Ready?""Would you care if I said no?"

She draws the curtain to the side and grins.

A wave of nostalgia washes over me as I step into the fortuneteller's kingdom. I used to be the girl running the show. The one everyone paid to get a reading. That was before I turned into a boring student.

Madame Josephine, a born-and-bred Roma, sits at a small table glaring into a massive Berg crystal. The woman is beautiful despite her age. I totally dig the golden coins around her neck and the low-cut V-neck blouse showing off her cleavage. "I've been expecting you," she says, not looking up. "Take a seat."

I hesitate. "Look, I don't need—"

Her sharp gray eyes meet mine. The blood drains from her face. "You?"

I'm not sure what to make of the freaked-out look she gives me. "Have we met?"

The woman's head snaps in Bonnie's direction, who, by the way, appears as confused as I am. "Are you out of your mind, child?"

Bonnie cups her elbows. "No. Are you?"

Madame Josephine's eyes widen, and she explodes out of the chair. "How dare you bring an untouchable into my home, Bonnie."

"A what?" Bonnie and I say in unison.

"An untouchable," Madame Josephine repeats.

Bonnie smirks. "Like Eliot Ness?"

Horror washes over Madame Josephine's face. Then, after a long period of awkward silence, she meets my gaze. "Get out of my place and leave me be."

I'm close to losing my shit, but something tells me it wouldn't help my case. Drawing in a deep breath, I swallow the anger growing inside me. "I have no idea what the hell is wrong with you, lady, but I can assure you I'm not an..." *What was it she thought I was again? Ah, yeah.* "An untouchable."

The woman stumbles backward. "You're lying."

My temper takes over. "Am not!"

Bonnie steps between us. "All right, let's all just calm down." She faces Madame Josephine. "Whatever you think she is, you're wrong. We came to you for a reading. That's all."

"Let's just go, B. I'm clearly not welcome here."

"No," Bonnie says, standing her ground. "Not until she tells us why she's acting like you're the devil incarnated."

Madame Josephine's gaze drifts back and forth between Bonnie and me. After what feels like forever, her shoulders sink and her face softens. "You really don't know, do you?"

She's pissing me off. "What don't I know?"

A sigh ripples through her. "Even if I wanted to read for you—which I don't—I couldn't."

"Why?" Bonnie sounds as mad as I feel.

*Does it really matter? The woman is clearly nuts.*

A muscle in Madame Josephine's jaw pops, and she backs up farther. "Untouchables are immune to the magic of other witches. It's what makes them the most powerful and most feared witches of all."

I've had about enough. "She's clearly been hit on the head. Let's go."

I start to turn and walk away, but the crazy woman stops me. "Wait," she orders.

"What? You gonna accuse me of sacrificing babies?"

"I can prove I'm right."

"How?" Bonnie's voice is rough and deep.

Madame Josephine looks at me. "Has someone

ever been able to read you?"

"You mean my cards?" I don't even know why the hell I'm still talking to her, but I guess a part of me is curious.

Madame Josephine shakes her head. "Cards, aura, emotions?"

I don't know any other aura readers, and I'd never felt the need to get a tarot reading, but I think of Alex and Jesse. Two of the best hunters in the world, with the most sophisticated instinct when it comes to detecting witches. They never recognized me for what I truly am. "I'm not sure."

"Have you ever been hexed?"

What the hell is she trying to say? "Not that I know of. Why? What does it matter?"

"It confirms what I just said," the woman replies. "Other magic does not touch you."

Bonnie, who's been awfully quiet, cocks a brow. "If she was untouchable—and I'm not saying she is—then how the hell are you able to read her?"

"I can't," she croaks.

This is total bullshit. "You say you can't read me, yet you claim to know I'm an untouchable? No offense, lady, but you're nuts." I pivot, ready to get the fuck outta here and never look back.

"I've seen you in my dreams, Amanda," Madame Josephine shouts after me. "Darkness will claim you. There's no escaping it."

Bonnie slams the rusty iron door behind her.

"Maybe it wasn't such a great idea after all," she murmurs as we walk down the alley and back to the street.

"Gee." I give her a look. "You think?"

Chapter 7

Pissed at the world, I barge through the back entrance of the diner. Madame Josephine can kiss my sweet little ass. I was declared evil before I was born. Why should I give a fuck about this untouchable business?

*It would explain Mother Dearest's premonition, though.* Me, as the queen of the underworld, bringing about the end of the world? Hilarious. I might be a selfish bitch, but it takes more than that to become Satan's new bride.

*Like being an untouchable?*

I fucking hate the voice in my head.

Ready to rip someone's heart out, I march to my door-less locker. Some days are better spent in bed. *This* is one of those. I change into my stupid uniform and get ready to endure Lindy.

The swing door hasn't shut behind me yet when Lindy's shrill voice echoes through the kitchen. "Amanda! Office! Now!"

*Office? I'm in trouble.* Bracing myself for what's to come, I follow her to the rat-hole. Plaster crumbles from the ceiling, and I swear I hear mice squeaking.

None of that seems to bother Lindy. "Sit down," she orders, pointing to a moldy leather chair across from her.

"Nah, I'm good."

"Sit. Now." *I bet there are dead rats under the cushions.* I choke back disgust and do as she says. My skin crawls as the fucked-up leather sinks beneath me. *I need a shower. Or two.*

Lindy's narrow eyes pierce a hole in my chest. The woman must have invented the evil eye. "Wanna spill the beans, or are you going to pretend you don't have a fucking clue why you're here?"

*Spill the beans?* The bitch makes being late sound like I've emptied the register. "I know I'm late, but—"

"Late?" She throws her head back and laughs. "You think this is about the twenty minutes I will cut from your wage?"

Actually, five minutes, but I'd be crazy to tell her. Wired, she jumps from her chair. Her auburn-colored pixie hair stands on end. "Try again, Amanda."

Studying her hard features, I look for hints. The thing is, Lindy always looks mad. *I miss seeing auras.* "I have no idea what you're talking about, Lindy."

The walrus of a woman advances toward me. Hatred darkens her mean piggy eyes. "After everything I've done for you," she snaps. "You dare lie to my fucking face?"

Having no idea what exactly it is she thinks she's *done* for me, I cock a brow. "I'm not lying."

She plops her substantial weight on a less than sturdy table, bending the material like it's freaking rubber. "Oh, you're not?" A wicked grin appears on her lips. "Then let me ask you this: how many times have I told you no hitting on my customers?"

Just the thought of regulars like Barry the pervert or filthy Jack sends repulsive shockwaves through me. I'd have to suffer from eye cancer to hit on one of them.

Lindy clenches her stubby fingers around the edge of the table. "What's the matter, girl? Ain't got nothing to say?"

"Do you even hear yourself? What makes you think a girl like me"—I get up and show off my body—"would hit on *your* customers?"

She looks clueless. "So you're saying Mr. Prada asked for your schedule for no other reason than your waiting skills?" Her nasty laughter rings in my ears like freaking tinnitus. "Do you think I was born yesterday?"

*I think you were born in freaking hell!* "Who the fuck is Mr. Prada?" I have my suspicions, but I need Lindy's confirmation.

"Quit playing blonde. It's not like this place is crawling with guys in fancy suits."

No doubt in my mind she's talking about Legend, and while it bugs me the guy asked her for my schedule, I don't see how it gives her the right to treat me like a piece of shit. Done listening to her crap, I meet her gaze. "I'm only gonna say this once, Lindy." My tone is sharp. "I'm not dating Mr. Prada or any of your other fucked-up customers."

"That better be the truth," she yells after me as I stomp to the exit.

I clench the doorknob so tight, my knuckles pale. "Ever read the *Wizard of Oz*?"

"Don't get smart with me, girl."

I peek over my shoulder. "I'm not getting smart with you. Just wondering if you know what happens to wicked bitches." I clear my throat. "I mean witches."

She squeaks and throws her shoe against the door, barely missing my head. "Get the fuck outta my face and do something useful for a change!"

*Gladly.*

Infuriated, I stalk out of the office and into the diner, where I spot the next evil. It lurks at table five. The second the Nun, and Bitch aka Jules, and Bitchier aka Ava lay eyes on me, they put their heads together and start whispering. I'm sure as hell no angel, but it's days like these when I wonder how the fuck I deserve this shit.

I want to ignore the morons, but I'd probably lose my job if I did, so I prepare myself mentally for another standoff, grab three menus, and amble over to their table.

"Hello, Amanda," Chelsea says. "Didn't know you'd be working today."

That's a lie. My schedule hangs on our fridge. I throw the menus on the table and scowl. "What do you want?"

Roommate From Hell puts a hand on her heart. "Gosh, why do you have to be so rude all the time?"

"Don't know." I give her my best fake smile. "Why do *you* have to be so annoying all the time?"

Chelsea opens her mouth. No words come out.

I pull notepad and pen out of my apron. "What can I get you ladies? Frog legs? Puppy eyes? Virgin blood?"

Chelsea flinches. Ava looks like she's about to vomit on the table, and Jules seems downright scared.

"I don't have all day," I remind them.

"C-Coffee and p-pie," Chelsea stammers.

I jot down the order and stride back to the kitchen. I swear, if this day gets any worse, I'll put a coma hex on myself.

"There you go," Joe says, handing me three slices

of apple pie.

"Thanks," I murmur and walk back to the bitch squad.

I put the plates down and pour their coffees. "Anything else?"

"Yes, one more thing." Ava's voice is surprisingly sharp.

I cock a brow and wait. She keeps quiet. *What the hell is wrong with these girls?*

"Amanda!" Lindy yells. "You ain't getting paid for small talk with your friends."

I shiver at the word *friends.* Those girls are stupid bitches, not my fucking friends.

"It can wait," Chelsea says more to her friends than me.

"Suit yourself," I hiss before I stomp back to the counter.

Keeping a safe distance from table five, I refill napkins. Ava's hand shoots up. "Waitress," she says, as if she doesn't know my name.

"Go," Lindy orders, nudging me in the ribs so hard I think she might have cracked one.

I give my boss a dirty look and saunter to the table. "What do you need?" I sound as annoyed as I am.

"The bill," Ava says with a mischievous grin.

I spin on my heels, ready to get their check so they can get the hell outta my face, but Chelsea stops me. "Wait."

I peek over my shoulder.

"There's something else." She sounds so innocent, it's hard to believe she's a racist bigot.

Ava wears a smug expression and drums her too-long fingernails on the tabletop. The sound drives me nuts.

"Are you dating Bridge DeLuca?" Chelsea asks, clearly uncomfortable with the topic.

Growing increasingly irritated, I knit my brows. "I don't think that's any of your business."

"Actually, it is." Ava's voice brims with confidence.

*Is she for real?* I cross my arms. "Yeah? How so?"

Ava tilts her chin at Jules. "Bridge is already spoken for."

Jules blushes and looks out the window. I knew she was into him. Saw it when she approached him in the hallway, but DeLuca plays in another league. Even the bitch squad should have realized that by now.

I meet Jules's gaze. Unrequited love sucks, and I'd feel sorry for her if she wasn't part of NYU's *Mean Girls*. "No offense, but DeLuca isn't exactly I-put-a-promise-ring-on-your-finger material."

Ava purses her glossy lips. "Bridge is a good guy." She jumps up and gets in my face. "He deserves better than a devil-worshipping freak. So stay the fuck away from him or—"

"Or what?" The darkness in my voice makes Chelsea and Jules flinch.

"Or you'll regret it," Ava warns.

I tried to play nice, but they just crossed a line, and there's no going back. "Listen to me very carefully. If any of you dares to come to my workplace again to threaten *me*, it'll be the last thing *you* do." I glare at each of them in turn. "*Capiche?*"

Unlike Jules and Chelsea, Ava doesn't even blink. "We're not scared of your devil's craft, Amanda."

A psycho grin tugs at my lips. "Oh, but you should

be."

Ava balls her hands into fists. Looks like Ms. Church never heard physical violence is a sin. "You are the worst kind of evil there is."

Chelsea and Jules are on their feet too. "Let's go, Ava."

"Yeah," Jules says. "She's not worth it."

*How about that coma hex now?*

\*\*\*\*

Lindy is famous for payback, but this time she's outdone herself. It's twenty past eleven, and instead of screwing DeLuca, I'm scrubbing the greasy exhaust hood in the diner kitchen. Gross doesn't even begin to cover how disgusting that thing looks. I'd bet my ass no one has touched it since the Noachian flood. What's even worse is the freaking cleaning agent Lindy insisted I use. The translucent liquid burns away my fingertips like pure acid. Why the fuck couldn't I keep my mouth shut when she accused me of dating Legend? *Because I possess a little thing called dignity.*

Putting away the pans, Joe watches me from the corner of his eye. "Why don't you let me help you, *principessa?*"

I wipe grease off my cheek and look down. "Nah, don't worry. I'm almost done." Of course, I'm lying. I could stay all night and the thing would still look like shit, but Joe works here full-time. He deserves to go home to drown this day with plenty of grappa—or whatever else it is Italians drink when they want to get wasted.

He frowns and then, as if he were struck by lightning, he smites his forehead. "*Dio mio,* I almost forgot." He gets on his knees, opens a drawer, and pulls out a tiny bottle filled with yellow liquid. "Here." He tosses it to me. "Use this. It works miracles."

I almost fall from the ladder catching it. "What is it?" I ask, ogling the liquid suspiciously.

"Mama's secret recipe," he whispers.

Still not convinced anything can remove the grease from the exhaust hood, I unscrew the bottle. *What the—* "Whoa, smells like freakin' poison."

Joe's warm laughter fills the kitchen. "It's no poison, principessa." He looks over his shoulder, making sure we really are alone, and adds, "Vinegar, lemon, eucalyptus, and baking soda. It removes every stain in seconds."

I pour some of the stuff onto a cloth and scrub the metal surface with it. Jesus freakin' Christ, it works. The grease dissolves as if it's never been there, and the hood sparkles. "You're a genius," I shout, happy I might get some sleep after all.

"Mama knows best," he says proudly.

I don't necessarily agree with that statement. In Joe's case, however, I'm inclined to make an exception. "Thanks, man."

He winks and grabs his bag from the counter. "Goodnight, principessa."

"Night, Joe."

Scrubbing like a lunatic, I'm so focused on the task at hand, I almost suffer a heart attack when I hear a loud bang come from the storage. Lindy left hours ago. I should be alone.

I decide not to check on the noise, because I really want to be done with the exhaust hood. Minutes fly by and nothing strange happens. Then an icy breeze flows over the nape of my neck, sending shivers down my spine. *What the hell?* I don't suffer from ghost-sickness, but I'll be damned if I don't recognize the supernatural when it touches me.

I step down from the ladder, scanning the kitchen. The pans on the hanging pot rack move. Clanging against each other, they create a spooky melody. "Who the hell is this?" Gotta admit, I'm a little freaked out.

"Manda," a faint, barely audible voice whispers.

*Hell, no. That can't be—*

"Manda, help me."

"Alex?" I shout, horrified.

"Manda, please." Definitely Alex's voice.

I stumble backward. My hip knocks against the counter. *Could Alex be—*No, I'd know if something had happened to him. I'd feel it. *But the nightmares.*

A violent wind gusts through the kitchen, and when it touches my arm, I freeze like a deer in headlights. Whatever is here isn't Alex's ghost. I'm sure of it, because its touch left a mark of pure evil.

"Manda." Alex's voice thunders in my ears and another loud bang rings from the storage.

This ain't no rat. I ignore the horror chewing on my guts and slowly walk toward the source of the noise. *You can do this,* I tell myself, opening the door.

Utter darkness stares back at me. I take another step, searching the wall for the light switch. A flesh-creeping howl echoes off the walls. *Shit, what the—*

I blink several times, but I still see it. The shadow of a gigantic dog manifests a couple of feet in front of me. Its eyes are a fiery red, and its shadowy teeth look like they could bite a head off without much effort.

My heart drops into my belly and a scream forms in the depth of my soul, but it never comes out. *Run,* the voice in my head orders. My fucking feet won't move.

"Save me, Manda. You're the only one who can." Alex's voice floats through the darkness, and I swear the dog smiles.

"Amanda?" A hand lands on my shoulder, and I jump higher than I ever thought I could.

Ready to show off the round-house kick Jesse once taught me, I pivot and see DeLuca.

He stares at me as if I lost my marbles on the kitchen floor. "Wow, what's with you?"

I'd answer, but I'm too busy scanning the room for the gigantic shadow dog.

"Hey," he says calmly. "Is everything okay?"

Nothing is okay. Not only did I hear Alex begging me for help, I also saw a larger-than-life dog with fiery red eyes that seems to have disappeared into thin air.

DeLuca switches the light on and snaps his fingers in my face. "What the hell happened? You look like you've seen a ghost."

*A ghost? Nah. More like a demon dog.* Slowly regaining control, I ogle DeLuca. "What are you doing here?" My voice is laced with suspicion. I'd texted him earlier and canceled our sex date, so why the hell did he show up here?

He shrugs. "Thought I'd pick you up. You know, brighten your night with some mind-blowing Magic Bridge tricks."

I'd laugh at him using his own nickname to describe what kind of dirty things he has up his sleeve, but I'm still too startled by what just happened.

"Amanda." He cups my cheeks. "Are you sure you're okay?" He sounds genuinely worried.

"Yeah," I assure him, my gaze once again

wandering to the spot where the creature stood seconds ago. "Let's get the hell outta here."

He flashes me a mesmerizing smile. "Whatever you say, sugar."

DeLuca stands behind me when I lock the diner. "You shouldn't leave the front door open when you're alone. Any scumbag could just walk in and mug you."

Something tells me getting mugged is the least of my worries.

Chapter 8

*Two weeks later.*

It's Saturday morning, aka my only day off. I could have slept in, finished my essay on Freud, or spent a lazy day on the couch reading a Stephen King book. Due to temporary mental incapacity, I let Bonnie drag me to the Victoria Secret's store in Soho instead. She didn't leave me much of a choice when she barged into my room and threw me out of my warm bed. It's not why I came along though. The second I laid eyes on her, I knew something was wrong. Saying she looked like hell wouldn't have done her someone-road-killed-my-puppy-and-left-it-to-die expression justice. I didn't have the heart to brush her off.

"This one's nice," I say, holding up a peach lace bra with a matching thong.

Bonnie hardly looks at it. "It's kinda girly."

We've been roaming the store for hours—push-up, full coverage, demi, strapless—we've checked them all out. Somehow Bonnie doesn't like anything. Scary. Following her to the lounging bottoms, I seize hold of her arm. "All right." I spin her around. "What's up?"

"Nothing." She shies away from making eye contact.

I might not have had any nightmares lately, but ever since I heard Alex's voice in the diner and saw that monstrous dog, I'm on edge. Meaning: I'm not in the mood to beat around the bush. I cross my arms and tilt my head. "Cut the crap and tell me what this shopping spree is really about."

She bites her nails. "It's nothing." She glances at a kissing couple near the sports bras. "Really." Who is she trying to convince, me or herself?

I point to the shadows under her eyes. "Then why the fuck do you look like you've been up all night crying?" Her honey-colored skin may mask some of the red spots accompanying nasty tears, but there's no mistaking the swollen face and puffy eyes.

She pulls the corners of her mouth down and gives me a dirty look. "I didn't cry," she insists. "Just didn't sleep well."

Ticked off, I pull a face. "Bonnie Marie Lacroix. You've got about two seconds to tell me what the hell is going on with you, or so help me God, I will try that truth spell on you. A word of advice? I wrote it when I was seven. Chances are it goes horribly wrong, and you'll be damned to speak the truth for all eternity."

Her eyes widen. "You wouldn't—"

"Try me."

When she realizes how serious I am, her shoulders sink. "It's Jason." She fiddles with the ribbons of her alabaster boho blouse. "He…he kinda fell for me." Most chicks would be overwhelmed with joy, but for Bonnie the three magic words equal the end of the world.

"Did you break up with him?" Considering her track record, I already know the answer.

She nods sheepishly. "Yesterday."

The girl doesn't need a new bra. She needs a new

lover. Preferably one who'll never use those diabolic words. I might not be able to provide her with said guy, but I can give her the next best thing. I throw an arm around her shoulders. "Breakfast at Landmark?"

She shrugs.

"C'mon," I say, pulling her toward the exit. "I'm buying."

She bats her thick irresistible lashes at me. "Dessert, too?"

I smile at her reassuringly. "All you can eat, baby girl." Bearing in mind how much Bonnie *can* eat, I probably shouldn't have said that, but I'd rather be broke than see her so unhappy.

****

New York Saturdays aren't necessarily crazier than any other day. The city is always crawling with selfie-addicted tourists and busy residents. Yet it took us half an hour to get to Little Italy—I blame Bonnie's snail-walk—and another twenty minutes to get a table at Landmark. No need to say it was way past breakfast time when we finally sat down. Fortunately—for Bonnie, not my bank account—Landmark also offers yummy lunch.

"You're killing the poor thing again," I groan, watching her poke her chicken souvlaki with the fork.

Keeping her eyes on the meat, she sighs heavily. "Isn't that what I do best?"

I shove a forkful of tasty falafel in my mouth. "Assaulting dead meat?"

She puts her cutlery down and frowns. "Killing things."

I'm used to Bonnie's melodramatic-drama-queen streak, but I've never seen her so disturbed over a breakup. "Let me get this straight, B." I take a sip of my icy soda. "You broke up with the poor bastard because he confessed he's irrevocably in love with you, and now you're miserable because you regret breaking up with him?"

She almost chokes on an olive. "I don't regret a thing, and that's the problem."

Either I'm too tired to understand Bonnie-language, or she's talking crazy. "Explain," I order, nibbling on my fries.

She slams her head against the table, barely missing the plate. "There's something wrong with me, Amanda." She looks up, and her eyes are glazed. "Every time a guy professes his love for me, my tummy aches and all I want to do is run. As fast and as far away as possible."

I wipe my mouth on a napkin and knit my brows. "You're totally overreacting. Jason wasn't exactly boyfriend material." *He isn't even screw material.*

Bonnie's leg rocks against the table, a clear sign the conversation makes her uncomfortable. "I'm an enchanting, nineteen-year-old chick who's never been in love." She's frustrated and angry. "Gosh, maybe I should see a shrink or join Chelsea and become a nun."

Bonnie as a nun? Hilarious. She'd probably spend most of the day in the confessional, committing sins with a priest instead of confessing them. Swallowing the hysterical laughter climbing up my throat, I lock my gaze on hers. "Cut it out, B. There's nothing wrong with you. Period." She gives me a killer look, but I don't care. "Love is an illusion. An invention of the brain to save humanity from extinction." I shrug. "Totally overrated if you ask me."

A muscle thrums along her jaw. "Says the girl who took a bullet for a hunter?"

*Home run.* Scared I might lose it if we go down this road, I opt for a quick topic change. "By the way, where the hell is the Nun? Haven't seen her in days." For all I care, Chelsea could have been deported to Guantanamo Bay, but talking about her is better than broaching the Alex topic.

Bonnie gives me her best how-the-hell-do-you-not-know look. "Haven't you heard?"

"Haven't I heard what?"

A spark ignites in her glazed eyes. Seems like good old gossip can cure self-doubt and insecurity in a heartbeat. "One of her friends—what was her name again?" She pushes an index finger against her temple. "Jackie? Jenny? Julianne?"

"Jules?"

"Yes," she says. "That's the one."

My interest piques. "What about her?"

Bonnie rests her elbows on each side of her plate and leans in. "She's been missing for a couple of days."

My eyes widen. "What? How? I mean, why?" I can't form a coherent sentence. What the hell is wrong with me? It's not like I care about the girl.

Bonnie leans back. "There are several theories. They range from urban legend material to rational explanation. Which one would you like to hear?"

"How about the official one?" I grumble, feeling a bit twitchy all of a sudden.

Bonnie picks her fork up and shoves a piece of chicken in her mouth. "Apparently, her best friend...damn, I'm so fucking bad with names."

"Ava?" I offer.

She waves her fork in the air. "Yeah, so that Ava chick found a letter in Jules's room. Said something like she needs a time-out and some distance from some dude she fell for."

*That would be DeLuca.*

"The dean and the police took the note as indication there was no foul play." Bonnie pauses. "Happens all the time, you know. College kids running away from pressure or a broken heart."

Plenty of people run away from their problems. The thing is, Jules doesn't strike me as one of them. She might be a bit heartbroken over DeLuca, but that's hardly enough to provoke a prissy girl like her to throw away her future. "All right," I grumble. "What's the R-rated version?"

Bonnie averts her gaze. "Can't believe you haven't heard," she mutters under her breath. "The whole campus is talking about it."

"'Bout what, B?" I'm certain I don't want to hear it. I probably should, though.

"Remember what you said to the Nun and her friends when they came to the diner?" she asks.

"I said a lot of things, B. Gotta be more specific." I'd told Bonnie all about that day two weeks ago. Okay, I'd told her everything that happened before the creepy monster-dog incident.

She bites her lip. "The part where you threatened them."

I almost laugh. "You mean *after* Bitchier threatened me?"

She nods. "That Ava chick and the Nun are convinced you had something to do with Jules's disappearance. At least, that's what they're telling everyone who's ready to listen. It's also the reason Chelsea is avoiding you. She's staying with Ava at the moment."

In a flash, everything makes sense: the weird looks I get when I walk into my lectures, the fact most students keep an arm's-length distance from me, hell, even Professor Penrose's weird I'm-here-for-you-if-you-need-to-talk offer. "You're kidding," I say, breaking into harsh laughter.

Bonnie sighs. "I wish."

Enraged, I reach for the soda and clench my hand around the glass. It doesn't matter what I do—starting a new life without magic, leaving everything I love behind. When it's all said and done, I'll always be labeled evil.

"Hey." Bonnie squeezes my arm. "Don't let these bitches bring you down."

Faking a smile for Bonnie is hard. I give it my best shot. "C'mon, B. I wouldn't be Amanda Bishop if I did, right?"

She slams her fist on the table. "Damn right, girl. Let them talk. It only means your life is much more interesting than theirs."

*Much, much more interesting.*

Bonnie pushes her chair back and points to the restrooms. "Be right back."

Staring at my half-eaten falafel, I can't stop thinking about Jules. I haven't touched a hair on the girl's scalp, yet somehow I feel at fault for her disappearance. Stupid. I'm a powerful witch and all, but it's not like my thoughts can make a person vanish into thin air.

I'm beginning to get a seriously fucked-up

migraine when a familiar voice calls my name. "Amanda?"

The first thing I see are the expensive Italian leather shoes, followed by casual low-hanging jeans, a baby-blue cotton shirt, an armful of odd-looking religious tattoos that spread over the neck, and last but not least, arctic-blue eyes ogling me.

"I thought it was you," Legend says, flashing me a bright smile.

What I want to say is leave me the hell alone. What I say is, "Hey."

Without asking for permission, he grabs Bonnie's chair and takes a seat. "It's been a while, huh?"

I narrow my eyes at him. Not sure how he measures time, but two days aren't a while in my book. The past two weeks, he's shown up at the diner every time I worked a goddamn shift, and I'm beginning to wonder if I need to get a restraining order.

He grabs some fries from my plate. "This is where you hang out when you're not working the diner?"

I'm not in the mood for small talk, but I'm especially not in the mood for small talk with *him*. "Look, Legend"—I point to the restrooms—"my friend should be back any minute."

His lips part, but before he can say a word, Bonnie returns. "Hey," she says, eyeballing Legend as if he's a freaking meal deal.

In a very polite gesture, Legend rises from his chair and offers it to Bonnie. "Sorry."

My best friend beams at him, and I want to puke. "I'm totally into sharing," she assures him, using her flirty voice.

*Seriously, I think I'm getting sick.*

Legend grins, then his attention swivels to me. "I should be going." Pulling a business card out of his pocket, he puts it on the table next to my plate. "I've wanted to give you this for a long time." He winks. "Call me sometime. I have a business proposition to make."

I glare at the card. *Business proposition, huh? What a rotten liar he is.*

Bonnie's eyes are glued to Legend's back. It's only when he closes the door behind him as he leaves that she looks at me. "Wow. Who the hell was that?"

"A customer." A very weird customer.

She grins like the Cheshire cat. "Maybe I should get a job, too."

I give her a look. "No. No, you shouldn't."

\*\*\*\*

I'm in my room, applying mulberry-colored lipstick and glaring at the bullet scar on my chest. Every time I show off cleavage, I'm forced to think of that night in Bakersfield. I'm forced to think of Alex. I wonder what he's up to these days? Killing some of my kind? Screwing some of his kind? Business as usual, I guess. Not that I care. Just curious.

I look at the digital clock on my nightstand. Shit, DeLuca should be here any second. I don't feel like hanging out with him, but he'd insisted we meet. The guy is starting to become a problem, and I need to get rid of him. As soon as I find another cure for my nightmares, that is.

"Wow," DeLuca moans, standing in the doorframe. "You look stunning, sugar."

*Think of the devil, huh?* I shove the lipstick in my bag. "How did you get in?" Not the nicest way to say hello, but it's the best I can do today.

"Bonnie," he says, stalking toward me like a starving lion.

Of course, she'd let him in. I must force her to watch more of those true crime shows, where the perpetrator is someone the victim knows. Maybe she'll stop trusting everyone.

Fighting the overwhelming urge to crawl into my bed and hide, I grab my favorite faux leather jacket from the closet. DeLuca's hands land on my waist.

"Sure you want to go out?" he asks, breathing me in. He pushes me against the closet. "We could…" He traces kisses down my neck. "Do more fun things here, sugar." More fun things probably involve the hardness pressed against my ass.

"Stop…calling me that," I moan as his hand travels down my belly and right into my tight leather pants.

He pins my hands above my head. "Or what?"

My lips part, but before I can say something, DeLuca's tongue dives into my mouth. We'd kissed a lot. This time it's different. Darker. More aggressive. It feels as if he's punishing me for something.

He's moving me. I'm faintly conscious of it, but the kiss fucks with my senses. Hell, it fucks with me, and not in a good way.

The bickering voice in my head screams *stop*. I can't. I'm not in control. DeLuca takes over.

My lips sting. I'd never been kissed so mercilessly.

His hand is inside my panties, feeling me up. "That's how you like it, huh? Rough and slutty."

I'm a big fan of dirty talk. Alex and I? Let's just say, we could have written a dictionary of words that drive people over the edge. But the way DeLuca does it kinda creeps me out. "Bridge," I choke out, short of breath.

He puts more pressure on my sweet spot, causing my back to arch. I've heard stories about body and mind wanting two different things. Never thought it could happen to me, though.

Reaching for the hem of my shirt, he spins me around. "Still with me, sugar?"

I'm not.

The room starts spinning. My head thumps like crazy.

And DeLuca's touch no longer affects me, because I'm caught up in flashes of what looks like *An American Werewolf in London.*

\*\*\*\*

*A howl rang through the darkness.*

*Red eyes looked up.*

*Crimson teeth snarled.*

*Blood splattered against a wall.*

*Flesh torn.*

*I heard a voice. At first it was distant, and I could barely make out what it was saying.*

*The voice grew louder. "Manda, help me."*

*My heart, literally, stopped beating. My lungs refused to draw in oxygen. And my mind felt like it was about to shatter into pieces.*

\*\*\*\*

"Alex?" I whisper, tears blurring my vision.

DeLuca pulls back. "Who the fuck is Alex?"

Chapter 9

I'm lying in my bed, holding my phone, eyes glued to the ceiling. Been here ever since I threw DeLuca out, which was right after he rose hell 'cause he thought I was seeing someone else.

The unusual vision still screws with my head. I've had my fair share of premonitions—hundreds, if not thousands. They always came in different shapes. Some concerned the past, others the future. Some could have been prevented, and others prescient. This one was different, though. Not only had it come in obscure flashes, it also felt as if whatever I saw was happening at that moment. A freaking live broadcast.

Now, almost nine sleepless hours later, the sun is up. Green House, our residence hall, is alive—I hear the noises our next door neighbors make—and I'm still wondering why I haven't called Alex. I know I'll have to eventually. There's no denying he's somehow connected to all the weird things happening. The nightmares, the creepy shadow dog, and the fact I heard him call out for help twice? As a witch, I can hardly write that off as coincidence.

It's not like I haven't tried to contact him. I must have dialed his number a thousand times in the past few hours. Finding the courage to press that godforsaken green button seemed impossible, though. I blame the fucking *what if* battle raging inside my head. *What if I call him, and he shows up here? What if I don't call him and something awful happens? What if he hangs up because he doesn't want to talk to me? What if he sounds happy to hear from me? What if he's in danger?* Stop.

I let go of the phone and press the heels of my hands against my temples. Anxiety is a bitch, and I better pull it together before I turn into the witch version of Holden Caulfield. Not that I have anything against the too smart, self-aware protagonist of *The Catcher in the Rye*, but I firmly believe teen angst should have an expiration date.

I look at the digital clock on my nightstand, and my stomach dips a bit. In a little more than an hour, I'm supposed to sit in Penrose's lecture. DeLuca will be there too, asking questions like, "Why did you whisper some dude's name while I had you pinned against the closet?" Good times.

*Can't avoid the inevitable.*

Gathering the last bits of energy buzzing through my numb body, I get up and stumble to the bathroom. I climb in the shower.

Dipping my head back, I embrace the hot water pouring down my lethargic skin, but every time I close my eyes, I shiver. The blood, the torn flesh, and the fiery eyes haunt me.

I turn the faucet, increasing the temperature from hot to I'm-gonna-end-up-in-the-ER-with-second-degree-burns.

*Why does shit like this keep happening to me? Did I not pay my karmic dues when I helped Alex save Jesse and those kids? Don't I deserve a freakin' breather? Some plus points on the cosmic scale?*

I rest my head against the shower wall, hoping the heat will burn away all the shit that's bothering me. It doesn't. Nothing can wash away the void this premonition has left inside me.

The hot spray smears the makeup from last night. The scent of my jasmine perfume is replaced by the harsh smell of sandalwood soap. Hell, how I wish everything else would go away as easily. *It won't.* Yeah, and I gotta stop pretending it will.

By the time I wrap my hair in a towel and slap on a little makeup, I'm certain of three things: I need to get rid of DeLuca before his I'm-a-lovesick-obsessed-asshole act gets worse, my new life sucks, and I will call Alex, consequences be damned.

I just put on my panties and bra when loud banging against the front door startles me. Bonnie is still fast asleep, the Nun has a key, and I'm not expecting any visitors. I step into loose jeans, pull a sweater over my head, and walk out of the bathroom.

One thing's for sure; whoever is knocking doesn't know a thing about patience. The door vibrates, and if I didn't know better, I'd say someone's trying to break it down.

"Jesus freakin' Christ, I'm coming." I yank the door open, ready to unload a shitload of anger, but when my brain processes what my eyes see, I can neither move nor talk.

Blood.

Bruises.

More blood.

Alex.

*What the—*

"Can we come in?" Jesse's voice hits me like an

uppercut to the jaw. He's steadying his more dead than alive brother and looks miserable.

The nightmares, the vision, Alex's desperate pleas—it all comes back in this moment, flooding my system like a monster wave.

"Manda?" Jesse is completely out of breath, and I'm not sure how much longer he can hold the barely conscious Alex.

I open the door wider. "C-Couch. Take him to the couch," I stammer, wondering if I'm having a nightmare with open eyes, or if my abilities have increased and I'm experiencing a vision without even knowing it.

"Shit," Jesse hisses as he lays his brother down, almost losing his balance. His hands and clothes are as bloody as Alex's. The expression on his face is more disturbing than any horror movie I've ever seen.

The initial shock fades, and something else takes hold of me. Red-hot merciless rage. I slam the door shut and look at Jesse—mostly because I can't look at half-dead Alex, who's bleeding like a pig. "What the fuck happened?"

Jesse kneels next to Alex, not taking his eyes off him. "Can we postpone the Q&A session? In case you haven't noticed, my brother is kinda bleeding out here."

*In case I haven't noticed?* The crimson soaking into our cream couch is sort of hard to overlook. I suppress the desire to yell at Jesse and run into the bathroom to get clean towels.

I really want to know what the fuck is going on, because I hate to act first and ask questions later, but one look at Alex, who fades in and out of consciousness, tells me this isn't the time for questions.

I shove Jesse out of the way. "Step back."

He gives me space so I can examine Alex's battered body. *Where the hell is all this blood coming from?* There's a nasty cut running from his left eyebrow all the way down to his jaw. Sort of looks like he had a date with Freddy Krueger, but common sense tells me it's not the primary source of the bleeding. I rest my hand on his good cheek and shake him a little. "Alex?"

Nothing.

"Hey." I slap him softly. "Can you hear me?"

His eyelids flutter. He doesn't answer.

"Open your fuckin' eyes, Alex." I sound like a hyena, but I don't give a shit.

"Am I...in hell?" he chokes out, eyes still closed.

*So he hears my voice and thinks he's in hell, huh?* Charming. Despite the fact he acts like a jerk even when death comes knocking, I breathe a sigh of relief. As long as he can speak, he can't be dead. "You're gonna be okay, Alex."

"Liar," he whispers, a fresh burst of pain flickering across his face.

"Old habits die hard," I say, mostly because I want him to stay with me.

He tries to crack a smile. His agony transforms it into a weird grimace.

My gaze goes from the cut on his face to his torn shirt. "I'm going to pull your shirt up, you hear me?"

I think he nods, but maybe it's just my imagination. *What the—*

Four long claw marks run over his ribcage. They're deep. Too fucking deep.

Jesse nudges my hip. "Can you help him?"

*Help him?* I look up. "He needs a fuckin'

81

ambulance, man." Jesus would be better, though.

"No," Alex mumbles as I press a towel against his chest. "No hospital." The stubborn jerk tries to sit up, though he can't even lift his arm. The more he moves, the more blood gushes out of the wounds, coloring the white towels dark sangria.

*Where does he think he's going? If he keeps this up, he'll visit the morgue.* Holding Alex down with one hand, I glare at Jesse. "You shouldn't have brought him here." I tilt my head at Alex's torn chest. "He needs a doctor."

Anger, frustration, fear—it's all carved into Jesse's face. "We can't take him to a hospital."

I give him the WTF is wrong with you look. "Why?"

He runs a bloody hand over his chin. "It's complicated."

*Complicated?* His brother looks like he ran into a horde of backwoods cannibals. My stomach twists into little knots. "A Facebook status is complicated. This"— I point to Alex's torn chest—"is something entirely else."

"Fuck. You think I don't know that?" He paces the room. "I wouldn't be *here* if I could have taken him to a hospital," he shouts, unleashing his anger at me.

I clench my jaw. I'm about to throw the remote control against Jesse's head, but the door to Bonnie's room flings open in time to prevent another Remington from getting hurt. "Jesus, keep it down," she barks, bumping into Jesse's rock-hard chest wearing nothing but an old oversized shirt.

"Whoa." Jesse steps back. For a fraction of a second, he eyeballs my best friend's bare legs. As I said, old habits die hard. Even when your brother is about to bite the dust.

"Who the hell are you?" Bonnie's wild curls stick out in every direction. Her gaze drifts from Jesse's blood-soaked shirt to his grief-stricken face. "Jesus, is that—"

"B!" I try to draw her attention.

She slowly turns her head. "Who the hell is—" The color drains from her face when she sees Alex, half dead, on our couch. "Oh. My. God." Her eyes widen with terror. "Is that who I think it is?"

I nod and return my focus to Jesse. "You've got about two seconds to tell me why we can't call an ambulance, or I swear I'm outta here." I'd never leave Alex like this—not him, not anyone—but Jesse doesn't know that.

"Damn." He throws his hands in the air. "The police are looking for him. Happy? Can we save my brother now?"

"What?"

Tears burn in his eyes. "Please." His gaze flies to Alex. "I don't have time to explain, but you're all he's got. Don't let him die, Manda."

How the hell am I supposed to keep him alive? "I'm a fuckin' witch, Jesse, not God."

"Guys!" Bonnie stands over Alex, slightly green. "I don't think this is normal," she says, pointing to Alex's rolled-back eyes.

I put a hand on Alex's forehead. He's burning up. I check his pulse, which is stronger than I expected. But for how long?

I push all the questions to the back of my mind. "B?" She meets my gaze. "Get the rosemary oil, St.

John's wort, and the first-aid kit. ASAP."

Bonnie lifts the towel off Alex's chest and knits her brows. "The cuts are way too deep for herbs," she objects.

She's right, but it's not like we have anything to lose. "Just do it," I hiss. "And you." I cut my eyes to Jesse. "Needle, thread, and absinthe."

He scans the room, ready to spring into action. "Where do you keep that stuff?"

Bonnie hauls him to the kitchen cabinet. "Here," she says, opening a drawer.

"Alex?" I caress his cheek. "Open your eyes."

He doesn't.

"Stay with me, Alex." I honest to God can't remember the last time I sounded so fucking desperate.

The absinthe bottle in Jesse's hand trembles. "Amanda, is he…is he—"

"He has a pulse," I assure him, index finger pressed against Alex's carotid artery. Not sure for how long, though.

Jesse hands me the absinthe, a silver needle, and plenty of black thread. "What exactly are you going to do?"

*What's it look like?* "We need to stop the bleeding. The only way to do that is to patch him up."

Bonnie puts the stuff I asked her to get on the table. When she sees the funky expression on Jesse's face, she says, "C'mon," and pulls him away so I can work. "She knows what she's doing."

*God, I wish I had her faith in me.*

"You sure?" He doesn't sound convinced.

Bonnie cocks a brow. "We're talking about Amanda Bishop, right?"

For some inexplicable reason, Jesse relaxes. "You're right," he mutters under his breath. "She won't let him die."

Miracles aren't exactly my expertise, but I'll try my best.

Alex is still out cold when I pour the fiery, high-percentage alcohol over his torn chest. It must hurt like a motherfucker, 'cause his eyes pop open. "Fuck," he whines as surely the burning sensation rushes through him.

"Don't be such a baby," I say, choking back a shitload of unpleasant emotions.

"Always the bitch, huh?" He coughs.

"Hey," I bark when he shuts his eyes. "Look at me."

"Tired."

"I know, but you gotta keep those pretty eyes open." I can't have him go into shock or fall into a coma.

"O...kay," he whispers. I'm not sure he can keep his word.

I wipe the booze off his chest. Hands shaking like crazy, I examine the cleaned cuts. It's bad, life-threatening, if-he-doesn't-bleed-out-he'll-die-from-sepsis bad.

"Manda?" Alex's voice is hoarse and weak.

"Shhh...Don't talk, okay?" I open the rosemary oil and pour the thick liquid over his chest wound. It's the best antibacterial fluid I have. Unfortunately, it stings like hell.

Alex flinches. He stiffens under my hand as the fresh pain sinks its claws into his skin. "You..." His eyes lock with mine. "Like that?"

"Are you kidding?" I say, watching the oil drip into the cuts, covering the torn flesh like a protective film. "You bleeding onto Chelsea's pope pillow? That's a freakin' dream come true."

He tries to smile. Gasps for air instead.

"Someone get me a lighter," I order.

"Here." Jesse hands me Alex's Zippo.

I reach for the scissors in the first-aid kit and hold the tips in the flame.

"Have you done this before?" Jesse asks as I move on to the needle.

"Yeah." I was seventeen when I cut my hand on broken glass. Since fortune-telling didn't come with insurance, I'd Googled *how to stitch someone up* and found a few videos. Even with painkillers, it had hurt like hell, but I'd done it.

He doesn't believe me. His stare tells me so. I wouldn't either.

Once the needle is sterile, I try to thread it, but my hands are too shaky. "A little help?" Bonnie is right there. I show off my trembling hands. "I can't do it."

"I got it." She threads the needle like a pro and hands it back in seconds. "You good?" she asks, concern filling her cognac eyes.

I'm a lot of things—terrified, desperate, confused, angry—but good isn't one of them. "Peachy," I mumble, looking for any debris in the wounds. There's none.

Bonnie squeezes my shoulder. "You got this."

I almost laugh, but when I see Jesse's horrified expression, I keep my mouth shut and reach for the scissors. I remember the video said something about cutting away loose or jagged flesh to prepare the edges, and that's exactly what I do.

Bonnie wraps an arm around Jesse's shoulders. "She's not gonna let anything happen to him. Trust her."

*God, I hope she's right.*

I push self-doubt and fear to the back of my mind and focus on Alex. "Hey." I snap my fingers in his face. "You still with me?" He nods, but the emptiness in his irises scares the living shit outta me.

*Open eyes, restless soul.* I ignore Gram's voice. No way Alex is going to die. Not today. Not here. Not now.

"Say if you need me to stop, okay?" I push the needle through his skin.

He doesn't even flinch. He just lies there, unresponsive.

I use my thumb and index finger to press the torn skin together and keep stitching. "B? Can you prepare some lavender-rosemary tea?"

"Sure." She circles Jesse's wrist and pulls him along. "C'mon, I could use a hand." Bonnie is perfectly capable of brewing tea, but Jesse needs distraction, and despite her deep-rooted hate for hunters, she tries to give him some.

An hour later, my fingertips burn like hell, but Alex is stitched up. He went in and out of consciousness the entire time. Forcing the tea down his throat wasn't easy, but I managed. I stare at my masterpiece of red flesh and black thread. *Not bad for a rookie.* "Done," I mutter, rubbing the St. John's wort on his chest before adding Band-Aids.

"Sure he's still breathing?" Jesse's voice is shallow, his eyes clouded. "He's asleep."

"It's the tea," Bonnie explains. "The stuff is almost

as good as an anesthetic." I brush Alex's hair back. "His head needs a few stitches, too." It's not nearly as bad as his chest. With all the practice I'd had, I manage to close it within minutes.

"Is he going to be okay?" The sorrow in Jesse's voice is heartbreaking.

"Dunno." I wipe my bloody hands on a clean towel. "He lost a lot of blood."

"Fuck. Fuck. Fuck. Fuck." Jesse kicks the wall like a maniac, causing the plaster to crumble. "This is my fault. I should have come to you sooner."

My gaze shoots up. "What do you mean sooner?"

Jesse scrubs his fingers through his un-styled hair and frowns. "There's something I need to tell you."

My belly hurts, and my heart pounds painfully fast. "What's going on, Jesse?" I'm not sure I really want to know.

His gaze drops to the floor. "It's complicated."

I swear, if I hear that word one more time, I'll lose my fucking mind and strangle him. Hands balled into fists, I advance toward him. "You better open your mouth before I start throwing punches."

"He's going to kill me." He glances at Bonnie. "I promised him not to."

I bring my fist up, ready to hit him in the face, but Bonnie steps between us. "Hey. You can kill him later." She winks at Jesse. "No offense."

He shrugs. "Some taken."

Bonnie continues, unimpressed. "Point is, if the Nun comes back and sees him"—she points her head at Alex—"she'll alert campus security. You don't want that, do you?"

I frown. Of course, I don't want that. Campus

security would call the cops, and according to Jesse, Alex—a freaking FBI agent—is a fugitive. I draw a deep breath. "All right." I sound defeated. "Let's get him to my room and cover up the couch with a sheet."

"Good idea," Bonnie murmurs.

Jesse shoves his hands under Alex's arms, and Bonnie and I grab his legs. "Ready?" he asks.

We nod and lift him. Carrying dead weight is harder than I thought. The three of us barely manage to get him to my bed.

Out of breath, I tuck Alex in and face Jesse. "You've got some serious explaining to do, Little Remington."

Chapter 10

I open the windows to let in some fresh air. The rusty iron scent of Alex's blood permeates the place. Add the herbs and absinthe, and I get an idea of what serial-killer-operated B&Bs must smell like.

I soak my hands in lemon to get rid of the dried crimson while Bonnie pours three cups of coffee. Her curls are still a wild mess, but she's changed into a pair of old jeans and a shirt that reads, I Don't Have A Dirty Mind, I Have A Sexy Imagination.

"You take milk or sugar?" she asks Jesse.

To say Little Remington looks hung up would be the understatement of the century. His usually tanned skin is snow white. The chocolate eyes are puffy and red. He looks like hell. Nevertheless, he's trying hard to keep it together. "Just black," he mutters, leaning against our old recliner.

I'm still mad at him 'cause of the *it's complicated* shit, but seeing him like this breaks my non-existent heart. I wish I could take his pain and desperation away. The thing is, there ain't no spell in the world to fix his hopeless situation. I might have been able to stop Alex's bleeding, but without a real doctor, there's no guarantee he'll pull through.

Rubbing my wet hands on my jeans, I trudge toward him and plummet down on the coffee table. I've got a million questions. *Why the hell is Alex on the run from the police? What did Jesse mean when he said he should have come to me sooner? How the fuck did Alex get hurt in the first place?* I wait for the coffee before I go all witch-interrogation-bitch on him.

"Manda?" Jesse's voice is broken. I get the feeling it's pretty much the current status of his soul.

I look up. "Hm?"

"Is he..." He clears his throat. "Is Alex going to make it?"

I rest my elbows on my knees and press the heels of my hands against my tired eyes. For as long as I can remember, I've told people what they wanted to hear. Will I be rich? *Of course, honey.* Am I going to have a breakthrough as an actor? *Dude, you'll be the next Brad Pitt.* Does he love me? *Until death do you part.* Never had second thoughts about lying. Probably because the people I'd lied to wouldn't have believed the truth anyway. False hope was better than none. But I can't lie to Jesse. He's been through enough in the last couple of months. The last thing he needs is false hope.

"Manda?" "I don't know, Jess." Shifting to the edge of the table, I shove my hands between my knees. "I really don't."

Silent tears roll down his cheeks. He doesn't even bother to wipe them away. "I can't lose him."

"You won't," Bonnie says, surprising us. I give her the have-you-gone-mad look, but she hands Jesse his cup and ignores me. "Why don't you tell us how this happened while we wait for your brother to wake up?"

Jesse takes a seat on the arm of our recliner. I almost expect another *it's complicated* statement, but the expression on his face tells me what I'll get will be worse. "You remember that friend of mine who sold his soul?"

How could I ever forget the reason behind Jesse's zombie excursion? I do, after all, still have the scars caused by it. "Yeah, and?"

A moment of silence passes. "Well," he says, covering his face with both hands. "He was less a friend than a brother."

*A brother?* Since *when does he have more than one?* I cross my arms. "Thought you and Alex were the only Remington boys?"

His already dark eyes turn black. "We are."

I squint. What he's saying is impossible. I laugh. "You're kidding, right?" I rest a hand on my belly and laugh some more. "Brother? That would mean—"

"Alex sold his soul," he blurts out, his face a picture of misery.

My heart misses several beats before it slams against my ribcage like a prisoner trying to escape his cell. "Come again?"

Jesse puts his cup down. "The reason I went looking for someone to break a deal with a demon was Alex, Amanda."

His words sink into my soul, causing a total eclipse of my heart. Everything around me ceases to exist— Jesse, Bonnie, the apartment—all swallowed by a black hole. It's as if someone has pulled the rug out from under my feet or I'm caught in one of those disturbing falling dreams. Only there'll be no waking before I hit the ground.

"Manda?" Jesse sounds wretched. "Say something…please?"

Not a single word leaves my dry mouth.

Bonnie stands beside me. I think she's squeezing

my shoulder. I'm too numb to be certain. "Let me get this straight," she says, voice even, eyes sharp. "Alexander 'I kill everything and anything that's supernatural' has..." She takes a deep breath. "Signed a pact with the devil?"

Jesse nods, and I hit rock bottom. I try to hold my head up, try to be strong—'cause that's what people say you should do after you fall—but I'm not sure they know how it feels when your world burns and crashes. How could Alex, of all people, make a deal with the devil? He's a hunter, for Christ's sake. Righteous, honest, caring—the last person you'd expect to find in hell. *No. No. No. No.* This can't be happening. It can't be true. Then I think of the way Alex acted when I'd asked him why Jesse was working a case by himself, his odd behavior when I'd had that vision of Anna, who had fallen in love with jerk-face. Eventually, I hear Baron Samedi, the rogue reaper who helped Francoise the bokor and Walter the pedophile abduct little girls. *"I'm willing to grant you one wish and one wish only...Why don't you ask your little hunter friend over there? Until we meet again, Alexander."* Fuck. Does that mean I paid with Alex's soul when I got Isobelle, the ten-year-old the bokor killed because she knew too much, out of purgatory? Could the reaper have saved him from hell?

"Amanda?" Bonnie is on her knees in front of me. "Are you okay?"

Angry is what I should be, flaming mad she even asks me such a question. For the very first time in my life though, there's no spark left inside me. The blazing fire is extinguished, and it left nothing but smoke and ashes.

"Manda?" Jesse stares at me as if I'm from another planet. "Your silence is fucking terrifying."

"I've never seen her like this," Bonnie assures him. "Think she's in shock or something."

*"When you fall, baby girl, you gotta get up. Gotta get up and move on."* Gram's voice thunders in my head.

I close my eyes and take a few deep breaths. My mouth is drier than the Mojave Desert when I speak. "If what you're saying is true, then how is he still alive?" Demons aren't exactly famous for mercy. If you sign a deal, they reap your soul. There's no stopping them.

"That's the thing," Jesse says. "He still has twelve days."

Bonnie peeks over her shoulder at Jesse. "What?"

"His contract ends in twelve days," he repeats.

"Doesn't make sense," she mutters, confused. "Demons aren't allowed to reap before your time runs out."

He nods. "I know."

Bonnie knits her brows. "Then why the hell does he look like a victim of *Teen Wolf*?"

Frustration bleeds into Jesse's features, hardening his jawline. "I don't know. I wish I did, but I don't."

"Why?" I hear myself ask.

Jesse cuts his eyes my way. "What?"

"Why did he do it?" Money, fame, sex—those are the usual suspects when someone strikes a deal with hell. Not in Alex's case. He's too fucking righteous.

Jesse's gaze drops to the floor. "I don't know."

"Bullshit," I bark. "You're his brother. There's nothing you don't know about him." My voice is cold and distant. I blame the ice running through my veins for it.

"I'm telling you the truth, Manda." He looks me right in the eye. "He wouldn't tell me."

Bonnie gets on her feet. "How about you start at the beginning? Tell us everything you know."

He thrusts his fingers through his hair. "Remember that night when you walked away?"

I raise my brows. "You mean the night Alex pointed his gun at me 'cause he thought I was a cold-blooded killer-witch?"

Jesse nods. "After you were gone, he went through a pretty rough time. Day drinking. Bar fights. Hell, sometimes he disappeared for days at a time."

None of that sounds like Alex. He's no saint, but I've never seen him drink during the day or pick a random fight like all the other idiots I used to screw.

"It was bad," Jesse says. "He only came around when Carter, our FBI supervisor, threatened to fire him."

"Why are you telling me this?" His behavior after we broke up is hardly relevant.

He sucks in air. "One day, after he'd just come back from one of those mysterious trips, I saw a cut on his palm. At first I didn't think much of it, but when I got a good look, I recognized it…a sigil."

"What happened then?" Bonnie asks.

"I questioned him over and over about it. Begged him to tell me how he got it, but you know Alex." He gives me a look. "He's a stubborn jerk. Told me to mind my own fucking business."

*Yep, sounds like the Alex I know.*

"Then five months ago," Jesse continues, "after a very boozy night in a strip club, he finally came clean."

He blinks fresh tears away. "Told me the truth about what had happened that night."

"And what truth would that be?" I grumble, growing increasingly impatient with him.

A pained smile crosses Jesse's lips. "Over boobs and bourbon, my brother confessed what he'd done. Said he had five months left until the demon would drag his soul to hell, and when I demanded to know why he'd done it, he just said"—he imitates Alex's husky voice—"'I love you, little brother, but some things are mine and mine only.'"

Bonnie heads over to Jesse and folds a hand over his shoulder. "So that's when you started looking for the bokor, huh?"

"Yeah. I heard he'd gotten a few guys out of their deals, and since I had to promise Alex not to ask Amanda for help, I figured he'd be my best bet."

"He made you promise not to tell Amanda?" Bonnie's voice is an octave higher than usual. "Why the fuck would he do that?"

Jesse traces the edge of his cup. "He thought she wouldn't care if he lived or died. I think he was still mad at her for leaving."

I dig my nails into the palm of my hand, expecting the pain to chase away the deadness. My skin is already red, the claw marks deep, and I still don't feel a thing.

"What an asshole," Bonnie barks. She looks at Jesse. "No offense."

A half-hearted smile is on his lips. "None taken."

A moment passes and then he gets up and walks toward me. "Manda," he says, kneeling before me. "I know I should have told you the truth in Bakersfield. Almost did in the hospital. But I'm here now, and I'm begging you…Help me save my brother from hell."

I stare at him in disbelief. A pact with the devil is shatterproof. Once you've purchased a ticket to hell, there's no going back, because it's non-fucking-refundable.

"Say something," he pleads.

I still wait for anger and madness to hit, but I remain calm. "What do you want me to say?"

He puts two fingers under my chin and lifts my head so we're eye to eye. "Say you'll help him. Say you'll save him. Say anything, Manda."

I jerk my head to the side and rise. "Anything, huh?" I pace the room. "How about this? When I summoned the reaper, and he told me he'd grant me one wish only, you kept your mouth shut. You could have saved him back then." I stop dead in my tracks and face him. "Sorry, man, but now it's too late. And this time, it ain't *my* fault."

A heart-wrenching sadness fills his eyes. "So Alex was right? You really don't give a shit if he lives or dies?"

I cross my arms. "You don't get it, do you? He's already dead, Jesse. Even the big guy in the sky can't save him."

"Amanda," Bonnie shouts. "What the hell is wrong with you?" She points to Jesse, who's at the brink of a breakdown.

I couldn't have hurt him more if I'd hit him with a fucking baseball bat. "He deserves the truth," I mutter before I spin on my heels and move to my room, slamming the door behind me.

****

I lie close to Alex. Hand on his chest, I feel his

heart beating, listen to him breathing while he's far away and dreaming. It's past midnight, and the numbness inside of me slowly subsides. The pain crawling through the crumbling deadness isn't much better, though. Hell, who am I kidding? It's so much worse.

I lost Alex the day I'd met him. Hey, I'm not a dreamer. Him being a hunter and me being a witch meant we were headed in two different directions. That was okay as long as I knew he still had one—a future that is.

"What the fuck were you thinking?" I murmur, brushing the hair out of his face. Damn, even with the ugly stitches running from his left eyebrow all the way down to his jaw, he's still perfection. Michelangelo himself couldn't have captured those flawless cheekbones, let alone those desirable lips.

I hate crying. Hate everything testifying to my weakness, but Alex is going to die. His soul will be dragged to the fiery lakes, and there's nothing I can do about it. How could I have been so blind in Bakersfield? Why hadn't his aura betrayed what he'd done? *Witches can only see so much, and Alex did a great job hiding his little secret.*

Tears well up and spill down my cheeks. Like Jesse, I don't bother to wipe them away. What's the point? There's plenty more where they came from.

I stare at his peaceful face. How could he do this to his brother...to me...to his—*Don't go down that road.* Easier said than done.

Slowly shifting to the edge of my bed, I lift the blanket to check if there's fresh blood on his bandages. I breathe a sigh of relief when there's none, but even if he survives the wounds, he could still die in a couple of days.

I tuck him in. "One righteous jerk-face hunter you are. I mean, a deal with the devil, Alex? Really?"

Why the hell did he do it? Does it really matter?

I never meant to care for Alex. Never meant to care for anyone but myself. Look at me now. Where did all my selfishness go? What happened to the girl who believed no one could ever break her heart?

"I need to talk to her," Jesse says outside my room.

"You gotta give her some time," Bonnie mutters. "She'll come around."

Jesse raises his voice. "My brother doesn't have time, Bonnie."

"Okay." She sounds exhausted. "I'll talk to her, but you gotta stay here. Understand?"

Talking to Bonnie or anyone else is the last thing I want to do, but when she knocks, I can't bring myself to deny her entry.

"Hey." She sticks her head in the door. "Can I come in?"

I shrug.

She drags a chair from my desk to the bed. "How you holding up?"

I shrug again.

For some time, she sits there quietly, looking at Alex, looking at me. Bonnie knows how quickly my temper can take over when someone rubs me the wrong way, and when she sees the tears in my eyes, I can tell she's scared to say the wrong thing.

What's the right thing to say in a situation like this though? Bonnie might not use her abilities, and she might hate her magical heritage, but she, too, knows there's no way out of a deal with a demon.

"His head looks good," she says when she finally breaks the silence. "Seems like you've got some hidden talents."

I keep my mouth shut.

She shoves her hands between her thighs, and another noiseless moment passes before her eyes lock with mine. "What are we going to do about this?" She points her chin at Alex.

I swallow the pins and needles in my throat. "There's nothing we *can* do, and you know it."

Bonnie's lips slip into a frown. "Says the girl who cured a zombie without an antidote?"

I give her a look. Not that I don't appreciate what she's trying to do, but I can't handle false hope. "Zombies are one thing, B. Deals with the devil, or one of his demon bitches, is something else entirely."

"Someone once told me every poison has an antidote."

I wipe my damp cheeks. "Have you ever heard of anyone who got out of a deal, B?"

She sighs. "I haven't."

I bite on my lip. "That's what I thought."

"But I'd also never heard of a zombie cure."

I hadn't expected a "but" from her. Not from the most rational person I've ever met. "What are you saying?"

She shifts to the edge of her chair. "What I'm saying is the Amanda Bishop I know wouldn't just accept his fate. She'd move heaven and hell, and I mean that quite literally, to save him."

A messy lump forms in my chest. Emotions crush me. "Just leave me alone, B." I run my fingers through

Alex's sweaty hair. "Please?"

"All right." She gets up and walks to the door. "But ask yourself this," she says, hand around the doorknob. "Can you really live with the fact you didn't even try to keep him alive?" Then she's gone.

Chapter 11

*Eleven days to hell*

Alex slept through the night. I didn't. Couldn't. His short breaths, cold hands and feet, and the swelling of his tongue worried me. I knew those were symptoms of anemia, and since our apartment wasn't equipped for a blood transfusion, I sent Bonnie and Jesse to Chinatown to get some blood-building herbs. Little Remington thought it a clear sign I hadn't given up on his brother. He was wrong. I just couldn't sit back and watch him die when there *was* something I could do.

I look at the digital clock on my nightstand, and my heartbeat quickens. I've already missed my lectures. Now it's close to two p.m., and my shift at the wicked bitch's diner started almost half an hour ago. Between worrying about Alex's current condition and wrapping my head around the reality he's going to be Hellboy's new pet, the diner completely slipped my mind. Pretty stupid, considering I need this job to pay for housing and tuition. There's no way I could have left him, though. He hasn't come to yet, and Bonnie and Jesse are still MIA in Chinatown.

*I better ring my ruthless boss before I kiss my job goodbye.* I can't exactly tell Lindy the truth, so I decide calling in sick is my best option. I work up the courage to give the wicked bitch a buzz and reach for my phone.

My palms are dotted with sweat, and I pace the room. When my tyrannical boss picks up on the third ring, I hold my breath. "Lindy's diner," she barks into the speaker.

*I'm so dead.* "Hey, it's me."

"Now, now, if that isn't Miss I-Ditch-Work." She almost sounds cheerful, which terrifies me. "You calling to say you're doing the night shift." It might sound like a question, but Lindy doesn't do questions.

I'm in front of the window. "I can't do the night shift." I draw the curtain aside and glare at the clouded sky. "I'm…I'm kinda sick."

"Kinda sick?" She bursts into laughter. "Sorry, hun, but I thought you just said you can't work because you're,"—she laughs harder—"sick. Hilarious, isn't it?"

Her shrill voice gives me an aneurysm. In twenty-years of miserable life, I've never let anyone talk to me like this. Then again, I've never depended on a job. Until now. My stomach sinks. "I puked my guts out, Lindy."

"And you think I care because?" She couldn't sound more hateful if she spit venom in my face.

Swallowing the lump in my throat, I think of McSorley's Old Ale House down the street. Bonnie had gotten me an interview there. I never went. Thought I could make it on my own. *Pride's a bitch, huh?*

"I ain't got all day," Lindy shouts. "You coming in or not?"

"I'm contagious," I blurt, hoping she cares more about the health of her customers than mine.

"Is that so? Well, let me tell ya something, missy. I wouldn't care if ya had the plague. Now, you either get your ass over here, or ya can find yourself a new job, and I sincerely doubt anyone other than the strip club down the street will hire such an incompetent blonde disaster like you."

I'm tempted to put a hex on her ass, but in view of my recent luck, it would go horribly wrong, and my already monstrous boss would transform into Godzilla. "You can't fire me because I'm sick," I try to reason with her.

"Watch me," she barks. *Fuck.* Losing this job, no matter how fucked up it is, means giving up my new life. I can't let that happen, but neither can I turn my back on Alex. *Shit.* I forget all about dignity and pride and get ready for a first. "Please, Lindy. I need this job," I beg. "Don't matter." Her voice is bitter. "You've got twenty minutes to haul your butt to the diner." Then she hangs up on me.

*I'm soooo screwed!* I don't think screwed quite cuts it.

"Manda?" Alex croaks.

I shove my cell in the back pocket of my jeans and spin. "Hey." A smile I don't feel shoots over my lips. "Look who's returned to the land of the living." He explores the cut on his face. It's going to leave a nasty scar. "Very funny, Manda."Boy, he looks miserable. The small blood vessels around his left eye are damaged, and a big shiner has developed. The massive blood loss paled his skin, and he's shaking with chills.

I saunter toward him. "How do you feel?" I ask, checking his pulse.

Alex pushes his elbows into the mattress, trying to sit up. "Awesome." I don't believe him for a second. Why should I? Ever since he walked into the Salty Dog

Tavern in Harpers Ferry, West Virginia, three months ago, he's done nothing but lie to me.

"Wait, I'll help you." I shove a few pillows under his head. "Some water?" I mutter, reaching for the glass on the nightstand.

He nods, and when I pass him the glass, he downs half of it at once. Then he scans my room. "Where's Jesse?"

"In Chinatown with Bonnie, getting some blood-building herbs for you," I explain while I pull the blanket away to take a look at the bandages. No fresh blood, but the veins around the wounds are darker than they should be—almost black. Odd. I've never seen anything like it, but it can't be good.

I plop down next to him and check his temperature with the back of my hand. I'm not a clinical thermometer, but I'm pretty sure his forehead is way too hot. "I'm gonna check if the Nun has some ibuprofen in her room."

I get on my feet, but Alex winds his cold fingers around my wrist. "Manda." His glassy eyes lock with mine. "Ain't no ibuprofen going to save me. You know that, right?"

A scream forms in the depth of my soul, but I swallow it. "All I know is you lied to me, Alex." I want to sound mad. Defeated is all I manage.

His gaze drops to his scarred knuckles. "What was I supposed to do? Tell you the truth?"

I give him the Amanda Bishop psycho-killer look. "Of course not. I mean, why the fuck would you tell me you sold your soul, right?" He draws circles with his thumb onto my palm, as if he's trying to ease the thunderstorm brewing inside me. Doesn't work, though.

"Why did you do it?"

He looks out of the window. "I had my reasons."

I almost laugh. "Oh really? Then tell me, Alex. What could possibly justify deportation to hell?"

He scans my bookshelves, avoiding my eyes. "You're not going to let this go, huh?"

I raise my brows and keep quiet.

"I can't tell you, Manda. I really can't."

I wrench my wrist out of his grip. "You can't? Like you couldn't tell me the truth in Harpers Ferry or like you couldn't pick up a goddamn phone to tell me you're going to bite the dust?" I sound like a madwoman, but today madness comes as a two-for-the-price-of-one bargain.

His lips part. When he sees the fury blazing in my eyes, he quickly shuts his mouth.

No matter how hard I push the topic, he won't tell the truth. He's too damn stubborn. Drawing a deep breath, I try a different approach. "Wanna tell me who went all Wolverine on you? Clearly wasn't the demon you warmed up to, or else you'd be dead."

"Don't know," he murmurs. "One minute I was sleeping in my cell, the next I woke up with excruciating pain in my chest."

I arch a brow. "And you never saw what or who attacked you?"

"There was a shadow, I think. And I'm pretty sure I heard snarling before I blacked out, but other than that"—he shakes his head—"nothing."

*Snarling?* I remember the fractured vison. Had I witnessed the attack? "When did it happen?"

He presses a hand against his chest and flinches. "Last night."

A relentless pang hits me in the chest. Had I seen a live broadcast of Alex's attack? Or worse, could I have prevented it from happening if I had called him?

"Manda?" Alex's hand lands on my arm. "You look like someone forced a raw steak down your throat."

I shove my shaky hands into the pockets of my jeans and ignore his comment. "Care to share what an FBI agent is doing in a prison cell?"

"Long story," he says, breathing heavily through the pain.

"Give me the blurb version."

"A couple weeks after Bakersfield, Jesse and I quit the bureau." He forces a smile. "Figured I'd better enjoy my last hell-free days."

"In prison?" I blurt out.

He rolls his eyes. "No, Manda. Not in prison. We hit the road. Went to all the places we've never been before. Grand Canyon, Disney World, Warner Brother's Studios—"

"I get it," I say, holding up my hand. "You thought seeing some stupid theme parks was more important than finding a way out of this mess." I wave for him to continue. "Moving on."

"There is no way out of this," he grumbles, casting me a sidelong glance. "We were heading toward Niagara Falls when I got a call from the United States Penitentiary in Hazelton. I bet you can guess how surprised I was when the operator asked me if I'd accept a call from an inmate named Francois Matthieu."

A muscle in my jaw pops and my eyes widen. "Psycho-bokor-asshole called you?" I'd heard he was moved to a federal prison in West Virginia, but why on earth would he call Alex, the hunter who put him behind bars?

Alex applies pressure to his chest and nods. "He wanted to make a deal. Said he could get me out of this mess if I helped him get out of prison."

"What did you say?" I ask, though I already know the answer. Alex is like the United States of America—doesn't negotiate with terrorists, or in this case, child-abusing bokor dicks.

He smiles. "That he can shove his offer up his ass. I'd rather spend an eternity in hell than let a monster like him walk. But when Jesse heard what he'd offered, he insisted we go and talk to him."

I raise my brows. "Talk to him, huh?" I don't think talking alone could have convinced Francoise.

Alex's chest rises and falls quickly. "Things took a pretty bad turn once I sat in a private visitor room with him."

I rub my aching temples. "Define bad."

He glares at his hands. "Let's just say Francoise got himself a date with his pal, Samedi."

"You killed him?"

He gives me the if-you-believe-that-for-just-a-second-you-clearly-don't-know-me-as-well-as-I-thought-you-did look and lets out a sharp breath. "No, I didn't kill him. But something or someone did. Snapped his neck right in front of my eyes. It happened so fast, I never saw it coming. Goes without saying what the guard thought when he walked in."

I need a second to process the news. Francoise is dead. Not that I'd shed tears over the asshole, but the fact he was killed by an invisible hand in the middle of a state prison blows my mind.

"Why didn't you call Carter?" I ask after the initial shock loosens its grip on me. He could have surely gotten him out of that fucked-up situation.

Alex scrubs a hand over his good cheek. "I did. He said he needed a few days to pull some strings. Whatever attacked me obviously didn't feel like waiting. The cops who found me called an ambulance. Jesse subdued the paramedics. The rest"—he tilts his chin at me—"is history."

This shit is worse than I thought.

Alex's eyes grow distant. "He should have let me die."

The blood in my veins turns into lava. "What's that supposed to mean, jerk-face?"

He knits his brows. "C'mon, Manda. You know I'm already dead."

"For a guy who fought evil all his life, you sound pretty okay with the prospect of being some demon's new boy toy."

He shrugs. "Who wouldn't want to be the boy toy of Helen of Troy or Cleopatra?"

*Cleopatra and Helen of Troy?* He clearly takes Dante's *Inferno* too literally. I ball my hands into fists. If I have to listen to this crap for another minute, I'll end up killing Alex myself.

I stalk to the door, but he stops me. "Hey," he croaks. "Where are you going?"

I'd love to say to hell, but then I'd have to spend an eternity listening to his so not funny jokes. "Kitchen," I mumble. "Fixing you some soup."

\*\*\*\*

I found four boneless chicken breasts, onions, carrots, celery, and zucchinis in the fridge and decided to make chicken vegetable soup. I'm considerate like that. Not that he deserves my kindness after he kept the crucial fact that he's going to burn in hell from me, but whatever.

The meat is boiling, and I'm almost done chopping the vegetables, when my gaze drifts to Chelsea's room. I really hope she stays gone, because she'd either call an exorcist if she saw Alex, or worse, alert campus security.

Throwing the carrots into boiling water, I glare at my watch. Bonnie and Jesse should have been back by now. I'd texted them after leaving my room, and they assured me they were on their way. Isn't it funny how when I start telling the truth, everyone else around me becomes a fucking liar?

"Manda?" Alex's voice echoes through the kitchen. I peek over my shoulder and almost chop off my index finger. Hand pressed against his ribcage, Alex leans against the door frame of my room. How he's standing on two feet beats me.

"What the fuck do you think you're doing?" I drop the knife and run toward him. "Are you insane?"

A cocky grin on his lips, he shrugs. "I dated you," he says, adding fuel to the blazing fire in the pit of my stomach.

I put his arm around my shoulders and lead him to the couch. "What is it with you?" I ask as I help him sit. "Are you that eager to die?"

He puts his feet on the coffee table and frowns. "Can't blame me for not wanting to spend the last days of my life in bed, can you?"

*Low blow. Very. Low. Blow.* Ignoring the pain his comment caused, I head back to the kitchen to throw the remaining vegetables into the boiling soup.

He scans the apartment. "So, you really did it?"

"Did what?" I ask, adding plenty of chicken stock to the water.

"You know…going to university, becoming a boring student." If I didn't know better, I'd say he was disappointed in me. That would be stupid. He hated my old lifestyle.

"Even have a normal job," I announce proudly. *Had, Amanda. You* had *a normal job.*

He throws his head back and laughs. "Are you fucking with me?"

I stir the soup and give him a look. "Shut up and lie down, will ya?" I sound like a general. I guess I can always enlist in the army if they throw me out of NYU because I can't pay tuition.

"Whatcha cooking?" he asks as I put the lid on the saucepan. "Smells delicious."

I pour a cup of cold coffee and pull myself onto the kitchen counter. "Chicken vegetable soup."

Alex beams at me. "You remembered my favorite soup?"

How could I ever forget? After I'd accepted a ride from the boys, and before Alex and I started screwing, he caught a bad cold—fever, dry cough, headache. He hadn't been whiny about it like most guys, but his throat had become so sore, he started sounding like Mickey Mouse on crack. I'd taken pity on him and offered to prepare his favorite soup, which turned out to be chicken vegetable.

"Sue me," I snarl through gritted teeth.

He rests his head against Chelsea's pope pillow and sighs. "Why do you always have to be such a bitch,

Manda?"

I sip cold coffee and look over the edge of the cup. "Same reason you always have to be such a jerk. It's in my nature."

A moment of silence passes, then he pushes his hands into the couch and straightens. "Can I ask you a favor?"

I jump off the counter and walk toward him. "You can try."

Alex turns his head to look at me. "I know you don't allow yourself to care about people, but when I'm gone, I need you to look after Jesse. Can you do that for me?" The sadness in his eyes is too much to handle.

I avert my gaze, choking back the lump of emotion crawling up my throat. "What were you thinking, striking a deal with hell, Alex?" *Seriously, what the fuck had he been thinking?* Leaving Jesse to deal with the aftermath of his choice, forgetting there are people who care about him—that's so not the Alex I know.

He reaches for my hand and threads his fingers through mine. "Please, Manda, I can't leave this world not knowing Jesse will be taken care of."

In this instant, the levee holding back all the anger and wrath inside of me breaks. "You have to know he'll be taken care of? Why didn't you think about your brother *before* you bargained with your fuckin' soul, Alex?" He opens his mouth, but I'm not done yet. "You know what's funny? All this time I thought I was the most selfish person to ever walk this earth. I've been wrong. 'Cause nothing I've done beats what you did to the people who love you."

His malachite eyes are darker than ever. "Are you done?" I could yell all day at him and never be done, but before I get a chance to keep going he says, "You think this was easy for me? I'm a goddamn hunter, Amanda. Selling your soul to the other side is about the worst thing my kind can do. Make no mistake." He meets my eyes. "I hate myself for what I did, but I'd do it again in a heartbeat."

Alex might be the only person on this planet who can detonate a bomb inside my soul with a single sentence. I'm ready to hit him in the face, but the door swings open, and Bonnie and Jesse walk in just in time to save Alex from getting another shiner on his right eye.

"What the hell?" Jesse barks, glaring at his brother. "Why aren't you in bed, man?"

Alex rolls his eyes. "Would you relax, li'l bro? I'm not dead *yet*."

*Keep up the attitude, and I'll change that.*

Bonnie pushes past Jesse and puts the grocery bag on the coffee table. "So," she says, giving jerk-face the once-over. "You're the infamous Alexander Remington, huh?" She extends a hand. "Well, it's not a pleasure to meet you, but I'm glad you aren't bleeding all over our apartment anymore."

Alex's expression says I-can-see-why-the-two-of-you-are-friends and smirks. "And you," he says, shaking her hand. "Must be the best friend."

She throws her curls over one shoulder. "In the flesh."

Jesse walks over to me. "Seriously, what the hell is he doing up when he should be in your bed?" He sounds so not amused.

I cross my arms. "I don't know. But you better take him back before I do the demon a favor and send his sorry ass to hell before his time is up."

"You fought?" Jesse's gaze drifts from me to Alex. "Again?"

"She started it," Alex mutters.

Something inside me cracks, and I lunge forward, ready to beat the fucking crap out of Alex. Too bad Bonnie wraps her arms around my hips and holds me back. "Whoa. What the hell, Amanda?"

I glare at Alex, who grins like the Cheshire Cat, and struggle to free myself. "Let the fuck go, B."

"See," he says to his brother. "That's exactly what I'm talking about. Zero self-control."

I narrow my eyes at him. "Oh, that's rich, coming from a hunter who'd rather go to Disney World than find a way to save his goddamn soul."

Alex's face turns to marble. "Why the fuck does everyone think I need saving?" He sounds really pissed. "I made my choice. Now I'm gonna live with the fucking consequences. Do I make myself clear?"

There it is again, the tedious urge to rip his head off.

"Why don't we all calm down?" Bonnie suggests, her arms still wrapped around me.

Jesse rolls his eyes. "Trust me, B, you're preaching to the choir."

If I wasn't so fucking mad, I'd ask my best friend since when she became okay with Jesse, a hunter, calling her by her nickname, but I got more important things on my mind. I shoot daggers at Alex. "Know what? I don't give a shit about *your* choice. I'm a witch. I don't do free will."

"What are you saying?" Alex asks, jaw clenched.

"Yeah," Bonnie whispers. "What are you saying,

Amanda?"

I blow out some anger and step back. "I'm saying I don't care what he wants. I'll get his sorry ass out of this deal if it's the last thing I do."

Jesse straightens and beams at me. "Does that mean—"

"Your brother won't go to hell, even if I have to fight Lucifer himself." That said, I stomp to the bathroom and slam the door.

## Chapter 12

Tang kuei, rehmannia, and peony—Bonnie and Jesse got me everything I need. Emptying the Chinese herbs into the mixer, I stare at the pig liver on the counter. Bonnie bought the disgusting thing. Said her coven has used it since the dawn of time to increase red blood cells. I don't know about the blood cells, but I can testify to the increasing urge to puke caused by looking at it. I pinch my nostrils together, grab the liver, and throw it on top of the herbs.

They say good medicine tastes bitter, but when I push the On button, and the stuff merges into a thick merlot liquid, my stomach threatens to erupt. I'd feel sorry for Alex—who actually has to drink the stuff—if he hadn't acted like a jerk a few minutes ago. It's a good thing Jesse hauled his butt to my room before I came out of the bathroom. Only God knows what I'd have done had he provoked me some more.

"Can I talk to you?" Bonnie says, testing the waters. She has firsthand experience when it comes to my short temper, and after the performance I gave—almost jumping down Alex's throat—she probably lives by the "better safe than sorry" motto.

I keep my eyes on the mixer. "Sure. Shoot."

She leans against the counter, crosses arms and legs, and gives me a dubious look. "You promise not to kill me?"

"I'll try my best."

She doesn't really buy it. I can tell by the way one foot rocks back and forth. "I know you were pissed at Alex, but"—she draws a deep breath—"are you aware of what you did back there?" She points her head at the living room as if the play is still being performed.

I cock a brow and sigh. "Yeah, B. I'm aware of what I did."

She leans closer. "Really? 'Cause you didn't just swear to Alex you'd get him out of an unbreakable deal, you also planted a whole lot of hope in his brother's heart."

What's wrong with her? Wasn't she the one who gave me a pep talk yesterday? "What happened to 'the Amanda Bishop I know would move heaven and hell?'"

Bonnie massages her forehead. "I meant every word. But two things." She holds her index finger up. "One, you can't save someone who doesn't want saving." Her middle finger flies up. "Two, what happens to Jesse if you can't keep your promise? Did you consider that when you announced you'd fight Lucifer himself for Alex's soul?"

A sharp pain jolts through my ankh tattoo. I never saw it like that. Never considered what my promise would do to Jesse. Fuck, what is it about Alex that turns off every rational thought? It's as if every time he opens his mouth, I'm blinded by the overwhelming need to prove him wrong. Been like this since Jesse asked me to join them for a drink and Alex said I probably had somewhere else to be. Of course, I'd sided with Jesse, and we all know how well that turned out.

"At least tell me you've got a plan," Bonnie murmurs.

I switch the mixer off and frown. "It's not exactly a plan."

She raises her brows. "Then what is it?"

"A place to start," I say, pouring the stinky liquid into a glass. Gram's grimoire is our best shot. If there's a way to fix Alex, it will be in the book.

"You really wanna do that?"

Do I want to go to Salem and face my annoying-as-hell sister? Hell, no. But I can't just let Alex be hauled to hell, can I? "We'll hit the road as soon as Alex feels a bit better."

"God," she moans. "You really must lo—"

I silence her with a look. "Don't even think about saying that out loud."

She holds her hands up. "Whatever. I just hope you know what you're doing."

*Me too, B.*

\*\*\*\*

Loaded with soup and the stuff from the blender, I kick my door open and move toward Alex. He's not happy to see me. I'm not happy to be here either.

Jesse sits next to him, but the second he lays eyes on me, he gets on his feet and retreats to the door. "Try not to kill each other." His gaze drifts from me to his brother. "Okay?"

I put the bowl of soup and the glass on the nightstand and fake a smile. "I'll be on my best behavior."

"Alex?" Jesse grumbles, giving his brother a look.

He rolls his eyes. "Just get outta here, man."

That's what Jesse does, but not without shooting Alex one last warning glance.

Wordless, I adjust the pillows and help Alex sit up.

"Hey." Jerk-face flinches as I let him down. "How about being a bit nicer? I am a dying man, remember?"

*I could smother him with one of the pillows and no one would ever know.* The thought conjures up a smile, but I push it away. "Drink," I order, handing him the glass.

He ogles the red liquid suspiciously. "What is it?"

I shrug. "Herbs."

He takes a sniff and makes a face. "Herbs, huh?"

Totally running out of patience, I cock a brow. "Stop acting like a wimp and drink up, Alex."

Unwillingly, he tastes it. "That's"—he wipes his mouth—"nasty."

"Finish it. It'll help."

Once he gulps down most of it without vomiting in my face, I lift his blanket. "Like what you see?" he asks as I pull up the bandages to check on the wounds.

I hate the cocky grin on his face, but when I realize there's no fresh blood or purulence, I smile. "Looks good." With the exception of the blackish veins. It appears they have spread farther up toward Alex's heart. I have a bad feeling about this, but I try to keep a lid on my emotions. No need to scare Alex, or anyone else.

His eyes find mine. "Had a good nurse."

"Stop sweet talking me."

"Just trying to be nice," he says. What he means is: just trying to piss you off some more, Manda.

"Don't." I rub St. John's wort onto his chest, apply new bandages, and hand him a bowl of steaming soup. "Eat."

He sighs. "What are you, my mother?"

If I was his mother, I would have drowned him in

the tub when he was a baby.

He spoons his chicken vegetable soup and watches me with hooded eyes. "Still mad?"

Mad? Me? That's just ridiculous.

He blows on his spoon and looks up. "C'mon, Manda, how long can you keep that silent avenger thing going?"

We'll see.

He puts the bowl down next to him and cups my cheeks. "Manda." I want to yank back, but for a half-dead dude, he has a pretty tight grip. "You really want us to part on bad terms?"

I swallow the fire climbing up my throat and keep quiet.

Hamstringed, he lets go of me, seizes hold of my shirt, and pulls me onto the bed. It happens in the blink of an eye, and I'm too startled to put up much of a fight. "What the hell?" I bark as a bit of soup lands on my bed. "You crazy or something?"

"More like something," he says, pressing me against his warm body.

"Let go of me," I order, struggling to break free from his death grip. Not a chance. He's determined to keep me next to his heart.

"I know you hate me right now," he whispers, running his fingers through my hair. "But deep down, you gotta know what I said out there was the truth. Even you"—he puts a finger under my chin and lifts it up—"the great Amanda Bishop, can't get me out of this deal." There's so much pain in his eyes, I want to break down and cry.

I shift closer. "How do you know?" My voice is ruptured. "You won't even let me try, Alex."

He traces my spine. I shiver from his touch. "Why do you care so much?" he asks, sounding surprised. "I almost killed you three times."

I bury my head in his neck and breathe him in. "Remember what I said in the car before we walked into pedophile Walter's lake house?" Just thinking of the hell-hole where the asshole raped those poor girls makes me shudder. I feel him nod. "I didn't lie, Alex. I *do* care about you. I know I shouldn't, because of the whole Natural Born Enemy thing, but we were once friends."

He chuckles. "You call all that bitching and fighting friendship?"

I look up and bat my lashes at him. "It's how I show my undying love. Ask Bonnie. She can literally sing a song about it." I think of Puddle of Mudd's "She Hates Me" and smile.

Alex stares at the ceiling. "I almost got you killed in Bakersfield. No way I'll put you at risk again."

I shove an elbow into the mattress and steady my head on my hand. "Would you drop the Bakersfield thing already? You didn't pull the trigger, Alex. Walter did. Besides, it's highly unlikely a look at my gram's grimoire will kill me."

Alex closes his eyes and says nothing. His chest rises and falls peacefully, as if he's making peace with something. Just when I'm all set to accept the fact he doesn't want my help, he says, "I'll make you a deal."

I raise my brows. "Haven't you made enough of those lately?"

"Maybe, but…" He shifts to his side and looks me in the eye. "I have a feeling you're going to like this one." Judging by the smug smile plastered across his face, I'll hate it. "I'll let you try to get me out of this deal," he continues. "But in exchange for my full cooperation, you have to promise you'll look after Jesse if you fail."

"Deal," I say faster than a bolt of lightning.

"Seriously?" He glares at me with a lack of certainty in his breathtaking eyes. "You're ready to take on responsibility for someone other than yourself?"

"Of course." I tap a finger against the tip of his nose. "Wanna know why?"

He furrows his thick brows. "Humor me."

"Because Amanda Bishop never fails."

The expression on his face is a cross between you-must-have-lost-more-brain-cells-in-that-coma-than-I-thought and oh-hell-what-did-I-just-get-myself-into. I extend my hand and wait for him to shake it. Jerk-face hesitates. "What's the matter? Scared a witch saves your sorry hunter ass *again*?"

A spark ignites in his eyes. "No, but since you seem out of your mind at the moment, I'm going to sweeten the deal for me and ask you to stay with me tonight."

"I'm not going to—"

"Trust me," he says, a sheepish grin tugging at his full lips. "I'm in no condition to offer you mind-blowing sex."

"So we're talking about good old, no touching, no kissing sleep?"

He nods.

"All right," I snarl. "But just so you know, you're already pressing your luck."

He shakes my hand. "Well, I guess we have a deal."

"Again," I say, glaring at the ceiling. "It's kinda turned into our thing, huh?"

He traces the dark shadows beneath my eyes and smiles. "Always figured bitching and fighting was our thing."

"That too," I whisper as exhaustion weighs down my eyelids.

Chapter 13

*Ten days to hell*

When I blink my eyes open, I'm pressed against Alex's chest. My cheek rests on his heart and his leg is wrapped around my thigh, keeping me close. It feels like a lifetime since I last woke in his arms. Honest to God, never thought it would happen again.

*Never say never.* Life has a way of doing whatever the hell it wants.

I look him over. He's in better shape than last night. His skin is not as pale—seems like adding pig liver really wasn't such a bad idea—and despite the fact he'll be dragged to hell in ten days, he appears at peace.

*Wish I could say the same about me.*

Determined not to wake him, I carefully shove his leg to the side and crawl out of the warm bed. The winter sun breaks through my window. I'm guessing it's around ten o'clock, which the clock on my nightstand confirms. If Alex downs more of the herb-liver shit, we could hit the road tomorrow. Get to the grimoire and find a way to fix this crappy situation.

*That is if he doesn't get an infection.*

While gathering my toiletries and a change of clothes, I make a mental note to text Melinda, my sister. She will freak if she hears I plan to bring two of the most dangerous hunters to a witch residence, but who cares? The grimoire is as much my heritage as it is hers.

I tiptoe out of my room and catch a glimpse of Jesse. Feet dangling over our too short couch, he snores like a panther. Pretty damn cute.

I saunter toward him, grab a blanket from the recliner, and cover him. Then I just stand there and watch him sleep. I wonder who he'd be without his brother?

*Best case scenario: a globetrotting, younger and hotter version of Hugh Hefner. Worst case scenario: a fucked up, always drunk, HIV positive dude, who hits on everything with two legs and boobs.*

God, all of this is so wrong. Jesse and Alex are like Twix—two parts of a yummy chocolate bar. I can't picture them existing separately.

*How the fuck could Alex believe his brother would be okay without him?*

Does it matter? All I have to do is honor my promise and get him out of this godforsaken deal. Then I'll hopefully never know how bitter a Twix bar would taste without its other side.

I take a quick shower and blow dry my hair. The scent of fresh coffee wafts through the bathroom, and instead of applying mascara, I follow the delicious smell to the kitchen.

"Why aren't you in class?" I ask the second I spot Bonnie next to the coffee machine.

She gives a lazy shrug. "Too damn tired." I have to take her word for it, 'cause she still looks like Miss Universe.

Jesse must think so, too. He's sitting on the recliner, watching my best friend with eagle eyes. There's something uncannily familiar about the look he gives her. I can't quite put my finger on it. *Damn, how I miss seeing auras.*

Since the life-saving liquid is still brewing, I walk over to him and ruffle his hair. "How did you sleep, Little Remington?"

He pulls a face. "You know I hate when you call me that, right?"

I grin. "Makes it all the more fun."

He rolls his eyes. "How's Alex?"

Bonnie's gaze drifts to me. "Yeah, how is he?"

"Probably brain damaged," I say, sauntering to the kitchen to prepare a bowl of cereal.

Jesse ogles me with a disturbed expression. "What?"

I grab the milk from the fridge and sigh. "Your brother promised his full cooperation for the 'save Alexander jerk-face Remington from hell' mission."

Jesse is on his feet in no time. "Are you serious?" His eyes sparkle like black diamonds, but his happiness fades when reality hits. "Shit," he mutters under his breath. "Do I want to know what you had to do to convince him?"

I'm all set to assure him I didn't put a hex on Alex when someone knocks on the door. My gaze flies to Bonnie. "You expecting someone?"

She cocks a brow and points to the blood-soaked couch. "Have you seen this place?" A simple no would have sufficed, but Bonnie wouldn't be Bonnie if she went with simple.

I put the bowl on the coffee table and walk to the door. "Who's there?" No one answers. It's days like these I miss a spy hole.

The color drains from Bonnie's face. "What if it's

campus security?" she asks, coming toward me. "Or worse, the cops?" Ever since her oldest brother got arrested, she stays at least a hundred feet away from the boys in blue.

From the corner of my eye, I see Jesse cover the couch with a blanket and reach for his Glock.

Another loud knock hits the door.

Drawing a deep breath, I circle the door knob and open it. Fuck, I wish I hadn't. I raise my brows. "What do you want, DeLuca?"

"We need to talk," he says, arms crossed.

I'm not up for another jealous rampage. Alex might be asleep, but if he wakes up and walks out of my room, DeLuca will throw a fit. And Alex? Well, there's no way of telling what he'll do. I give DeLuca a look. "I'm a little busy right now. You think your I'm-acting-like-an-alpha-male-dick act can wait?"

His amber eyes narrow to slits. "Nope."

I can't even say "fuck off" before he pushes past me. I slam the door behind him and frown. "Sure you can come in, douchebag."

"Wanna tell me what the fuck is going on with you?" he snarls through gritted teeth.

I'm at the brink of scratching his eyes out. "With me? I'm not the one trespassing like an idiot."

He ignores my comment. "Why weren't you at work or in class?"

*What the hell is this?* "I don't think I have to account for my movements to you, DeLuca."

Something incredibly dark passes through his eyes. "That's all you have to say?"

Nope, there are plenty of insults on the tip of my tongue, but Jesse speaks before I can unload on him.

"Who the hell is that?"

Like a cyborg on a mission, DeLuca spins. "Is that him?" He peeks over his shoulder, glaring at me as if I committed all the deadly seven sins at once. "Is that Alex?"

A wicked smile crosses Jesse's lips. "You dating him?" I hate the way he looks at me. So judgmental it's almost as if Alex stands in front of me.

Before I can explain, DeLuca stalks toward Jesse. He gets right into his personal space. "Are you the motherfucker who screws my girl?"

"Your girl?" Jesse bursts into laughter.

DeLuca's spine turns to iron. "You think this is funny?" He balls his hands into fists. I'm positive he's about to strike.

"DeLuca," I snap, seizing hold of his royal blue thermal shirt. "Get the fuck out of my apartment. Now."

He yanks his arm out of my grip. "I'm not going anywhere until you tell me the truth, Amanda."

*I have a fugitive in my bedroom who looks like he ran into Wolverine. And by the way, said fugitive also happens to be my ex-lover, who sold his soul.* Yeah, because that would go so well.

We engage in a stare-down. Neither of us is ready to give up. Out of the blue, Jesse walks up beside me and throws an arm around my shoulders. "Honestly, sis, you have crappy taste in men."

DeLuca's eyes widen. "Sis?"

Jesse raises his brows at him. "Got a problem with that?"

Embarrassment washes over DeLuca, coloring his face a nasty shade of red. "I-I…had no idea."

Jesse shrugs. "How could you? You were too busy

barging in here and calling me a motherfucker, right?" He doesn't look pissed, but his voice is sharper than Michonne's katana on *The Walking Dead*.

DeLuca brushes the angled fringe out of his face and frowns. "Man, I'm sorry. I didn't mean to—"

"Be an asshole?" I blurt out. "Yeah, too late."

"I was just worried," he says, trying to justify his behavior.

"Last time I checked, I made it pretty clear we're not exclusive. I can write it down for you if it helps."

He watches me with heavily hooded eyes. "I wasn't worried about you being with someone else."

I knit my brows. "Oh, really? So you're acting like an asshole just for the sake of it?"

His gaze drops to the floor. "No…yes…not really."

"All right," Bonnie interrupts. "Why don't we give him a shot and let him explain himself?"

What the fuck is there to explain? DeLuca is one step away from becoming a case for *Stalked: Someone's Watching*.

Jesse gestures for him to talk. "We're listening."

*I'm not.*

DeLuca swallows hard. "When you didn't show up for class, I went by the diner. Your boss said she fired you."

Jesse cuts his eyes my way. I know what's on his mind. No super-cool aura-reading ability needed. He understands I lost my job over Alex.

"Go on," I mutter, ignoring the amazed, yet guilt-ridden look Jesse gives me.

"I figured you'd show up today." DeLuca sucks in air. "When you didn't, I thought those guys must have gotten to you."

The need to strangle him grows inside of me like a weed, but then I hear what he's just said. "What guys?"

"You haven't heard?"

Oh God, here we go again. Would I fucking ask if I had?

"What haven't we heard?" Bonnie says and groans. Unlike me, she plays the game.

The blood drains from DeLuca's face, and for a fraction of a second, I consider shoving the Chinatown Special down his throat. "They," he says, fighting for composure, "they found Jules." Bonnie stumbles backward, as if she already knows what he's going to say. "She's dead."

*This week keeps getting better and better.*

Jesse's gaze shoots to me. "Who's Jules?"

"The girl your sister threatened before she disappeared," DeLuca explains.

"I didn't threaten *her*," I hiss. "I threatened *all* of 'em."

Jesse runs a hand over his face and sighs. "Not again, Manda." He's referring to Mister Sinister. He, too, bit the dirt only days after he'd dared to piss me off.

"I didn't touch her," I shout, feeling a little crazed.

"Those guys in fancy black suits think differently," DeLuca counters.

"Do they think I'm some kind of virgin-killing alien or something?" I hide behind sarcasm. Truth is, I'm slightly worried. Jules is dead, the whole campus knows what went down in the diner—well, they know what the Nun and Ava told them—and the *Men in Black* are looking for me.

"What guys?" Bonnie's voice is hard, her features

even harder.

DeLuca throws his hands in the air. "I don't know who they are." He stares at Jesse. "They showed up in Penrose's class today. Told us the police had found Jules's mutilated body in Washington Square Park. Everyone sorta went into shock. Ava broke down, I think. The guys didn't care. They went to Penrose and demanded to know where they could find"—his eyes lock with mine—"*you*, Amanda."

*I'm beyond fucked.*

Chapter 14

Ever watch one of your favorite TV shows and wonder why the fuck the writer insults your intelligence by starting a new episode with one of those annoying-as-hell recap sequences? Always thought they didn't give the viewer enough credit. As if we're brain dead, or unable to put one and one together. Now, while Jesse navigates the Mustang through the way too familiar streets of Salem and Bon Jovi's "Wanted Dead or Alive" blasts through the speakers, I wish a screenwriter would do a little "Previously on *The Stab-worthy Witch*" summary for me. Presumably, it would be along the lines of: Amanda tried to start over, found herself haunted by creepy nightmares, and learned her ex-lover sold his soul to a demon, and our incredibly sexy villainous witch is once again accused of a brutal homicide, but the *Men in Black* are already on her heels. Bet I forgot something, but it's sorta hard to keep track of the plot twists in the freak show I call my life.

"Manda?"

I look up, meeting Jesse's eyes in the rearview mirror.

"Is he okay?"

Alex's head rests in my lap. Cold sweat runs down his cheeks, and he shivers uncontrollably. Nothing about him screams "okay." In fact, he looks downright awful. I wish we could have given him another day to heal, but after DeLuca dropped the bomb Jules was dead, we—Jesse, Bonnie, and I—figured it would be better to hit the road immediately. Or should I say immediately after Jesse got rid of DeLuca. Little Remington had to come up with some lame excuse about a sick aunt. DeLuca didn't buy it. But what was he gonna do? Tie me to a chair?

I run my fingers through Alex's damp hair. "He's—"

"Awesome," Alex murmurs, a fresh burst of pain making his jaw clench. He digs his hands into the rear bench and lifts himself. "Still can't believe you hauled my hurt butt on a five-hour drive so we can skim through some stupid book."

That "stupid book," as he calls it, predates the Salem witch trials. Before it was given to my grams, it belonged to none other than the legendary Victoria Bishop—my great-great-great-great-great-grandmother. If one can believe the legends, she was one of the most powerful, kick-ass witches to ever walk this earth, making her grimoire a well-respected and feared resource in the witch community.

"Show a little respect," Bonnie barks from the passenger seat. "You're talking about family heritage."

Alex arches a brow. "Still don't see why you guys pulled me out of bed as if the house was on fire."

I look out the window, feeling guilty for not telling him the truth about our sudden departure. It was Jesse's idea, though. He claimed his brother had enough on his plate. No need to add a dead student and the *Men in Black* to the menu.

Bonnie shifts in her seat. "Sorry, Amanda, but the great Alexander Remington really isn't as badass as you painted him. Whiny? Yeah. Badass? Hell to the no."

Alex flashes me a smile. "Badass, huh?"

I ignore the stabbing pain behind my right eye and rest my head against the cool window. "Shut up, Alex."

"Shut up," he says, having a hard time breathing. "*Badass* Alex."

I give my best friend a look. *Thanks, B.* Knowing Alex, I'll never hear the end of it.

Bonnie faces Alex. "I kinda liked you better when you were unconscious."

Alex presses a palm against his chest. "Ouch. A witch doesn't like me. That hurts." He grins. "Not."

Bonnie is a millisecond away from losing her temper, but Jesse interrupts her. "I think I've got the wrong address." His gaze drifts from his GPS to the First Period Colonial house halfway down Broad Street.

"No you don't," I snarl.

"You serious?" Jesse sounds surprised. I don't blame him. The Bishop residence is one of the oldest and finest in Salem.

"Dead serious," Bonnie says proudly. She's always loved this house. Then again, her memories of it are happier than mine.

Overwhelmed, Jesse pulls into the driveway and kills the engine. "Damn, Manda." He can't take his eyes off the house my ancestors built when they arrived in the New World. "You neglected to mention you're a rich witch."

I cup my elbows. "I'm not rich. My family is."

A cocky grin lights up jerk-face's lips. "Where's the difference?"

I yank the door open and stretch my numb legs. "*You* wouldn't understand," I guarantee him. He loves his family. I hate mine.

I get out of the car and stare at the charming ivory façade. To an outsider, it must appear the perfect home. They have no fucking clue how many bloody battles the walls inside have witnessed. Mom and Dad's endless fights, my terrified screams when Mother Dearest locked me in the attic, Dad's death, Melinda's bloody wedding day—the list is endless.

"Amanda." Bonnie stands next to me. Her eyes are filled with concern. "Are you sure you're up for this?" I fake a pretty convincing smile. "It's not a big deal, B." Just the thought of Miss-I'm-so-much-better-than-you'll-ever-be turns my stomach upside down. Other than that, I'm superb.

She rocks her heels into the pebbles covering the driveway and pulls her curls into a bun. "And you're absolutely certain he's not here?"

My heart beats a little faster, and I swallow the bitter taste in my mouth. "He's with Melinda's friend." I'd texted her before we left and made sure Leandro wouldn't be anywhere near the house while Alex and Jesse are here. Of course, she agreed. His well-being is the only thing we agree upon.

Bonnie bites her lip. "And you're okay with that?"

Melinda's friends are stuck-up housewives with a *Sex and the City* complex. So, no, I'm not even remotely okay with it. "It's none of my business, B." I sound cold and distant.

She lifts her brows. "But—"

"Guys," Jesse yelps, having a hard time steadying his brother. "Can we move?"

I take the longest, deepest breath ever and stagger to the door. A dull ache roars through my chest, and my belly cramps, yet I do the unthinkable. I ring the bell.

"You look like shit," Bonnie says to Alex.

"Charming friend you've got," Alex grumbles.

"I'm just honest," Bonnie defends herself.

Alex's skin is slightly green, and he looks as if he's about to puke on Melinda's porch. I make a mental note to check his wounds later.

"Manda?" Jesse stares at my balled hands. "You sure your family is okay with us being here?" He pauses. "You know, considering we're hunters and all." *It's bad enough to invite hunters into your home. Incredibly stupid to let them anywhere near the grimoire.* Melinda's words, not mine.

"It's just my sister. She's cool with it." He didn't expect an honest answer, did he?

"Good. We don't want to cause any trouble," he says seconds before the door flies open.

Melinda's teal-blue eyes drift from my heels to my face. She doesn't approve of my outfit or makeup. I can tell by the way she wrinkles her nose. "Amanda."

"Melinda." Yep, it's pretty much how I picture a reunion of the Evil Queen and Snow Queen. Cold hate.

My not-so-beloved sister pushes past me and pulls my best friend into a tight embrace. "It's good to see you, Bonnie."

Bonnie hugs her back, giving me an apologetic look.

I shrug it off. It's not her fault my sister abhors me. Plus, the feeling is mutual. Just one look at her ginger fishbone braid and old-fashioned Jackie O costume reminds me why I'd rather eat glass than tell anyone we're related.

Perfect Housewitch pulls back and turns to Alex

and Jesse. "I'm sorry," she says, straightening her jacket. "Where are my manners?"

Alex peers at her. "Been wondering that, too." Hunter-heroic is the biggest jerk on this planet, but no matter what Jesse did, he'd never treat his brother like this.

For a moment, she stands there speechless. It must be the first time someone questioned her manners, and the look on Perfect Housewitch's face is priceless. But Melinda wouldn't be Melinda if she couldn't hide her emotions behind a brilliant smile. "I'm Melinda Bishop." She extends her perfectly French-manicured hand.

"I know," Alex grumbles, paying no attention to my sister's hand. "We spoke on the phone, remember?"

Melinda throws her fishbone braid over one shoulder and beams at him. "I certainly do. Thank you, again. My sister"—she casts me a sidelong glance—"obviously thought it wasn't necessary to inform her family she had been shot."

*Don't kill her. Don't kill her. Don't—*

"Yeah, well, picking up a phone is sorta hard when you're in a coma," Alex counters.

"Y-You're right," Melinda stammers, totally thrown off her game. Then, because she doesn't know what else to do, she points to the hallway. "Please, come on in."

We follow her to the living room. The distinct aroma of lavender pricks at my nostrils. *Lavender in December, keeps the sorrows tender*, Grams used to say. Perfect Housewitch doesn't strike me as low-spirited.

"Hey." Bonnie nudges my hip. "Sorry about the

hugging stunt. I had no idea she'd—"

"Please," I say as we reach the living room. "It's not your fault my sister is a bitch." I give her a half-smile. "Besides, between the two of us, you *are* the more likable one."

Her cognac eyes darken. She looks abnormally serious by Queen B standards. "Still doesn't make it right."

*It doesn't.* Thing is I knew what I was in for when I chose to come here. I study the photos on the fireplace. Grams and Melinda on her first day of school. Mom and Dad on their wedding day. Mom and Melinda in the garden, and at least a dozen photos of Leandro. The picture-perfect family. Looks can be deceiving. No one knows that better than I do.

"Please take a seat," Melinda says, directing Jesse and Alex to the sofa. "May I offer you a cup of tea?"

Jesse smiles. "Sounds—"

"Why don't we just cut the crap?" I snap, unable to take more of her I'm-polite-and-kind shit.

She fiddles with the buttons of her jacket and exhales sharply. "Mind your manners, Amanda. We"— she tilts her head to Alex and Jesse—"have guests."

Storms usually start as a breeze. The revulsion in Melinda's eyes triggers an instant tornado. "Just give me the grimoire, Melinda. Then you can go on living your pathetic life, pretending I don't exist."

She blushes. "Amanda, please—"

"What?" I bark, planting my hands on my hips. "You think they haven't noticed I'm as welcome here as the devil is in heaven?"

"I'll get the tea," she says before striding to the kitchen.

I ignore the looks I get from Alex and Jesse.

Bonnie's hand lands on my shoulder. "You've gotta relax, Amanda." She chooses her next words with great care. "She's trying."

"To do what?" I laugh. "Make me go crazy? Or push the knife deeper into my back?" I slip my trembling hands in my pockets. "She's doing a damn good job at both."

"Just give her a chance." Bonnie tries her famous golden retriever look on me. "Please?"

Melinda had all the chances in the world. I don't intend to waste another one on her. Too bad I don't have the heart to destroy Bonnie's hope. "Whatever." I groan, stalking to the sofa.

"You good?" Jesse asks as I drop down next to him. *I've survived worse.* "Why wouldn't I be?"

He moves closer. "Oh, I don't know. Maybe because you walked right into World War W?"

I squint. "World War W?'

He shrugs. "You know, World War Witch."

I throw my head back and laugh.

"It ain't funny," he snorts.

I ruffle his hair. "I fought World War Z, Little Remington. I'm pretty sure I can handle one lousy desperate housewitch."

A small smile pulls at his lips. "Even if said witch happens to be your big sister?"

Valid question. Before I get to answer, Melinda returns, loaded with tea and biscuits. "I hope you all fancy Earl Grey," she says, pouring four cups.

*Fancy? Seriously, who the hell talks like that?*

Once she hands everyone but me a cup, she takes a seat on Gram's old sunflower armchair, crossing her legs gracefully. "There's sugar and milk on the tray."

Alex, who's not just a jerk-face but also the most observant guy I've ever met, looks at the photos on the fireplace, then at my sister, then at me. His expression is a cross between your-sister-sucks and I-can't-believe-what-I-see-with-my-own-eyes. He straightens. "No tea for you?"

"I—"

"She doesn't like tea," Melinda blurts, visibly annoyed.

*So now she speaks for me, huh? Fuckin' awesome.*

Alex ignores her like he usually ignores me. "Manda?" His voice is razor sharp and for once, I'm not the reason behind it.

I take a few deep breaths to disarm the nuclear bomb in the pit of my stomach. "She's right." I grin. "I don't drink that pussy shit."

Melinda flinches as if I physically hurt her. "Language," she warns, pursing her coral lips.

I fake a mesmerizing smile. "You're not my mother. But speaking of the devil, how's Miss Florida doing? Her new husband realize yet what a bitch she is?"

Jesse's jaw drops.

Bonnie covers her face with both hands.

Alex almost chokes on good old Earl Grey.

*Good times.*

The teacup in Melinda's hand trembles. "Aren't you the least bit ashamed of yourself? Talking about your own mother like that in front of—" She surveys Alex and Jesse. Then she shakes her head. "If Grams were here, she'd—"

"Tell you to mind your own fuckin' business?" I

hiss. "Yeah, no kidding." The woman would have never scolded me for speaking the truth. Mother Dearest is a bitch. Grams knew that. Melinda does, too.

Perfect Housewitch winces. Her perfect façade crumbles. "Mother was right about one thing; your evil streak gets worse by the day."

A wicked smile curves up my lips. "I may be bad, but I'm perfectly good at it, sis."

She looks sullen. "There's nothing good about the way you behave."

Alex's biceps flex. "Whoa." He gives Perfect Housewitch a sinister look. "Easy there. She's still your little sister."

Melinda puts her cup on the table and flashes him the fakest smile I've ever seen. "I appreciate your concern for my sister, Alexander, but this is a family matter."

*Translation: stay the fuck out of this, hunter.*

He narrows his eyes at her. "Funny you say that. From where I stand, you don't exactly treat her like part of your"—he points to the photos—"*family.*" Alex is just getting started. I see it in the stiffness of his muscles. Jesse takes over before the situation escalates. "Maybe," he says, "we should all focus on why we're here."

"He's right," Bonnie mutters. "We've got bigger fish to fry."

Perfect Housewitch gets on her feet. "You're absolutely right, Bonnie. I'll get the grimoire." She pierces a hole through my brain with her eyes. "But just so we're clear, Amanda. The book doesn't leave this house."

I jump up. "Are you fuckin' with me?" I'm close to

ripping Melinda's heart out.

Perfect Housewitch wiggles her stupid nose. "You didn't think I'd let you take the grimoire on a road trip with two hunters, who could very well use it to make our kind extinct, did you?"

I want to pull my hair out and scream. Strangle her with my bare hands. Bite her head off. But I don't. As much as I hate to admit it, she has a point. That book in the hands of the wrong people could be fatal—for all species.

"I need some air," I say, rushing out of the room before I do something I'll later regret.

*Like turning my snuff film fantasies into reality?*

Yep, something like that.

## Chapter 15

I stomp out of the house. Bone-chilling cold hits me in the face. I inhale sharply, but exasperation punches the air out of my lungs. I'd known what I was signing up for when I reached the conclusion the grimoire was our best shot. Yet, I started to think coming here was a mistake. Being around Melinda is like being around a freaking succubus—she sucks the energy right out of you. But what am I supposed to do? Head home, buy popcorn, and wait for the premier of *Drag Me To Hell* with Alexander Remington in the lead role?

*Why the hell not? He's a righteous jerk who treats me like the source of all evil most of the time. Not to mention he tried to kill me. Not once. Twice.*

He also refused to leave my side when pedophile asshole's bullet sent me to the ICU in Bakersfield.

*He didn't stay because he cares. He stayed because he felt responsible for what happened.*

Alex is still one of the good guys. Why else would he have given up his only shot at getting out of this deal to free Isobelle's soul from purgatory?

*He's good. I'm not. That's the fuckin' problem.*

I sit on the porch swing, pull my knees to my chest, and stare at the herb garden. I'm not trying to convince anyone I'm good. Hell, no. I accepted who I am a long time ago. Mother Dearest made sure of it.

\*\*\*\*

*Autumn had always been my favorite time of the year, and with All Hallows' Eve looming around the corner, Grams and seven-year-old me had spent most of the day in the herb garden, collecting the necessary ingredients for the sacrifice. I reckoned sacrifice a strange word for offering herbs to assure the safe journey of our ancestors' souls, but our kind—white witches—considered plants living, breathing creatures, harvesting them only with great respect.*

*"Manda, darling?" Grams pointed at a plant with grayish leaves and purple flowers "Can you get a bit of sage? We'll need to dry it for the smudge sticks."*

*I smiled at her and hopped toward the plant, arms dangling at my sides. Out here, with Grams, I was free to be me. Laughing came easily, and, occasionally, I even forgot about the horror awaiting me inside the house.*

*I was one step away from the sage when a black-capped chickadee landed in front of me. The tiny creature tilted its round head and looked me right in the eye. The bird's white cheeks and its rusty brown flanks were beautiful. I got a bit closer. Usually, birds took off when you breached their private space. Not this one. The little creature was bold and not the least bit scared of me.*

*Gram touched my shoulder. "It likes you."*

*Puzzled, I looked up. "Why is it still here? Aren't all birds supposed to be in the south by now?" Unlike me, they didn't like the chilly autumns plaguing Salem.*

*Grams got on her knees so we were face to face. "This little man," she said, her voice having that unique, soothing ring to it, "belongs to a species of survivors, Manda."*

*I narrowed my eyes at the cheeky bird. "He doesn't look like it." He appeared small and fragile. Nothing like how I pictured a survivor. "You're right, darling. But do you remember what I said about judging a book by its cover?"*

*I grinned. "You said never to do that, right?"*

*Pride colored her aura a brilliant orange. "That's right." She beamed at me. "Now, this bird might look vulnerable, but it has quite a few aces up its sleeves."*

*"Like what?" I asked, curious. "Well." Grams took my hands in hers. "The reason it doesn't leave Salem like all the other birds, for example. This small thing"—her gaze drifted to the curious bird—"has the unique ability to lower its body temperature during cold winter nights, and its memory is so good, it can always relocate the caches where it stores food." I knit my brows. "So black-capped chickadees are super birds?" Grams's sweet laughter flooded the garden. "You could say that, I guess." I admired the small creature, but a part of me wondered why it was so determined to stay in Salem. If I had wings, I'd have been long gone.*

*Grams pulled me closer. "You're a survivor too, you know?" I wanted to tell her I didn't feel like one when Mother's voice made my belly dip. "Amanda Caroline Bishop, where are you?"*

*Grams gave me a half-hearted smile and straightened. Her purple aura changed to a dull gray, and I knew right then and there I was in some serious trouble. "Better answer her, Manda."*

*I didn't want to answer her, but I also didn't want to spend the rest of the day locked away in the attic.*

*"Amanda!" she yelled as she stomped over the*

*freshly mowed lawn. The sharpness in her voice scared the hell outta me.*

*I dug my nails into my checkered skirt and gasped for air. "I'm here, Mom." I sounded like a mouse. Felt like one, too.*

*Mother's shiny copper hair cascaded down her shoulders—she looked a lot like the poisonous red-haired chick on* Batman, *minus the tight green suit— and her brand-new pink pumps, the ones I wasn't supposed to touch, dangled from her hand. "What in God's name did you do?" Her ice-blue eyes pierced through my soul.*

*I looked at the long black scratch that ran over the full-length of the heel and stumbled backward "I-I...I-I..." I was too terrified to form a coherent sentence. "I—"*

*She grabbed my wrist and turned it violently. "You what?" Mom possessed timeless beauty—round face, striking cheekbones, and full lips—but when she spoke to me, her soft features always turned to granite.*

*"Mom, you're hurting me," I whined as sharp pain shot through my arm.*

*She wore that satisfying smile. The one reserved for when she locked me away in the attic. "How many times have I told you these shoes are not to be touched?"*

*I didn't know what to say. Mother wouldn't believe the truth. She never did. I looked at Grams for help. "I didn't touch 'em," I said, filled with the desperation of a seven-year-old. No shoes, no matter how pretty, were worth upsetting my mother. Like the black-capped chickadee, I had a very good memory. Knew exactly what was in store for me if I disobeyed her.*

*Gram's shiny blue aura said she believed me. She always did. Arms crossed, she faced her furious daughter. "Let her go, Maria."*

*Mother ignored her and twisted my wrist some more. "Everything coming out of your dirty mouth is a lie."*

*I bit back my reaction to the pain running from the tip of my fingers all the way up to my shoulder and shook my head. "That's not true," I insisted. It really wasn't. I had never lied to my mother. I wondered if she'd like me better if I did.*

*She narrowed her cold blue eyes at me. "There's something wrong with you, Amanda." Her gaze slid to Grams. Then she wrinkled her nose. "It's the evil running through her veins."*

*I'd never understood what she meant by that. Mom kept saying I was wrong and evil. I didn't feel evil or wrong. Unless Mom looked at me like that. Tears pricked my eyes. I blinked them away. "I'm not wrong, Mom. I didn't touch your shoes."*

*Mother's flawless skin turned a nasty shade of red. "You…You…" She let go of my arm and pushed me to the ground. "You're my biggest mistake, Amanda." She straightened her skirt and arched a brow. "I should have aborted you when I had the chance."*

*"Stop it, Maria!" Grams's aura was red and full of wrath. "She didn't touch your shoes."*

*Mother frowned. "Then who did, Mother?"*

*Grams helped me up and brushed the dirt off my back. "You have two daughters, remember?"*

*"Melinda would never—"*

*Grams shielded me from Mother's loathing gaze. "Are you really that blind? You're corrupted by the hate for your own flesh and blood."*

*"My own flesh and blood?" She laughed bitterly. "If it wasn't for you, she'd never been born. And we both know the world would be a better place without her." That I did understand. Mom didn't want me. She'd never wanted me.*

\*\*\*\*

The wooden porch boards creak under heavy boots. I push the memory back to where it belongs—oblivion. Scared, seven-year-old Amanda no longer exists. She's as much history as the Salem witch trials.

"Manda?"

From the corner of my eye, I see Alex leaning against the door. "What?" I snap, not in the mood for smart-ass comments.

He joins me on the swing. "Your sister is—"

"A bitch?" I rest my chin on my knees and shrug. "Yeah. Guess the Bishops will never win a *Brady Bunch* award." We're so screwed up, we make the Montagues and Capulets look like saints.

He glares at the dim sky. "Just ignore her. She—"

"Don't do that, Alex."

His gaze travels over my face, eager to read me. "Do what?" He sounds genuinely confused.

I claw the ailing wood of the bench and force my spine into a straight line. "Don't pity me." Taking shit from Melinda, I can handle. Alex's compassion, not so much.

He shifts closer, a storm brewing in his malachite eyes. "Is that what you think I do?"

He can barely stand on two feet. I don't see what other emotion could have forced him to get up and come out here. "Yeah, Alex. I think that's exactly what you're doing. The only other explanation for your contradictory behavior would be a dissociative identity disorder."

His leg brushes mine, and I move away. "You're being a bit dramatic, don't you think?"

He isn't the cause of my anger, and I try to keep my cool. The thing is, deep down I'm always mad at him. "Am I, Alex?" I focus on the oak tree overhanging the driveway. "One minute, you call me a selfish witch, and the next, you try to make me feel better. I don't know how to deal with your mood swings."

Alex scrubs his hand over his tired face. "It's complicated."

There is that infuriating word again. I fucking hate it. "Oh, sure. It's complicated, huh? Well, let me tell you something. From where I'm standing, it's pretty simple."

He raises his brows. "Enlighten me, then."

Our eyes lock. "You're a jerk with a hero complex."

I expect a snarky reply or a cocky grin, but Alex catches me off guard when he folds his hands in his lap and says, "It's not like that."

My throat tightens. "Then *how* is it?"

He keeps quiet, gazing at the garden or the oak tree, but not at me.

I get on my feet, overwhelmed by some unexplainable disappointment. "That's what I thought," I mutter, ready to walk away.

Alex grabs my arm and pulls me back down. "Wait."

I'm so fucking tired of all the drama. "Why, Alex? Why the fuck should I wait?"

A muscle in his jaw pops. "I know I don't always treat you right." He pauses and thrusts his fingers through his hair. "But you have that certain something that brings out the absolute worst in me."

*I'm the one he's blaming for his shitty behavior? That's fan-freakin'-tastic.* I pull my hand out of his grip and laugh. "Congratulations, jerk-face. You just passed the 'domestic abuser' exam with flying colors." Always blame the victim, right?

Realization flickers across his eyes. "No, Manda. I didn't mean it like that."

I cup my elbows and sigh. "Funny, 'cause that's exactly how it sounded."

"Manda." He reaches for my hand, but I'm done with the touching thing and step back. "You're really making me do this, huh?"

I have no idea what the hell *this* is.

He bites on his lower lip and draws a deep, probably very painful, breath. "You know what I see when I look at you?"

I cock a brow. "An evil, stab-worthy witch you'd like to kill?"

"Most of the time," he confesses. "But I also see a girl who doesn't give a shit about other people's opinions. Someone who's strong enough to do what's right, no matter what anyone else thinks about her."

My jaw drops. I check his temperature with the back of my hand. "Nope, no fever. Maybe your head injury is worse than I initially thought."

He pulls a face. "Don't make this any harder than it already is." His malachite eyes pierce mine. "All I'm trying to say is, Isobelle and all the other kids you saved back in Bakersfield would disagree with your sister."

Something in his eyes cripples the rational side of my brain. "But you wouldn't?" I blurt out, tongue faster than my brain.

He averts his gaze. It's all the answer I need.

*Sometimes, Manda, survival is about inner balance. We accept the things we can't change and focus our energy on the ones we can,* I hear Grams say.

Damn, the woman had been smart.

I extend my hand. "C'mon." He looks up. "Let's get back inside before good old Earl Grey gets cold."

Alex's gaze slides from my hand to my face. The surprise on his face is amusing. Guess he thought I'd blow a gasket. He takes my hand and smiles. "Manda," he says as we walk back in.

I look at him.

"You were right. That stuff really is pussy shit."

\*\*\*\*

It's late in the afternoon. The wind howls, rattling branches against the west side of the house. I'm confined to an uncomfy wooden chair, digging through 1,862 handwritten papyrus pages of the grimoire. My ass is numb. My eyes hurt like freaking hell.

"Anything?" Jesse asks, feverishly drumming his fingers against the table. Unlike Alex, who's watching reruns of *Judge Judy* on the couch, and Bonnie, who's in the kitchen with Melinda, Little Remington refuses to leave my side.

I rub my temples and stare at the page.

"Sleeping Pouch:

Place the following ingredients in a small pouch under your pillow. It shall keep the bad dreams away and help you find some rest.

Fresh lavender,

A spoon of dried amber,
A pinch of ghostplant,
Green jade."

"Nope," I say, looking up from the weighty book. "Not yet." Jesse presses a palm against his forehead. "Anything I can do to help?"I glance at his tapping fingers. The sound is driving me nuts. "I could really use some Red Bull." More like a whole case of the stuff but whatever. "Coffee wouldn't hurt either."

He bursts out of his chair. Running errands seems like a welcome distraction. "Ask and you shall receive." He sounds like a man on a mission. The Red Bull Slash Coffee mission.

Bonnie sticks her head through the kitchen door. "Did I hear Red Bull?" She sounds like she needs the stuff more than I do. Understandable. She's spent the last few hours with Perfect Housewitch.

Jesse nods. "I was just about to go get some."

She leans against the doorframe, bats her lashes, and gives him one of her famous even-the-pope-couldn't-resist-me smiles. "Mind if I come?"

There's an odd spark in Jesse's eyes. "You can point the way."

*Point the way, huh?* Something tells me he doesn't need a living GPS. The sidelong glance Alex casts his brother says he thinks so, too.

"Let me get my bag," Bonnie says cheerfully.

I'm close to asking Little Remington what the hell he's doing, flirting with my best friend, who happens to be a mambo.

Alex beats me to it. "What are you doing, Jess?"

He reaches for the car keys in his pocket. "Getting Amanda an energy drink," he says matter-of-factly.

"Why, need anything?"

Alex's malachite eyes burn through his brother. "Yeah." His voice is deep and commanding. "I need you to be careful."

*Translation: Don't be a fucking moron and screw a witch. Been there. Done that. Didn't end well.*

"You coming?" Bonnie shouts from the hallway. She must have taken the shortcut through the kitchen.

"On my way." Jesse winks at Alex and then he's gone.

"Why do I get the feeling those two are up to no good?" Alex says as the door in the hallway slams.

*Because they are.*

I shrug. "Relax, Alex. They're both adults." I don't sound very convincing, 'cause deep down, I'm a little worried too.

Alex rolls his eyes. "If *you* say so."

I shake my head at his undertone and get back to the book.

"To Summon a Knight of Hell:

Like heaven, hell has its own hierarchy. Knights of Hell, also known as archdemons, are the leaders of the twelve demonic legions. These creatures are extremely vicious and dangerous. Summoning them, therefore, can have fatal consequences. If, however, you must do so, follow these instructions closely:

Find a crossroad in a cemetery. Draw a circle of salt and juniper around you (under no circumstances must you leave the protective circle during the ritual). Light twelve black candles around the circle, and one red candle in the center, next to you. Carve the demon's sigil into your palm. Use your blood to draw the demon's sigil on the ground in front of you. Focus on the demon you want to summon and repeat three times:

In this night and in this hour,

I call upon the darkest power.

Come to me,

I summon thee.

Come to me,

I set you free.

May fate spare you the need to call upon those brutish creatures, for they have no remorse and will not show you mercy. Blessed be, my child."

"A spell to summon a knight of hell? Thought you descended from white witches," Alex says, peeking over my shoulder. I'd been so focused on the wicked stuff I didn't hear him coming.

I flip a page. "I do, Alex." Never heard of a rogue Bishop witch.

He gives me a don't-bullshit-me-I'm-a-hunter look and walks to the fireplace. "Then why would your ancestors need to summon a douchebag of hell?"

*Very good question.* I have no freaking idea why a spell like that is in the grimoire. Our kind—the ones who practice white magic—aren't allowed to consort with demons. It's pretty much against the code and punishable with exile.

"Manda?"

"Sometimes you've gotta work with what you're given," I say, more to myself than to him. "I had to summon a reaper to get Isobelle out of purgatory, remember?" Whoever wrote this spell must have had an equally good reason.

Alex doesn't look convinced. He leaves it at that, though. Or maybe, he's just too busy studying the family photos on the fireplace. "Who's that?"

I look up. When I see the picture he's pointing at, my heartbeat accelerates.

"Manda?"

"He's...my nephew," I whisper, mouth dry as I gaze at his beautiful, innocent smile and the cat-like shamrock-colored eyes.

Alex grabs the photo and saunters toward me. "Your sister has a son?"

Pressure starts in my stomach, slowly rising to my chest and throat. *Breathe. You gotta breathe.* I gasp for air, but the stabbing pain radiating from under my ribs to my back makes it kinda difficult.

Alex snaps his fingers in my face. "Earth to Manda?"

*Pull it together.*

I ignore the blood-rush in my ears and nod. "Yeah."

Jerk-face studies the angelic face. "What's his name?"

"Leandro." My voice is hard, my face frozen.

"Nice name," he says. "How come we haven't met him yet?"

I flip a few pages and shrug. "He's with one of Melinda's friends."

Alex flings himself into a chair next to me. "Is he a warlock?"

I want to hide in the kitchen. Run as fast as I can and never look back. Instead, I swallow the needles in my throat and sigh. "He's what we call a hereditary."

Alex laughs. "Sounds like some kind of aristocrat."

Keeping my eyes on an entry about spirit animals, I shake my head. "Simply means he descends from witches." It also suggests there's a good chance he's gifted. He's too young to be absolutely certain.

Alex places the photo on the table in front of him. "What about his dad? Is your sister married?"

"Was married," I snarl. "She's a widow."

Alex's eyes pop. "I'm sorry. I didn't mean to—"

"Don't be." Pity is the universal reaction when people hear a twenty-three-year-old is widowed. In Perfect Housewitch's case, totally unnecessary. "My sister has crappy taste in men." Her husband had been the most arrogant English prick I'd ever met. The dude's pompous behavior drove me nuts. Granted, he hadn't deserved such a cruel death, only hours after he said "yes," but Grams had warned Melinda. She'd chosen not to listen.

Alex stares at me. I pull the book closer and pay no attention.

Eventually, comforting silence falls over the room. No more bloodcurdling questions from Alex's side. No more half-truths from mine.

Then, as if life hasn't screwed me enough, Alex says, "You know, he looks one helluva lot like you. Same eyes. Identical smile."

I should come up with a snarky reply. Something like, "Mesmerizing beauty is a family trait," or "Guess God tried to make it up to him since he'd punished him with a mother like Melinda." When I see the suspicious look in Alex's eyes, though, I forget all about it.

I push the chair back. "I'm gonna get some water."

Chapter 16

Good news: Bonnie and Jesse are back with plenty of Red Bull and coffee, and Alex has long since returned to the TV. He stopped his interrogation, but not because he wasn't curious. Hell, he'd have given an arm and a leg to question me some more, but Melinda and I got into each other's faces, and he heard the whole thing go down. Keeping his mouth shut was healthier.

Bad news: I'm still hovering over the damn book. Lucky me, huh?

Bonnie shoves a can of Red Bull my way. "Find anything?"

"*Nada*." Not a single reference to deals with demons, let alone how to break them. Maybe Alex is right. Maybe there is no fixing him.

Jesse hands his brother a takeaway cup from Gulu-Gulu Café on Essex Street. Then he looks at me, worried. "You look like crap, Manda. You should get some rest." Judging by the sound of his voice, I'd say he sees the defeat on my face.

"He's right." Bonnie squeezes my shoulder. "I can take over."

Ten days to hell and only a couple of hours until Leandro returns. No way am I stopping now. "I appreciate your insults. Really do. But we're on a clock, in case you forgot."

Bonnie lifts her chin. "All right, Miss Stubborn." She pulls a sandwich out of the grocery bag and throws it on the book. "But you gotta eat something."

I toss the sandwich aside. "Make yourself useful, B, and check hunter-heroic's wounds, okay?"

She murmurs something. I pay no attention.

"Anam Cara—Soulmates:

Souls are older than mankind itself. They are the most complex creation and possess infinite power, for they are not only immortal but also divine.

Mother Nature forged the life essence in sacred flames, thereby creating the first gods: Yahweh and Asherah, Ra and Hathor, Zeus and Hera, Jupiter and Juno, Tabaldak and Glooscap, Izanagi and Izanami, and Shakti and Shiva. The mighty gods ruled earth under the watchful eye of Mother Nature. The sacred fire bore them many powerful children who, in their own rights, were gods themselves.

For millions of years, the deities lived peacefully together, protecting earth. But the more gods born, the harder it was to maintain peace. Soon, they engaged in a sanguinary battle, killing each other mercilessly.

Mother Nature banished the remorseful gods to heaven and the unrepentant to hell. In a desperate move, she decided to split future souls so each being only carried half of the divine energy. The sacred fire no longer bore gods, but humans and animals.

Every coin has two sides—yin and yang, good and evil, male and female—and the soul of a human is no different. Each creature only carries half of the divine energy. The other part resides within our Anam Cara.

Soulmates are destined to meet, drawn to each other like a moth to the flame. They accept each other as they are and share a love so fierce, it might be destructive at times. It's a deeply rooted, sacred connection. One that cannot be broken. The link between two souls is so strong, neither heaven nor hell can claim one of them if the other objects.

Blessed be, my child."

I can't take my eyes off the page. *Does that mean what I think it does?* I need a goddamn translator. "B, get your ass over here."

"What's going on?"

From the corner of my eye, I see her curious expression as she marches toward me. Jesse is right behind her, excitement gleaming in his eyes. "Did you find something?"

I refuse to encourage his enthusiasm and push the book toward my best friend. "I need you to read that."

I don't have to tell her twice. Her eyes fly over the words. The expression on her face is a cross between WTF and is-this-for-real. "Oh. My. God."

I jump out of my chair and pace the living room. "Tell me it means what I think it does." Awesome. I sound as thrilled as Jesse looks.

Her eyes lock with mine. "I-I think so," she stammers.

Jesse clenches his fists. "Guys? Care to share why you look like you've seen a ghost?"

Alex stretches his arms above his head. "She ain't that pale when she sees ghosts," he assures his brother.

I shut them both out and concentrate on Bonnie. "Have you ever heard of this?"

"Never."

"You think it'll work?"

She shrugs. "It's worth a shot, I guess."

"Jesus Christ!" Jesse's excitement turns into irritation. "Can you guys quit the secret witch language and tell us what the heck you found?"

I ignore Little Remington and stomp to the couch. "Just to get a few things straight," I say to Alex, "you're the only one who signed this deal, right?"

"Who else would have signed for my soul?" He sounds annoyed. Looks it, too.

I cross my arms. "Yes or no, Alex?"

He runs a hand over his stubble and scowls. "Yes, Amanda. I'm the only one who signed the deal." A fat smile creeps over my lips. "Awesome." Because if the whole Anam Cara shit is true, I have just found his do-not-pass-hell, do-not-pay-with-your-soul card. "Enough." Jesse throws his hands over his head. "One of you. Will tell me what the fuck is going on, or I swear I'll...I'll..."

*Strangle us with bare hands?* Yeah, no shit. "Chill, Jess."

He's on the brink of losing his shit. "Talk. Now."

My eyes flick up. "I might have found a way out of this"—I look at Alex—"fiery situation."

Jesse's eyes grow wide. "Seriously?"

"Wouldn't lie about it."

Alex narrows his eyes at me. "Judging by the look on your face, I'd say it involves child sacrifice."

"Worse," Bonnie says. She likes messing with jerk-face's head.

Alex pales. "What?"

I'm all game when it comes to screwing with Alex. Can't stand the horrific expression on his face, though. "Keep calm and trust your awesome witch friend, Alex."

"Amanda," Jesse and Alex yell. They sound like a heavy metal choir.

*Melodramatic much?*

Considering how fucking impatient they are, I should keep them on the tenterhooks a bit longer. I don't. "Short version?" They both nod. "According to this book, hell can't claim your soul if your Anam Cara objects."

"My what?" Alex is clearly not getting any of this.

"Your soulmate," Bonnie explains.

Alex laughs. "This some sort of joke?"

My expression is grim. "No. This is me saving your sorry hunter ass."

He's still laughing, until he realizes I ain't fucking around. Then he sorta freaks out. "Have you guys lost your mind?"

"Why else would we try to save a hunter?" Bonnie grumbles.

Jerk-face cups my chin. "Amanda," he says, voice hard as stone. "You can't be serious."

I squint. "I can and I am."

He shakes his head. "First, I don't believe in this whole soulmate business, and second, even if I did, I only have ten days. How am I supposed to find what other people search for their whole lives within ten fucking days?"

Jesse shoots daggers at his brother. "Shut up for a second, will ya?" He looks at me. "What you're saying is we have to find Alex's soulmate so she—"

"Or he—" Bonnie cuts in.

"Can do what?" Jesse continues. "Write an objection letter to hell? Hire Keanu Reeves as an advocate for human-hell rights?"

Jesus, I've only just read the stuff. "I guess she'd have to claim ownership of his soul." Can't blame me for sounding a bit crazy. I'm making this shit up as I go.

Jesse plops onto the table. "And then this nightmare would be over? There'd be no hellfire at the end of my brother's tunnel? No demon dragging him to the pit?"

*I sure hope so.* "That's what the book says."

"Don't tell me you're buying into this madness," Alex snaps.

Silence settles over the living room.

"Shit. You fucking are," Alex barks when he sees the look on his brother's face.

Peeved, I arch a brow. "A little optimism wouldn't hurt, Alex." It's not a perfect solution, but it's all we've got.

Alex glares at me. "There's a fine line between *optimism* and *delusion,* Amanda. And you just crossed it."

Bonnie, now sitting on the table next to Jesse, swings her feet and sighs. "I'm the last person who wants to be on team Alex, but how *are* we supposed to find his soulmate in ten days?"

The book says soulmates are destined to meet. Chances are Alex and his already crossed paths. Problem is he must have gotten to know a hundred chicks while roaming the country.

"Manda?" Jesse sounds worried. "You do have a plan, right?"

*Not really.* "Let's do a spell," I suggest.

Bonnie almost falls off the table. "Are you fucking crazy?"

Little Remington knits his brows. "Why? Sounds

like a good idea to me."

Bonnie jumps down and faces Jesse. "Do you have the slightest idea what happens if a love spell goes wrong? Are you aware it's black fucking magic?"

"What?" Jesse is startled. "Why would a love spell be black magic?"

I frown. "Because our kind believes love is divine. Tampering with it can upset the natural order."

"Yeah," Bonnie adds. "Not to mention it can turn ordinary people into obsessive, stalking psychopaths."

"Enough," Alex shouts. "No way any of you is tapping into black magic." He gives his brother a look. "We're still hunters, remember?"

"There must be another way." Jesse speaks to himself, not to us.

I go to the book and re-read the entry. "According to this, 'soulmates are drawn to each other, accept each other as they are, and share a love so fierce, it might be destructive at times.'" I meet Alex's eyes. "Can you think of anyone who stirred up such feelings?"

"I can," Jesse says.

All heads turn to him. "Spill it," Bonnie orders.

He grins, and I already hate what he's about to say. "Seriously? Am I the only one in this room who thought of Amanda?"

My heart stops beating.

Alex's jaw drops.

Bonnie just stands there, thinking. Until she says, "Can't believe I'm saying this, but 'a love so fierce it might be destructive' *does* kinda sound like the two of you."

Alex regains control over his mouth. "Okay. I've listened to all this soulmate bullshit, but if any of you thinks a hunter"—he points at himself—"and a witch"—he points at me—"could be fucking Anam whatever, you must be living in an alternate universe."

"He's right," I croak. "Alex and I are destined to hate each other, not..." The word won't even cross my lips.

Alex lowers his gaze. "Exactly. I mean, how am I to accept her as she is when she's a goddamn witch?"

Punch in the gut. *Well done, jerk-face.*

Bonnie gets in Alex's face. "Know what?" Her voice is colder than dry ice. "I think you're right. An asshole like you could never be Amanda's soulmate. She's too fucking good for you."

Alex grins from ear to ear. "Oh really? Too *good*?"

My best friend balls her hands into fists. "Yeah, Alexander. Too fucking *good*."

Jesse steps between them before one of them can kill the other. "Let's all take a deep breath and calm down, okay?"

"No." Bonnie snaps. "Amanda is trying to save your brother's life, and all *he* does is blow shit in her face."

"I never asked her to save me," Alex says, defending himself. "Never asked for her fucking help either."

"Then why show up at our place?" Bonnie counters.

A dull ache in my head flares to life. "That's enough," I shout, close to losing my temper and murdering both of them. I turn to Jesse. "I'm not his soulmate. Moving on."

Bonnie's lips part. "But—"

"I said moving on." She knows me well enough not

to push me and keeps quiet. My gaze flies to Alex. "How about you write a list with every girl you've ever, even just remotely, experienced the described feelings?"

Alex pulls his brows together. "Then what, Manda? Are we going to call them and say, 'Hey, sorry to bother you, but do you think we could be soulmates?'"

I am not in the mood for his smart-ass act. "No, Alex. We're not going to call 'em. We'll pay 'em a visit and ask 'em to claim your soul."

Bonnie cuts her eyes my way. "You cannot be serious. You'd risk exposing witchcraft, Amanda."

*She's right. Reading someone the cards or sharing herbal recipes with 'em is not the same as asking a total stranger to claim a soul.* But we're running out of options.

"You'd have to test them first," Melinda says.

Where the hell did she come from, and since when is she in on the "Rescue Alex from Hell" mission?

Perfect Housewitch fiddles with the half-peeled potato in her hand. "If you test them, you'll only have to share the truth with the right one," she says matter-of-factly.

Bonnie, Jesse, and Alex stare at her with dropped jaws. I, on the other hand, cross my arms and cock a brow. "And how do you suggest we do that?"

She grows uneasy with all our eyes on her. "There's a ritual," she says. "It'll help you determine if she's his soulmate."

"Haven't seen a ritual like that in the book."

Her gaze drops to the potato in her hand. "The ritual is in *my* book," she confesses. "You need hair or blood of both—Alex and the girl."

I want to ask Perfect Housewitch since when has she had a grimoire of her own, but Alex starts talking. "Oh, that's just great." He shakes his head like a mad man. "So, we have to drive around the country to find every girl I've ever had feelings for, only to knock on her door and ask for her blood?"

Melinda nods. "You could put it that way."

Alex's gaze shoots to me. "Do you know how fucking crazy that sounds? Crazy even by your standards, Manda."

Going up against a bokor and his zombie slave isn't exactly sane either. We'd done it nevertheless. "Just write the damn list, Alex."

Jesse grabs a pencil from the table, pulls a small notebook out of his pocket, and shoves it against Alex's chest.

"You guys are fucking nuts."

Jesse smirks. "Shut up and go to work, Romeo."

"Amanda," Melinda says. "May I talk to you for a second?" She pushes the kitchen door open. "In private."

*I knew there was a catch to her sudden helpfulness.*

Perfect Housewitch leans against the kitchen counter, crossing her ankles. It's sort of weird. Melinda is nothing like Grams, but she sure as hell inherited her perfect posture and lady-like manners. "We have to talk, Amanda."

"Go on and talk then."

I totally expect one of her famous you're-a-disgrace-to-the-family speeches. Something else entirely comes out of her mouth. "Bonnie mentioned you're doing well at NYU?"

"So?"

Melinda drops her hands to her sides. "Can we have a normal conversation for once?"

That's the most hilarious thing I've heard all day. I suppress the laughter climbing up my throat and knit my brows. "Nothing about us is normal, Melinda. Just cut to the chase and tell me why the hell you hauled my ass to the kitchen."

She draws a deep breath. "I know you want to help Alexander. Believe me, I do, but I need you to stay out of this."

*Twilight Zone* alarm. First, Perfect Housewitch comes up with a ritual to determine who Alex's soulmate is, and now she wants me to stay out of this? "Do you have a brain tumor?"

She squints. "What? No."

*No brain tumor, huh? Okay. Maybe a concussion?* "Did you hit your head?"

She brushes a strand of hair out of her face and straightens her skirt. "Amanda." Teacher voice is back. "Stop this nonsense, would you?"

I reach for a juicy red apple from the fruit basket and take a bite. "Sure thing," I mumble, mouth full. "But first you're gonna tell me why the hell you came up with that ritual if you want me to stay the hell out of this."

Her bottom lip quivers. She looks pretty upset. "I offered my help because, like you, I don't want him to die. I'm certain you understand why."

I let the apple roll from one hand to the other. "We're on the same page then?"

She nods. "We are."

"Then where's the fuckin' problem, Melinda?"

My choice of language makes her flinch. She

doesn't scold me, though. Terrifying.

"I have a bad feeling about this," she admits. "Especially, after Grams—"

*Not again.* "Stop right there. If Grams were worried about me, she'd tell me herself." Melinda's mouth opens in surprise. I'm done and walk to the door.

"Amanda, think about L—"

I turn my head. "What the hell do you think I'm doing, Melinda?"

Chapter 17

*Nine days to hell*

After being squeezed in the car for almost sixteen hours, and listening to Alex and Jesse's endless stories about Diana, the first girl on the list, we finally reach Cross Hill, a typical southern small town where folks still wave at each other from their porches and regard strangers with as much caution as they would alien invaders.

The atmosphere in the Mustang is a mixture between colorless and doom and gloom. Six names. Six states. Nine days left. Long story short: Alex is screwed. We all think it. Only hunter-heroic is brave enough to admit it.

"How can you be sure she still lives here?" Bonnie asks, pushing the gas pedal a little harder. Lake Greenwood is about fifteen minutes from Cross Hill, and we all want to get out of this goddamn car.

I still can't believe she came along. I'd told Bonnie to go back to NYU. I had this covered. She said something along the lines of, "If you think I'll let you do this on your own, you clearly don't know me, Amanda."

Alex moves closer to me and meets my best friend's eyes in the rearview mirror. "I'd appreciate it, if you could keep those pretty eyes of yours on the road before you wreck the love of my life." Jerk-face hates when someone else drives his car.

Bonnie cocks a brow. "And I'd appreciate it, if you'd answer my question."

Alex frowns. "Diana ain't never gonna leave this place. She loves it here."

I gaze out the window, tired of hearing her name. *Diana.* The girl he met when he was seventeen. The chick who, apart from all the others, knows the truth about him—hunter and all. The black-haired Asian beauty who puts a smile on jerk-face's lips every time someone mentions her.

Jesse unbuckles his seat belt and turns. "How are we going to play this? Knock on her door and ask for her blood to perform the ritual?"

"No way," Alex barks.

I squint. "Why not? Thought she's in on your dirty little secret."

Jesse runs a hand over his tired face. "She's right, man. Diana knows what goes bump in the night. Firsthand experience, remember?"

I almost forgot. *Diana.* The girl Alex saved from a shtriga. Just for the record, shtrigas are witches. Their coven, formed by a woman named Aradia, dates back to fourteenth-century Italy. Her followers are devoted to the Goddess. Unfortunately, every coven has rogue members, spoiling the reputation of the whole club.

Alex shoots Jesse a flinty look. "After four years of radio silence, you expect me to knock on her door and ask her to perform a soulmate ritual to save me from hell?"

Bonnie jerks the steering wheel to the right, and Alex almost lands on my lap. "I swear," he says, "you're a worse driver than my brother."

She cuts her eyes to Little Remington. "Before we go all soulmate on that Diana chick's ass, we need to make sure she's not married." Despite Bonnie's free-love-I-should-have-been-born-in-the-60s attitude, she's a firm believer in the sacred bond.

"She's not married," Alex says matter-of-factly.

I want to ask how he knew if he hasn't seen her in four years but clench my teeth, keeping my mouth shut. *He probably stalked her on Facebook or something.*

I inhale warm air streaming through the rolled-down window when I see a street sign—Dixon Price Road. We're almost there. I should be excited. Diana could be Alex's lifeline, his ticket out of hell, but my belly cramps, and I don't even know why.

"That's her house." Alex points to the baby-blue lakefront home with the number 211 painted on the garage.

"We need a plan," Jesse says as Bonnie pulls into the driveway. "Like, right *now*."

I tie my hair into a high bun. "One step at a time, okay?"

Jesse knits his brows. "What's step number one?"

I yank the door open and gratefully stretch my legs. "We knock on the door, Jess."

I feel Alex's eyes piercing my back. "It's not too late to call this shit off." His hand lands on my shoulder, and I turn my head. "I mean it, Manda. Let's spend my last days doing something fun."

I pull a wry face. "Oh, you mean like going to Disney World?" He nods. "Sorry, but a bunch of knights in shining armor and their naïve princesses isn't my idea of fun." That said, I get out of the car and ogle the idyllic house. There are about a million places I'd rather be. For the sake of Alex's soul, I'll grit my teeth.

Once everyone is out of the car and Bonnie locked it, we stroll past the garage to the double glass doors. I'm not trying to be a bitch, but who the fuck lives in a house with glass doors? *Cinder-freakin'-diana.*

Jesse brings his fist to the door. "Ready?"

Alex touches his forearm. "Don't, man. Just don't."

"Do it," Bonnie orders.

Jesse looks at me. I nod. He knocks.

Two seconds pass before Alex says, "No one's home. Let's get outta here." His jaw is tense, his shoulders stiffer than a Steiff Teddy Bear.

Jesse shifts his head. "Dude, give her a—"

The door swings open. An elderly woman with an apron around her waist greets us. "Can I help you?"

They all stand there like idiots. Awesome. "Hey." I fake my best smile. "We're friends of Diana. Is she home?"

The woman smiles. "The Wongs are on a fishing trip. They won't be back until tomorrow."

*We're fucked. We're more fucked than fucked. We're the most fucked up people in the State of South Carolina.*

"Would you like to leave a message?"

*Oh, yeah. Tell Diana we'll be back for her blood.*

"No, ma'am. Thanks. We'll come back tomorrow," Bonnie says.

Dismay poisons the air as we head back to the car. None of us anticipated a situation like this, and by the look on Jesse's face, I'd say the anticlimactic moment hit him right where it hurts—not his crotch, his heart.

"Maybe it's a sign from above," Alex says once

we're back in the car. "We should move on to the next name on the list."

Not gonna happen. "No. We'll come back tomorrow like we said we would." Sure we're on a very tight schedule, but even without the psychology lectures I've attended, I'd be certain there's a reason why Diana was the first girl on Alex's list.

"I'm with Amanda," Bonnie says.

Jesse nods. "Me too." He faces his brother and smiles. "Think it would be best if we stayed at Lady Amelia's. With the cops on your ass and all."

"Lady Amelia, huh?" Alex sounds unsettled.

Bonnie turns the key in the ignition and the Mustang roars to life. "Who the hell is Lady Amelia?" she asks, backing out of the driveway.

"She runs a B&B in Cross Hill," Jesse explains.

Bonnie glares at her reflection in the rearview mirror. "Sounds good. I could really use some beauty sleep." Bullshit. Bonnie's skin looks as smooth as ever and there are no signs of bags under her eyes.

Alex nudges my leg. "There's something you guys should know."

"What should we know?"

"Lady Amelia is…was…a—"

"Hunter," Jesse finishes for him.

The jarring sound of the brakes howls through the car as Bonnie stops it in the middle of the road. "Are you off your rocker? We are not going to spend the night in a hunter-owned B&B."

Jesse tries his famous I-can-melt-your-heart smile on my best friend. "Relax," he says. "Amelia is cool. She'll understand."

\*\*\*\*

*Understand my ass.* The instant Bonnie and I crossed the threshold, a hunting rifle points at us.

"Alexander Ethan Remington," the gray-haired, tattooed woman yells. "You're nutty as a fruitcake if you think I'll let those...those *witches* stay in my house." She might be old, but her posture says: fuck with me, and I'll shoot your ass.

Jesse tries to sooth her with a calming gesture. "Would you calm down?"

Pulp Fiction Granny shifts the rifle's shaft back and forth between Bonnie and me. "You ain't gonna tell me when to calm down, son. This is my fucking house. My fucking rules. Clear?"

Alex takes a step toward her. "We understand, Amelia, but it's an emergency." He's close enough to yank the rifle out of her hand, but she'd still have enough time to shoot at least one of us.

The scar on my chest itches, and I feel the overwhelming urge to run. "We're not your enemy," I assure her, not taking my eyes off the rifle.

She eyeballs Alex. "What kind of emergency justifies working with witches?"

Bonnie's face slips into a frown. "The one where his soul will be dragged to hell in nine days unless we save his sorry hunter ass." Her voice is so even, no one would guess she's talking to a woman with a rifle pointed at her heart.

Amelia gawks at Alex. "Explain," she orders, slightly lowering her gun.

Alex's lips stay sealed. Jesse takes matters in his own hands. "Alex sold his soul, Amelia. We have nine days to get him out of this deal, or he'll end up as some demon's bitch."

Pulp Fiction Granny's shoulders sink. She studies Alex closely. "That true, Alexander?"

Alex's smile doesn't reach his eyes. "He pretty much nailed it."

"*You* made a pact with the devil, and now you think his whores will help you?" There's so much hate and disgust in the words, it's hard to ignore. "You're a hunter, Alexander, you should know better than to trust those obnoxious creatures."

Bonnie lunges forward, ready to hit Amelia in the face. "I'll show you ob—"

"Enough." Jesse holds B back. Then, he faces Amelia. "These girls are our friends. You won't to talk to them like that. Understood?"

Bonnie's eyes burn brighter than Sirius itself. She's had a thing for Jesse since the moment she, half-naked, bumped into his chest. But standing up for us gained him her respect, the most important thing for her.

"He's right," Alex says to my surprise. "Hate it all you want, but they *are* our friends." He stands next to Jesse. "You wanna shoot them? Gotta shoot us first."

*Oh. My. God. First Perfect Housewitch offers her help, and now Alex goes against another hunter for us? For witches?* Either I'm on *Shutter Island*, or he's been Facultied. In other words: controlled by otherworldly parasites.

Amelia thinks it over then puts the rifle on the reception desk. "I can't believe you," she mutters, hands dropping to her sides.

Alex shakes his head. "Don't care. This is a hunter B&B, and we *are* hunters. So can we stay or not?"

Hunters—like witches—have a code. Their most important rule is to always help a brother or sister in need. Good old Amelia doesn't have much of a choice. "All right. You can stay, but there are rules."

Alex gestures for her to continue.

She holds up a finger. "One, you will share a room. Can't have those witches roaming freely in my house. Two"—another finger comes up—"if they try anything, I'll personally send them to purgatory." Her voice is as cold as ice, and I get the feeling she's secretly praying we'll mess up.

Alex nods in agreement.

"And"—a third finger shoots in the air—"no magic in my house."

I look at Bonnie. "Damn, B. Guess that means child sacrifice will have to wait till tomorrow."

Amelia clenches her hands and moves to the reception. "You can stay in Miss Daisy's room. It's big enough for all of you."

Glaring at her back, I think of Hedwig, the mambo who'd treated Alex, a hunter, with as much respect as she treated her own kind. Amelia could really take a page from her book.

We follow her up the stairs to the last room on the left. Without a word, she unlocks it. Jesse, Bonnie, and Alex walk in.

I try to follow, but Amelia holds me back. "I know who you are," she whispers. "If you hurt that boy again, *witch*, I will push a dagger through your evil heart. Understand?"

I want to ask her what the hell she's talking about, but when I see the repulsion in her pale, gray eyes, I yank my hand out of her grip and slam the door in her face.

*I hate hunters.*

## Chapter 18

*I looked over my shoulder. Glowing red eyes were only a few feet behind me. I sprinted past the king-sized iron gates of the cemetery, straight into the woods.*

*The creature was fast. Faster than any dog I'd ever seen. The muscles in my legs jerked as I picked up speed. Branches snapped beneath my feet. The cold wind beat violently against my face.*

*The beast howled as it chased me through the woods. Its paws galumphed over the dried soil, heading straight toward me.* Don't stop. It's going to get ya.

*I'd faint if I kept up the speed. Hiding behind a tree, I braced my hands on my knees and tried to breathe. Every time I drew in some air, it felt as if someone was stabbing me in the chest.*

*"Manda?"* Alex? Impossible. He's dead. *"Manda, please. Help me." His voice echoed off the trees.* Don't. It's a trick. *"Why won't you help me, Manda?" He sounded so weak and vulnerable, it fucking killed me.*

*Tears pricked the corners of my eyes. The rational side of my brain urged me to get the fuck outta there, but this was Alex screaming for help. I couldn't turn my back on him.*

*I pressed my thumb into my sweaty palm, hoping the pain would chase away the fear. It didn't. I stepped away from the safety of the tree. "Alex?" I whispered.*

*He stood a few feet away, face pale, eyes misty.*

177

"*Please, help me,*" *he said as the blood-thirsty creature strode out of his shadow like a hungry panther.*

Told ya it's a trick.

*I looked from the beast to Alex. If I ran, the thing would rip me apart. A scene from* Django Unchained *flickered across my mind's eye, and when the dog-like creature bared its teeth, I decided I had no intention to end up like poor d'Artagnan.*

*I forced my spine straighter.* "*Good dog,*" *I said, approaching it slowly.* "*I won't hurt you and you won't hurt me, right?*"

*The beast bent its head slightly, and when it didn't jump me, I took another step in Alex's direction.*

"*Can you get me outta here?*" *Alex's panicked voice drew the bloodhound's attention to him.*

No way the both of you will get outta here alive.

*I hated the voice in my head, especially when it was right.* "*Listen to me,*" *I said, meeting Alex's bleak eyes.* "*It can only chase one of us.*"

*As if it understood what I said, the beast's red eyes slid from Alex to me.*

"*If I say run, you will run. Got it?*"

*Alex glared at the hellhound and shook his head.* "*I won't leave you.*"

*I took a deep breath and smiled.* "*Yes, you will. You will run, and you won't look back.*" *I swallowed the glass shards in my throat and took another step toward the beast but kept my eyes trained on Alex.* "*I'm a witch, remember? I can take care of myself.*"

"*I-I...Shit.*"

*I closed the little gap between the dog and me, and when I had its full attention, I shouted,* "*Run, Alex. Run.*"

*He did, and I threw my whole weight onto the creature, wrestling it to the ground. It was a fight I was destined to lose. The beast pinned me down, its red eyes only inches from mine. The distinct smell of sulfur stung my nostrils as its breath beat against my face.*

You're fuckin' crazy, *I told myself as sharp teeth penetrated the skin on my neck.*

*"Amanda!" Alex screamed from a distance.*

*It was too late. I'd taken his place, and the creature was merciless.*

\*\*\*\*

I yank my eyes open. There's no forest. No beast. Just Miss Daisy's room.

*Another nightmare. Great.*

I wipe the sweat off my forehead and sit up. A glow from the silvery moon penetrates the windows, casting an unearthly light over the dark room. I pull my shaking knees to my chest and focus on Bonnie's snoring to calm my heart. She's spread over the full length of the bed, sleeping peacefully. They all are. Alex and Jesse are curled up on the other bed. End credits of *The Omen* roll over the TV screen. We must have all drifted off while watching the movie.

Drained from the fucking nightmare, I get on my wobbly feet. My damp tank-top and yoga pants stick to my skin. Drops of sweat course down my collarbone. All I want is a hot shower to wash my messed-up emotions away, but while staggering toward the bathroom, I freeze. A spine-chilling howl echoes off the walls.

*Am I still dreaming?*

I scan the room, looking for the beast, prepared to get attacked by its sharp teeth. There's nothing.

*Your mind's playing tricks on you.*

I inhale sharply. These nightmares are fucking with me. I need to get a grip. I take another step and the TV starts flickering. White noise rings through the darkness. Another howl thunders through my ears. The door leading to the hallway clicks open.

*What the fuck?*

I've seen enough horror movies to know what happens if I'm dumb enough to walk out of this room. Always bitched about the stupid blonde chick who got herself killed because she didn't understand the rules in her genre, but when I spot a creepy shadow through the ajar door, my feet take on a life of their own.

*Don't do this.*

Too late. I'm already in the hallway. The shadow is gone. Several dim bulbs on the walls flicker. An electric buzz charges the air.

*This ain't good.*

The scent of brimstone crawls into my nose. I shake like a leaf as a pair of hellish eyes appear at the far end of the long hallway. One second, I'm looking right into them. The next they're gone.

*Go back in the room and wake the others.*

Muffled voices roar through the house. My heart beats fast in my chest. I follow the sound nevertheless. Digging my nails into my palms, I round a corner and head down the stairs. The golden chandelier in the lobby swings back and forth.

*There's no draft.*

The voices grow louder. I tiptoe to the dining room and hide behind the door frame.

"I can't believe they brought them here," a man with a deep, husky voice says.

"We should kill her while we can," another one says.

"No," Lady Amelia barks. "You won't start a hunter war in my house."

A chair moves. "This is madness. You know what they say about her."

"I do," Lady Amelia assures him. "But the Remingtons are still hunters, and she's with them."

I guess it's a fair assumption they're talking about Bonnie or me.

"The Remingtons?" The one with the husky voice laughs. "Are you really trusting Alex's judgment when it comes to this whore? He's blinded by her."

Nope, not Bonnie. Me.

"He's right," the other says. "Alex has heard the rumors. He had dozens of chances to end her, but—"

"Enough." Amelia raises her voice. "She's not to be touched. Anyone who does will answer to me. Clear enough?"

Boots walk across the wood floor in my direction. "You're as crazy as they are," Husky Voice grumbles.

I have no idea what rumors they're talking about. But I'm certain about one thing—if they find me here eavesdropping, I'm a dead witch. I spin on my heels, my hip knocking into a lamp. I catch it before it falls.

"What was that?" Amelia asks, alert.

"Don't know." Husky Voice is on high alert.

The safety on a gun is removed. "Let's find out," the other man suggests.

Panic settles in. No freaking way I can outrun them. Terror overrides the natural flight instinct, keeping me at the spot.

*I'm dead. I'm so fuckin' d—*

A hand covers my mouth. I want to bite. Scream. Fight. I'm in a death grip, being hauled into a closet.

It's dark. I can't see a thing. Clawing the stranger's arm, I struggle to free myself.

"Manda, calm the fuck down."

*Alex?*

"I'm going to take my hand off your mouth, but you have to be real quiet. Can you do that?"

The second I realize it's Alex, and not some demon or hunter who wants to kill me, I relax and nod.

"Anything?" Husky Voice barks outside the closet as Alex slowly removes his hand.

"No," Amelia replies. "Check the upper floor."

Boots rush up the stairs. Then there's silence.

Alex's hot breath tingles on my skin. He spins me around. It's too fucking dark to see his face. "Are you suicidal? They would have killed you." He sounds scared. My hand rests on his chest. I feel his heart racing beneath it. He *is* scared.

I should thank him for saving my sweet ass, but I'm too vexed. "You don't say. Thought they'd ask me to join their PJ party."

I can tell he's frowning. He always does when I annoy him. "What the hell are you doing down here?" He's so close his lips brush the corner of my lips.

I want to ask him about the rumors his hunter pals mentioned, but all of a sudden the closet is too fucking small. Alex is too damn close. Panic creeps over me. Not the kind I felt minutes ago. The one only hunter-heroic can cause.

I try to step back. His strong hands hold me in place. "Manda?"

His touch sparks a fire in my stomach, and those

flames burn hotter than hell. "I-I…" I can barely breathe, let alone talk. "H-Heard something."

"You should have woken us up." He takes my face in both hands and sighs. "You should have woken *me* up."

I should have. That way I wouldn't have ended up in a fucking closet with him. I suppress the butterflies in my belly and clear my throat. "Can we go now?" I whisper, fighting the need to take possession of his delicious mouth.

"They're searching the house. We gotta stay put for a while."

I hear the creaking of the upper floor. But I begin to wonder if taking my chances with three murderous hunters would be less fatal than being stuck here with Alex.

"Relax." His voice is softer. "They ain't gonna hurt you." He brushes his thumb over my lips. "I won't let them."

It's when he says stuff like that I consider the dissociative personality disorder theory to be true. Less than forty-eight hours ago, he raised hell when Jesse suggested I was his soulmate. Now he's hiding me in a closet so his kind won't kill me.

He cups my cheeks. "Manda?"

My chest rises and falls quicker than a rocket. Don't even get me started on my treacherous heart. I press my back against the wall. "Hmm?"

He slides his hand under the edge of my shirt. I flinch as his warm fingers touch my belly. "Can I ask you something?"

I swallow the desire to rip his shirt off and nod.

He thrusts one leg between mine. "Do you have a

bucket list?"

I try not to think about the throbbing sensation in my panties. "No," I croak. "Do you?"

His hand travels up my stomach, stopping right under my bra. "Not exactly," he whispers. "But if I did, this would be on it."

Having a mind of its own, my body arches against his hand. "Being stuck in a closet?"

"Being stuck in a closet with *you*," he corrects.

I didn't know it possible for him to lean in farther, but he does. "Promise me something, Manda." He draws circles on the skin under my two ladies. "If this whole soulmate shit ain't gonna work, this is how we'll spend the last day of my life."

*Soulmate.* The word hits me like a roundhouse kick. We're stuck in the closet of a hunter B&B because we're looking for Alex's fucking soulmate. The love of his life. My brain takes over. I push him away.

"Whoa," he says. "What's with you?"

I want to screw a guy who's looking for another girl. That's what's with me. "Stay back," I warn when I feel him coming closer again.

"Manda." He sounds bewildered. "You on drugs? Why the sudden change of heart?"

"Was on drugs," I say, crossing my arms. "Now I'm clear as day."

"What's that supposed to mean?" He raises his voice, obviously no longer concerned about Lady Amelia or the other two assholes.

*It means I'm not the kinda girl who takes a back seat.* "Nothing," I snap. "Just stay the hell away from me until we're outta here, all right?"

184

Chapter 19

*Eight days to hell*

Bonnie points to the vibrating phone in my lap. "You not gonna get that?"

"No," I snap as Jesse pulls into Diana's driveway. I've had enough douchebag trouble for a millennium. No need to get some more from DeLuca.

Bonnie casts me a sidelong glance. "What's eating at you? You've been on bitch crack all morning."

Alex watches me through the rearview mirror. He demanded to ride shotgun so he could stretch his legs. In reality, he just didn't feel like sitting next to me. I felt the same way about him. Jerk-face has acted like an asshole ever since I left his horny hunter butt in the closet. Hilarious. *He* treated *me* like a piece of witch meat, but I get the cold shoulder treatment?

"Amanda?" Bonnie nudges me. "You just gonna ignore me like you ignore poor Magic Bridge?"

"Magic Bridge?" A cocky grin curls Alex's lips. "You exchanged a Mustang for a Pony? Wow. That's...lame."

I gaze out the window and bite my lip until I taste copper. Most days, I simply want to strangle Alex. Today, I wish I had a brazen bull, the medieval torture device. I'd love to see him roast to death.

Bonnie puts a hand on Alex's shoulder. "Anyone

ever told you what an asshat you are?"

"Witches throw that shit at me all the time." He looks back over his shoulder. "Right before I send them to purgatory."

Jesse pulls the key out of the ignition. "Guys, can we all get a grip?" Always the peacemaker, just like B.

I yank the door open. "Yeah, the sooner we find jerk-face's other miserable half, the faster we can all go back to *our* worlds."

We stand on the porch of the lake house like a third-rate version of the Scooby Gang as Alex's gaze lands on me. "Everybody stick to the plan."

Sneaking into Diana's bedroom to steal her brush? Great plan. Doomed to fail I'd say.

After an eternity in front of Cinder-freaking-Diana's glass door, Jesse knocks. Alex fiddles with the sleeve of his worn leather jacket. He's nervous. Hundred bucks say it has less to do with the prospect of saving his soul and more with the reunion of his first love. But hey, who am I to judge? I'm just the girl he wants to screw in a closet if things go haywire.

"Coming," a contralto voice sings.

When the door flies open, I stand face to face with Miss Asia. It's not her flawless skin or her silky black hair that sparks a cruel fire in the pit of my stomach. It's the way her eyes light up when she sees Alex. "Oh my God, Alexander Remington?" She puts a hand over her heart. "Is that really you?" The chick looks as if she's about to faint.

*Alex.* The Justin Bieber of all the Dianas in the world.

"In the flesh," he says, an impish grin tugging at his lips. "It's been a while, huh?"

Diana doesn't answer. She's too damn busy throwing her arms around Alex. "I can't believe it. I thought I'd never see you again."

Alex wraps his strong arms around her and pulls her close. "You didn't think you'd get rid of me that easily, did you?" There's something so intimate and tender about their hug, it's hard to imagine they haven't seen each other the last four years.

Diana steps back. "You brought friends?"

"You remember Jesse?" he says, pointing to his brother.

Diana's smile widens. "Wow, look at you. All grown up."

He smiles that smile, the one that wets the panties of the whole female population. "And you're still quite the beauty, I see."

Bonnie elbows Little Remington. "Thanks for introducing us, moron."

Jesse directs the I-drive-you-over-the-edge smile at my best friend. "Diana," he says, never taking his eyes off Bonnie. "Meet the incredible, extra awesome Queen B."

Diana grins. "It's nice to meet you, Queen B."

Bonnie winks at her. "Just B to you."

And as if the whole reunion isn't bad enough, Diana spins on her heels and faces me. "And you're?"

I want to be nice. Every word coming to mind is either bitchy or downright mean. So I stick with the saying, if you don't have anything nice to say, keep your stab-worthy mouth shut.

Alex frowns. "That's Amanda."

Diana's gaze drifts from him to me. She's totally trying to read us. I know, because I invented the look she's wearing right now. "Nice to meet you, Amanda."

"Likewise," I lie.

Diana bats her black lashes. "How did I deserve a visit from my favorite hero?"

*I need to throw up.*

Hunter-heroic throws his arm around Diana's shoulders. "We were in the neighborhood, and I told them all about your wicked coffee. Any chance we could bribe you into making some?"

*Smooth move. Gotta give it to him.*

Diana laughs and opens the door for us. "Well, you better come in. Won't serve the best coffee in the country on the porch."

The way Alex has his arm around her makes me want to scratch my eyeballs out and feed it to the beast that haunted my dreams last night.

"Hey," Alex barks. "You coming?"

*I'd rather not.* But I follow them inside nevertheless.

Diana leads us down a hallway to a sunroom. The furnishings are a perfect blend of old-fashioned and modern. Light streams through the massive front window, illuminating the room in a beautiful orange light. Family photos decorate the walls.

*Diana.* The girl with the perfect life.

"Make yourselves at home," she says, pointing to ebony rattan chairs circling a glass table.

The gang gathers around the table. I don't join them. "Do you live all by yourself in this big house?" Bonnie asks, sounding like a creeper.

A genuine smile touches Diana's doll eyes. "Oh, no. I live with my parents."

"Of course you do." Shit, did I just say that out

loud?

Alex narrows his eyes at me.

Jesse sighs.

Bonnie shakes her head.

And Diana? Well, she pretends she didn't hear me.

"You just missed my mom. She's gone to get some books for me. Should be back soon, though." The chick has a beautiful voice.

"What about your dad?" Jesse sounds a bit like the wolf in Red Riding Hood—suspicious and way too nosy to be trusted.

Diana gestures at a little shed next to the pier. "Gutting the fish. Amanda," she says, walking up beside me. "Why don't you take a seat? I'll go and get the coffee."

Alex is on his feet in no time. "Need a hand?"

"Absolutely." She sounds a little too enthusiastic for my taste.

The second the two are gone, I fling myself into one of the stupid rattan chairs. "All right," Bonnie murmurs, not the least bit amused. "What's the matter with you?"

I examine my nails. They so need a manicure.

Jesse studies me. "Amanda, is this about last night?"

*What does he know about last night?* I want to ask. My stubbornness keeps my mouth shut.

Bonnie looks from me to Jesse. "Someone gonna tell me what I missed?"

Jesse's gaze slams into mine. "Why don't you ask Amanda?"

"No idea what you're talking about."

"So you're saying you and Alex didn't leave the

room last night to do"—he makes a face—"you know what?"

One side of my mouth curves up. Not that I find his accusation funny, but the shy look on his face is. "You should watch less porn, Jess."

Bonnie's eyes go wide with surprise. "Wait a second. Are you insinuating they had sex?"

*She's quick today.*

Jesse raises his brows. That's all the answer Bonnie needs to go all mambo-bitch on my ass. "Please tell me you didn't screw that moron." Her voice is a mixture of annoyed-as-hell and I'm-begging-you-to-say-no.

I tap my long nails against the glass. "No, B. Told you I don't make the same mistake twice."

Little Remington calls bullshit. It's written all over his remarkable face. "Then where were you?"

I'm not in the mood to think or talk about the rumors, the closet, or the disappointed expression on Alex's face when we went back to our room, but neither Jesse nor Bonnie will drop this. "I heard noises and followed them downstairs. Alex came to get me. End of story."

Jesse crosses his arms. "Yeah, right."

"It's the truth. Believe it or not, I don't care." Okay, it's a half-truth, which in my opinion makes the best lie.

"The truth, huh? Then why the fuck are you guys acting like kids all day?" I expected such a counter from Jesse, not my so-called best friend.

When I don't answer, Jesse reaches over the table and pats my hand. "Manda, I have to ask. Are you okay with all of this?"

I pull my hand away. "Why wouldn't I be?"

He leans back in his chair and crosses his legs. "Maybe, you still l—"

"Stop right there," I bark, holding up a hand.

He grins. "Why? Because it's true?"

"Because it's a whole lot of bull, and you know it." Alex and I give love a bad name. We fucking hate each other most days, want to kill each other on the others.

Jesse's mouth snaps open. Before he can object, Alex and Diana come back loaded with coffee and sweets.

Diana serves Jesse and Bonnie. "I hope you like it."

Bonnie wraps her fingers around the steaming cup and takes a sniff. "Smells awesome."

A proud smile crosses Miss Asia's lips. "It's an old family recipe."

Alex hands me a cup, leans in, and whispers, "Can you act like a human being for a change?"

I gulp down half the cup at once, secretly hoping booze is part of the family recipe.

Once Diana makes sure everyone has been served, she takes a seat next to hunter-heroic. "Alex said you guys are on a road trip?" Diana says to me of all people.

I manage to nod.

Her doll eyes light up. "That's pretty awesome. Cross-country trip is on my bucket list too, but I can't leave my kids. They'd be heartbroken."

*Can't leave my kids?* My hands tremble, and I swallow wrong.

Diana jumps up. "Oh gosh, are you okay?"

I'm coughing my lungs out. Do I look okay? I want to tell her to go fuck herself, but I'm a little busy dying. Talk about wicked coffee.

While everyone else stares at me, Miss Asia rockets into action. "She can't breathe," she says as she yanks the cup out of my shaking hands.

Alex gets on his feet. "Shit. We gotta do something."

*Oh really? Thought you guys would just sit back and watch me die.*

Diana hits me on the back. A jolt of electricity rushes through my veins as her petite hand connects with my body. It's painful. Diana must feel it, too. She jumps back and glares at me as if I'm the devil incarnate.

Alex shoves her to the side and knocks some air into my lungs. I'm not sure how many times he has to hit me until I'm finally able to suck in oxygen. "Thanks," I croak, drawing in a long, deep breath.

Diana stumbles back. "Is she…a-a…w-witch?"

*Awesome.*

Alex holds both hands up. "I can explain," he says.

Back pressed against the large window, she shakes her head frantically. "Please, don't hex me," she begs in terror.

Bonnie puts her cup down and gives me a concerned look. "You okay?" When I nod, she faces Diana. "Calm down. We're not going to hurt you."

Diana's doll eyes almost pop out. "We? You're a w-witch, too?"

Bonnie flinches. She hates being called a witch. "She's a mambo," Jesse explains.

To say Miss Asia looks freaked out would be the understatement of the year. Her gaze lands on Alex, and it lacks the gentleness from before. "I can't believe you. After everything these creatures did to me…" She fights off tears. "After everything I've been through, you have the nerve to bring witches into my house?"

This is bad. Diana's father is in the shed, her mother will be back any moment, and the girl looks like we're some home invaders trying to kill her. *Why the hell did I have to choke on the coffee? I should have known she was a sensitive.* Most people who survive a hex develop sensitivity to the supernatural.

I swallow the bitter taste in my mouth and get up. "Listen," I say as calmly as possible. "I know you're scared. Alex told us what the shtriga did to you, but we won't hurt you." I cross my heart. "I promise."

She ignores me and glares at Alex. "Why are you traveling with witches?"

He approaches her carefully. "I can explain, and I will, but you need to calm down first, okay?" When she doesn't slap him, he puts a hand on her shoulder. "Please, Diana, you have to trust me. You know you can."

I sit down on the rattan chair and sigh. This is ridiculous. We don't have time for shit like this. "You have two options," I blurt out. "Option one, you can throw us out and I promise we will never come back." I get dirty looks from everyone, including Miss Asia. "Option two, you sit down and listen to what we have to say and help us save Alex's life." I shrug. "Up to you."

She drops her arms. "What is she talking about?"

Jesse leans against the window next to her. "We'll tell you, but you have to get a grip first."

Her hands shake like crazy. "I'm listening."

Alex and Jesse take turns telling the story. Diana is so focused, she doesn't even blink. Her expression

193

changes from surprised to confused to downright horrified.

"Let me get this straight, Alex. You want me to give my blood to a witch so she can perform some creepy ritual that will reveal if we"—her finger drifts back and forth between her and Alex—"are *soulmates?*"

Alex's gaze drops. "I know how crazy it sounds, but—"

"That pretty much sums it up," Jesse says.

"That's not crazy." She glides down the windows until she sits on the floor. "It's insane."

Alex kneels in front of her. "I completely understand if you're not up for it." His malachite eyes meet mine. "I told them this was a bad idea."

Diana shakes her head. "A bad idea?" She gets on her feet. "Alex, why do you even believe these creatures will help you? How can you trust them after everything that happened to your sister?"

*Sister? Since when do Alex and Jesse have a sister? And what does she mean, after everything that happened to her?* I'm close to asking, but when I see the warning expression on his face, I keep quiet.

He clenches his fists. "Leave Natasha out of this, Diana. She ain't got nothing to do with any of this."

"Manda and Bonnie aren't like the shtriga that hexed you," Jesse says in a desperate attempt to change Diana's mind.

"They are witches, aren't they?"

A part of me feels the urge to slap Miss Asia. She's an American, for Christ's sake. Prejudice shouldn't be in her genes. I decide to cut her some slack, though, because being hexed really does suck.

Alex's features soften. "You're right." He cups her cheeks. "They are witches. But she"—he points his head at me—"saved my brother's life, Diana."

Diana squints. "That true?"

Jesse walks up beside me and throws an arm around my stiff shoulders. "Yep. This one's badass." Fear clouds Diana's eyes, and he adds, "Not in an evil way, of course."

Bonnie, who has been quiet until now, rises from her chair. "Do you work for the Triad?"

Diana is caught by surprise. "What? No. Why?"

"You're Asian," Bonnie says matter-of-factly. "Don't you *all* work for the Triad?"

"Of course not," Diana murmurs, offended.

"Well, honey, it's the same with witches. We're not all evil." The girl has a way with words. She could run for president and totally win.

The wheels in Diana's head turn. There's a whole lot of guilt in her eyes. "How does that ritual work?"

"I'll burn a spell with Alex's and your blood on it. Should the smoke of the candle turn red," I fake a smile, "well then, congratulations. You've found your soulmate."

"And if not?" she asks.

"We'll move on to the next girl on the list," Jesse says.

Diana glares at Alex. "You have a list?"

He blushes and shrugs. Diana frowns. "And what if I am the one? What happens then?"

The question catches me off guard. If Diana is the one, they'll get the happily ever after most people only dream of. *And I'll lose him forever.*

"Then you'll be one of the lucky girls who gets to

live with the person she's fated to be with," Bonnie explains.

Something that looks a lot like fear crosses Alex's eyes. Seems like hunter-heroic isn't up for a long-term commitment just yet. Jesse sees it, too. He smiles at his brother and says, "Can we do the ritual *before* we plan my brother's wedding?"

"Okay, but if anything happens to me—"

"You can call Amelia, and she can send me straight to purgatory," I suggest.

Diana obviously knows Amelia. "Deal." She gazes out the window at the old shed near the pier. "What about my parents, though? We can hardly tell them the truth."

Jesse taps his index finger against his temple. "Let's do the ritual at Amelia's. That way, Diana's parents won't catch us doing magic."

I'd ask him if he's totally lost it, but my jaw is on the floor.

"Excuse me?" Bonnie's curls stick out in every direction. "Did you forget that woman's stand on magic in her house?"

Jesse beams at her. "Relax. I got this."

\*\*\*\*

Half an hour later, we tottered into the lion's den. Lady Amelia, aka Pulp Fiction Granny, reacted as badly as I thought she would. The hunter was running outta fucks she could give about Alex's situation, and the harder Jesse and Alex tried to talk her into helping us, the more aggravated she got.

If it wasn't for Diana, she would have sent us all straight to hell. Miss Asia accomplished what Jesse and Alex couldn't. She convinced Pulp Fiction Granny not to shoot us and talked her into letting us do the spell in her precious hunter B&B. Goes without saying, Amelia demanded to be present during the ritual. I had no problem with that.

"That all you need?" Alex asks, positioning the white candle in the center of the small table in front of me.

I stop scribbling and look up. "No, I need a knife and a lighter."

"Knife?" Pulp Fiction Granny barks. "Why the fuck do you need a goddamn knife?"

Bonnie frowns. Her patience wearing thinner and thinner. I don't blame her. The old woman has a way of making the best of us feel evil. "We need Alex and Diana's blood for the spell."

"Don't worry," I add. "It's just a drop."

"It better be," she warns, hugging the rifle closer to her chest. It wouldn't surprise me if she took the thing to bed at night.

"Anytime with the blood," I say, pointing to the piece of paper on the table.

Alex pulls a pocketknife out of his jacket, extends the blade, and pierces his index finger. Crimson soaks into the letters, smearing some of the words in the process.

"That's enough." I face Diana. "Now you."

Alex wipes the knife on a towel, holds it under the flame of his Zippo to sanitize it, and hands it to Diana.

She slices her finger. "Shit." She flinches. "That looks so much less painful on TV." She squeezes the cut over the paper, and blood drips on it. "Enough?" she asks, face pale.

I nod and put the spell back on the table. "Give me

the Zippo," I order.

Alex throws it over. I light the candle and focus on my breath. *So this is it. The moment of truth.* I close my eyes and try to calm my pulse. The only way I'll be able to do this ritual is by disconnecting my brain from my soul. *If Diana is the one, Alex is saved.* I can move on with my new life and never think about him again. *Because that worked so well last time, huh?*

I draw a deep breath and picture Aphrodite, not as a naked woman who rises from the foam of the sea, but as a strong chick who's brave enough to follow her heart. Her face takes form, and I start chanting. "I call upon you, Aphrodite, goddess of love, beauty, and delight. These lovers seek your advice. Show us if their souls were forged in the same fire, or if their feelings are guided by desire."

I repeat the spell until a warm feeling touches my heart. Then I hold the blood-smeared piece of paper to the flame and watch it burn. The paper chars and crumbles. The smoke remains as black as the night.

"That can't be good," Jesse whispers.

"She's not his soulmate," Bonnie says.

"I'm sorry," I whisper, unable to look him in the eye.

*But am I?*

Chapter 20

Diana isn't the one. Alex is still going to hell. Yet, I'm in a suspiciously good mood. So was Diana when she left Amelia's. She'd wanted to help Alex, but a huge part of her had been relieved when the smoke didn't turn red. Diana had been really worried about her kids at the shelter where she works. She kept saying she didn't have time for love, because the kids took up most of her day. In my opinion, she just wasn't ready to give up her freedom. Knowing your soulmate, however, would inevitably lead to that. No more test-drives needed. No more experiences gained. I might not be her biggest fan, but she deserves to live life to the fullest, which, believe it or not, includes a couple of heartbreaks.

"I need a pit stop," Jesse grumbles, eyes on the road. Unlike Diana, he'd been hit hard by the result of the ritual. Crossing one name off the list had reduced his brother's chances of survival and put him in a very dark place.

Alex points to a road sign. "Take the next exit. We can stop in Auburn."

"Sounds good. I'm starving," Bonnie says, head resting against the cool window of the Mustang. She's been awfully quiet since we got in the car, and I can't help but wonder if it's because we're headed to New Orleans, where her brother is rotting in a prison cell.

I shift closer to my best friend. "You good?" I keep my voice down so the boys don't hear me.

She forces a smile. "Yeah, why?"

*Maybe because you swore to never set foot in that city again?* "Just checking."

About two miles from the interstate, Jesse pulls into the parking lot of Toomers Coffee Shop. Getting out of the car feels good and the prospect of steaming coffee makes my addict-heart beat a little faster. It's after eight, and they close in a little less than an hour. That's more than enough time to fill our groaning stomachs and down some black gold.

"What do you want?" Jesse asks, joining the long queue. He must be in a worse state than I thought. Doesn't even pay attention to the hot chick in the mini-skirt right in front of him.

I pull out my purse. "Triple-shot Americano."

He eyeballs me. "Put that away, Manda."

I hate when someone pays for my stuff. I'd argue with him, but I don't want to be the person who changes his mood from pissed off to murderous.

"You guys can grab a seat. I'll get the drinks," he murmurs.

Bonnie nods. "I'll stay with him." She points her chin at an empty table. "You two go ahead."

Alex pulls me along. "Come on."

"You should talk to him," I suggest as we sit down. "He's hurting."

Refusing to meet my gaze, he runs a hand over his stubble. "It's better that way."

*Excuse me?* Did he just say it's better if his brother is in pain? What the hell is wrong with him, lately? Did the prospect of an eternity in hell scramble his brain?

"Wow, Alex. You sound more and more like me."

He presses a hand against his ribcage. "We both know this plan won't work," he says, his breath shallow. "It'll be easier on him if he starts accepting it now."

Despite his shitty way of showing it, I know he's trying to protect his brother. So I decide to let it go for now.

"Amanda?"

Full name, huh? Can't be good. "Yeah?"

Shoving the napkin holder from one hand to the other, he's trying hard not to meet my eyes. "Can I ask you something? You don't have to answer if you don't want to."

The edges of my mouth curve up. "Fifteen."

He looks up. "What?"

"The age I lost my virginity," I say, trying hard not to laugh. Not that losing my virginity had been comical, but the surprised expression on Alex's face totally is.

Leaning back in his chair, he shakes his head. "Funny."

"Not really. The dude kissed like a llama, grunted like a sick pig, and—"

He makes a face. "Okay. Okay. I got it."

Resting my elbows on the table, I sigh. "All right, no more kidding. Ask and you shall receive." I grin. "Or not."

He looks away and draws a long breath. "That Magic Pony dude and you…Are you guys a thing?"

"A thing?" I laugh. "Are you asking if we dated? Screwed? Are in a relationship?"

His shoulders stiffen. "Are you?" His eyes search mine. "In a relationship, I mean?"

I knit my brows. Where the hell does the sudden interest in my love life come from? "Why do you care?"

His expression is indecipherable, and I'd give my non-existent fortune to be able to read his aura. "Just curious, I guess. Must be one helluva guy if he tamed the great Amanda Bishop." Is that envy in his voice?

I raise my brows at him. "First of all, I'm not a horse, Alex. No one *tames* me. Secondly, the only thing DeLuca and I had going was sex." *I needed it to forget about you.*

I could swear he flinched. It was too quick to be certain. He clears his throat and straightens. "So you're still going around breaking young boys' hearts?" His voice is sharper, eyes like stone.

This is the perfect beginning for another battle in World War A, but I'm not in the mood to go down that road. I flash him a smile. "But Billie Bridge is not my lover. He's just a guy who claims I am the one."

He shakes his head. "Are you really singing Michael Jackson right now?" he asks, a smile tugging at his lips.

I wink at him. "The King of Pop always gave perspective."

"You're un—"

"Triple-shot Americano for you." Bonnie puts a hot cup down in front of me. "Latte for asshat." She hands Alex his cup. "And"—she takes a seat next to me—"lots of cupcakes for me."

"Thanks, B."

"You won't try to slip the money in my shirt when I sleep, right?" Jesse's voice is less edgy than five minutes ago. I wonder what, or should I say who, changed his mood.

Bonnie beats me to an answer. "Have you met her?"

These people know me too damn well. Scary. "Give me a break." They're both giggling. "Both of you."

They all smile, even Alex. "Three against one, huh? Not fair."

Alex grins. "You can handle it."

"Damn right I can." I sip my steaming Americano. "Now cut the crap and tell me all about the mysterious girl in New Orleans."

"Melissa." Jesse's playful tone suggests the girl is nothing like Diana. "Hot, always-ready-for-a-surprise Melissa."

Bonnie arches a brow and smiles. "I like her already."

Wish I could say the same thing.

A flicker of annoyance crosses Alex's face. "Shut up, Jess. Melissa is a real sweet girl."

Jesse almost chokes on his mocha. "Yeah. A real sweet stripper."

My jaw drops. "Shut. Up." I look at Alex. "Seriously? You were in love with a stripper?"

He squints, and I realize how wrong that question sounded. Unlike most of my female counterparts, I have the highest respect for strippers. What I really meant to say was, how on earth did Captain Righteous end up falling for a bad girl?

"She's cool," Alex defends her, casting Jesse a grumpy look.

"As I said, I already like her," Bonnie throws in.

Alex nods at her gratefully, then faces me. "She's

been through some real bad shit. Her job doesn't define her."

"Whoa," I say, the cup almost slipping from my hand. "I'm not judging her. I'm judging *you*, Alex."

Chapter 21

*Seven days to hell*

Vexed, Bonnie searches her bucket bag for the key to the apartment. The girl's mood was shitty when we drove here, but now that we're in the city of her nightmares, she's giving Jason—yep, *Friday The 13th* Jason—a run for his money.

Jesse scans my best friend's perfectly rounded butt. "I can't believe you own an apartment in the French Quarter."

I lean against the wall, trying hard not to laugh my ass off. "She doesn't own *an* apartment, Jess. Her family owns the whole building." Along with a couple of other flats and several nightclubs.

Alex's brows shoot up. "Thought you guys couldn't use your gifts to win the lottery?"

Bonnie shoves the key in the lock. "What are you trying to say?" Her tone is dark. Doesn't sound like her at all.

Alex flashes her a mocking smile. "C'mon, B. You gonna pretend it's a coincidence both your witch families are loaded?"

Any other day, I'd be in his face, but my adorable never-losing-her-countenance best friend is on a roll and beats me to it. "It's Bonnie, not B. And did you know there's a special place in hell for bigots,

Alexander?" She sounds so sangfroid, it's a little scary.

Alex sneers. "What did you just call me?"

Bonnie kicks the door open and shoots him a look over her shoulder. "A bigot." She grins creepily. "But in case your small hunter brain can't comprehend the word, I'll give you another—prejudiced asshole."

"That's two words, *B*," Alex counters.

She puts a hand over her heart. "Oh my gosh. He can count."

*Whoa, what's gotten into her?* I've never seen her talk to someone like this.

Alex is close to bursting. Jesse, who'd been amused until a few moments ago, changes the topic before the argument turns into a full-blown cat fight. "You spend a lot of time here?" he asks Bonnie.

From all the things he could have said, he brings up New Orleans? *Congrats, Jess. You just scored a ten on the major-topic-change-fail scale.* I slam my hands over my eyes, bracing myself for Hurricane Bonnie to hit.

It never happens. My best friend just shrugs. "Used to. Not anymore." Then she walks inside, and Jesse follows.

"Hey." Alex grabs my arm as I stagger to the door. "What's her goddamn problem?"

She hates this city. That's what's her problem. Wasn't always like that. I remember the last time we were here together. We had the time of our lives—made out with steamy guys, downed lots of Ramos Gin Fizz, and danced our asses off. Unfortunately, the night took a pretty bad turn when Gabriel, B's oldest brother, was arrested for rape. Yep, that's life. One minute you're celebrating Mardi Gras, and the next you're sitting in a police station, waiting to give a statement. Bonnie's family is practically royalty in NOLA, and Gabriel's arrest quickly turned into one of the city's biggest scandals, changing my best friend forever.

Alex gives me a thoughtful look. "Manda?"

He'd cut B some slack if I told him, but I'm not a snitch. It's her story to tell, not mine. "Just leave her alone, okay?"

He cocks a brow. "Leave her alone? She just called me a bigot, Amanda."

A slow grin spreads over my face. "Truth hurts, huh?"

Dropping his shoulders, he shakes his head. "Witches," he hisses. "Don't you just love them?"

I wink at him. "You once did, remember?"

He looks pissed. Before he can retaliate, I move inside.

The scent of fresh lilies climbs up my nose. Bonnie's mom loves them, and crazy as she is, she demands her employees stock each building, inhabited or not, with the flowers.

Once I get to the living room, I find Jesse on the antique leather couch. Hands folded between his knees, he wears a frustrated expression. "Where's B?" I ask, scanning the room.

He looks at me helplessly. "Kitchen, I think."

"Sharpening her knives?" Alex murmurs behind me.

His comments start to piss me off. I grab him by his jacket and haul him toward his brother. "Sit down and be quiet."

He pulls back. "What am I, your dog?"

*A Chihuahua at best.* I press my palms against his back and shove him to the couch. "Sit. Down. Stay."

My eyes meet his dark green ones. "Got it?"

Alex shakes his head. "You're—"

"Hot when I'm giving orders?" I grin. "I know."

He mumbles something under his breath. Good thing I can't hear him. If I did, I might be the one sharpening the knives in the kitchen.

I eye Jesse. "I'll be right back." He nods and I add, "Don't touch anything." I narrow my eyes. "For your own good." Who knows how many cursed objects they have lying around here?

Bonnie's head rests on the granite countertop when I walk in. She sorta looks like she's cemented to the cold stone. "Hey." I pat her back. "How you holding up?"

She snarls.

"You know I'm not the sharing and caring type," I say. "But if you wanna talk…"

She shifts her head to the side and looks up. "Can I ask you something?"

I press my hip against the kitchen island. "Shoot."

"How the fuck did you fall for a guy like Alex?"

*Didn't see that one coming.* "He's kinda like mold. Grows on you with time."

Her brows fly up. "You realize mold is toxic, right?"

I shove my hands in my pockets. "I'm self-destructive like that." I look her over. "But we both know Alex isn't the reason you're on edge, right?"

Bonnie lifts her head and says nothing.

"Look." I take a step toward her. "I'm the last go-to person for family counseling, but—"

"Stop," she begs. "I appreciate you getting out of your comfort zone for me, but I don't want to talk about

Gabe. Not now. Not ever."

I hate to see her hurting, but what good would it do, pretending Gabe doesn't exist? "He's still—"

Resentment flushes her cheeks. "Don't even go there. Brother or not, for all I care, he can rot in his prison cell for all eternity."

Bonnie can say what she wants, but deep down she misses her big brother. God, the girl practically worshipped him all her life, and beneath all the anger, she still loves him. But what he did to that girl didn't just ruin her life, it also ruined Bonnie's. Took away the one thing she held dearest—respect.

Painfully silent moments go by before she speaks again. "I should hit the shower." She peers at the clock on the microwave. "Rick's Cabaret opens in less than two hours."

Right. Strip Club. I'd almost forgotten why we were here. "You sure you're okay with the plan?" Doesn't matter what she says, I'm 100 percent sure she isn't. How could she be? The plan involves her using magic. A special kind of magic—manipulation.

She draws a long, pained breath. "I don't really have a choice, do I?"

I'm torn between saying "no" for Alex's sake and shouting out a loud "yes" for B's. I take the coward's way out and say nothing.

Bonnie frowns. "Guilty doesn't suit you."

It doesn't, but it's sure as hell how I feel. I came up with the idea. Melissa—the second girl on Alex's maybe-soulmate list—has no idea the supernatural exists. We can hardly ask for her blood like we did with Diana. I figured if Alex and Jesse could keep her busy, Bonnie and I would sneak backstage to get our hands on her brush.

*Here we go again with the stealing a brush plan, because that worked so well last time, right?* What else are we supposed to do? Scalp her while she's giving a lap dance?

I massage the nape of my neck. "I'm sorry I dragged you into this mess." I truly am. Alex isn't her problem. He's mine. Yet Bonnie ditched classes to help out a hunter she doesn't even like.

"Wow." Her lips curve up. "Did you just apologize?"

I roll my eyes. "Don't get used to it."

She folds her arms and smiles. A real smile. "Maybe I should let you talk me into using my magic more often." I give her a look and she goes on, saying, "Think about it. I could make the Nun support a gay group or have her do a naked fertility dance on campus."

The moment she mentions Chelsea, I instantly think of dead Jules and the *Men in Black.* Not the right time or place to worry about it. I push the thought away and grin. "Talk her into losing her uptightness, and I'll carve my apology in stone."

Bonnie giggles. "Deal." Then her eyes darken. "I still want to desperate-housewife your ex, though."

I squint. "You want to shoot him and stage it as a suicide on Wisteria Lane?"

Bonnie elbows me. "No, Amanda." She wiggles her brows in typical B-style. "I want to drown his sorry ass in bleach." A devilish smile crosses her lips. "From what I've heard, it works miracles on mold."

I laugh so hard tears blur my eyes. "God," I croak, wiping my damp cheeks. "I love you, B."

"Who doesn't?" she replies, hands landing on my shoulders. "Come on, we gotta get ready. I won't hit a strip club looking like this."

I eyeball her. There's nothing wrong with the way she looks. Ask Jesse, he'd agree in a heartbeat. But while she doesn't have a mean bone in her body, she certainly has two-hundred-and-six vain ones.

****

I don't know what I expected to find behind the doors of Rick's Cabaret. Presumably something along the lines of *Zombie Strippers*—without the zombies. What I see is something entirely else. The place is old-school, porn Hollywood. Dim lights, black walls, red leather chairs, and at least a dozen waitresses in bikini-tops. Dudes of various ages roam around, drinks in one hand, notes for the dancers in the other. *Who needs seventy-two virgins in paradise if there's Rick's Cabaret?*

Jesse's eyes burn brighter than the sun. He's fixated on a sleazy, sexy, blonde stripper snake-dancing to raunchy music. "Honey, I'm home."

I catch Bonnie frowning and nudge the little player in the ribs. "Behave," I warn as we walk up to the blue-lit bar.

"He doesn't even know how to spell that," Alex says, groaning.

Jesse gives us a smug smile. "Who won that spelling competition in grade school again?"

Alex casts me a sidelong glance and sighs. "The word the teacher gave him was *naughty*."

"It's all about having your priorities straight," Jesse says, his chocolate eyes connecting with Bonnie's. "Right?"

What happens next sends Alex and me into a state of complete shock. In the blink of an eye, Bonnie leans against Jesse. Her too short, too tight red lace dress presses against his chest. "Priorities, huh?" Her lips are seconds from sealing the deal, and Little Remington is frozen. Doesn't move or breathe.

Bonnie smooths her thumb over Jesse's jawline and bites on her lower lip. "A well-formed butt pressed against your crotch, hands diving into your hair, lips exploring your delicious body—that on the top of your list?"

Little Remington swallows hard but manages to nod.

Just when I think she's about to attack him, Queen B steps back and laughs. "Men." A hint of disappointment roughens her voice. "Show them a couple of boobs, and they'll only think with their cock." She waves her hair over her shoulder and saunters to the redheaded bartender. If this isn't the definition of giving someone a cold shoulder, then what is?

Alex stares at his brother.

"Not a word," Jesse murmurs and walks away.

Alex blows out a long breath. "Should I be worried?" he asks, watching his brother mingle with the crowd.

*I am.*

"Manda?"

"Hm?"

"You gonna answer my question?"

I put a hand on his shoulder. "Let's go find Melissa." That wasn't what he wanted to hear, but it's better than the truth.

He searches the crowd, but not for Melissa. "I'll

catch up with you," he says when he spots Jesse chatting with the sexy blonde stripper who just got off stage.

I look for Bonnie, hoping she's more focused on the mission, but I can't find her. Annoyed with all of them, I turn to the door. "I'll check upstairs."

"Sure," he murmurs, body there, mind long gone.

I go up a level. A set of black velvet ropes appear. Intoxicating music thrums through the club, the sort you can't stop moving to. My right hand grows heavy. The ankh on my skin stings like a vicious cobra bite. Something's off. I can taste it on the tip of my tongue—a wicked bitter flavor.

I force my feet to move. Seedy red light brushes plush black armchairs. Shadows move through the gloomy room. I blink several times until my eyes adjust to the darkness. Slowly, the silhouettes take on the form of men. Old, young, bald, sexy—their looks couldn't be more different, their charisma not more alike.

I smooth the silver cami dress I borrowed from Bonnie and move closer to the hexagram-shaped stage in the center of the space. Heads turn in my direction. Several guys stop dead in their tracks and glare at me openly, completely unashamed. They must mistake me for a dancer, I tell myself, ignoring the hungry gazes.

A few middle-aged dudes at a table in front of the stage look over their shoulders. Their manners are a cross between I-want-to-Ted-Bundy-her and can-I-get-a-private-lap-dance. Creepy.

I keep my gaze trained on the stage, hoping—no, praying—Melissa shows. She doesn't. Neither does any other dancer. In my peripheral vision, I see someone approaching. I walk in the opposite direction, straight to the red-lit bar.

Leaning against the counter, I observe the weird crowd. Something's fishy. My alarm bells ring louder than Big Ben. *Why are you still here? Move your ass back downstairs.* I should listen to the voice in my head, but somehow I'm drawn to the sinister atmosphere, seduced by the smell of sin and danger. God, what's the matter with me?

A group of young, rich douchebags gathers next to me. They're barely older than I am, but stand there like they own the world. I hate guys like them. They look heavenly, but reek of asshole.

I try to be oblivious of them, but the way the one with the black mamba tattoo on his neck eyeballs me— as if I'm some kind of happy meal—makes my skin crawl. He's drooling all over his expensive suit.

He strolls over with a confidence that's both scary and impressive. I look the other way, hoping he'll get the hint. He doesn't. "How much for a private dance?" His hoarse voice gives me chills.

I don't mind being mistaken for a stripper, but the way his lips curve into a sinister grin tells me he knows I'm not one. One side of my mouth shoots up. "You couldn't afford me," I assure him.

He looks me over. "You sure about that, sweetheart?"

I hated him before he called me sweetheart. Now I pretty much despise his existence. "Damn sure," I say, meeting his midnight eyes.

He shifts closer. The scent of musky aftershave lingers between us. "Would you bet your soul on it?"

I cock a brow. "Why don't you try your cheap pickup lines on someone who falls for your *Cry-Baby*

Walker act?" A deaf man could hear the villainy in my voice. Unlike some females, I don't dig guys who act like they're the next big bad in town. In fact, I find them as repulsive as the knight-in-shining-armor brigade.

His smile slips away. "Big mouth for such a small witch."

I snap my head up. "What did you say?"

His lips come dangerously close to my ear. "I said...big mouth for such a small *girl.*"

Time to get the hell outta here. I spin on my heels, ready to make a run for the velvet curtains. The asshole grabs me by the wrist and pulls me back. "Are you crazy?" I bark, trying to break free.

He shoves me against the bar. My tailbone knocks against the wood, sending a dull pain up my spine. "Where do you think you're going, sweetheart?"

Okay, I've had it. I ball my free hand into a stone-hard fist, ready to punch the freak in the face. Shame I never get to strike, because good old hunter-heroic shows.

"You have two seconds to let go of her before I wipe the counter with your face." Alex's voice is deadlier than the mamba on the dude's neck.

Mamba-Guy's attention goes to Alex. "Boyfriend?"

Alex flexes his muscles. "I won't say it again."

Amusement flickers in Mamba-Guy's eyes. "Wannabe boyfriend then."

Alex steps closer. "One."

*It's the fist-fight countdown.*

Mamba-Guy tightens his grip on me. "We're not done," he threatens and pushes me into Alex's rock-hard chest. "Here, bro. You can have the ho."

Alex's body is rigid. "What did you call her?"

I've had enough testosterone for the night. I reach for Alex's hand. "Come on."

He doesn't move.

"Now, Alex."

Still frozen.

I sigh heavily and haul his stubborn butt out.

Once we're behind the curtain, he stops dead in his tracks. "What the hell were you doing up here with that guy?" There's murder on his face, ice in his voice.

"I was looking for Melissa, jerk-face."

He arches a brow. "And you mistook her for a snobby guy with a bad tattoo?"

*Is he on crack or something?* "What the hell is wrong with you?"

He squints. "With me? What the hell is wrong with *you*? You're gone for less than ten minutes, and look what you've gotten yourself into."

"I had it under control," I snap. "You're the one who came barging in to feed your fuckin' hero complex."

A slow-burning fire spreads in his eyes. "Next time, I'll stand back and watch you drag yourself out of your own shit."

"Good," I bark. "'Cause I don't need a hero."

"Fine." He crosses his arms. "From now on you can clean up your own messes."

"Perfect," I shout in his face.

"Great," he yells.

"Awe—"

"Um, guys?" Bonnie cuts me off.

"What?" Alex and I holler at the same time.

She stands on the stairs and looks bewildered. "W-we have a problem."

Chapter 22

The alarming feeling I had on the second level follows me downstairs, and I don't like it. What bugs me even more is the unsettling look on Bonnie's face as she leads us through the packed club, past red leather chairs and less creepy but equally horny dudes, to a private area sectioned of by sangria-colored ropes.

The blonde stripper—yep, the one Jesse was hellbent on getting to know better—sits on a plush couch next to Little Remington.

"Dude," Alex groans. "Don't tell me you—"

"Alex," Jesse cuts him off. "This"—he points to the long-legged dancer with the Victoria's Secret body—"is Esmeralda."

"Hi," Alex says, waving lazily.

"She's a friend of Melissa's," Jesse explains. "You should sit down and hear what she has to say, bro."

"I'm good standing."

Bonnie walks toward him. "No, Alex." She hauls him to a chair across from his brother. "You should really sit." The softness in her eyes and voice is surprising, considering she wanted to desperate-housewife him not long ago.

Alex, still electrified from our little dispute, blows out a long breath. "All right." He flings himself onto the chair. "I'm listening."

Jesse nudges Esmeralda's bare leg. "Tell them

what you told us."

*Us?* I'm pretty sure this is a private lap dance room. So what were the *three* of them doing here? Scratch the question. Some things are better left unanswered.

Esmeralda shifts to the edge of the couch and shoves her hands between her thighs. "Your brother said you're friends with Melissa?"

Alex nods. "Yeah. She ain't working today?"

I might have lost the ability to read auras, but I'm still absorbing emotions like a vacuum cleaner, and the sadness in Esmeralda's eyes takes my breath away. Her gaze drops to her white knee-high go-go boots. "She's not," she says, voice trembling.

Alex squints. "Is it her day off?"

Esmeralda shakes her head.

Hunter-heroic's shoulders tense. "Did she quit?"

Tears well up in Esmeralda's eyes. A sharp pain slices through my chest. *Oh no, this is—*

"She's missing," Esmeralda whispers, eyes hooded.

*Bad.*

Alex jumps up, and I half expect him to aim his fist at the drywall. "Say that again?"

Esmeralda wipes her wet cheeks. "Two weeks ago, Melissa left work but never came home. Her mom freaked out, filed a missing person report." She rubs her palms on her nurse slash slut costume. "Cops didn't do much. Guess she's just another stripper casualty to them."

Ever seen a lion before it attacks? The terrifying look in its eyes before it jumps its victim? The blood-curling roar it lets out? Well, that's pretty much Alex right now. A predator looking for a kill.

"Alex." Jesse casts his brother a worried look. "I'm sorry, but there's more." He pats Esmeralda's shoulder. "Tell him."

Panic creeps into her pretty face. "If Barry finds out, he'll—"

"He won't," Bonnie says. "I give you my word." She always keeps her promises. It's why she's the only person I've ever trusted.

Esmeralda's leg trembles. She scans the room. When she's certain it's just us, she says, "Melissa isn't the only girl who's vanished. In the last couple of weeks, three of our dancers have disappeared."

I lean against the wall, tired of more shit being thrown our way. Shouldn't the freaking universe grant us a minute to catch our breath? Like in books when the characters get a chapter or two to reflect on what has happened to them? I press my foot against the wall and cross my arms. "Define disappeared."

She lifts her gaze. It's the first time I get a good look at her face. I can't help but wonder if she's even legal, that's how young and vulnerable she looks. "The first two girls were new," she says. "Didn't think much of it when they didn't show for work. Figured they found better jobs. A better life. But Melissa wasn't like the others. She needs this job and..." She struggles with her voice. "She'd never quit without telling me."

A sick feeling savages my stomach. I still refuse to jump to horrific conclusions. "Maybe she took a time-out?"

Alex glares at me. "She didn't."

Esmeralda looks at the lighted wall clock "Shit," she murmurs. "I've got five minutes to haul my butt on stage." She heads to the curtains. "You going to hang around for a while?"

"We'll be right here," Alex promises.

A grateful smile tugs at her lips. "Great. I'll see you in a bit."

The second Esmeralda is gone, Alex faces Jesse. "You and I, we both know what's happening here."

An odd tension creeps over Little Remington's face. "He's back."

Bonnie squints. "Who's back?"

The lines around Jesse's chocolate eyes deepen. "We never told you how Alex met Melissa, huh?"

*Frankly, I don't wanna know.*

Alex scrubs his fingers through his hair and plummets down on the chair. "A year ago, around Halloween, Carter asked us to investigate a case in New Orleans." His voice cracks. I get the feeling his heart is too. "Multiple prostitutes and strippers had gone missing. Their mutilated bodies were later found in the swamps."

Bonnie's eyes pop open. "That's terrible."

Alex's voice loses the edge. "Yeah. They had cuts all over their bodies and the alligators did quite a job on them."

"We surveyed the city's brothels, strip clubs, and the streets for over a month," Jesse explains. "That's how we met Melissa. She approached us when she heard we were FBI."

Alex nods. "Yeah. She pointed us toward one of her customers."

"The asshole held a knife to her throat when she did a private dance for him," Jesse grumbles. "Girl barely escaped."

"Turned out, Melissa wasn't the only one he attacked," Alex says. "Working girls all over the city had heard of him. Didn't take long to track him down."

Bonnie's natural curiosity is awakened. "Did you arrest him?"

Both Remingtons stare at the floor. Jesse flushes. "We tried. But—"

"The guy knocked us out and disappeared," Alex finishes, voice harder than stone.

I almost laugh. "Both of you?" I find that hard to believe. These guys aren't just muscles and brains. They're trained hunters. Taking them out wouldn't be easy.

He gives me the one-more-word-and-I-hang-you-upside-down-on-a-flag-pole look. "He used magic, Amanda. Black magic. We didn't stand a chance."

Bonnie shivers. "Hold on. Are you saying there's a stripper-ganking, serial-warlock-killer on the loose?"

Jesse shakes his head. "That's where we get to the creepiest part of the story. The guy wasn't a warlock. He was human."

"Impossible," I say. "Humans don't have that kind of power."

Bonnie shoves her hair back. "Amanda is right. I mean, how can you be so sure he wasn't a warlock?"

Alex jumps up. "We're hunters, remember? We can sense witches."

Bonnie crosses her arms. "You can, huh? Then how come you didn't know Amanda was a witch?"

Alex averts his gaze. "I don't know." He must have asked himself the same damn question a million times. Judging by his rigid muscles, he never found an answer.

"She's the only witch we weren't able to sense,"

Jesse adds.

*"You're an untouchable."* Madame Josephine's voice taunts me. God, I need a break from the mess I call life. But if there is such a thing as an untouchable, the douchebag who killed these girls could be one.

"Okay," Bonnie mutters. "Let's say the dude—whatever he is—is back in town. What now? With the hellish deadline hanging above our heads, we don't exactly have time to hunt him down."

"We'll call Carter for backup," Jesse suggests.

"You are fugitives," I remind him. "Carter would have to call the cops."

"Yeah," Jesse says. "But he won't. He knows Alex didn't kill Francoise."

*Makes sense.* Carter helped us in Bakersfield. Why wouldn't he help us now?

"Sounds like a plan. But since we're already here." Alex points to the curtain. "We should have a little chat with Barry. See why he wants to keep a lid on the whole thing."

I have a super-bad feeling about this. "I don't think that's—" The ringing of my phone cuts me off. DeLuca. *Awesome.* He's texted, too.

"You wanna take that?" Alex grumbles.

I open WhatsApp first to read the messages. At least a dozen say "call me," but the last one makes me want to hurl. "FBI looking for you! Call me ASAP!"

"Manda." Jesse looks worried. "Everything okay?"

The blood drains from my face. "Yeah," I croak, forcing a half-hearted smile. "I gotta make a call, though."

Alex raises his brows. "What, Pony-Boy can't wait?"

How he knows it's DeLuca, I don't know. Don't have time to think about it, either. "I'll be right back," I say, ignoring Alex's murderous expression.

Chapter 23

The music in the club is too damn loud. I rush outside, regretting it instantly. Bourbon Street at night is slightly crazier than Walmart on Black Friday. Granted, no one is on the hunt for a new laptop or fancy clothes, but everyone sure as hell wants to buy a good time and lots of booze. The best place to get both is the famous French Quarter, with its breathtaking Spanish-influenced architecture.

I try not to pay attention to the buzz around me and key in DeLuca's number. It rings once, twice. "Amanda?" he squawks. "Is that you?"

"No, DeLuca. E.T. hijacked my cell to phone home."

"Jesus," he hisses. "I was worried sick. Where the hell are you? Wait, is that music? Are you...at a *party*?"

DeLuca keeps shooting questions at me, and I don't listen to half of them. A selfie-taking, shitfaced guy bumps into me. "Watch it," I snap, close to bursting.

The douchebag doesn't apologize. He's too damn busy staring at my boobs. "Damn, I love this city," he mutters, never taking his eyes off my two ladies.

*Something must have gone terribly wrong in the creation process of* men. Yeah, their brains were delivered to their freaking penises.

"Amanda?" DeLuca shouts, tearing my eardrum in the process. "What's going on?"

"Hold on." I walk down the small alley leading to the staff entrance of Rick's Cabaret. It's deserted and quiet.

"Amanda?"

Has no one ever told the guy patience is a fucking virtue? "I'm here."

"You going to tell me why the goddamn FBI interrogated me yesterday? They're looking for you. And Chelsea? She had to be taken to the hospital because she found a *blood*-soaked couch in your apartment. Whose blood? Are you on the run? Did you...did you kill Jules?"

Wow, those are sure as hell a lot of questions. Too bad I don't intend to answer any of them. "What did the FBI guys say?"

"They just asked a lot of odd stuff. Like if you and Jules had issues, if you've ever done something weird, if animals had gone missing in the neighborhood. What does any of this even mean?"

Questions only a hunter would ask. *Awesome.* I lean against the cool brick wall. "Did they mention their names?"

"Agents Marple and Brown."

Why do I get the feeling those guys are less FBI and more fans of British crime fiction? I mean, really? Marple and Brown? As in Miss Marple and Father Brown? Sorry, not buying it. "What did you tell them?"

"Nothing. It's not like I know anything."

*True.*

"Sugar"—his tone softens—"are you in trouble?"

I laugh. "Always, DeLuca."

"Stop fooling around." His voice is sharp. "This is serious. Goddamn *FBI* serious, Amanda."

*Goddamn hunter serious would be more accurate.* "Rel—"

Metal squeaks. The back door of Rick's Cabaret swings open and as if this night didn't suck bad enough, Mamba-Guy and five of his creepy friends stroll toward me.

Shivers roll down my spine.

Ankh hurts.

*I'm fucked.*

"Amanda, you still there?" DeLuca sounds as freaked out as I am.

"Any chance you've got B's number?" I whisper.

"Why?" he barks. "What's going on?"

"I need you to call h—"

Mamba-Guy yanks the phone out of my hand and ends the call. "Hello, sweetheart. Long time no see," he says, a sinister grin on his prominent face.

Who the hell does he think he is? I ball my fists. "Give me my phone."

"No. Told you we weren't done yet."

The way he looks at me gives me the creeps. Everything about him—his demeanor, the cocky grin on his lips, the devilish expression—screams psycho, but I can't keep my provoking mouth shut. "Oh, we are," I assure him, pulse quickening, elbow itching to deliver a jab to his face.

His asshole friends surround me like a horde of starving vultures. "Deliciously feisty," the black-haired, sunglasses-wearing dude moans.

I cock a brow. "McDonald's is down the street, pal."

Mamba-Guy laughs. "We're not big on *fast* food, sweetheart."

My chest tightens. This is bad—I'm-in-bigger-trouble-than-usual bad. I look for an escape route. There's none.

The one who looks a bit like Chucky from *Child's Play* wiggles a strand of my hair around his index finger and smirks. "We like it nice and slow, baby."

Lava courses through my system, melting the part of my brain begging me to keep my mouth shut. "You think I'm scared of a bunch of rich kids?" I slap Chucky's hand hard enough to make him cringe. "Sorry to disappoint you, but I've handled worse scum than you."

Mamba-Guy gets in my face. A flash of anger is in his eyes. "It's funny how you refer to us as scum, little witch."

Here we go with the witch again, and this time he can't talk his way out of it. I heard it loud and clear. No music around to make me doubt my ears. I cock a brow. "Charmatic or Buffyatic?"

Mamba-Guy's face turns into a canvas of confusion. "What?"

I flash him a devilish smile. "You keep calling me witch. I assume you're either a *Buffy* or *Charmed* fanatic." I stare at his too-sharp face. "Shame, you kinda look more like an *American Horror Story Freak Show* guy, huh?"

His buddies laugh. Mamba-Guy shoots them a look, and they shut their holes. He locks his midnight gaze on mine. "Your kind always thinks they're so smart." Mamba-Guy spits on the ground. "But you're really just our whores. Mud under our boots."

*Our whores? Our boots?* **Something** tells me this isn't a figure of speech. I stiffen. "Who the hell are you?"

He throws his head back and laughs. When he looks at me again, I get a glimpse of his real face. Garnet eyes stare back at me. Gruesome decayed skin hugs red flesh. Ugly would be too nice a word to describe his wicked grimace.

I eyeball his friends. They, too, are on the Ugliest Things Alive list. I choke back a scream. They're—

*Demons! You pissed off a bunch of fuckin' demons.*

I'm dead. Not I-was-killed-by-the-spirit-of-a-kid-and-linger-in-limbo dead, but six feet under, pushing up daisies, exanimated dead. These creatures are vicious and merciless. Worse, they're immune to spells unless you know their names. I doubt they're dumb enough to give them to me.

Flight instinct kicks in, but there's nowhere to go. The asshole wraps his hand around the nape of my neck and pulls me closer. "Where do you think you're going, sweetheart?" He looks at his friends and grins. "This party is just getting started."

"Let go!" I scream, digging my sharp nails into his decaying hand.

Laughter echoes off the walls. "Sorry, baby. We can't do that," Chucky says.

"Get ready," Mamba-Guy orders. They walk to different spots, forming a pentagram around their asshole friend and me.

"What, you gonna kill me right here in the middle of Bourbon Street?" What ever happened to the Don't Draw Too Much Attention to Your Demon Activities rule?

"Kill you? Sweetheart, when we're done with you, you'll *wish* we'd ended your pathetic life." He nods, and his creeper friends start chanting. I don't understand a single word they're saying. Never even heard the language.

I'm outnumbered, and out-powered.

*Any time now would be good, hunter-heroic.*

The air around me catches fire. I might be a smart-ass, but I'm not naïve enough to believe I stand a chance against six demons. Still need to try, though. I straighten and gaze into Mamba-Guy's garnet eyes. "Tell me, what do demons do in a strip club? Did hell run out of slutty demons?" Buying time seems my best chance to survive.

He grabs my face and jerks my head to the side. "So much attitude."

Sharp pain jolts through my chin, but I don't flinch. Speak no fear, see no fear, hear no fear—that's how you make it on the street. Should work with demons too. I shrug and grin. "WWA."

"What?"

"Witches With Attitude," I say.

Mamba-Guy raises his brows. "What's that? A private witch whore club?"

I smirk. "No. It's code for: I'm straight outta Salem and gonna kick your ugly demon ass." How, I'm not sure yet.

His sulfur breath beats against my cheek. "Yeah? And how are you going to do this, little witch? Your magic can't hurt us."

I smile sweetly. "You're right. But…" I bring my knee up and slam it into his crotch.

Cupping his groin, he cries out in pain. "Fucking

bitch!"

I shrug. "Looks like you're less immune to my knee."

I start running, but the asshole catches my hair and hauls me back. He pushes me to the ground. "Do that again, and I'll cut out your fucking eyes."

I forget about the pain in my back and pull myself up. "You know, for a demon, you're throwing around pretty lame threats."

"Shut up," he warns, his garnet eyes catching fire.

The chanting around me grows louder. The air is so fucking hot, it sizzles. "Something's wrong," Mamba-Guy mutters. He glares at one of his friends. The guy looks like a bad imitation of James Dean. "Why is she still conscious?"

James Dean Wannabe stops chanting and narrows his eyes at me. "Don't know. The spell should have taken her out by now."

*Untouchable, huh?* "Looks like your magic can't hurt me, either. So how about we call it even?"

Mamba-Guy clenches my arm. "Are you deaf? I said shut up."

"I'm not one to follow orders," I say matter-of-factly. The dude stares at me as if I'm totally nuts. I use his momentary bamboozlement to fold my hand around his withering wrist, turning it with full force.

He cusses under his breath, but instead of letting go, he pulls an athame out of his expensive designer jacket. "You are starting to piss me off, little witch." He pushes the blade against my neck, slicing my skin.

Warm crimson runs down to my collarbone. I grit my teeth, swallowing the pain. "Why are you doing this?"

"Because I can," Mamba-Guy says, cutting my dress in two. It—or rather what's left of it—lands on the cement.

Ain't that great? I'm basically dying in my underwear.

"How is she still standing?" Chucky asks behind me.

Mamba-Guy shrugs. "She's strong. But not strong enough. Keep chanting."

While I stand there and wait for my death, I think of three things. One, I'm glad I picked the black lace bra and panties. At least I'll look hot when I'm reaped. Two, who thought I'd end up in hell while trying to save Alex from it? Three, I'm going to miss jerk-face.

Minutes go by, or maybe just seconds, before Chucky screams, "Stop."

"What's the matter?" Mamba-Guy barks.

"Look at her back," Chucky says.

Mamba-Guy faces James Dean Wannabe. "Hold her."

Like an obedient little demon dog, James Dean Wannabe thrusts his fingers through my hair and hauls me toward him, making this the second time I'm almost scalped. "Behave," he warns as his friend examines my back.

"Shit," he hisses. "That's the mark."

*The mark?* Is he talking about my ankh-shaped birthmark? The reason why I got the ankh tattoo on my wrist in the first place?

They all stop chanting and stare at me with fear in their eyes.

"It's *her,* isn't it?" Chucky says.

"Amanda Bishop." Mamba-Guy spits out my name

as if it's pure venom. Hilarious, bearing in mind he's the one with the deadly snake tattoo on his neck.

"We're dead," Sunglasses Boy barks.

James Dean Wannabe pushes me to the ground. My knees smash against the asphalt. "That fuckin' hurt," I shout. Fresh blood spills on the cement. The distinctive scent of rusty iron crawls up my nose.

"I told you there was something off about her," Chucky says to Mamba-Guy. "The runes didn't affect her."

*Runes?* What runes? Seriously, what is going on?

I'm about to ask just that when Bonnie's voice thunders through the alley. "Amanda?"

*Not good.* "Stay a—"

"What the fuck?" she screams when she spots me on the ground, half-naked.

I want to scream "run," beg her to get Alex and Jesse, but the demons jump into action. Without any warning they lunge forward—all six at once. It happens so freaking fast, I can't do a thing about it. *Fuck. Fuck. Fuck. Fuck.* They're going to kill her. She'll die in the city of her nightmares, and it will be my fucking fault.

I wait for the sound of tearing flesh and breaking bones. What I hear is something else entirely. "Playing with toys that don't belong to you, I see." Bonnie's lips move, but the blood-curdling voice coming out of her mouth isn't hers.

I stare at the bizarre scene. Bonnie still standing? Check. Her eyes white like snow? Check. Demons kneeling before her? Check. The shadow dog—yes, the one from my nightmares—next to her growling? Check.

Mamba-Guy's head is bowed. He's the first of the demon horde to speak. "We didn't know it was her."

"Yeah," James Dean Wannabe whispers. "We wouldn't have touched her if we had."

I get on my feet, fighting shock and panic. "What did you do to my friend?"

Bonnie's white eyes gaze back at me. "She's a mambo. What do you think I did to her?" There's not a trace of hostility in the voice. Quite the contrary. It's almost gentle.

White eyes plus mambo? *Equals a demon riding her.* In short, she's possessed. Oh boy, and here I thought this day couldn't get any worse. I hate when I'm wrong. "Get the hell outta my friend." I sound slightly crazy.

Bonnie aka the thing inside her steps forward, the shadow dog on her heel. "I won't harm your friend, love. You have my word." Then it approaches James Dean Wannabe. "You were saying?"

"We stopped when we saw the mark."

"Of course you did," the thing says.

This whole I'm-looking-at-my-best-friend-but-listening-to-a-demon thing creeps me out.

"Can we leave?" Chucky asks. "It was clearly a mistake."

Mamba-Guy nods. "My bad. Won't happen again."

"It won't," the thing confirms. "Your business in this club draws to an end. Demon-strip-paradise will be shut down."

I'm hit by a bolt of lightning. The men upstairs weren't men at all. They're all demons. That's why they stared at me. It's why my ankh hurt, too.

Mamba-Guy lifts his gaze. "But—"

The thing inside Bonnie wiggles her index finger, and the dude's mouth snaps shut.

I smell the fear of the other demons. It poisons the air like acid rain. "We never meant to cross you," James Dean Wannabe whines.

"I'm afraid…" The ground shakes as if an earthquake is hitting the city. "It's too late for apologies." The thing raises Bonnie's hands in the air, and the demons levitate.

"Don't do this," Chucky begs.

The thing laughs. "Rule number one in hell?"

"Show no mercy," James Dean Wannabe blurts out.

The thing winks at him. "Exactly." Then the demons fly against the wall. The impact is so hard I hear their bones cracking. What happens next is a freaking nightmare. The shadow dog jumps at them. Blood splatters. Teeth sink into rotten skin. Screams penetrate the night. Then there's silence.

I look over the mutilated bodies. All I see is blood and more blood. They're deader than dead. "Shit," I hiss as my best friend approaches me.

"Sorry about the mess." It shrugs. "But I hate when someone touches my things." The shadow dog is by its side. The demon pats its head, and the dog leans in.

"W-who are you?" I stammer, surprised I still have a voice.

A sinister smile tugs at its lips. "Your question should be what can you do for me, love."

"What the hell is that supposed to mean?" I shouldn't yell at a demon who just killed six of his kind and has a hellhound as a pet, but lunacy corrupts my brain.

It stops a few feet in front of me and tilts its head to the side. "All in good time, love." It gazes at the dead demons. "The girl you're looking for, by the way…well, she's no more. Don't waste your precious time."

The girl is Melissa. How the hell does the thing know about her? "How—"

"I'm inside your friend, remember?"

"How could I forget?" I mutter.

"Amanda?"

*Jesse?* I look over Bonnie's shoulder. Alex and Jesse run toward us, guns drawn. *Now they're coming? Great timing.*

"What the fuck?" Alex barks, ogling the dead demons.

The thing turns around, and both hunters stop dead in their tracks.

"Oh my God," Jesse utters, hands shaking. "Is she—"

"Possessed," I say, hoping it will keep them from shooting her.

The thing laughs. "I'm a sucker for reunions, but I have some business to take care of." It turns to me. "See you soon, love." And just like that, the color returns to Bonnie's eyes.

Alex glares at my half-naked body and my bloody neck. "Someone tell me what the fuck just happened?"

*I wish I knew.*

# Chapter 24

*Six days to hell*

I limp to the antique couch in Bonnie's family's apartment, wearing nothing but bra, panties, and Alex's leather jacket. The cut on my neck is still bleeding, and my knees hurt like hell, but I'm too wrapped up in what just happened to care. Demons doing business in a strip club is odd. A thing possessing my best friend, scaring the shit out of demons, and saving my ass is...I don't even know what *that* is. Oh yeah, and then there was the news Melissa is no more. All in all, this has turned into a nightmare on Bourbon Street.

"You got something to clean her neck?" hunter-heroic asks Bonnie.

She hasn't said a word since the thing left her body. Even now, she just nods and rushes to the bathroom. Jesse watches her like a hawk. He, too, lost the ability to speak. Part of me wonders if he's scared of Bonnie now that he knows what she's capable of. Then I see the worry in his eyes and consider the possibility he's not scared of her, but for her.

Alex examines my neck. "You going to tell me what happened?"

"I already told you." Twice. Okay, I might have left out some parts. Crucial parts, but Alex doesn't need to worry about FBI slash hunters looking for me, the fact the demons were terrified when they saw my birthmark, or that Melissa could be dead. Neither do I want him to know the thing came to save me.

He reaches for the first-aid kit, which my mute best friend put on the table. "Tell me again," he orders, reaching for gauze pads to clean my injury.

I frown. "I was talking to DeLuca when these assholes attacked me. Bonnie came running." I give her an apologetic look. "Next thing I know, her eyes are white, the thing inside her kills the demons, and the two of you come running. Oh yeah, and then you made me walk down Bourbon Street in panties and bra. End of the story."

Alex sprays antiseptic on the wound and wipes it gently. "That's all, huh?" He's not buying it. It's written all over his handsome face.

"Yes, sir."

He raises his brows. "What do demons do in a strip club, and why did one of them kill the others?"

I pull back and rest my head against the comfy couch. "I don't know, Alex." I really don't. "And we don't have time to think about it." A Black Forest clock stands across from me. "It's past midnight, which means you've got six days, and there are still four names on that list."

"She's right." Looks like Little Remington finally found his voice. "I'll call Carter. He'll take care of Rick's demon Cabaret. We"—he tilts his chin at his brother—"need to move on."

Alex's squints. "What about Melissa?"

*She's dead.*

"Carter can look for her," Jesse suggests.

Alex's lips part, and my witchy-senses tell me

there's an argument in the air. But I've had about enough for one night. "B?" She looks at me. "Can I take a shower?"

She rolls her eyes. "Why do you even ask?" I'm glad to hear her vocal cords are still intact. "I'll get a towel."

"Thanks," I say, heading to the bathroom.

I get rid of my underwear and turn to start the shower. Bonnie walks in with the towel. She looks wretched. "Need anything else?" she croaks, not looking at me.

I've known the girl most of my life. The only other time I've ever seen her so broken was when Gabriel was arrested. "B?"

"Hm?"

"Are you mad at me?" It's a selfish question, but I need to know.

"Mad at you?" She sounds confused. "Why would I be mad at you, Amanda?"

I reach for the towel and wrap it around myself. "That thing," I say, sitting on the edge of the Jacuzzi tub. "It's my fault it possessed you."

She eyeballs me as if I'm completely nuts. "It's not your fault," she murmurs, joining me on the edge of the tub. "I'm a mambo. Spirits and demons don't need an invitation to ride me, remember?"

I'm aware of that. It's one of the reasons she doesn't use her gifts. She dwells in the illusion that magic won't touch her if she doesn't touch it. We both know it's not true, though. At the end of the day, we are what we are—witches. And what defines us is who we are. In Bonnie's case, it's the sweetest soul and best friend one could wish for.

"I'm worried," she says after a long period of silence.

I slowly let out the breath I'm holding. "Don't be, B. We'll find Alex's soulmate, and I'm pretty sure the thing won't come back." Okay, truth be told I'm not really sure about the thing not coming back, but I am 100 percent certain we'll get Alex out of this mess. At least it's what I'm telling myself.

Bonnie shakes her head. "I'm not worried about Alex or me." She's more serious than ever. "I'm fucking worried about *you*, Amanda."

"Me?" I tighten the towel around my chest. "Why would you be worried about me?" She's the one who was possessed, and Alex is going to hell. I don't see why she's concerned about me.

Her eyes are red and glazed. "That demon..." She stares at me and shudders. "It wants you, Amanda. It wants you bad. I felt it when it was inside me. It felt like starving while someone holds a beef steak under your nose."

I try to smile it off. Problem is, she's right. I, too, felt the desire of the thing. "Hey." I rest my hand on her leg. "One drama at a time. Let's save Alex first and worry about demon dude later, okay?"

She shakes her head. "What if all of this is connected?"

I squint. "Connected how, B?"

She rises to her feet and starts pacing the bathroom. "I don't know. But think about it. The nightmares, Madame Josephine claiming you're Eliot Ness, Alex showing up at the apartment half-dead because he sold his soul, and now that demon saving you? Does that sound like a coincidence to you?"

It doesn't. And there's more. The two FBI hoaxers interrogating DeLuca, Jules, the *Men in Black*, but I'd be insane to mention any of it. "Guess it's just a shitty month."

She stops in front of me. "What if this isn't about Alex, Amanda? What if all of this is about you?"

She's losing me. "How is Alex selling his soul about me, B?"

She drops her shoulders and sighs. "I don't know. It just doesn't add up."

I get on my feet, paying no attention to the pain in my knees. "I know you love me," I say, folding my hands over her shoulders. "But you need to stop worrying. I'm like a cat. Always land on my feet."

She studies me closely. Then after what feels like forever, she says, "Yeah, but cats only have nine lives."

I force a half-hearted smile. "I'll be fine."

"Promise?"

I cross my heart. "Scout's honor."

"All right." She strolls to the door. "I'm gonna kill my mom's bourbon stock."

"Leave some for me," I order.

Hand on the doorknob, she looks over her shoulder. "Amanda?"

"Yeah?"

"You think he's scared of me?"

*He,* as in Jesse. God, I'm not sure I like that she cares about his opinion. Who am I to judge, though? "Nah. He's seen worse." He's been worse.

"Good," she mumbles before she moves her butt out of the bathroom.

**** 

Canary rays slice through the massive window

241

front, flooding the living room with bright light. Too fucking bright for a girl who's been up all night. Sleep doesn't come easily when your head reels with information you can't process. Feeling like a vampire, I squint and stagger to the ebony table. "Careful," I say, handing Jesse his eighth cup of coffee. "It's hot."

He traces the gray circles under his eyes. "Thanks."

"You look like shit. Why don't you get some rest?" Between informing Carter about the demon activities at Rick's Cabaret, making sure Bonnie wouldn't end up in the ER with bourbon poisoning, and calculating the most efficient routes to the rest of Alex's maybe-soulmates, he scratched sleeping from his to-do list.

"It's almost seven," he grumbles. "No time for sleep." We'd agreed to spend the night in NOLA and hit the road early in the morning.

I sip my coffee and take a seat next to him. "How is it going?"

He shoves the iPad away. "It's fucking hopeless. I've calculated every route at least a dozen times. There's no way we'll make it to all of these girls in time."

I cut my eyes to Alex. He's snoring on the couch. The prospect of an eternity in hell obviously doesn't bug him as much as it bugs his brother.

Jesse lifts his cup. "What are we even doing, Manda? Diana was a dead end, Melissa is missing, and the other girls are scattered all over the country. You really think we can save him?"

I put my hand over Little Remington's. "We still have six days."

"Exactly," he mutters. "Six days. No way we'll find his soulmate in time."

I grab the list Alex wrote. Jesse had approached the issue with math. Let's see what my witch sense says. I skim through the remaining names.

Sarina, Poulsbo, Washington.

Viktoria, Miami, Florida.

Anna, Westminster, Vermont.

JJ, Winter Harbor, Maine.

*Anna.* She's the chick I saw on my vision quest when trying to locate Jesse back in Bakersfield. The girl definitely had feelings for Alex, but I doubted she was Alex's soulmate. He liked her, but when Anna asked him if he loved her, jerk-face had thought of me. The witch that *ruined* him—his word, not mine.

"That Anna chick," I say, pointing to her name. "Is our last option."

Jesse raises his brows. "Why?"

I shrug. "Because your badass witch friend says so."

He ogles me suspiciously, but I won't share with him what I'd seen. There's a little thing called privacy, and I happen to respect that.

"Even if she's our last option"—he pushes the iPad under my nose—"it's still a twelve-hour drive to Miami, forty-eight hours from Miami to Poulsbo, another fifty hours to Winter Harbor, and six hours to Westminster."

One doesn't need to be a math genius to know we're screwed. Rubbing my temples, I try to think of a solution. Easier said than done after a sleepless night.

Jesse rubs his jaw. "Any bright witch ideas?"

"We split up." Bonnie stands in the doorway. Her curls are soaking wet from a shower, and she changed into skinny jeans and a shirt with My Attitude Depends

On You printed on it.

Jesse's jaw drops at the sight of her tight jeans. My best friend's cheeks flush a bright red, and I literally smell sex in the air. It's pathetic really.

"Hey." I snap my fingers. "Can you guys undress each other later?"

Bonnie strolls toward us and grins. "Someone's in a mood."

Jesse clears his throat and averts his eyes. "You were saying?"

Bonnie reaches for my coffee. "My best friend has spent too much time with your grumpy brother. That's what I'm saying."

Jesse smiles. "No, about splitting up."

She downs my coffee. "Efficiency: produce a specific outcome with a minimum amount of waste, expense, or unnecessary effort."

Jesse's gaze flickers up. He looks at Queen B as if she's the answer to all his prayers—totally impressed. Great. Now he's not just mesmerized by her beauty but awed by her brain.

I frown. "Unlike you, I haven't slept, B. So why don't you cut the I-major-in-computer-science-and-economics crap and get to the point."

Bonnie flings herself on the table. "We're two witches capable of doing the spell and two hunters." She meets my annoyed gaze. "Do the math, Amanda."

I think I'm having stroke-induced hallucinations. No way Bonnie, the girl who hates being a mambo, just suggested she'd do the spell. "You don't do magic, remember?"

She tosses her hair to one side and massages the nape of her neck. "It's not really magic. Just one lousy spell."

*One lousy spell, huh?* "Still magic," I snarl through gritted teeth. "Besides, splitting up? That's fuckin' crazy." I look at Jesse for support. "Right?"

"Don't know, Manda." He stares at the list. "We could cover more ground if we each do half." He draws a deep breath and finally dares to look me in the eye. "We'd double the chances of saving him."

"Save who?" Alex asks, voice thick with sleep. I'm glad he's awake. He'll never agree to Bonnie's stupid plan.

Bonnie rolls her eyes. "You, you moron. Ain't nobody else in this room who sold his soul."

"They want to split up," I blurt out. "Told 'em it's a stupid idea, but they won't listen."

Alex digs his elbows into the couch and pushes himself up. "One hunter, one witch?" His expression is unreadable.

Jesse nods. "It's our only shot, bro."

Alex staggers toward us. I wait for an explosive argument in which he tells his brother how ridiculous it would be for us to go separate ways and he'd never allow him to ride with a witch. I'm getting something completely else. "Sounds legit," he says, eyes on me.

"What?" I shout, jumping up. "Are you crazy? It would be one witch, one hunter. Meaning: Jesse would be alone with one of us. He'd be alone with"—I pause for dramatic effect—"a *witch*, Alex."

Something passes through his eyes. God, I wish I could read his aura. Maybe then I'd understand why he's talking crazy.

Alex squeezes my shoulder. "Relax, Manda. Jesse can take care of himself." Our eyes lock. "Besides, I trust you." He smiles at Bonnie. "Both of you."

I cross my arms. "Dude, are you on meth?" It's either that, or he was abducted by aliens last night, and I'm talking to his clone.

He raises his brows. "You asked me to trust you in Bakersfield." He shrugs. "Congratulations. Now I do."

My mouth snaps open. "But—"

"Then it's settled," Bonnie cuts in. She faces Jesse. "Find us a cheap rental."

*Us?* "Sounds like you already picked your teammate," I grumble, murder on my face.

She smiles innocently. "You really think I'll voluntarily sit in a car with Alexander Asshat Remington?" She tilts her head to Alex. "No offense."

He holds up his hands. "None taken."

"Plus," Bonnie goes on, "what if he's attacked again? Between the two of us, you're much more capable of protecting him."

*Is this some sort of sick joke?* I'd ask, but my jaw is lying on the hardwood floor.

"Bonnie's right," Alex says.

I shoot daggers at him. "Dude, did hellfire fry your brain cells?"

He doesn't answer.

Jesse abandons his web search for car rental companies. "Look," he says, a hint of sorry in his voice. "It's three against one. Absolute majority."

*Democracy sucks.*

## Chapter 25

A warm breeze wafts through the rolled down windows of the Mustang. I try to keep the inferno inside my soul under control. Not an easy task, taking into account how angry I am. Every now and then, when I push the gas pedal a little harder, Alex casts me a worried glance. I'm too fucking mad to acknowledge it. Splitting up must be the stupidest idea of the year. Why can't he see that?

*Does it matter?* It's too fucking late anyway. Jesse and Bonnie are en route to Poulsbo, Washington, in their fancy rental car, and I'm driving to Miami with hunter-heroic, who looks like crap. His forehead is covered with sweat, and it's obvious he's in pain. He's been like this since we walked out of the car rental company in New Orleans, where Queen B and Little Remington got a car, which is why, despite my tiredness, I insisted on driving.

The silence must trouble him because he shoves a cassette in the player. *Who listens to cassettes anymore?* I swallow the snarky comment on the tip of my tongue and focus on the road.

He presses the play button. Styx's "Renegade" blares through the speakers, and I can't help but smile. I love this song. And he knows it.

****

*The distant lights of the dive bar floated through*

*the car. I couldn't believe I sat here waiting for Little Remington to screw the brunette bartender he'd flirted with all night. It was wrong for more reasons than one. I hadn't had much of a choice, though. They'd offered me a ride, and I'd accepted. None of them claimed they'd change their ways while I was with them.*

*Alex fiddled with the radio, changing station after station, on the hunt for a good song. There were none. "You cold?" he asked, searching through a stack of old cassettes.*

*"No," I said, teeth chattering. "I'm shaking because you're so damn hot, I can't keep my libido in check."*

*His smile was smug. "Good. Almost thought I'd have to get my old football jacket from the trunk."*

*I made a face and hugged the fabric of my thin jacket closer. "You insinuating I'm some dumb cheerleader?" Crazy how strong my voice sounded, bearing in mind I was freezing to death here.*

*He pulled a cassette out of the stack and bit his lower lip. "I would never do such a thing." He met my eyes. "I happen to like cheerleaders," he said, shoving the ancient relic into the player.*

*I gazed out the window. "Shocker. A guy like* you *digs cheerleaders. What a surprise."*

*Led Zeppelin's "Stairway to Heaven" echoed through the car, and Alex shifted in his seat to face me. "A guy like* me*?" Curiosity blossomed in his eyes. "Care to elaborate?"*

*I let out a long breath. "You know, the type who thinks every girl needs a savior, wears worn-out leather jackets to come across as the ultimate alpha-male, and listens to Zeppelin because that's what damsel-in-*

*distress-saving, leather-jacket-wearing, alpha jerks do, right?"*

*His eyes went wide. "All right." He held up a warning finger. "You can insult me all you want, but don't you dare defame Led Zeppelin. They are gods, and I won't have blasphemy in my car."*

*I choked back laughter and cocked a brow. "Says every guy who never listened to a real rock band."*

*He drew closer. His warm breath beat against my cold cheek. "That's rich, coming from a chick who listens to Justin Bieber and One Direction."*

*I gave him a look. "First of all, there's nothing wrong with One Direction, but if you ever call me a Belieber again, you'll need to invest the poker money you just won in plastic surgery, capiche?"*

*A mischievous grin tugged at his lips. "Okay, smart-ass." His voice challenging. "Hit me with your best shot. What's your favorite rock song?"*

*I didn't have anything to prove to jerk-face, but after he'd accused me of listening to teeny brat Bieber, I was hellbent on defending my honor. "Fine," I said, pulling out my phone. "Get ready for some real music." I scrolled through hundreds of songs until I found it— my all-time favorite.*

*Alex's jaw dropped. "Is that—"*

*"Styx's 'Renegade.'" I shrugged. "Beats 'Stairway to Heaven' any day."*

*"Not bad," he muttered, clearly surprised my playlist didn't consist of pussy pop and cuddle rock.*

*The tune vibrated through my system. I sang along, feeling each word as if written for me and me only. The cold, Alex—I forgot all about it as I lost myself in the rhythm. Great music could make me oblivious to how fucked-up my life was.*

*"Why is it your favorite?" Alex asked as the music faded.*

*The question caught me off guard and brought back unwanted memories. The first time I'd heard the song, I sat on my drunken dad's lap. He'd made it his mission to introduce me to* real *music. Frankly, I think he'd just wanted to piss off my mom. She hated rock. Anyway, I was five or something, and as I sat there, I couldn't help but picture myself on the gallows. In my case, though, there was no mother to mourn me. In fact, there was no one to give a damn if I was dead or alive.*

*"You okay?" Alex asked. He looked at me as if I were a broken engine that needed to be fixed. I hated it.*

*I straightened and put my poker face on. "Sure." I forced a smile. "Your turn." I seize hold of his jacket. "And try to be a bit more original than Zeppelin, okay?"*

*He dug through a pile of cassettes until he found the one he wanted. "Ready?"*

*I grinned. "Give it to me, baby."*

*He rolled his eyes and shoved the cassette into the player. "Gotta work on your Offspring voice, Manda."*

So he does know good music, huh?

*I rested my head against the seat and waited for the song to start. It took me three seconds to recognize it. "'Knockin' on Heaven's Door'?"*

*He smiled. "Best song* ever.*"*

*There was definitely a theme to his music taste. "You're a heaven kinda guy?"*

*The rainbow color of his aura indicated confusion. He locked his mesmerizing eyes on mine. "What's a heaven kinda guy?"*

250

*I held his gaze. "Means you're the kinda man who thinks there'll be peace when you're done." I tilted my head to the side and shrugged. "Makes sense, considering you're a righteous jerk most of the time."*

*He stared at me, eyes wide. "You saying you don't believe in heaven and hell?"*

*"Sure I do." I looked at my ankh tattoo, then back at him. "Look around you, Alex. We're surrounded by hell. It feeds people the illusion there's a reward at the end of the tunnel—seventy-two virgins waiting for you and you only, eternal peace, unconditional love, forgiveness. It makes the righteous kill to climb up that stairway to heaven, but in the end, when they take their last breath, it laughs in their faces and tells them how dumb they've been to ever have believed they had a shot at heaven."*

*"Wow." He blew out a long breath. "Who fucked you up so bad?"*

Life, Alex. Life.

\*\*\*\*

"Manda?" Alex's hoarse voice brings me back to the present. "You going to keep this silence up, or are you going to woman-up and tell me why the hell it bothers you so much to ride with me?"

I eyeball him. He looks even worse than he did two minutes ago. His eyes are bloodshot. He's so pale he could be mistaken for an albino. I need to check his wounds. Sooner than later would be a good idea.

"Manda." He snaps his fingers in my face.

"It doesn't bother me," I finally say.

He flashes me a pained smile. "Yeah. Right." Of course, he doesn't buy my lies. Alex never does.

"Riding with you doesn't bother me." I hold the

steering wheel in a death grip and sigh. "I just don't understand why you agreed to splitting up."

He presses a hand against his ribcage. "I'm going to be real honest with you, okay?"

I knit my brows. "Um, okay."

"We both know I won't find my soulmate. People like us aren't cut out for relationships, let alone soulmates."

A wave of anger hits me. I dig my nails into the steering wheel, trying to keep my cool. "What are you saying?"

He frowns. "I'm saying we both know I will die, and when I do, I don't want my brother watching."

Heat flushes my cheeks, and my knuckles turn as white as bones. "You're using me?" *Wow, did I say that out loud?*

He turns to the window. "I'm not *using* you, Manda. It's just…Jesse doesn't think straight. You saw what he did back in Bakersfield to get me out of this. He'd never let me go."

Jesse won't. But selfish witch Amanda will? That's so Alex, I don't even know why it still shocks me. I take a deep breath, suppressing the raging storm inside of me. "You're a selfish jerk, Alex."

He glares at me. "*I'm* selfish?"

"Yes. Yes, you are."

"You don't know shit," he hisses, peeved.

Bitter laughter roars through me. "You're right. I don't know why a guy like you decides to sell his soul. Don't care either. Because no matter how noble your reasons might seem to you, you still chose the easy way out. You decided to leave behind the people who love you and rot in hell. Sorry," I say, looking him in the eye. "But that's a page right out of the *Amanda Bishop is Selfish* book."

I half expect him to throw a fit or strangle me. He starts coughing his lungs out instead.

"Alex?" He pushes one hand against the dashboard and covers his mouth with the other. Something is wrong. There's blood on his palm. My heart skips a beat. "Alex, what the hell is going on?" He glares at his bloody hand, gasping for air.

I jerk the steering wheel to the left and stop the car on the side of the road. "Alex?" I unbuckle my seatbelt. "Talk to me." I sound hysterical. Hell, I am hysterical.

"I'm okay," he chokes out.

He doesn't look okay to me. I don't even bother with the don't-bullshit-me look. I shove his shirt up. The gauze pads are blood-soaked. *Fuck!* Our eyes lock. "I need to take a look."

He nods, and I slowly peel the pads away. I expect purulence, but the cuts don't look bad. Wish I could say the same about the black veins spread all over his belly and chest. What the hell is that? Sepsis? I don't think so. Last time I checked, sepsis caused red streaks, not black veins. Maybe he's suffering from another kind of infection? "We need to get you some antibiotics," I mutter, replacing the bandages carefully.

He wipes blood off his lips. "You need a prescription for those, and I'm not breaking into another pharmacy." He's talking about the Bakersfield incident. To cure Jesse from his zombie state, we had to get our hands on Physostigmine. According to the grimoire, it reverses the symptoms of the zombie drug. We never got to test the theory, though.

"Relax. We won't commit a felony, I promise. Just

need to stop at the next grocery store to get some herbs."

"Manda." Alex puts two fingers under my chin. "I need you to understand something." His eyes are soft, his voice gentle.

"Can we postpone the I-can't-be-saved talk?" I'm not in the mood to talk death after I watched him cough blood.

"Manda." He cups my cheeks with such desperation, it makes my heart sink. "I need you to hear this."

The sadness in his eyes is too much. I look away. "What do I need to hear, Alex? That you have no regard for your life? That you accept hell out of selfless reasons? Or that you don't want your brother to watch you die but have no problem making me watch?" Damn, I had no idea how hurt I am.

His shoulders sink. "I don't want to die. Don't want to go to the pit either. But what I did, Manda, I'd do again." He ogles my lips. "You don't have to like or understand it." He caresses my cheek with his thumb. "But you have to accept it, just like I did."

Something in my chest cracks. I think it's my non-existent heart. For the first time, I see fear in his eyes. He's terrified of hell but made his amends because…he accepted it?

I'm not sure what to say or do. Kiss away his hopelessness or beat the fucking pessimism out of him? I push his hands away and lean back. Thick black clouds cover the sun, and I can't help but smile at the cliché. I used to make fun of pathetic fallacy. Thought it was hilarious how authors like Fitzgerald used the easy way out to describe emotions. Little did I know, sometimes the weather really does portray the state of a human's soul.

I turn the key in the ignition and face Alex with a real smile. "You've got one thing wrong, Alex."

"What's that?"

"I'm a witch," I say. "I don't have to accept anything."

Chapter 26

Viktoria Mogilova is the definition of beautiful. High cheekbones, full lips, long red-brown hair, and curves Jennifer Lopez would kill for. According to Alex, she's Russian. It's quite obvious. She holds her head up high and walks through the world as if nothing could hurt her—invincible.

In a perfect world, she should be the one.

Alex could be happy with her.

They would have a shot at a good life.

Shoulda, woulda, coulda. Truth is, the world isn't perfect. And Viktoria isn't the one.

"Let's go," Alex says, squeezing my leg gently.

He isn't disappointed, broken, or depressed. I am. I still stare at the multi-million-dollar estate on Bay Road, home of Viktoria and her newly-wedded husband, Michael, trying to convince myself she only married him for the money.

She didn't. When I knocked on their door, pretending to be a helpless chick whose car broke down, I saw the love in their eyes. They looked at each other as if nothing else mattered in the world. For a notorious liar like me, it's easy to spot a fake. What Michael and Viktoria have is the real deal. I knew right then and there Florida was another dead end. Viktoria had already found her soulmate, and his name wasn't Alex.

"Come on, Manda. Start the engine." Alex's voice is soft, not pushy.

How can he be so calm when his soul is at stake? I press my lips together and glare at the star-sprinkled sky. "What time is it?"

"Almost eleven," he says, sipping on the garlic, ginger, thyme, and cinnamon tea I made for him.

One more hour to midnight. One day closer to the hellish deadline. *Awesome.* I blow out some air and move nearer to Alex. He's not as pale as he was hours ago, but I don't like the dark shadows under his eyes. "How do you feel?" I wish I sounded less worried.

He smiles a weak smile. "The stuff tastes like poison," he says, holding up the paper cup. "But I think it helps." After the coughing incident, we'd stopped at the next grocery store to get the ingredients for an antibiotic mixture. Easy. Getting hot water wasn't. I'd asked a Starbucks barista for four takeaway cups of boiling water. The dude scowled as if I'd just committed the worst coffee shop crime ever. Changed his mind when I shoved twenty bucks over the counter.

I turn the key in the ignition. "It's a twenty-seven-hour drive to Winter Harbor, right?"

"Give or take an hour."

"We better get going then," I say, backing the car out of the parking slot.

\*\*\*\*

*Five days to hell*

Yawning, I try to keep my eyes on the road. My sight is blurry and my mind drifts to dark places. Alex's soul lost in the everlasting flames of hell. Him never getting the chance to meet...*Don't go there.* Why not? In five days this will be reality, and unless JJ or Sarina turns out to be the one, there's nothing I can do about it.

Apparently, Alex notices how drowsy I am. "Let's get a room."

I smile, because it's so much better than breaking down and crying. "That an indecent proposal, Alex?"

A boyish grin tugs at the edges of his mouth. "If you call sleep indecent, then, yes, Manda."

"We can sleep when we're dead. In your case, that would be in five days," I remind him.

"Manda." He loses the humorous tone. "I know you mean well. But"—he points to the road—"a blind eighty-year-old wouldn't drive such wiggly lines."

"Shut up, Alex."

He unbuckles his seatbelt and faces me. "Your eyes are bloodshot, you're yawning like a lion, and if you don't take a break, you're gonna get us both killed with your reckless driving."

I'm about to argue with him when the car next to me honks like crazy. For a fraction of a second, I freeze. I'd drifted way too close to his Chevy. *Shit.*

"All right." I pull the car to the right. "Have it your way. But don't you dare blame me if we don't make it in time."

"I won't," he promises.

Pit stop in Savannah, Georgia. Great. I navigate the car into the driveway of the Sleep Inn, a cheap, two-star hotel right next to the I-95N exit. It looked passable on the outside. Should have known better than to judge a motel by its façade. The A/C doesn't work, the room smells like old carpet, there's scum on the shower glass, mold in every corner, and don't even get me started on the cockroach wandering over the filthy bed sheets.

Alex escorts the cockroach out of the room. I might

not like these creatures, but I raised hell when he tried to kill it. We've got enough shitty karma to battle. No need to add to the list. "Sure you wanna stay here?"

"Hell, yeah. I love a fucked-up motel room," I lie.

He shuts the door and gives me a look. "You hate cockroaches, Manda."

I also hate the idea of sharing a room with hunter-heroic, but Bonnie was right about one thing: Alex needs protection from himself and the creature that ripped his torso open.

I throw my bag on the left bed. "I'll live. Besides"—I bat my lashes at him—"I have hunter-heroic with me. He's gonna take care of all the cockroaches for me."

He saunters toward me. Presenting a mesmerizing smile, he scrubs his fingers through his untamed hair. "What happened to 'I don't need a knight in shining armor'?"

"I don't," I say, flinging myself on the bed. "But I do need a knight in cockroach armor."

"Okay, Mrs. I'm-not-scared-of-demons-but-little-cockroaches, I'll hit the shower."

I push myself up on my elbows. "Need some help?"

I don't realize how wrong it sounds until Alex laughs. "That an indecent proposal?"

I scan the tight black shirt hugging his six-pack.

He stares at me with a fire in his eyes that's hard to ignore. "Manda, is it?" He's fucking serious.

I pull my gaze from his chest, mad at the throbbing sensation between my legs. "Get outta here, Alex."

If I didn't know better, I'd say he looks disappointed.

After a moment of awkward silence, he grabs a change of clothes and disappears into the bathroom. I exhale sharply. Jesus, what is wrong with me? He's going to hell, and I'm sincerely considering screwing him? What happened to the girl in the closet refusing to play second fiddle? Damn, this is exactly why I didn't want to split up. Alex and I, alone? That's as cruel as putting cocaine under the nose of an addict.

I'm spread out on the disgusting bed, listening to the sound of hot water spraying Alex's god-like body. My imagination runs wild. Gosh, it would be so easy to strip down and join him. So deliciously tempting to trace his wet chest down to a more sensitive area. He'd be game. I remembered what he'd said to me in the closet. *If this whole soulmate shit ain't gonna work, this is how we'll spend the last day of my life.* But this isn't the last day of his life, and I need to get a fucking grip. Forget about the wetness in my panties and move on.

I'm still battling the hunger for Alex's touch when my phone vibrates. Queen B. Damn, I never told her Viktoria turned out to be someone else's soulmate. My thumb glides over the accept button. "Hey, baby girl, I'm sorry I—"

"I'm not a girl, but I don't mind you calling me baby," Jesse says in a playful tone.

I smile. "Sorry, man. Thought you were Bonnie. Why you calling me from her number?"

"Is Alex with you?" he whispers.

"He's in the shower," I say.

"Good."

"Why are we whispering?" I ask in a hushed tone.

He clears his throat. "Can you go somewhere else?"

I'm not sure I like this. "Hold on."

I amble out of the room and lean against the wall in the empty hallway. "Where are you guys?"

"Colorado Springs. You?"

"Savannah," I reply quickly.

"Oh."

I draw a deep breath and push the bottom of my shoe against the wall. "I'm sorry, Jess. Viktoria is happily married. She isn't *the* one." I should tell him about the blood coughing thing and the black veins, too. Don't have it in me to hurt him some more, though.

"We still have options," he murmurs.

"We do." Very few options, but options nevertheless.

There's a long pause. "Carter called me."

My pulse quickens. I have a knot in the pit of my stomach. Both are omens I'm about to get bad news. "What does he want?"

Silence.

"Jesse?"

Painful silence.

"Dude!" I bark, losing my temper. "What's the matter with you?"

"I don't know how to say this."

"Just the way it is, Jess."

"All right, but you can't tell Alex. Okay?"

I squint. "Um, sure."

"Carter said a couple of hunters are looking for you. Some work for the Paranormal Analysis Unit of the FBI, others are freelancers. They think you killed that Jules chick at NYU." He's talking faster than Eminem raps. "I assured him you had nothing to do with the girl's death. He already figured that out and called his guys back, but there's nothing he can do about the ones not working for him."

*Agents Marple and Brown, huh?* My throat tightens. "That's not all, is it?"

"No," he admits, an edge to his voice that scares me.

I hate when people make me wait. Especially when my pulse throbs against my neck and my palms are dotted with sweat. "Spill it, Jess."

"Carter and his people raided Rick's Cabaret. The demons were gone."

The light bulb on the wall flickers. Chills run down my spine. I scan the hallway. I'm alone but feel like I'm being watched. I blame it on lack of sleep. "That's good, right?"

"Yeah."

"But?"

"They weren't just gone, Manda. They were killed. All of them. Carter describes the scene as a demon *Chainsaw Massacre.*"

"What?" I'm having a hard time processing the news. Tearing a bunch of demons apart is one thing. Slaughtering a whole club full of the nasty creatures something entirely else. "How is that even possible?"

"I don't know," he says, sounding as miserable as I feel. "But two things. You need to be damn careful—there's no way of knowing how many hunters are looking for you—and you can't tell Alex any of it. He'd freak."

I press my back against the wall to steady my weak knees. The light flickers again, and I swear I hear a dog howling. "What the—"

"What is it?"

The lights go off, and I'm in the dark except for the exit sign at the end of the hall. My heart thunders in my ears as I hear it again. The howling of a dog.

"Amanda!"

"Gotta go, Jess." I end the call and scan my surroundings. There's a large shadow at the end of the hallway. It moves toward me.

I could go back inside. It would just be one step. The shadow comes closer, floating down the long hallway. Hell, I really should move. The air is electrified. More howling echoes off the walls. What the—

"Manda?"

*Alex?*

I spin and the lights go back on.

Alex stands in the doorway, a towel around his waist. "Whatcha doing out there?"

My jaw is clenched. "I…I—" My gaze drifts to the spot where the shadow was moments ago. There's nothing. It's gone.

Alex cocks a brow. "You?"

I write the incident off as a hallucination caused by sleep deprivation. "I was just looking for a vending machine," I say.

The trembling in my voice raises his suspicion. His eyes land on the phone in my hand. "Did you find one?"

I compel a smile I don't feel. "No." I shove the phone in my pocket and walk toward him. "Let's go inside. I need some sleep."

"Yeah, you do. You look like shit."

Feel like it, too.

I take a quick shower. When I come back, the

lights are dimmed, and Alex, still wearing nothing but his towel, is lying on the left bed. My bed. Arms crossed behind his head, he looks me over. "What, no towel today?" He refers to the scenario in Bakersfield where I may or may not have dropped my towel to piss him off.

I pull the St. John's wort and a couple of fresh gauze pads out of my bag. "I'm gonna take a look at your chest."

"You can look wherever you want. I ain't got nothing to hide." His voice is smoky.

I sit down next to him and rub some of the sticky stuff onto his cuts, deliberately ignoring the blackish veins. "How long?" I ask, not meeting his eyes. I'm crazy, not suicidal.

"How long what?"

I tape the gauze pads to his chest. "How long since you got laid, Alex?"

"By you?" He flashes me a sexy-as-hell smile. "Too. Damn. Long."

"I'm not going to fall for your shit, Alex."

The playfulness in his eyes flickers out of existence. "You sure you and Pony-Boy aren't exclusive?"

I untangle my hair tie and put it on the nightstand. "This DeLuca obsession of yours is getting real awkward. Want me to call him and see if he's up for a date?"

He leans against the headboard. "What a funny bunny we are today."

I turn and look him in the eye. "Cut it out, Alex. I don't wanna fight." Not after the news I just got. Not after the shadow I saw. Not five days before he goes to hell.

He raises his brows. "Are you okay?"

I climb under the sheets. "Yes, hunter-heroic. I am. Now move to *your* bed."

He turns on his side, resting his head on one elbow. "Are you really throwing me out of your bed when I only have five days to live? That would be plain cruelty."

I pull the blanket over my chest. "Do whatever the hell you want, but make no mistake, this ain't no invitation for sex."

He smiles. "Damn shame."

I frown. Sure, it's dumber than dumb to sleep next to a guy who drives my lady parts crazy, but he's hurt and I don't want to sleep alone. Maybe I did hallucinate, and there was no shadow. Maybe the bulb flickered because it was about to burst. But what if my mind hasn't played tricks on me? What if there really was someone in the hallway? One of the hunters looking for me or worse, the demon from Rick's Cabaret?

I reach for the lamp. "You good to sleep?" He nods and I switch off the light, bathing the room in darkness.

For a while, we're both quiet, me trying to sleep, him watching me like a hawk. I literally feel Alex's gaze roaming over me. It makes me all kinds of giddy and restless.

His leg brushes against mine. "Manda?"

"Hm?"

"What's with you and your family?"

I dig my nails into the sheets and glare at the ceiling. What is it with him and his sudden interest in my personal life?

"Manda?"

Exasperation simmers under my cool façade. "My sister and I, we don't get along. In case you haven't noticed, we're from two different planets."

"What about your mom?"

Why do I feel like I'm being interrogated by Detective Bitcher? I mean, I don't ask him about the mysterious sister Diana mentioned. "Haven't seen her since she threw me out of the house four years ago. It's very unlikely—as in demons-and-angels-make-out unlikely—I will see her anytime soon. Can't ruin her picture-perfect family for her new rich husband."

He sighs loudly. "Wow, she really threw you out of the house?" He pauses, probably wrapping his head around the reality I call life. "What could possibly justify a mother treating her own flesh and blood like that?"

I don't want to talk about Mother Dearest or my past. Alex is a stubborn son of a bitch, though. He'll never let me sleep until he gets what he craves—an answer. "Before I was born," I explain, voice trembling. "My mom had a vision."

"She had the same gift as you?" Alex queries.

"No." I'm not sure why the hell I'm telling him any of this. "She only had visions when she was pregnant with me. Anyway, I was some sort of queen of the underworld, bringing upon the end of the world." I turn, facing the bathroom door, and close my eyes. "Probably doesn't surprise you, huh?"

His hand travels from my shoulder down to my fingers. "I'm sorry," he whispers, his breath warm against the nape of my neck. "No kid deserves to grow up like that."

I swallow the desire to conquer his mouth. I ignore the heat rising in my belly. "Get some sleep, Alex."

He throws an arm across me, pulling me against his warm chest. I try to resist, but it's been a while since I felt so good. "Night," he whispers, his body melting with mine.

I stare into the darkness and try to get a grip on my heartbeat. Why does he have to be so close? Why can't he see having him in my bed, knowing I will never have him in my life, is fucking torture? I close my eyes.

*One sheep.*

Alex's hand wanders over my ribs, down to my hips.

*Two sheep.*

His fingers brush my leg.

*Three sheep.*

He draws tiny circles on my inner thigh.

*Ah, fuck the sheep!*

I throw the blanket to the side and sit up on the edge of the bed, my feet dangling over the gross carpet.

"Move your ass back to bed," he orders, patting the free spot next to him.

"The mattress is too soft," I lie. "I'll try the other one."

He murmurs something about me being full of bullshit, but I ignore him because I can no longer ignore the need in my loins.

## Chapter 27

*Four days to hell*

Piles of snow cover the flat roof of Bobby's Bar, located a few miles outside Winter Harbor. I've seen my fair share of shitholes, but the old cement chunk, painted dark red, looks like the devil's favorite hunting ground.

Icy wind blows through dead trees and beats against the bar. Hugging my coat closer, I glare at the neon sign above the door. Several letters are gone, but I think it says We Don't Serve Women. You Must Bring Your Own.

Close to the entrance, I stop moving. "Sure that JJ chick works here?" I ask, teeth chattering. December in Maine is a vicious little bitch.

Alex grabs my arm and hauls me toward the entrance. "Absolutely. Now, come on, it's not as bad as it looks."

*Not as bad as it looks, huh?* Agree to disagree. Ever since we crossed the state border, I'm plagued by this weird feeling I'm in deep shit. Like something terrible is about to happen. I only wish I knew what.

"Wait," I say, wrenching free of his grip. "How do you wanna play this?"

He tilts his head and grins. "We'll go with the truth this time."

I cross my arms, not liking the truth path he's on. "You just going to walk in there and say, 'Hi, JJ. Long time no see. Oh, by the way, I sold my soul and need you to do a soulmate ritual with me'?"

Alex purses his lips. "Amanda." His voice is so stern it sends chills down my frozen spine. "Don't freak, okay?"

I stumble backward. My brain connects the weird feeling and Alex's strange reaction. "Oh no," I bark, putting more distance between me and the bar. "Don't tell me she's—"

"A hunter," he finishes for me.

"Hell to the no!" The lump in my throat is choking me. "I'm not going anywhere near another hunter." I have a couple on my tail. That's more than enough.

He runs a hand over the healing cut on his face. "Manda, JJ isn't a typical hunter. She's cool, I promise."

Last time the Remingtons said that about one of their hunter pals, I almost got shot by Pulp Fiction Granny. "Hunters hunt," I bark. "It's as simple as that."

He grabs the sleeve of my jacket and pulls me closer. "Listen to me," he says, his lips way too close to mine. "I won't let her hurt you." Our eyes lock. "Trust me?"

It's hard to tell him to go fuck himself when every cell in my body does a happy dance because he looks at me like I'm the most precious thing in the world. "Whatever," I grumble. "But if she *does* kill me, I'll haunt your sorry ass, even if I have to infiltrate hell."

He flashes me a cocky grin. "Seeing Amanda Bishop in hell, making the devil fear for his throne? I'd sell my soul all over again for that."

I nudge him in the ribs. "Your jokes suck, Alex."

He throws an arm around my shoulders and guides me to the entrance. "Wasn't a joke, Manda. I truly believe hell hath no fury like Amanda Bishop pissed off."

I lean in closer, soaking in the heat radiating from him. "Your compliments suck even more than your jokes."

He cups my cheeks, his expression dead serious. "I swear on the life of my brother, no one will touch a hair on your pretty little head." He kicks the door open. "Now, come on. It's freezing out here."

*Whatever.*

I scan the bar like a lethal redheaded Russian spy, assessing possible dangers. There are two customers; one has his head on the counter and looks like he's sleeping, the other gulps down a beer and stares at an old-fashioned TV hanging on the wall. It's not even noon, and these guys look wasted. They ain't no hunters. I relax a bit.

We stroll to the counter. Unless JJ is a sixty-year-old barkeeper with hygiene issues, I don't think she's here.

"Hey." Alex addresses the grumpy dude behind the bar.

He ignores him.

Alex casts me a sidelong glance and shrugs. "Maybe he's deaf?"

The bartender's brows shoot up. Nope, definitely not hearing-impaired.

I shove Alex out of the way and smile at Mr. Grumpy. "Excuse me," I say, leaning over the sticky counter. "Is JJ in?"

The guy turns his back to me and reaches for a beer bottles. "Never heard of her."

I cock a brow and grin. "Interesting how you assume JJ is female. You know, since you've never heard of her and all."

I have his attention. He spins, looking me over. The edges of his lips turn down in disgust. Honestly, I'm a bit startled. Usually, men of all ages give me the I-want-to-screw-you-right-here look, not the get-out-of-my-bar-you-freak glance. "You got a problem with your ears, girl? Said, I don't know *her*."

I ball my hands. The dude's wife might be okay with him talking to her like that. I'm not. "What the fuck is your p—"

Alex moves closer to the counter. "We're not here to cause trouble," he assures him. "But we need to talk to her."

Mr. Grumpy sniffs his snot back. "JJ ain't working here anymore. Girl left town," he says and spits on the floor.

Reading auras or not, I'm still the best lie detector there is, and this douchebag is full of bullshit. "You are one of the worst liars I've ever had the pleasure to meet."

Mr. Grumpy curls his hands into fists and draws closer. "Did you just call me a liar in my own bar?"

I dare say his murderous expression is supposed to scare me. Wrong girl. A lopsided grin on my lips, I move closer. "You heard me."

He slams a fist on the counter, waking the I-take-a-nap-in-a-bar dude in the process. "Get out of here. Now."

Alex cups my elbow. "Let's go, Manda."

He tries to pull me away, but I'll be damned if I move. All the shit bugging me for days comes crashing down on me in this instant, igniting a firestorm in the pit of my stomach.

"Manda." Alex's eyes plead with me, but when I see red, no one in this world can stop me.

I yank my elbow out of Alex's grip and bend over the counter, getting right in Mr. Grumpy's face. "Ever heard of the Cosa Nostra?" My voice is so calm, it scares me a little. And Alex? Well, judging by the look on his face, I'd say it scares him a lot.

Mr. Grumpy glares at me, totally confused. "The what?"

"The Sicilian mafia. Their fashion sense is real classy." I trace a button on his dirty shirt. "They're experts when it comes to tying a tie. If you want, I can show you how it's done. Won't take long. All I need is your tongue." I start to feel a little crazy. Psycho crazy to be exact.

The old man tries to laugh my threat off, but I can tell I got to him. There's a whole lot of uneasiness in his eyes. "Are you threatening me, missy?"

I pull him half over the counter. "I don't do threats." His gray eyes go wide. "Only promises. So let's try this again, shall we? Where's JJ?"

"You're crazy as shit," he barks, pulling away.

Alex agrees. He yanks me back by my shoulders. "Are you nuts?" he asks once we're eye to eye.

"Just a little."

Alex is all set to give me a lecture on God knows what—pretty sure it involves respect thy elders and stop watching the *Godfather*—but a husky female voice delivers me from the pending evil. "Alexander

Remington, that really you?"

Alex and I both turn. A few feet away, next to a door I assume leads to the storeroom, stands the porn version of the poisoned-red-apple-eating, slumbering-till-prince-charming-kisses-me princess. Long black hair cascades down over her shoulders, tight leather pants accentuate endless legs, and full red lips scream "kiss me." I hate to say it, but the chick makes me want to change sides.

"JJ." Alex beams at her.

"You know these freaks?" Mr. Grumpy grumbles.

Murder on my face, I spin. "What did you just call us?" I really thought I had my temper issues under control. The word freak generally flips my bitch-switch, though.

In my peripheral vision, I see JJ roll her eyes. "Relax, Dad."

*Dad?* I look from Mr. Grumpy to the porn-fairytale princess. How on earth could a guy like him produce something like her? Her mother being Miss Universe is the only explanation.

JJ walks toward us and smiles at her dad. "He's very protective of me."

"No shit," I murmur.

The girl doesn't seem to mind my snarky comment. Perhaps because she's too wrapped up in jumping her ex-lover. "Man," she says, grinning from ear to ear. "It's good to see you." She points at the cut on his face. "Let me guess, your girl realized what a jackass you are?"

"She's not my girl," he states, annoyed.

"Yeah, I'm not his girl," I agree, more annoyed.

JJ throws her head back and laughs. "So you used

to be his girl before you realized what a jerk he can be?"

Hunter or not, I dig her spirit. "Nah," I say, waving it off. "Was smart enough to see right through his nice-guy act before I made that mistake."

Alex's face slips into a pissed frown. "I'm right here."

"We can see that." JJ pulls herself onto the counter. "All right, Remington. What can I do for you?"

Hunter-heroic stares at the floor. Gone is the tough guy who hunts evil witches and monsters. Arrived is a little boy who looks like he's about to tell his mother he ruined her favorite dress.

"That bad, huh?" JJ raises her brows. "Did he piss off a witch?"

"He's still pissing her off," I say matter-of-factly. "But—"

"Wait." JJ stares at me. "Are you..." She waits for Alex's verification. "Oh. My. Gosh. She is, isn't she?"

I squint. "I'm what?"

"Amanda Bishop?" JJ jumps to her feet. "The infamous witch who hornswoggled the great Alexander Remington?" She sounds downright impressed.

Alex slaps his hands over his eyes and sighs. "Her ego is big enough. She doesn't need you to go full-on fan girl over her."

JJ pays no attention to jerk-face. "Well," she says, looking me over. "I can see what clouded his witch-detecting senses."

She's really nothing like any hunter I've ever met. "Thanks?"

She winks. "Never thank me for the truth, sista." Then she ogles jerk-face. "Wanna tell me how I earned a visit from badass Amanda Bishop and her lame sidekick, Alex Remington?"

"Sidekick?" Alex hisses. "You remember who kicked your sweet little butt in the ring last year?"

She nudges me. "I'm gonna let you in on a little secret," she whispers. "I let him win." And that is the truth.

Wow, if she kicked Alex's ass, I don't want to get on her bad side. Yet I have to speed up this reunion. "Look, JJ." I hop on a barstool. "There's no easy way to say this, but this isn't a courtesy visit."

JJ walks behind the bar and grabs three sodas from the fridge. "You don't say." She shoves one bottle toward Alex and the other to me. "The jerk never just *visits*."

Alex narrows his eyes. "That's not true, and you know it."

"It so is," she says to me, popping the top off the soda. She takes a few sips and wipes her red lips. "Okay, I'm ready. What do you want, Remington? More importantly, why are you guys here *together*?"

Alex stares at the whiskey bottles on the dusty shelves. He won't spill the bad news anytime soon. Guys are such pussies.

"Long story short," I say when Alex's lips stay sealed. "Alex has four days until the demon he sold his soul to drags him to hell."

JJ throws her head back and laughs. When she realizes no one's laughing with her, she stumbles back, knocking her hip against the bar. "You serious?"

I nod.

Red-hot rage blazes through her hazel eyes. "You sold your fucking soul?" The panic in her voice is loud and clear.

Alex shoves his hands in his pockets. "Surprise," he says, eyes hooded.

She stalks toward him like a lunatic. Then it happens...*BAM.* She slaps Alex so hard, his head jerks to the right. I don't know what kind of reaction I expected, but it definitely was not that.

"Son of a bitch," she shouts, pulling all eyes to us. "How fucking stupid can you be? Selling your soul, Alex? Really?" Alex's mouth snaps open, but JJ isn't done yet. "You're a fucking hunter. The best I know, and here you are with a ticket to hell?"

Alex stiffens. His eyes grow darker than a forest at nightfall. "You think I don't know what a disgrace I am to our kind? Remember the first thing I taught you?"

She cups her elbows. "Never make a deal with a witch or a demon."

*Alex had certainly done both.*

"Damn right. I broke my own rules, and there's nothing worse than being untrue to yourself. So why don't you quit the judgmental shit, because ain't nobody can bring a harsher sentence on me than myself."

A deep, unforgiving pang hits me in the chest. There's so much hate in Alex's eyes. I think he wants to gut himself.

JJ isn't oblivious to Alex's self-loathing. "I'm sorry," she says, voice soft. "I didn't mean to sound like a dumbass."

Alex rolls his shoulders back and manages a lame smile. "It's okay. I would have slapped you, too."

She raises her brows. "Only difference? I would have hit back."

"Can we get our head back in the game?" I'm pissed. No fucking idea why.

JJ's dazzled eyes lock with mine. "What game? Thought a trip to hell was a one-way road?"

"Usually is," I say, shoving the soda from one hand to the other. "But we found a loophole, and we were hoping you might be able to help us exploit it."

"I'm listening," she says, impatiently.

Alex flings himself onto a barstool and waves JJ's dad over. "Bourbon, please?"

JJ and I both glare at him.

"What?" He rolls his eyes. "I need to be wasted to have this conversation."

"That bad?" JJ asks.

"Worse," he grumbles before he downs the shot JJ's dad passes him.

Chapter 28

We retreat to a table near the windows. Alex and I take turns filling JJ in. She doesn't cut us off, but stares at us as if we've lost our minds somewhere along the interstate when we mention the ritual, and occasionally downs some of the bourbon Alex insisted on bringing along.

Exhausted, I prop my elbows on the table and steady my chin on my folded hands. "That's pretty much all there is to tell."

JJ downs some bourbon and shakes her head. "Do you have any idea how insane all of this sounds?" She leans back, tapping her fingers on the table. "Going on a cross-country trip to find an alleged *soulmate*"—she scrunches her nose at the word—"so she can get him out of a deal God himself can't break?"

I see where she's coming from, but the grimoire has never failed me. "I know it sounds crazy. Believe me, I do. But our only other option is to sit back, buy nachos, and wait for the screening of *Drag Alexander Remington to Hell*."

She pulls her thick ebony hair into a high ponytail and frowns. "All right, let's say this plan isn't complete nonsense, and it could actually work. I'd like to know"—she looks at Alex—"why the fuck I am on that stupid list?"

*That supposed to be a rhetorical question?* I knit

my brows, completely dumbstruck. "Have you met yourself?" I ask, tongue faster than brain. "You're like the R-rated version of Snow White, girl. There's no guy on this planet who wouldn't have put you on his list." Hell, I'd put her on my list.

She laughs. "I think I just fell in love with you."

"Just being honest."

"And I appreciate it. I do. But I don't think good looks qualify for being someone's true love." She inhales sharply. "I mean, come on." Her hazel eyes pierce through me. "You're the chick he couldn't get over. If you're not it, then I doubt I'll be the one."

Alex almost chokes on his own salvia. "You think Amanda is on the list?" His voice trembles with...anger? Disgust? I can't tell.

JJ's eyes go wide. "Sweet baby Jesus." She leans over the table. "Don't tell me the possibility never occurred to you?"

"You high or something?" Alex barks. Valid question. Little Remington rooting for Team Amanda and Alex is one thing. JJ, a hunter who just met me, believing fate could be twisted enough to make natural born enemies star-crossed lovers? That's something entirely else.

"I wish I was high, Alex. Especially after the bomb you just dropped on me. But"—she tilts her chin at me—"after everything I've heard about the two of you, I'm surprised she wasn't the first name on said list."

"After everything you've heard?" I blurt out, shocked. Am I in a parallel universe? She's a hunter. Alex would rather die than have his pals know he'd screwed a witch. I think of the hunters at Lady Amelia's. They, too, sounded as if they knew what went down between us. *Did I miss the Alex screwed Amanda announcement in the* Hunter's Times*?*

JJ peers at me as if I'm from another planet. "You really don't know, do you?"

"What don't I know?" My voice is an octave higher than usual.

"JJ," Alex warns, eyes like flint.

She couldn't care less about jerk-face's threatening tone. "Every hunter on the face of the planet talks about you," she says, looking me in the eye. "*Hello.* A witch saving two hunters? That's like a Christmas miracle without Christmas, like Satan kissing puppies, or—"

"We get the message," Alex growls.

I snap my head in his direction, murder on my face. "Did you know about this?"

His attention stays glued to the bourbon bottle.

"Oh God, you did, didn't you?" I grab the bottle, hoping to drown my wrath. It doesn't work. Being on the radar of freelance hunters because they think I killed a girl is bad news, but *this* is...I can't find words to describe how fucked up it is. Not only do hunters all over the country know I exist, my kind has probably heard of it, too.

JJ reaches over the table and squeezes my hand. "Relax. Most of us think it was pretty heroic what you did." Her face is lit up with a big smile. "You didn't just save Alex and Jesse's asses. Damn, girl, you saved those kids, too."

"Relax?" I hiss, jaw clenched. "Do you have any idea what happens to witches who betray the code? They ain't getting an award for bravery, JJ." They're expelled and shunned at best. Tortured and killed at worst.

Alex drums his fingers against the table. "Always concerned about yourself, huh?" He faces JJ with a smug smile. "May I introduce to you the one and only, selfish, stab-worthy, unlikeable Amanda Bishop. And you're surprised she didn't make it on the list? Think again."

I claw the wooden table before I do something stupid like scratching his fucking eyes out. "You are such an—"

"Asshole," JJ cuts in. Alex's mouth snaps open, but the hunter girl I've grown to adore is on a roll. "Seriously," she says, shooting daggers at him. "We both know you *and* your brother would be dead now if it wasn't for her."

Alex crosses his arms. The grin on his face is gone. "Thanks for reminding me."

JJ straightens. "Know what? It's a damn shame you actually needed a reminder. Maybe someone should tattoo 'Saved by Amanda Bishop' on your forehead. Just in case you forget again." Her hazel eyes blaze. The girl's temper is worse than mine.

*Why am I not gay, again?* Because I have the hots for a guy who acts like I'm the worst creature on the face of the earth, that's why. Fucking shame they don't sell dignity at Walmart. I'd be the first in line.

Alex curls his hands into fists. "You done preaching?"

She's not. Rage flashes in her eyes. I, on the other hand, have heard enough insults for one day. "Let's focus on the real issue," I suggest, not sure why I sound so calm.

JJ's gaze travels over my face. She, too, must wonder why I haven't gone crazy witch-killer on Alex yet. A moment of silence passes. "Sure, let's concentrate on saving a prejudiced jerk-hunter."

*Man, can I marry her?* I smile. "You're really not a typical hunter, are you?"

She inclines her head at Alex. "If that's typical in your book, then no."

"Does that mean we can have your blood?" Being straightforward seems to work best with JJ.

Alex nudges me in the ribs. "Fucking smooth, Manda."

I glare at him, ready to bite his head off. "It's not like we're on a clock or something, right?"

JJ grins from ear to ear. "Sweet baby Jesus, I like that one."

Alex arches a brow. "Of course you do."

"So?" I say, paying no attention to the hostility in Alex's voice. "Are you in or out?"

JJ presses her index finger against her temple. "You seriously think I'd give my blood to a witch so she can do some eccentric ritual that's supposed to determine if Alexander Remington is my soulmate?"

I sigh. "Yep, that's pretty much what I thought."

"Hm."

"Well?"

"Well," she says, getting on her feet. "Do you have a knife?"

I beam at her. "You in?"

She winks at me. "It'll be my genuine pleasure to be the great Amanda Bishop's blood bag. And"—she cocks a brow at Alex—"if we can save him in the process? Well, I guess that's not bad either."

"You guys wanna get a room?" Alex murmurs.

"Don't tempt me, Alex." I had a feeling she was

flirting with me before. Now, I'm certain of it. She faces Alex. "I need a favor, though. Preferably before we get started."

Alex's hunter senses are reeling. I can tell by the excited look on his face. "What's up?"

JJ folds her hands in her lap. "I've been working a bad case. Could use a set of fresh eyes."

"What case?" For a guy who's turned his back at the PAU, he sounds thrilled at the prospect of working a case. Once a hunter, always a hunter, huh?

JJ scans the bar, making sure no one eavesdrops. "You remember Old George?" she asks, once she's sure I-take-a-nap-in-a-bar dude and my-life-is-so-fucked-I-get-wasted-before-noon fella are busy with something else.

Alex nods. "What about him?"

JJ sucks in air. "He's dead. Was killed two days ago."

Alex's eyes almost pop out. "You serious?"

Judging by the look on his pale face, we're stuck here until the curious case of Old George is solved.

JJ scowls. "You think I'd joke about the death of a hunter?"

Perplexed, Alex shakes his head. "What happened?"

JJ's smooth features harden. "A week ago, George comes in shit-faced, as usual. Talks about how he had a breakthrough on a case he worked years ago." JJ points over her shoulder at her dad. "My old man asked him what he was talking about, but George said he couldn't tell anyone, that he didn't know who to trust anymore."

Alex sinks a little in the chair. "What does that even mean? We're all hunters for Christ's sake. If we can't trust each other, then who?"

JJ presses her palms against the table and leans back. "Don't know, man. But George kept saying my dad ought to be careful. That nothing is as it seems. Couple of days later, he was found dead in his cabin." JJ swallows hard. "Slaughtered like a pig, Alex. Never seen anything like it."

"Then what?" I hate my damn curiosity. But something about this story makes the hair on my neck stand, and I'd like to know what caused the creepy sensation.

"I started digging through the old man's files," she explains. "Found at least a dozen cases in which the victim had been killed the exact same way."

"Serial killer?" I ask.

JJ flashes a half-hearted smile. "Unless serial killers are immortal, I doubt that. The oldest case dates back to the eighteenth century."

Alex explodes out of his chair. "You got the files here?" Hunter-heroic is in his element. Nothing is gonna stop him.

"They're at my place."

JJ and jerk-face would make a pretty good match. Both have a heroic streak, both love hunting, and both are smoking hot. They'd have an unconventional life together. Instead of going to the movies or on a date night, they'd probably kill a few witches or kick some demon ass, but they'd never get bored.

Alex is already halfway to the door. "Whatcha waiting for?"

JJ is on her feet in no time. "C'mon," she says to me. "I live right around the corner."

*And be the third wheel at a party?* I don't think so.

Some alone time can't hurt them. It could help re-ignite their old flame.

I examine my chipped nail polish. "I think I've ruined my reputation badly enough. No need to add to the myth of the witch that helps hunters."

Alex shakes his head. "You are—"

"Selfish? Not exactly news." I tilt my head at the door. "Now get the hell outta here and hurry the fuck up. In case you forgot, we're here to save *you*."

"We won't be long," JJ promises. Alex's annoying mouth opens, but she puts a hand on his shoulder and shoves him out the door.

\*\*\*\*

I have no idea what JJ's definition of "not long" is. In my dictionary, it's much less than six hours. The waiting is driving me nuts, and I start to wonder if I should have gone with them.

*Holding the candle while they get all sweaty?*

Who says they're having sex? For all I know, they lost track of time while digging through Old George's files.

*Coming up with lame excuses because you can't handle the truth? It's called denial.*

"Hey," JJ's dad barks from across the bar. "How much longer you gonna occupy my table? I've got paying customers here."

I look around. No one. Even I-take-a-nap-in-a-bar dude and my-life-is-so-fucked-I-get-wasted-before-noon fella fled the sinking ship. Unless his customers are invisible, it's his way of telling me to get the hell outta here. I shouldn't have offered him a lesson in Sicilian ties.

I press a palm against my leg to stop it from

tapping and smile. "Chill, old man. Alex and JJ should be back any minute." Or not.

He casts me a sidelong glance. "Sure hope so. Witches are bad for business."

As much as I like his daughter, I can't stand the guy. Hellbent on staying calm, I pull my phone out of my bag and type a text to B. *How is it going?*

Takes five seconds till my phone rings. "Hey." I sound grumpier than usual.

"You okay?" she asks, already knowing the answer.

"Any news?" A long period of silence follows. Not a good sign. "B?"

Her voice is unnaturally listless. "Good news is I didn't kill anyone while preforming the ritual. Bad news is Sarina is definitely not Alex's soulmate."

My heart drops. "You sure?"

"I did it twice, Amanda."

We're fucked. Sarina and JJ had been our best bets. Now we have to scratch one girl from the list, leaving only JJ.

"Have you guys been luckier?"

Sharp pain slices through my right eye. I put pressure on the eyelid before it turns into a full-blown migraine. "Dunno. We're in Winter Harbor at a bar. JJ's dad owns it. Well, I'm here anyway."

"What do you mean, you are? Where's Alex?"

*Oh, you know, he's off solving some stupid case or screwing JJ.* "He should be back any minute," I say, because the truth infuriates me.

"That Manda?" I hear Jesse say.

"The one and only," Bonnie replies.

"Tell her to wait for us in Winter Harbor. We can

be there in less than twenty-four hours."

"Amanda," Bonnie starts.

"I heard him," I grumble. "But unless you rented the Batmobile, I can't see how you'll be here that fast when it's a fifty-hour drive from Poulsbo." Besides, Alex is going to freak. What was it again he said? I don't want my brother to watch me die?

"We won't drive," Bonnie explains. "We'll catch a plane."

"What about the cops?"

"Let's just say I have a way of convincing people to do what I want."

*Is this a joke?* "You going to use your magic to get you on a plane?"

She sighs. "Listen, we're at the airport booking the tickets. I gotta go."

I'm not sure what to make of my best friend's sudden change of heart. She'd refused to use magic all her life, and now she wants to manipulate a whole airport? "Be careful," I murmur, but she'd already ended the call.

I throw my phone on the table and ogle the half-empty bourbon bottle. *Ah screw it!* If I have to spend hours alone in a hunter bar, I might as well make the best of it. I unscrew the poison and down a good portion. It tastes like crap but warms my cold heart.

"Tough day?" a raspy voice whispers.

I spin. Gunmetal-blue eyes stare back at me. A sexy smile lights up the sinister bar. *Oh my God.* "Bay?" Hot-you're-missing-out-angel-Texas-bartender Bay? "What the hell are you doing here?"

He smiles sheepishly. "Maniac, remember?"

*Right.* He did say he was from Maine.

He runs a hand over his shaved head. "Mind if I join you?"

It's sorta weird to run into the Texas bartender, who told me about the missing kids in Bakersfield, in such a small town as Winter Harbor. I check out his tight blue shirt and his intense eyes. Even weirder that I declined his offer to give him a lesson in dark arts, aka mind-blowing sex.

"Amanda?" He catches me staring.

Heat flushes my cheeks. "Knock yourself out," I say, pointing to the free chair across from me.

He plops down. "What are you doing here, angel? Thought you were headed to Bakersfield."

*Where I almost died, 'cause I had a face-off with a psycho bokor and pervert asshole.* "Got tired of the heat," I state nonchalantly. "What about you? Finally had enough of cowboy boots and sweet tea?"

His rich laughter echoes through the empty bar, making me all sorts of fuzzy. "Nah. I'll never get enough of that shit. Just visiting family."

My eyes go wide. "So you *are* from Winter Harbor?"

One arm on the table, the other thrown over the back of the chair, he nods. "Born and raised here."

I squint. "That's one helluva coincidence, us meeting here."

One side of his mouth curls up. "Is it? A coincidence, I mean."

I raise my brows, not sure where he's going with this. "Got a better explanation?"

"Sure." His grin spreads like an infectious disease. "Fate."

"Fate, huh?"

"There's one more possibility," he says matter-of-factly.

"You haven't been able to get me out of your pretty little head and are stalking me?" I sound like a telephone sex chick.

Bay leans back. "You don't have self-esteem issues, do you?"

"Nope."

He laughs. "Neither do I."

I study his well-formed chest and his very kissable lips. "You don't say." Guys like Bay never lack confidence. Why would they? They're the best the male species has to offer.

"Hey." Bay waves JJ's dad over. "Can we get a bottle of tequila?" The boy didn't just remember where I was headed, he also knows what I drink. Impressive.

The old man's wrinkled face hardens. There's something chilling about the pointed look he gives Bay. He grabs a bottle from the shelf and stomps toward us. "Anything else?" he barks, slamming two short glasses and a bottle of Jose on the table.

Despite the shitty way he's treated, Bay smiles. "Nah, we're good."

"Wait," I say as Mr. Grumpy turns to walk away. "Any chance we could get oranges and cinnamon?"

JJ's dad gazes over his shoulder. "Do I look like I run an organic grocery store, missy?" Before I can come back at him in typical Amanda fashion, he stalks back to the bar.

Bay arches a brow. "Wow, what did you do to him?"

"Ah, you know, just the usual stuff. Ordered bourbon, offered him a lesson in Sicilian ties. Nothing special."

Bay's jaw drops. "You're kidding, right?"

I pour two shots and grin. "I don't do jokes, remember?"

For a split second, Bay stares at me as if I've lost my freaking mind. Then he brings the glass to his lips and smiles. "Cheers to that."

I gawk at the tattoos crawling all over Bay's arm right up to his neck. I hadn't paid much attention the last time I saw him, but now he's so close I get a good look at the weird religious symbols. Runes, crosses, pentagrams, an om—every religion is represented. They look creepily familiar. I swear I've seen them before, but where?

"Like what you see, angel?"

I move the short glass from one hand to the other. "You into religion?" I ask, still trying to figure out why the tattoos ring a bell.

"The truth?"

I cross my arms. "No, Bay. Lie to me."

He leans in. I smell the tequila on his breath. "Girls dig the mysterious-guy look. The tattoos"—he points at his neck—"are responsible for half my fun nights."

"What's responsible for the other half?" I challenge him.

A devilish smile shoots over his lips. "The fact I'm a sexy beast with *incredible* skills."

I fill up his glass. "Ever heard that barking dogs don't bite?"

"This one does," he assures me, voice husky.

I already knew that. Emotion absorbing vacuum cleaner?

Bay leans back, making his chair rise on its two

legs. Balancing precariously, he studies me. "You gonna tell me what brings you to my hometown?"

"We're visiting a friend," I say, tracing the edge of the glass.

He narrows his eyes. "Who's we?"

"A friend and me."

"*A* friend, or boyfriend?"

I like that he's not beating around the bush and smile. "I don't do boyfriends."

A mesmerizing smile plays on his lips. "You know, I'm beginning to wonder where the hell you've been all my life."

*Busy dying for a dude who tried to kill me twice, got me shot once, and lied to me multiple times—that's where.* No more. I'll help Alex out of this deal, watch him ride off into the sunset with JJ, and never ever think about him again.

We kill half the bottle, have plenty of good laughs, and realize our mothers share the How to Make Your Kid's Life Living Hell gene. It seems the only thing Bay and I don't have in common is the dislike for our sisters. Unlike me, the guy adores his. She's also the reason he returned home.

I shove another shot toward him. "You do realize not going to college to piss of your mother is sort of stupid?"

He shrugs. "Yeah, but you should have seen the look on her face back when I told her I'd moved to Texas to serve a couple of old bikers in a fucked-up bar." He holds the glass up and grins. "Priceless."

I kinda know what he means. I would have given my left arm to see my mother's expression when Melinda told her I earned my living by reading cards.

"So what's next for you?"

Bay sighs. "Dunno. Don't care. I take life as it comes."

*Why did I walk out of that bar that night again?* He could have helped me get over jerk-face. Still can.

He brushes a loose strand of hair out of my face. "Amanda?" I look up. "How about that lesson in dark arts now?"

I make one last checkup of Bay before I let him haul my sexy butt out of this shithole. Strong arms that can grab you real tight? Check. Rock-hard chest? Check. Eyes you can get lost in? Check. Lips promising mind-blowing kisses? Check.

What about Alex, though? He'd lose his shit if he came back and I was gone.

*He's probably getting laid by JJ, or why else haven't they returned?*

"Shall we?" Bay's sexy-as-hell voice ripples through me.

I meet his eyes. There's no disgust or hate in them. No regret or disappointment. No you-were-the-biggest-mistake-of-my-life vibe coming my way. *Screw Alex.*

I'm about to say "hell yes" when jerk-face's voice thunders through the bar. "Hey, baby."

*Baby? Oh God, I'm hallucinating.*

A kiss lands on my cheek. "Did you miss me?"

*Oh boy, this is worse than a hallucination.* It's fucking real.

Chapter 29

*Did I miss him?* Like an idiot I stare at Alex. "Were you brainwashed by Hydra while you were gone?" It's either that, or they smoked a freaking bong in JJ's apartment.

The wooden legs from a chair scrape across the floor. Alex moves it as close to me as possible. Then he plunks down on it. Sitting straighter than a freaking candle, he looks Bay over. "We haven't met," he says to him, danger radiating from his eyes. "I'm Alex. And *you* are?" His voice is colder than a bucket full of ice.

Bay's whole demeanor changes in an instant. The muscles in his arms flex, turning them into deadly weapons. His spine is as stiff as iron. "Bay," he murmurs, extending his hand for a shake.

Jerk-face disregards Bay and throws an arm around my shoulders, scooping me against his side. "Sorry we kept you waiting." He speaks to me, but his eyes are fixated on Bay. "Took a little longer than expected."

"No shit," I grumble, still at sixes and sevens as to why Alex treats Bay like his archenemy.

Alex cups my chin, turning my head his way. "Well, I'm here now." He flashes me a cocky-as-hell grin. "You ready to go?"

Alex's lips are inches from mine. I'm scared I'll accidently kiss him if I so much as breathe. I cut my eyes to Bay. He doesn't look amused. I don't blame him. Until a few seconds ago, he was convinced I'd give him a lesson in dark arts. Now jerk-face is here, acting like a freaking caveman, hellbent on protecting what's his—or what he thinks is his.

"Baby?"

*What's with the baby shit?* The last time he called me that, he was a wasted wreck in Bakersfield and tried to hit on me. I scan the bar, searching for JJ. She leans against the bar, an amused smile tugging at the corners of her red lips. My eyes plead with her, begging her to tell me what the fuck is going on. She shrugs and keeps smiling. *So much for girls gotta stick together.*

Alex's grip on my chin tightens. He doesn't hurt me, but the pressure definitely draws my attention back to him. "We're gonna be late if we don't hit the road." His gaze is so fierce I wonder if he's trying to hypnotize me.

I'm still speechless. Bay, however, gets the message loud and clear. Chair legs drag across the floor as he stands. "It's pretty late. I better get going before my mom kicks my ass for missing dinner."

"Yeah, you better get going," Alex mocks him. "We wouldn't want to upset your mom." His malachite eyes pierce mine. "Would we, babe?"

*Enough of the babe shit.* I push Alex's hand away and get on my feet, dead set on keeping my word and getting the hell outta here with Bay. Hadn't reckoned what an asshole jerk-face could be. He circles my wrist and pulls me back down.

Bay eyeballs Alex's hand on my arm. He doesn't like what he sees.

"You do realize you're still here?" Alex grumbles.

Bay sucks in air and walks to the counter. He puts

a twenty-dollar bill on the table and peers over his shoulder. "See you around, angel." Then he's gone.

*Bye, bye, sex. Hello, jerk-face.* Madame Josephine had been wrong. I'm not untouchable. I'm fucking cursed.

Red-hot rage bleeds into my system. "You." I point a finger at Alex. "Explain. Now."

He leans back. "Ladies first," he counters, voice sharper than a butcher knife.

My brows fly up. Is he serious? He wants *me* to explain myself? Yeah, sorry. I might have lost my dignity along the way, but this is a road I'm not willing to go down. Ever. "I wasn't the one acting like a caveman, Alex. You, on the other hand? Wow. You nailed that shit."

He ogles me as if I've committed murder. "I'm acting like a caveman, huh? Well, you're acting like…" He shakes his head. "Throwing yourself at the next best guy? Really, Amanda? It's so pathetic, it's kinda funny."

Every muscle in my body tenses. My fingers itch to leave another goddamn scar on his face. That's exactly what he wants, though. Provoking a reaction, making me mad, so he can dwell in the satisfaction I care about his opinion. *Not gonna happen.* Refusing to play his fucked-up mind games, I smile. "Last time I checked, I could throw myself at whoever the hell I wanted."

He jumps up, knocking his chair over in the process. "Do you even know who that guy is?" He sounds beyond mad.

"Do you?" I counter calmly.

Something close to "I will fucking kill you" passes through Alex's eyes. I don't have to have second-sight to know he's about to throw a fit. Luckily—for him, not me—JJ comes to the rescue. "Guys." She's between us, waving her hands like a white flag. "Can we all pretend to be grownups for a moment?"

"Grownups?" Eyes on the door, I pour myself a tequila shot. "Why don't you tell that to jerk-face, who acts like I'm his fuckin' toy."

Alex yanks the glass out of my hand. *That's it.* I've reached my breaking point, and I'm not sure he realizes what he's in for. Jumping up, I get in his face. "What is your fuckin' problem, Alex? Are you jealous or something?"

He laughs so hard, even JJ's dad stares at him. "Jealous? Because of you and this Bay guy?" He draws closer. His fiery breath slaps my cheeks. His eye shade changes into a much darker seaweed. That's when I notice he, too, has reached breaking point. "Let me make this very clear, Amanda. You can screw whoever you want. The two of us"—he points a finger between us—"we're done. I couldn't care less if you banged the whole town. So don't get confused between me looking out for you and me being jealous." A devilish smile pulls the edges of his mouth up. "Because trust me, I'll only feel sorry for a guy stupid enough to fall for you."

*And here I thought I'd heard it all.* He'd been mean to me. He'd even tried to kill me twice. Never had he humiliated me like this. I wish I could say I'm less pathetic than other girls, that his words didn't hurt like a bitch. I wish I didn't have tears burning in my eyes. But above all this, I wish I could just be done with him.

I close my eyes, allowing a cold smile to form. He doesn't deserve my anger. Hell, he doesn't even deserve my coldness. "You know," I say, meeting his gaze. "I'd say go to hell, but I'm beginning to think it would be too good a place for you."

Alex's mouth snaps open, and JJ grabs him by the jacket and hauls him back. "Enough," she shouts. Her voice is rockier than the Grand Canyon.

Alex pulls back and shoots her a death-glare. "Stay out of this, JJ."

"Stay out of this?" Her cheeks redden with anger. "You think I should stand by while you behave like a fucking asshole? The girl you call selfish, Alex, stands in the middle of a hunter bar, knowing she could get ganked at any time. And for what? Because she believes a chauvinistic asshole like you deserves to be saved? If you had talked to me that way, I would have murdered you myself."

Alex's eyes go wide. His jaw is set hard. "I never asked her to—"

"I said enough," JJ warns, eyes narrow, fists balled. "You did what you had to do. I get that. But instead of acting like a fucking asshole, you could have told her the truth about Bay."

*What truth? And why is everyone acting as if Bay is the source of all evil?*

"Nothing to say?" JJ snaps at Alex.

His gaze drops.

"Classy," JJ spits in his face.

Not a word crosses his lips.

JJ blows out some steam and steps closer to me. "C'mon." Her voice is soft. Her eyes are, too. "Let's get you outta here. I bet you could use some air."

I don't think twice before following her. She kicks the back door open and leads me up some stairs. I'm glad the stairway is dark. I'd hate for her to see my glazed eyes.

When we reach the first floor, she studies me. "You okay?"

I swallow the lump in my throat and put on my best poker face. "He's a jerk."

She doesn't buy my I'm-cool-as-ice act but doesn't question it either. "I know it's not much consolation, but he likes you, Manda." She fumbles a key out of her tight leather pants and unlocks the door. "He likes you a lot," she says.

*Well, he has a crappy way of showing it.*

When I say nothing, she sighs. "C'mon." She walks into a small apartment equipped with a tiny kitchen, a sofa-bed, and an ancient TV. "Some of the bar staff crash here after long shifts. My dad is okay with Alex and you using it for the night."

Alex and me? I look around. There's only one bed. I'll be damned if I share it with him after what he just said.

JJ reads my expression and quickly adds, "You could always stay at my place." She bats her thick black lashes at me.

I heave a sigh of relief and fling myself onto the old sofa. "Thanks." I manage a smile. "I really appreciate it." The only other person who's ever stood up for me like she did is Bonnie.

JJ follows me over to the sofa, sits, and kicks off her killer heels. There's a moment of silence. I get the feeling she's giving me time to catch my breath. "You know he was just looking out for you, right?"

I've spent my whole life looking out for myself. Been my own hero when I needed one. Dried my own tears after I shed them. Nursed my wounds, never expecting anyone's help. I never asked Alex to protect me, and for as long as I'm breathing, I never will.

I melt into the soft fabric of the sofa. "I don't care why he did what he did, JJ. I'm done being his punching bag." Truer words, I'd never spoken. "I might not want him to rot in hell, but I will walk away from this if he dares treat me like that again."

JJ shifts closer. "I don't blame you. I'd have walked away the second he opened his goddamn mouth." She steadies her head with her hand. "But you should know…Bay? He's dangerous, Manda."

A shaky laugh escapes the depths of my tortured soul. Dangerously sexy, maybe. Dangerous as in criminal? No way.

"I'm serious," JJ insists, not a trace of humor in her voice.

I draw a deep breath. "Okay," I murmur, frustrated. "I'll bite. What makes a Texas bartender, here to see his sister, dangerous?"

JJ reaches over, tugging a strand of lose hair behind my ear. It's such a sweet gesture, I almost hug her. Almost. "You should really ask Alex."

I'm too tired to argue. Too vexed to just sit here. "I need some fresh air," I murmur, forcing myself away from the comfy sofa. "Get jerk-face. We'll do the ritual as soon as I'm back."

Chapter 30

I've been standing outside Bobby's Bar for a while, staring at the silvery moonlight slicing through heavy clouds. It's dark, cold, and wonderfully peaceful out here. No jerk-face trying to break me. No JJ determined to defend me. Only me, myself, and the night.

*I won't let anything happen to you...I'll only feel sorry for a guy stupid enough to fall for you...This is how I want to spend the last night of my life.* Correction. Only me, myself, the night, and the fucking voice in my head, reminding me of Alex's dissociative personality disorder. One minute, I'm high off his love. The next, I'm drowning in his hate. I keep asking myself what's wrong with him. How he can be so loving and protective, yet so mean and abusive? What I should ask myself, though, is what the fuck is wrong with me? How can I watch him throw me in the flames over and over? How can I risk everything to protect someone whose hate burns me so fiercely? I can't say what it really is that makes me so pathetic when it comes to jerk-face. I only know what it feels like and, right now, there's a carving fork in my airway, a throwing star in my heart, and blazing fire all over my skin.

I wipe my damp cheeks, hug my jacket tighter to my chest, and think of all the things I've compromised to feel another high. Honor. Dignity. Self-respect. And for what? A guy who loathes my very existence? Someone who thinks he's better because he puts the lives of others before his? Someone who's stupid enough to sell his soul out of false nobility?

*No more!* I've spent too much time dreaming of him calling my name. It's not worth the price. Hell, I'm a dark queen under the control of a white freaking knight, and somewhere along the way, I allowed myself to be foolish enough to believe in heaven and Alex. *No more!* I will not compromise who I am to climb the stairway of heaven and find a locked gate. I will not.

I lean against the brick wall of the bar and draw a long, pained breath. No matter what Alex did or said to me, he doesn't deserve hell. I know that. Yet, I'm no longer willing to pay for his ticket out with my heart.

"Are you sure, love?" a sinister voice calls.

I straighten and stare into the night. The trees across from me are still, but the sound of rattling leaves echoes through the darkness. "Who's there?" I shout, heart exploding in my chest.

A terrifying howl rings through the night. The neon sign above the bar starts flickering. I'm not alone. Someone's watching me. Chills roll over my spine. I see nothing, no one.

*Turn around and run.*

I walk toward the trees. "Who the fuck is there?"

The light of the moon breaks through the branches, falling onto a gigantic shadow. At first, I think it's the shadow of the aspen, but as I step closer, I see the shape is human.

I freeze.

Electricity charges the cold air. The shadow moves closer. "You really think you can let him die, love?"

The creepy voice raises the hair on my neck. I recognize it from my nightmares. It has tortured me for weeks.

Every bone in my body says it's the demon from Rick's Cabaret. The one who rode my best friend. The one who killed six of his kind without mercy. But I need to be sure. "Who. Are. You?"

The shadow cocks its head. "Wrong question. Again."

In my peripheral vision, I watch the light of the neon sign go out. I'm on high alert. "Yeah?" I spit out. "What's the right question, then?"

The thing takes another step in my direction. I get a glimpse of its otherworldly amber eyes. "The right question?" It laughs and draws closer. "I'll give you a little hint. What's your deepest desire? What do you want most in this world, love?"

"None of your fuckin' business," I snap.

It laughs harder. "You truly are one of a kind," it says, looking me in the eye. "Which is why I offer you my help."

"With what?"

"Your greatest fear, love."

I want to run, but I can't move. I open my mouth to scream, but nothing comes out.

An arctic finger touches my third-eye. It feels like death. I'm dizzy. Nauseous. The parking lot fades away. I'm somewhere else entirely.

****

*Alex sat next to Anna. He was fixated on the black smoke coming from the candle that just burned the spell. He was lost. So was his soul. Not that he hadn't known it deep down, but getting confirmation still sucked.*

*"I'm so sorry," Anna said, her hand on Alex's shoulder.*

*He managed a smile he didn't feel. "Don't be. I made my bed, now I have to lie in it."*

*Bonnie let go of the burning spell and looked at Jesse. "It's over." Her voice filled with pain and sorrow.*

*The color drained from Jesse's face. "There must be another way. We could fight the demon. Or—"*

*"No." Alex faced his little brother. "It's done, and you have to accept it." Alex walked toward Jesse. "Promise me you won't do anything stupid."*

*Jesse's whole body was tense. "You mean selling my fucking soul like you did?"*

*Bonnie stood up and reached for Jesse's hand, squeezing it gently. "You don't want to fight with him."*

*"Why not? He's a selfish asshole."*

*Bonnie cupped his cheeks. "That might be true," she said with soul-shattering softness. "But he's still your brother, and this is going to be the last conversation you have with him."*

*Jesse looked from Bonnie to Alex. The rage blowing through him turned into desperation. "Alex, please." Tears streamed over his pale cheeks. "Please don't leave me, man. I'm lost without you."*

*Alex glared at the old clock hanging on the wall. He only had a little more than five minutes. Determined to make the best of it, he pulled his brother into a bear hug. "You're not lost without me, man. Between the two of us, you've always been the stronger one. The one with the heart. It's time you live the life you always wanted. Travel the world. Be whoever you want to be.*

*Don't cry for me. Don't grieve for me. Live."*

*Jesse sobbed uncontrollably. He wrapped his arms around Alex. "I love you, man."*

*Somewhere outside a dog howled. Alex knew what it meant. He pulled back. "I love you, too, little bro. Always remember that."*

*Jesse refused to look at his brother.*

*Alex drew a deep breath and approached Bonnie. "Will you tell her that—" He couldn't say the words. He'd never had the guts to tell her. Now that it was too late, it made him a hypocrite to do so.*

*Bonnie pulled Alex into a tight embrace. "I will. I promise."*

*He smiled and stepped back. Then, as the howling grew louder, he walked out of the house right into hell.*

*The clock struck midnight as unbearable pain pierced through Alex's chest. Sharp teeth sank into his skin. Claws dug into his chest, ripping him apart as if made of cotton. He never saw his assailant coming, but seconds before he closed his eyes forever, he heard a voice. "I hope it was worth it."*

\*\*\*\*

When the vision fades, the thing is behind me, breathing in my ear. "The thought of losing him terrifies you, doesn't it? More so, because you already know you won't find his soulmate in time." I stand still. So does my heart. "Don't worry, love." It traces a shadowy finger down my neck. "I'm here. I can help you save him."

"H-how?" I stammer, not sure why I even speak to the creature.

"Amanda?" JJ's voice sounds distant. "Where are you?"

*Damn.*

The thing moves nearer. "I'm afraid I have to go. Find me when you're ready, and we can discuss terms and conditions."

*No, he can't go yet.* "Find you where?" I spin, looking for the shadow. It's not there. *It was, though.* I'm not crazy. Seconds ago, it spoke to me. Showed me what it believes to be my greatest fear. Taunted me by offering its help to save Alex.

From the corner of my eye, I see JJ running toward me. She scans the area like a hawk. "What in God's name are you doing here by the woods?"

I say nothing.

"Damn, girl." JJ sounds worried. "What's the matter with you? You're paler than my go-go boots."

*She's a hunter. Why does she care?*

"Seriously, what's up? You look like you've seen an evil unicorn."

*I gotta pull it together.* "Nothing." I can hardly tell her the truth. Chances are she'd tell Alex, which would result in a shadow hunt.

She cocks a brow. "Are you sure?"

I nod. "Let's go back inside and do the ritual, okay?"

Chapter 31

Alex stares at the ashes of the spell. "Guess we all knew this would be the result," he says, trying to sound cool about the fact the smoke stayed black. He isn't. I smell his fear. See his disappointment.

JJ pushes the heels of her palms against her eyebrows. "There's still one more name on the list, right?"

*There* is *one more name, but she isn't his soulmate either.*

"Yeah, don't worry about it." Alex sounds casual. "I'm not dead yet."

*But you will be. Soon.*

I think of what the thing said. Y*ou already know you won't find his soulmate in time... I can help you save him, love...Find me when you're ready, and we can discuss terms and conditions.* Terms and conditions sounds one helluva lot like a deal. And find it where? It's not like there's a shadow map on Google. Fuck, why am I even thinking about this? There's no way I'll strike a deal with it.

"Amanda." JJ's sitting on the floor, cross-legged. "You don't look so good."

I force a smile. "Just tired." *Of Alex. Of hope. Of life.*

Suspicion flickers through her eyes, but she keeps her thoughts to herself and faces Alex. "What's next?

Are you heading to the other chick?"

His eyes grow darker. "Jesse texted. They're on their way." He sounds miserable. Not only did the outcome of the spell bring him a step closer to eternal torture, but despite his efforts, Jesse will be present when he takes his last breath. "In the meantime," Alex continues, "we could work on George's case."

My shoulders stiffen. *Work George's case?* He's going to hell, for Christ's sake, and all he cares about is solving the murder of a drunkard? *Obnoxious, arrogant asshole.* What does he think hell is, a freaking cakewalk?

JJ's phone rings. She pulls it out of her pocket and glares at the screen. "Shit," she mutters under her breath. "I gotta go. Will you be okay?" The question is directed at me.

Alex answers. "We're not going to kill each other, if that's what you're asking."

JJ waits for my confirmation. I nod. He's a walking corpse. Why waste time and energy killing him?

"I'll see you first thing in the morning."

"Okay," Alex says the moment JJ shuts the door behind her. "What's the deal with you and your silent act?"

Ignoring the question and him, I amble to my bag to grab a change of clothes.

"Manda?" He strolls toward me, hands in his pockets.

I keep my eyes on the bag, searching for yoga pants.

"Oh, c'mon…" He grins. "Talk dirty to me. I know you want to."

What I want is for him to shut his goddamn mouth

and leave me the hell alone. I throw the yoga pants over my shoulder and make my way to the bathroom.

"Amanda." He seizes hold of my arm. "Are you seriously still mad at me because of that Bay dude?"

"Hands off me. Now," I command, voice sharp.

He works up a magical smile and scrubs his fingers through his hair. "Don't be like that. I did you a favor. The guy just wanted in your panties, or worse, to kill you."

*No more!* The chains of self-restraint break. The beast is unleashed. "You mean like you wanted in my panties before you pointed your Beretta at me?"

He intensifies that smug smile. "You have nice panties."

I wrench out of his grip. "And that's all you ever cared about, huh?" He's startled. Sorry, buddy, I'm just getting started. "Maybe Bay is dangerous. And maybe all he cares about is screwing me." I look him in the eye. "But unlike you, he doesn't treat me like a supernatural abomination. He treats me like a fuckin' human being."

"Human being?" He laughs. "You have no idea who that guy is, Amanda."

I grin. "Funny. Been thinking the same about you lately." Anger claws my gut. He's going to die. I might as well get the shit that's been bothering me off my chest while I still can. "Once upon a time, Alex, I thought you were good, and caring, and honest. Turns out I was wrong. You're just as bad as I am. A selfish liar."

His jaw clenches. "You're calling *me* a liar? Hilarious. Last time I checked, *you* were the one who lied to me."

"What was I supposed to do?" I bark, emotions getting the best of me. "Tell you I'm a witch so you could shoot me right away?"

With one long stride, he closes the distance between us. "You've never given me a real chance, Amanda. First, you lied and then, you walked away, pretending *we* never existed."

"What did you expect me to do? Wait till you changed your mind and pulled that damn trigger?"

"You honestly believe I would have killed you?"

We both know if it wasn't for Jesse, I'd be dead now. "You hated me, Alex. God"—I throw my hands in the air—"you still do. What was it you said again? Ah, yes. 'I'll only feel sorry for a guy stupid enough to fall for you.' "

Throwing his own words back at him makes him flinch. "I was mad when I said that."

A bitter taste crawls up my throat. "You're always mad or drunk when you say stuff like that. But it doesn't change the fact you did." I fold my arms. "The tongue might not have bones, Alex, but it sure as hell knows how to break 'em." I step back. "Know what? It doesn't matter. *You* don't matter. Because as you said, we're done."

I turn and head to the bathroom, ready to lock myself inside if it means I don't have to see his face anymore.

Too bad Alex corners me and pushes me against the door. "What do you want me to say, Amanda? I'm sorry I was looking out for you? Sorry you have the rare ability to make me lose my shit and say stuff I'll later regret?" His malachite eyes lock with mine. "Is that it?"

"No," I spit out. "I don't need your false apologizes, Alex. You've been treating me like shit ever since we met." I straighten. "Guess what? I'm done putting up with your fuckin' mood swings. I'm done putting up with *you*."

A hand lands on either side of my head. "Is that so? Then tell me this: why are you still here? Why don't you just go back to Pony-Boy and your new life? I mean, it's not like you really care about what happens to me."

"Fuck you," I snap as my palm connects with his cheek, leaving the mark of five angry fingers on his face.

For the longest time, he just stares at me. I try to shove him away, but jerk-face stands his ground. Doesn't move a freaking inch.

"Get outta my way, Alex." It's less an order and more a desperate plea.

Jerk-face wouldn't be jerk-face if he listened. Hell, he moves closer. His lips almost touch my cheek. "Did you ever care about me, Manda?" He pauses, exhaling sharply. "Did you ever love me?"

"Love is for children," I shoot back, heart thundering in my chest.

His breathing is shallow, eyes squinted. "That's not an answer."

I bite my lip, hardly able to control the million emotions overwriting my system. "I didn't." I look away. "I don't."

"Liar," he whispers.

I ball my hands, ready to punch him again. "You're a hunter, Alex. I was born to hate you." I barely recognize the coldness of my own voice.

He looks me in the eye and grins.

*Seriously, he grins. What's the matter with him?*

His gaze roams my face. "But you don't. You never did. Wanna know why?"

I tilt my head to the side, trying to escape his eyes. "No."

There it is, the cocky-as-hell grin I've grown to hate. He brushes his thumb across my chin. "Beneath all this attitude, Amanda, you're just a normal girl who wants to be loved. Sure, you pretend to be strong and selfish, but deep down you know damn well this strength you cling to so desperately is weakness." He draws a deep breath. "You're weak, Amanda Bishop. You're a weak little girl who never got over her mommy issues."

My chest tightens. He couldn't have inflicted more pain on me if he'd hit me. "I hate you, Alex." I push him hard. "I fuckin' hate you," I scream, slamming my hands against his chest over and over. "Falling for you was the biggest mistake of my life." Tears break free. "I wish I'd never met you. Wish I'd never gotten in that car with you. But above all this, I wish I didn't still care about you."

He lets me hit him. Doesn't stop me. I keep assaulting him until I drop my hands from exhaustion. "I hate you," I whisper, choking back salty drops. "I fuckin' hate you, Alex."

He cups my chin, looking me deep in the eyes. Then his mouth crashes down on mine. In that fraction of a second, he claims ownership of me, body and soul, and I'm too tired to fight him off. Too exhausted to keep the walls around my heart from crumbling. Too broken to refuse his healing lips. Because he's going to hell, and there's nothing I can do about it.

He dives inside, swirling the tip of his tongue against mine.

I breathe hard between the kisses, savoring the feel of his tongue against mine. Moaning, I put my arms around his neck as I kiss him back, sucking on his bottom lip and longing for more.

For a second, he pulls back. "I love the way we hate," he whispers, grabbing a fistful of my hair and pulling my head back. He trails kisses down my throat, taking his sweet time with every spot.

I close my eyes, aware of wetness between my legs. God, I feel higher than a kite as he grazes my bottom lip with his tongue. Yeah, I'm doing it again. I compromise myself to feel another high. Throw all my dignity out of the window to feel Alex just one more time. But I don't care. There's no love admission tonight, but I'll let him take this from me, 'cause it feels right.

Hands on my hips, he lifts me, pushing me against the door.

I wrap my legs around his marvelous body. When he kisses me again—like there's no tomorrow, like the world around us could burn to ashes, and we wouldn't know it—I forget everything else.

Alex slides his fingers down my chest, grabs the hem of my shirt, and pulls it over my head. "You have no idea how badly I want this." His voice is hoarse and sexy.

His hardness presses against me. A rush hits my belly, and the pulse between my legs pounds harder.

Alex rests his forehead against mine. "How badly I want you."

My lips land on his. We kiss, and there's nothing sweet or gentle about it. It's rough and angry.

I tug at his shirt and pull it over his head. I unbuckle his belt.

He carries me to the bed, his chest rising and falling with excitement and longing. He steps out of his jeans. Then he's straddling me, working on the buttons of my jeans while his tongue travels down my belly.

My jeans are gone. My panties are soaking wet.

I arch my back, relishing his lips on my skin. There's no doubt in my mind. What we have is sick and twisted. Wrong for all the right reasons, but as long as the wrong feels so right, I'm in flight. I pinch my heel against his delicious ass and pull him closer.

"Tell me what you want, Manda," he orders, shoving his hand into my panties. "Say it," he demands, flicking my pearl.

I dig my nails into his back and open my legs, inviting him in. "You, Alex." I shove his boxers down, freeing his impressive length. "I want you," I admit, rubbing the tip.

"I know," he says, massaging harder.

Fireworks explode in my belly, setting me on fire. I put my hands on his chest, push him off, and climb on top of him. I tease his erection with my tongue.

His eyes roll back in pleasure. "Fuck." He lays back, enjoying the pleasure my mouth gives him. He's close, but it ain't gonna happen yet.

I get up and step out of my panties.

He cusses under his breath as I sit on his hardness. His length fills me perfectly, stretching every muscle inside me.

"Oh God," he mutters as I ride him. Slow at first,

then faster, harder. The sound of our bodies pounding against each other echoes through the apartment. The world around us ceases to exist.

"Manda," he whispers, cupping my breasts, pinching my nipples so hard I almost scream. "What the fuck are you doing to me?"

I'm completely out of breath.

Alex wraps his arms around my waist, and with one swift move, he changes our position. I lie on my back. He dives inside and rocks my world. My boobs bounce like a fucking yo-yo.

"Don't stop."

He increases the tempo. "You're killing me."

Our eyes meet. The sweat on his forehead, along with that cocky to-die-for grin on his lips hits me in the heart. I've missed this. I've missed him.

He pushes into me, forceful enough to make my eyes flutter, my heart stop, and my body shatter into a million pieces.

"Fuck," he mutters, coming undone.

For a while, Alex stays on top of me. Then he rests his head on my chest, allowing me to run a hand through his hair. Time passes. No one speaks. No one moves. We hardly even breathe.

After what feels like a lifetime of silence, Alex rolls onto his side. "Manda?"

"Hm?" I murmur, looking at the ceiling.

He traces kisses down my collarbone. "I really do love the way we hate."

I close my eyes and let him pull me close. The heat radiating from his body warms my heart. Knowing he'll die freezes my soul.

Chapter 32

*Three days to hell*

When I wake up, I don't smell coffee, scrambled eggs, or bacon. I inhale the unmistakable scent of regret. I want to stay in bed, keep my eyes closed, and forget last night ever happened. I learned a long time ago to face my mistakes. To never run from what I did, 'cause at some point—when you least expect it—shit comes back, biting you in the ass. It's better to deal with whatever crap you've produced *before* it turns into karma.

I slowly blink my eyes open. The space next to me is empty. Alex sits at the small kitchen table, nose buried in the files he got from JJ. "Morning," he says as I throw the blankets away and sit up. "Sleep well?"

"Yeah," I murmur, totally aware he's staring at my back. "You?"

Alex's footsteps echo through the room. Moments later, he presses his full lips against my alerted skin. "Better than in a very long time."

He trails kisses down my neck. My heart skips several beats. Geez, what's with him? Shouldn't he be all what-the-fuck-did-I-do, rather than can-we-pick-up-where-we-left-off?

I lean down and grab my clothes from the floor. The ones I can find. "I need a shower," I choke out, walking to the bathroom.

Alex stands in front of me in no time.

*Quick son of a bitch.*

"Manda," he says, cupping my chin. "There's something I gotta say."

"What?" I didn't mean to snap at him, but my emotions are all over the place. I can't think straight.

He smiles. "I…"

*Should have never screwed you?*

"We…"

*Made a mistake?*

Some of the mischievous sparkle of last night is back in his gaze. "I'd do it again," he finally says.

My eyes go wide. My freaking jaw drops to the floor. I'm that close to asking him if he screwed out his brain cells last night when a loud knock on the door makes me jump.

"Alex? Manda?"

*JJ. Great.*

Alex ignores her. "Would you?"

"I—"

"Alex?" JJ yells louder. "You in there?"

She's probably going to barge in any second, and I'd rather not have her see me naked. "I gotta take a shower," I say, pulling away and slamming the bathroom door behind me.

I stay in there for as long as I can, letting the hot water wrinkle my skin. Looking like a granny is definitely better than coming face to face with Alex. To be completely honest, I even consider running. I mean, *I'd do it again?* How the fuck could he say something like that when we both know it was a mistake? *People do strange things when death knocks on their door.*

Yeah, I shouldn't take it too seriously. I'm pretty sure he'll change his mind about it *if,* and that's a big *if,* he makes it out of this alive.

Not in the mood for makeup, I get dressed and twist my wet hair up in a bun, securing it with more than a dozen bobby pins before I unlock the bathroom door.

"Hey," JJ says, a stupid grin on her face as I stumble into the living room. "Thought you drowned in there."

They both stare at me, and I kinda wish I had drowned. "Whatcha doing?" I ask, trying to change the topic.

Alex hovers over a stack of files. "Trying to figure out what George found that got him killed and how your boy, Bay, is involved in all of this."

I blow out a frustrated breath and stroll toward them. "So we're back on the Bay is dangerous track, huh?"

JJ shoves cold coffee my way. God, I hate the way she looks back and forth between Alex and me. It's obvious she knows what went down last night.

"He *is* dangerous," Alex murmurs, pointing to a few crime scene photos laid out on the table. To say the pictures are gruesome would be trivialization. All the victims died the same way—ripped torso. *Like Mister Sinister.* Whatever killed them also left a mark—a sigil. My money is on demons.

I take a sip of the delicious black gold and lean against the table. "Look, I get it's weird that these people were slaughtered like pigs and all, but to me it looks like a demon is responsible. And while it may be a super-freaky coincidence, the guy who pointed me toward the missing kids in Bakersfield is now here, it doesn't mean he's a demon."

"He what?" Alex's voice has a deadly ring to it.

Shit, I never mentioned that, did I? "Remember that night in Texas when I hit a bar and slept in the car?"

Alex nods.

"Bay was the bartender. He told me all about the missing kids."

Alex's eyes narrow. "And you didn't think to tell me?"

I cock a brow. "Why would I? It's not like you and I were on great speaking terms back then. Besides, Bay isn't a killer."

Alex pushes his chair back and presses his hands against the table. I think he tries not to strangle me. "You barely know the man."

I frown. "I'm a witch, remember? I can read people...Sense evil." Well, I could read people. I didn't exactly sense the demons at Rick's Cabaret, but still.

"Ever thought the fact you like him clouds your witch judgment?" He sounds angry. Furious, to be exact.

My mood is already lower than low, and him yelling at me doesn't help at all. "This is ridiculous," I snap. "My judgment is fine, but you might wanna check your hunter senses."

JJ rolls her eyes. "Don't you think it's time you tell her the truth, Alex?"

I fold my arms and eyeball her. "Why do I get the feeling I'm missing something here?"

Alex shakes his head. "Doesn't matter."

"The hell it doesn't, Alex. I put my whole life on

hold. I think I deserve the fuckin' truth."

JJ gives me a look I can't quite read. "She's right." She glares at Alex. "Either you tell her, or I will."

Alex draws a deep breath and scrubs a hand over his face. "You guys are killing me." Moments go by before he speaks. "Bay…"

"Yeah?"

He fists his hair. "Well, he's…"

JJ sighs. "He's a hunter, Manda."

My knees go weak, and my breath catches in my throat. "He's…a…hunter?" I shake my head. "Impossible. I would have sensed it." My witch senses might be a little rusty lately, but back in Texas they worked just fine.

Alex threads his fingers through mine. "Manda." His voice is so serious my heart starts racing. "Bay isn't a witch hunter."

I squint. "He's not?"

JJ is on her feet, too. "You've seen the tats on his arm, right?"

I think of the religious symbols and nod.

Alex scoops two fingers under my trembling chin. "Those tats are the mark of the Malleus Maleficarum Order."

Last time I checked, Malleus Maleficarum was a book, more commonly known as *Hammer of the Witches*. Some German dude wrote it in 1486 as a prosecution guide for witches. He pretty much unleashed hell on earth for my kind with that crap.

JJ flings herself on the table. "Long story short: it's a secret hunter organization, specializing in killing Knights of Hell. But the sons of bitches are reckless and never show mercy."

Alex's eyes lock on mine. "They're not like us, Manda." He pauses. "Last year, they killed a whole coven in Kansas because they believed they worked with a demon."

"It was a massacre," JJ adds. "They didn't even stop at the kids."

My chest tightens. "Are you serious?"

Alex squeezes my hand. "I once ran into their leader." His expression darkens. "A dude everyone calls Legend. Let me tell you, he ain't playing around."

*Legend?* Oh. My. God. That's why the tattoos on Bay's arm looked so familiar. Legend, the customer who stalked me, had the same markings. I remember what he'd said to me at the Landmark. *I have a business proposition for you.* Then I hear Jesse's voice. *Carter said a couple of hunters are looking for you.* Man, I am so fucked.

"What do you think he wants from me?" My voice comes out broken.

Alex shrugs. "I don't know, Manda."

I look at JJ. "No idea," she says. "But they have no honor. They kill everything standing between them and a demon."

"They might have killed George, too," Alex explains.

I stomp to the nightstand and grab the keys to the Mustang.

"Hey," Alex yells as I'm marching to the door. "Where do you think you're going?"

I tighten my death-grip on the doorknob. "I'm going to find Bay."

He blocks my path. "The hell you will," he barks, hand around my wrist. "You'll get yourself killed."

I give him a look. "Let. Go." I've been in the dark too long. It's about time I step into the light again.

"Okay." He knows there's no going back once I make up my mind. "But you're not going alone. I'm coming with you."

Arguing with him would be pointless. I yank the door open. "Let's go then."

JJ laughs. "Alex?"

He peers over his shoulder.

"Sure she ain't your soulmate?"

I fight the urge to hit her and walk outta there before I hear his most definitely insulting answer.

Chapter 33

Winter Harbor has a population of one thousand. In such a close-knit community, it was a piece of cake to find Bay's family home. I park the car down the street and glare. There are exactly five houses, and they all look alike. Nice fences, overwhelming Christmas decorations—I'd been ignoring the season until now—and white paint. The dude lives in *Pleasantville*. Isn't that just fan-freaking-tastic?

Alex rubs his jaw. "You sure about this?" he asks as we approach the porch. "This could be a trap."

I'm not sure about anything anymore, so I ignore the question and ring the bell.

In my peripheral vision, Alex reaches for his Berretta. *What's he gonna do? Shoot a fellow hunter?* "Alex, put that—"

The door swings open and a sweet, blue-eyed girl looks up at us. She's the spitting image of her brother—same eyes, same irresistible smile—but instead of a shaved head, she has long blonde curls and tattoo-free skin.

Alex shoves his Berretta back in the holster and frowns. *This* hunter obviously does have issues with killing innocent kids.

"Can I help you?" Her voice is so sweet she sounds a bit like Laa-Laa from the *Teletubbies*.

I wipe sweaty palms on my jeans. "We're looking

for Bay. Is he home?"

"Sure." She pivots. "Bay! You've got visitors."

Bay is in the hallway in no time. I ogle his bare chest and low-hanging jeans. Malleus Maleficarum Order member or not—the guy is mesmerizing.

"Amanda?" He sounds surprised. "What are you doing here?"

"We"—I point my head at Alex—"need to talk to you."

"Come on in," his sister says, eyeballing Alex as if he's the cover model of *Seventeen* magazine.

Bay narrows his eyes at jerk-face. He's not happy about his sister's offer but approves nevertheless. "You heard her."

Alex goes first, shielding me from Bay. There's nothing like seeing hunter-heroic in action. I tread on his heels like a moron.

Bay's hand lands on his sister's shoulder. "Sunny." She looks at her brother. "Why don't you check on the lasagna? Mom will freak if we let it burn."

Sunny doesn't want to leave. She'd much rather stare at Alex a little longer. The girl has taste.

"Now," Bay orders, realizing his sister crushing hard on jerk-face.

Her angelic expression darkens. "You sound just like Mom," the kid complains and stalks away.

Bay waits till she's gone then waves us over. "Follow me." He leads us to a small living room. There's a lit fireplace, a cozy sofa, and plenty of unnecessary Christmas decorations. Nothing in here suggests the guy is a crazy, kid-killing lunatic. Then again, Walter's lake house didn't scream child-pornography-ring-dungeon either.

Bay blocks the exit. "To what do I owe the pleasure?"

*Now what?* I can't just ask him if he's a freaking demon hunter, can I? I look at Alex for help, but he shakes his head, as if to say "don't look at me this was your idea."

"Amanda?" Bay's clearly not the patient type. "Want to tell me why you're here?"

I look him in the eye. The dude lied to me and probably stalked me. No way he gets to play the clueless card. "I think you know exactly why we're here, Bay. Or should I say, *demon hunter*?"

Alex's gaze flies to me. "One day," he mumbles, hand on his gun, "that mouth of yours is going to get us both killed."

Bay is rigid. He sorta stares at me as if I just walked out of *Halloweentown*. "I-I—"

"You what?" I bark, balling my fists. "You thought I wouldn't get to the bottom of your little charade?"

His shoulders sink. "It's not what you think."

I laugh. "Oh really? 'Cause right now I'm thinking you and your pal, Legend, are tailing me."

Alex's mouth snaps open. "What?"

I didn't want Alex to know about any of this. It's too late, though. "That Legend dude approached me in New York," I say. "Said he had a business proposal for me." I face Bay. "I'm beginning to think that was a whole lot of bullshit. Especially since I heard a bunch of hunters are out looking for me."

The blood drains from Alex's face. "How do you—"

"Carter," I mutter. "He told Jesse."

"Why the fuck didn't you tell me?" Rage flames in

Alex's eyes.

I frown. "Dunno, Alex. Maybe because I figured you had enough on your plate."

"Enough on his plate?" Bay interrupts. The guy is brave, considering Alex and I are on the brink of killing someone.

I snap my head in Bay's direction. "You don't get to ask questions, understand?" Alex opens his mouth, but I cut him off. "And you don't get to scold me for not telling you everything when all you did was lie to me. Are we clear?"

They stare at me like little boys.

"Now," I say, pointing a finger at Bay. "You better tell me what this is all about before I show you what real witches have up their sleeves when they're mad."

Bay brushes a hand over his shaved head. "It's complicated."

*I swear, I'm gonna throw punches at the next person who says "it's complicated."*

Alex's grip on his Beretta tightens. "Answer the question."

Bay arches a brow and grins. "Or what?"

He shouldn't have said that. Messing with Alex never ends well. "Or I'll make you."

Every guy with a brain would do as Alex says. Bay, however, stretches his brawny body. "Think I'm scared of you, Remington?" He sounds relaxed, but the look on his handsome face screams slaughter.

I stop the two testosterone-fueled idiots. "Drop it." I eyeball Alex. "I can fight my own battles, thank you very much."

Bay throws his head back and laughs. "Hear that, Remington?"

I narrow my eyes at demon-hunter-idiot. "Shut up and answer my goddamn question, Bay."

It's then he understands how fucking mad I am. He exhales sharply. "It's a long story, Amanda."

"The short version will do."

Alex laughs. "Hear that, moron?"

"You know," Bay says, a smile creeping into his hard features. "I've heard you're an asshole, Remington, but your reputation doesn't do you justice."

Like the demigod who owns a freaking hammer, Alex curls his hands, ready to punch Bay in the face.

*Gosh, what is it with guys and their fucking ego trips?* I give Alex a shove. "Stop." I glare at Bay. "Both of you. Or I swear I will put a fucking love hex on the two of you. Let's see if you still want to kick each other's asses then."

They both freeze. They look terrified. Most importantly, they shut their arrogant hunter traps.

A victorious smile rolls over my lips. "Now that we all know who's the boss..." I look at Bay. "You better start telling the truth. We witches aren't exactly known for patience."

"All right." Bay looks over his shoulder. "But not here. There's something you need to see."

Alex throws his hand on my shoulder. "The hell she'll follow you."

"Dude." I face him. "I can totally speak for myself." Then I look at Bay, who's grinning as if he wants Alex to lose his temper. "Show me what?" I ask, trying to break the eye-battle between the guys.

"You'll see." Bay walks toward the hallway.

He leads me up the stairs to the attic. Of course, hunter-heroic is right behind me. "This is a stupid idea," he mutters under his breath.

*Tell me something I don't know.*

We walk into a beautifully decorated room. Usually, attics are creepy. This one looks like a room in Buckingham Palace—flowers everywhere, an antique sofa in the center, white chiffon curtains at the window. There's an automatic coffee maker, for Christ's sake.

"Told you my mom is a neat-freak," Bay says when he sees the startled expression on my face.

*At least he didn't lie about that.*

"Cut the crap and tell us what we're doing up here." Alex is mad at Bay, mad at me, mad at himself 'cause he didn't haul my butt outta here when he still could.

Bay flings himself on the couch and pats the empty spot next to him. "I won't bite," he assures me.

I stay where I am. Far, far away from demon-hunting, lying-idiot Bay. "You've got two seconds before I *make* you tell the truth."

"I have no idea where to start," Bay grumbles.

"How about at the beginning?" Alex suggests, voice dangerously low.

Bay pays no attention to jerk-face. Instead, he locks his gunmetal eyes on mine. "Just to be clear, Amanda. I didn't follow you."

I laugh. "It was a coincidence you showed up here after your boss approached me in New York and a couple of hunters put out an APB on me?"

His already hard face turns to marble. "I'm not lying." He eyeballs Alex. "I'm here because of what had happened to old George. The last thing I expected was meeting you guys here."

I can't read his aura, but his voice is even. Not a

trace of deceit in it. "Keep going," I order with a queen-like hand gesture.

Bay gets on his feet and saunters to a desk near the round window. "I need to show you something."

He points to the desk. It's covered with newspaper articles. Some are recent, others date back decades. I scan the articles. They're all about weird animal attacks. "What's this?"

"Just read them."

I plop down on the chair and skim through them. *Torn ribcage, weird carvings in the chest...* They basically tell the same story.

Bay shoves an old book under my nose. "Now look at this."

Alex spies over my shoulder. "Hellhounds?" He laughs. "Are you serious?" Bay and I stare at him, but he continues, unimpressed. "They don't exist. Everyone knows they're just a myth."

"Actually," I say, meeting Alex's malachite gaze. "That's not completely true."

He narrows his eyes at me. "Are you fucking kidding me?"

Bay cocks a brow and smirks. "Sorry, pal, but she's right. Hellhounds do exist. Been hunting them for a while now."

I don't know what surprises Alex more, that hellhounds exist, or Bay claiming he's been hunting them. He crosses his arms. "All right, let me get this straight. You're a member of the Malleus Maleficarum Order, but instead of hunting Knights of Hell, you're hunting hellhounds?" Alex shakes his head. "This gets more absurd by the second."

"Alex," I warn as I see the pained expression on

Bay's face. "Why don't you just shut up for a second and let him explain?"

He holds up his hands. "Sorry, it's just"—he looks Bay over—"the thought of a guy like him hunting *hellhounds*? Hilarious."

Bay's jaw clenches, but instead of buying into Alex's jerk-act, he faces me. "A hellhound killed my dad," he says.

Alex raises his brows. "Come again?"

Bay presses his hip against the desk. Something incredibly sad passes through his shiny eyes. "I wasn't joking when I said my mom is like yours, Amanda."

"You told him about your mother?" Alex barks as if that's the most important thing right now.

I flip him off and focus on Bay. "Ignore him."

Bay cuts his gaze to Alex and grins. "With pleasure." He runs the heels of his hands over his eyebrows and sighs. "Anyway. The woman loves everything expensive and treasures her reputation above everything else. When my dad lost his job, and the bank was close to taking away our house, she completely freaked. Threatened to divorce him and take us with her." The pain in his eyes is real and heart-wrenching.

Jerk-face takes a seat on the arm of the chair. The smug expression on his face is gone.

Bay draws a pained breath. "One night, Dad went to this bar. I guess he needed some space from my mother." He shrugs. "Or maybe he just needed to get drunk. A weird guy approached him, said he could help him fix all his problems. All he wanted in exchange was his soul." The lines around Bay's eyes deepen. "The funny thing is, my dad never believed in the supernatural. The guy was the most rational person I've ever met, but with my mom breathing down his neck and the prospect of losing his kids, he took the chance."

Alex sighs. "Then what happened?"

Bay starts pacing the room. "My dad signed the deal. A year later, I found him in his bed. Dead. Slaughtered. The sheriff thought a wild animal somehow found its way into the house. Not that far-fetched, considering where we live. But when I went through his stuff after the funeral, I found his diary. He'd written it all down."

"It sucks what happened to your dad, but what has any of this to do with me?"

Bay pulls himself onto the desk. "Everything and nothing, Amanda."

My head hurts. "Could you be more cryptic?"

"When I was eighteen, I left Winter Harbor, looking for the demon who did this to my dad. That's pretty much how I met Legend and how I ended up in the Malleus Maleficarum Order."

"You thought they could help you track down the demon that brokered your dad's deal?" Alex asks.

Bay nods. "They taught me everything I know about demons and how they use hellhounds to reap their souls."

"I still fail to see what I have to do with any of this."

Bay catches my eye. "Look, Amanda, I don't know much. But you were right about one thing: the Order *is* looking for you. They sent out a text to every hunter in the country."

"A text?" I almost laugh. "What, don't they have a secret Morse code or something?"

Alex shoots daggers at me. "That's not funny,

Manda."

"He's right."

*Wow, did Bay just say Alex is right?* Maybe I'm in deeper shit than I realized.

"The Order thinks a Knight of Hell wants you. Legend went to New York, hoping you'd help him." He takes a deep breath. "You disappeared. Now every member has the same mission—kill you before the demon gets his hands on you."

Alex jumps up like a crazy person and grabs Bay by the collar of his shirt. "What did you just say?"

I almost expect Bay to punch him. Instead, he gives Alex an apologetic look. "Relax, man. I'm not going to touch a hair on her pretty head. Haven't told anyone she's here either."

"Relax?" I shout, exploding out of the chair like a rocket. "You just said some merciless hunters are out there trying to kill me, Bay. And why? Because they believe some stupid Knight of Hell is looking for me?"

"It's more than that," Bay says. "You're an untouchable, Amanda. If a Knight of Hell gets his hands on you, there's no way of knowing what would happen."

Alex lets go of Bay's shirt and stumbles back. I wait for the "what is an untouchable" question. It never comes.

I'd ask why he isn't surprised about this tiny little detail, but I've got more important things on my mind. "How is it that everyone knew I was untouchable before I did?"

"Look." Bay walks toward me. "I don't know how they know, but they do. And if you're smart, you'll leave the country *ASAP*."

I have a hard time wrapping my head around any of this. Bay being some sort of hunter, a secret order pining for my sweet little ass, Alex going to hell. Seriously, what the hell is this? A freaking horror film? *You forgot the Knight of Hell.* Right, how could I leave out the part where a lunatic demon wants me to do…Hell, I don't even know why the thing wants me. But I start to connect the dots, and I'm pretty sure said Knight of Hell was the one who saved me from the other demons. The one who said he could get Alex out of his deal.

"You okay?" Alex asks, concerned.

"No, Alex. I'm not okay." He reaches for my hand, but I pull back and glare at Bay. "Did you know I was a witch when we first met?"

He nods. "When I saw you in that bar, I didn't just know *what* you were. I knew exactly *who* you were."

"What?" Alex and I say at the same time.

Bay cocks a brow at Alex. "Word between hunters travels fast." He smiles and faces me. "When I saw the legendary Alexander Remington, who, by the way, is an even bigger asshole than I thought, parked in front of the motel—"

"Careful," Alex warns.

Bay rolls his eyes and continues. "Whatever. When I knew who *he* was, it didn't take much to figure who *you* were. Why do you think I told you about those kids? I'd heard of his brother and picked up on a rumor he'd gotten himself in trouble with the person responsible for the missing kids. Besides, they said the almighty Remington would never ride with a witch unless her name was Amanda Bishop."

Alex rubs his jaw. "And who is they?"

Bay smiles. "Let's just say your relationship is the most discussed topic in the hunter community."

Alex narrows his eyes. "What relationship?"

Bay eyeballs him. "You're saying you didn't sleep with her?"

Alex sighs. "Sure I did, but that doesn't make us the next hunter fairytale."

I frown. Last night Alex insulted me, screwed me, and now he acts as if Bay told him he's been sleeping with Satan's bride? "You're right," I say to Bay. "He *is* an asshole."

"I'm right here," Alex barks.

"Good," I mumble. "Means you definitely heard me."

"I should have told you what I am." Bay grins. "But I liked you, and witches generally hate hunters. Especially Malleus Maleficarum hunters."

Alex's shoulders suddenly stiffen. "All right, can we skip the part where you hit on her and get right to the part where you tell us why you haven't called your hunter pals yet?"

Bay shrugs. "As I said, I happen to like her."

My phone vibrates with a text from B. *At Bobby's. Where the fuck are you?*

*On our way*, I reply before shoving the phone back in my pocket. I slowly rise from the chair. "We gotta go. B and Jess are at Bobby's."

Alex nods.

I head to the door. "And Bay?" I say, looking over my shoulder. "I'd appreciate if you wouldn't call your Order pals."

"I won't," he promises.

"That better be the truth," Alex warns.

Chapter 34

The second Bonnie lays eyes on me, she knows something is up. "Oh, shit. You look like crap." JJ and Jesse sit next to her, nodding in agreement.

I shove my hands in my pockets and sigh. "Why, thank you, B. Nice to see ya, too."

She hops off the grungy barstool and walks toward me. Her cognac eyes roam my face. "Seriously, have you slept?"

"Probably not," JJ says, flashing me an "I know what you did last night" smile.

Immediately, Jesse picks up on it. "No way. Really?"

I clench my teeth, ready to tell them to go to hell, but Alex barrels through the doors. He walks straight to his brother and gives him a hug. "Good to see you, man."

Jesse studies the both of us. "What did we miss?" A deaf man could hear the undertone in his voice.

Alex shoots me a look.

I avert my eyes. My head still reels with information I can't seem to make sense of. The whole fucking world knows I'm an untouchable, some high-ranking demon wants me, a creepy Order has put a reward on my head, and Alex is going to hell. Good times.

Bonnie squeezes my arm. "Amanda, what's going

on with you?"

Alex's forehead is wrinkled. A sharp breath escapes his throat. "She's in trouble," he says.

JJ, Jesse, and Bonnie wait for an explanation, but I spin on my heels and head to the restrooms.

I press my hands against the sink and glare at my reflection. Bonnie was right, I do look like crap. My skin is raw and dry, the bags under my eyes are worse than ever, and my eyes are more brown than green. They often changed color when I was a kid. Grams used to say they reflected my emotions. If that's the case, brown means total bamboozlement.

I should focus on Alex and his problem, but I need to wrap my head around the reality that I've become the bull's-eye for a Knight of Hell and the Malleus Maleficarum Order. As a witch, I know damn well there's no such thing as coincidence. Alex being attacked before his time was up, him showing up at my place to ask for help, which then resulted in Legend putting an APB out for me, and on top of that, the demon who's gunning for me, offering his help? Call me crazy, but it sure as hell sounds as if all of this is part of something bigger.

I dig through my bag, searching for the card Legend had given me when we last met. It takes a while till I find it. When I pull it out, I'm not sure what to do with it. Bay didn't lie when he said his boss wants me dead. He must know what's happening to me. Maybe he can help me understand how my life turned from bad to freaking nightmare in a matter of days. Maybe he knows how we can save Alex. But isn't it pretty stupid to call the sheriff, even if you didn't shoot the deputy?

*It's not like he can kill me through the phone,*

*right?*

There's a good chance Legend knows more about the demon who claimed he could get Alex out of his deal. Not that I contemplate accepting a demon's help, but it would be good to know who I'm dealing with.

I put Legend's card on the sink and splash cold water in my face. "You got this," I assure myself. After what feels like forever, I suppress the gut-wrenching feeling in the pit of my stomach and dial Legend's number.

Every time the phone rings, my heart beats a little faster. I'm diverted to voicemail. "In case of an emergency, call Daryl—"

I hang up. I might have lost my marbles, but no way I'll call that Daryl dude. There must be another way to get to the bottom of this. A spell maybe? *I don't even know what I'm dealing with here.* What about a vision quest? *Haven't I had enough visions lately?*

Ah, fuck! I slam my fist against the wall, tearing the skin around my knuckles. Blood spills from the cuts. Pain shoots through my hand. *Awesome.*

"Amanda?" Bonnie's voice startles me. She's standing in the doorway, staring at me. "What the fuck are you doing?" She rushes toward me. "Wait," she says, opening the faucet and shoving my bleeding hand under the cool water. "Let me help."

*Let. Me. Help.* I remember the strip club and the demon who took over Bonnie's body. What had it said? *All in good time?* Guess the time has finally come.

A creepy smile crosses my lips. "Help, huh? Well, I could sure use your *help*."

Bonnie's jaw drops, and she freezes. She so knows I'm not talking about my hand. "What's going on?" Her voice trembles.

"You won't like it."

She shakes her head. "I already *hate* it."

\*\*\*\*

*Two days to hell*

It's past midnight when I get back from the occult shop in Farmington. I didn't do the 139-mile drive for fun. Hell, no. I needed some supplies, and it turns out Winter Harbor isn't exactly equipped for voodoo rituals. I've got the herbs and candles from the Enchanted Herbs & Botanical store in Farmington, and the cat bones…well, they were a bit harder to acquire. Good thing Winter Harbor has a pet cemetery, 'cause no way in hell I'd kill an innocent animal. Not that digging up the grave of the poor thing was any better, but at least the cat was already dead.

I stumble back into the bar, half frozen from the cold. The gang is gathered around a table. Guess they're working on George's case. Bay is there, too. He brought a box full of files and books. I'd be mad as hell at all of them, considering we should be on our way to Anna by now, but since I'm 100 percent sure she isn't our solution, I keep my mouth shut.

"Look who's back," Alex snaps. He's pissed at me. The only way I could get out of the bar without raising too much suspicion was claiming I needed a break from all the hunter crap.

Bonnie glares at jerk-face. "Leave her alone." Despite everything I've asked of her, and the fact she went all I-want-to-beat-the-fucking-crap-outta-you on my ass, she still stands up for me. I don't deserve a friend like her.

Chair legs screech across the floor. A moment

later, Bay holds a steaming coffee cup under my nose. "Here," he says, smiling. "You look like you need it more than I do."

"How thoughtful of you," Alex grumbles.

Jesse grins from ear to ear. "Someone's jealous."

JJ's gaze travels over Bay's brawny body. "He should be." Seems like she no longer thinks he's a threat.

"Shut up," Alex barks.

I'm too tired for their childish argument and down the coffee at once.

Bay's eyes go wide. "Wow. You really did need it, huh?"

I shrug and face my best friend. "B, I need to talk to you." That's code for I got the stuff, and we can get right on it.

She draws a long, pained breath and nods. "Sure." She follows me to the door leading to the apartment.

Alex mutters something under his breath, but I refuse to listen to him. He thinks I don't care about George and the demon hunters trying to whack me. I let him. That way he won't get in my way.

"You're fucking crazy," Bonnie barks as I empty the bag on the small kitchen table.

"That's not news, B."

"No, Amanda. This isn't your normal crazy. This is...hell, it's..." She shakes her head wildly. "I can't believe I let you talk me into summoning a demon so he could possess me." It's a lot to ask of her. Even mambos who practice their craft wouldn't invite demons into them, but we're running out of time and options.

I rest my palms on her shoulders. She's terrified.

"Summoning a demon isn't crazier than invoking a reaper." Or so I hope.

She knits her brows. "What if this is exactly what the thing wants?"

To convince Bonnie of my plan, I had to tell her everything—the visons of the hellhound and the demon, Legend and Bay being Malleus Maleficarum hunters who think a Knight of Hell is trying to get his hands on me, and most importantly Anna isn't Alex's soulmate. She completely freaked. Then she tried to talk me out of it. Eventually, once the initial shock faded, she came to the conclusion all of it was connected. I agreed but still wanted to talk to the thing, and B never could say no to me.

"I guess we'll find out soon," I say, burning devil's claw. The musky scent fills the room, and I start lighting candles.

Bonnie sits cross-legged on the floor. "I really hope you know what you're doing." Her voice is deeper than ever. She's scared out of her wits. Don't blame her. Giving a demon power over yourself is horrifying.

I sit across from her, knees folded against my chest. "You're gonna be fine, B." Something tells me the thing won't harm her.

The scent of devil's claw crawls into every corner of the apartment. I wipe my watery eyes with the sleeve of my shirt and focus on Bonnie. Cat bones in her hand, she closes her eyes and tries to control her breath. In many ways, voodoo and traditional witchcraft are the same. Both require a helluva lot of concentration and a clear mind.

Bonnie's chest rises and falls slowly. "Ready?" she asks, eyes still closed.

My gaze darts to the door. *Shit, did I lock it?* The hunters downstairs—especially jerk-face—have no idea what Bonnie and I are up to. Geez, they'd kill me if they found out we're summoning a high-ranking demon in a hunter bar.

I want to get up and check the lock, but Bonnie starts the ritual before I can. "*Seyè a fènwa isit la lapriyè mwen. Pran sa yo kado mwen te fè pou ou. Monte kò sa a Mwen ofri ou.*" B speaking Creole is sorta weird. No matter how much she hates that part of her, there's no denying her power.

The air grows hot and damp as she keeps repeating the incantation. Hot shivers curve down my spine each time the spell crosses her lips. My throat tightens, and I feel like I'm sitting in a sauna cranked to 212 degrees.

The flames of the candles blaze higher. She says the spell one last time, throws the bones, and then it happens; Bonnie's irises disappear, and I gaze into a white void.

"Hello, love." It's not Bonnie's voice I hear. Nope, it's something much darker and creepier—the voice from the woods, from my nightmares. "I'm glad you finally called. I was beginning to think I overestimated your intelligence." When I don't say anything, the demon possessing my friend asks, "Why so quiet, love?"

I swallow the stone in my throat and straighten my numb spine. "Who the hell are you, and what the fuck do you want from me?" God, I sound so much stronger than I feel.

"Who I am doesn't matter," it says, getting on his—Bonnie's—knees. "To be or not to be is the question."

"Drop the Shakespeare act and answer me," I snap, opening some space between us.

Laughter floats through the tiny apartment. The demon gets up and circles around me. Its proximity raises hair all over my body. "C'mon, love," it finally says. "Use your brain. Why did you call upon me?"

I'm tempted to cut the creepy smile out of the dumb-ass thing's face. Too bad it happens to be my best friend's face. "I want to know what you want from me."

It flashes brilliant teeth. "No, you don't."

I cross my arms. "Yes, I do."

It shakes its head. "No, love. You really don't."

*Great.* This could go on for an eternity. "All right," I bark, determined to send the asshole back to hell. "Tell me Mr. Smarty-Pants, why do *you* think I summoned you?"

"I'll give you a little hint," it says, still circling me. "The reason I'm here has to do with a certain hunter." It flashes a smile. "Am I right, love?"

I keep quiet.

"Oh, c'mon, now. I'm right, aren't I?"

Not a word comes out of my mouth.

The thing stops in front of me and bends down to my ear. "There's really nothing you wouldn't do to save your hero, is there?"

I jump up. "Shut the fuck up!" I hadn't asked Bonnie to let that thing ride her because of Alex. I'd never—

"You can't deny what your heart wants." He approaches me like a lion stalking its prey. "I can smell your darkest desire, love." The thing winks. "It's one of my many talents."

I glare into the white mist covering Bonnie's eyes and see a reflection of Alex. "You honestly think I summoned you to get Alex out of his deal?" I snarl through gritted teeth. "I'm a witch. I don't make deals with demons like you."

Scorching fingers caress my cheek. "Is that so, love?"

I'm here because I want answers. I'm here because that thing is probably the reason a bunch of hunters are out for my blood. I'm here because—

*God, why am I really here?*

I couldn't expect to get information out of a high-ranking demon, could I? I mean, what the hell was I thinking? That the thing would be kind enough to supply some answers?

I ball my fists, clawing my nails into the heel of my hand. "Let's say you're right and I summoned you 'cause of Alex. Would you do it? Would you let him out of his deal?" Knights of Hell have the power to cancel a contract. I've never heard of one who did, though.

His fingers curl around the nape of my neck. "Oh love," it whispers. "Can't you see? There's nothing I wouldn't do for you." Boy, I thought I'd seen strange stuff, but talking to a demon who wears my best friend's body while hitting on me tops it all.

The sun-like heat radiating from the creature is too much. I step aside, hoping the thing will give me some room to catch my breath. Surprisingly, it does. I try to get a grip on my racing pulse before I gaze into the white mist clouding my best friend's eyes. "And what do you want in exchange for your help?" A demon never does anything out of the goodness of its heart.

Hell, I doubt they even have one.

The demon paces the room. "Does it matter?"

"Of course it fuckin' matters," I almost scream. "You're a goddamn demon."

"I know what I am." The thing's voice turns sour. "Yet, I am your only hope of saving him." It tilts its head to the side and studies me. "And to answer your question, I think you already know what I want," it says, a reflection of myself flickering across its eyes.

Fear squeezes my gut so tight, I feel like I'm dying. "Y-you want—"

"You," it says cheerfully. In the blink of an eye, the demon is in front of me. "Your soul in exchange for Alexander's."

I stumble back. My hip knocks into the table. "You're crazy," I yell.

It laughs. "Oh love, don't act so surprised. Deep down you already knew." It closes the gap between us and runs the back of its blazing hand over my cheek. "You should feel honored. I've never given up a soul, but for you…" Its lips brush the edge of my mouth. I shudder violently. "I'll make an exception."

Refusing to show him how scared I am, I stand my ground. "Why?"

It narrows its colorless eyes at me. "What do you mean, why?"

I cross my arms. "Why would you make an exception for me?"

It grins like a moron. "Let's just say your soul is much more interesting than the hunter's. What do you say?"

Dying and going to hell? Scratch that. Dying and going to purgatory—that's where rogue witches end up—is insane. "How about..." I press an index finger against my chin. "Oh yeah, no freakin' way!"

The stupid grin on its lips drives me mad. "We"—it points a finger between us—"both know this whole soulmate trip is pointless. Are you really willing to let Alexander be dragged to hell?" It draws closer. "Before you answer, you should know—hell has a special place for hunters, and it's not filled with virgins."

"Fuck you," I spit out, flipping him the middle finger. "I can protect him. You can't drag him to hell if you can't get to him, can you?"

The demon walks to the bed and sits down. "So feisty. Love it." Its gaze roams over me. "There's just a tiny problem, love. I don't need to get to him. He's already infected."

A muscle pops in my jaw. "Infected with what?"

It tilts its head to the side. "A slow-spreading poison."

"You're lying."

It cocks a brow. "Am I, love? You saw him cough blood and I'm fairly certain you spotted the black veins crawling all over his body, didn't you? I mean..." It smirks. "Do you really think I didn't anticipate you trying to protect him from the hellhound? Why do you think he was attacked before his time?"

Shit. There's not a trace of bullshit in what the thing says. Worse, it makes total sense. *What now?*

After a long pause, the demon says, "I reckon you thought about the effect this choice of yours will have on the creature you're so desperately trying to protect?"

My heart leaps in my chest as something that feels a lot like pure madness floods my system. I stalk toward the bastard. "Don't you ever talk about him.

You hear me?"

"Ah, there's nothing quite like the fury of a m—"

"Shut up!" I don't give a fuck if this is an upper-level demon or not. One more word, and I will rip its head off.

"Don't be so rude. Hear me out first." It draws closer. "It's my understanding you're hunted by the Malleus Maleficarum Order." The sudden change of topic catches me by surprise. "You see, love," it goes on, "these hunters are nothing like your precious Alex."

"So I've heard," I snarl. "Fail to see how this is any of your concern, though."

The demon folds its hands into a praying position. "Alexander told you what they did to the coven in Kansas?"

*Can demons be strangled?* "So?"

"What do you think they'll do to your sister and the little one?"

One simple question. Thirteen undemanding words. Yet they shatter my world like a sledgehammer. *They killed everyone. Even the kids.* That's what JJ said. It never occurred to me they might do the same to witches I know. Bonnie, her family, Melinda, Leandro—could their lives be in danger because of me? A sharp pain slices through my brain, and my heart throws a fit.

The demon strolls toward me. "I can help you out of this mess."

"H-How?" I stammer.

"Easy," it says, shrugging. "Trade your soul for Alexander's, and I'll sweeten the deal by promising your loved ones protection. No one will touch them. Not even Lucy himself."

I shiver uncontrollably. Before I can say anything, I hear footsteps. Someone's coming up the stairs

The thing's gaze darts to the door. "I think our little chat must come to an end, love." Gracefully it reaches for my hand. I want to pull back, but my body is completely numb. "Consider my offer. Should you accept it...well, you know how to find me."

My palm burns. "What the fuck are you doing?" I whine, the scent of scorched skin in my nostrils.

"Drawing you a map," it says seconds before Bonnie's eyes roll back in her head and JJ comes barging in.

"Someone hungry?" she asks.

Chapter 35

Silence. It wafts through the apartment like carbon monoxide—invisible, toxic, and absolutely lethal. I'm cowering on the windowsill all by myself. Took ages to convince Bonnie to join JJ and the rest of the gang downstairs. I was terrified she might have heard what the demon said, but she didn't. I did my best to convince her the creature had been less than helpful. After I swore an oath—crossing my fingers behind my back—she said, "Told you it was a bad idea."

Knees drawn up under my chin, I watch the edge of the woods. Moonlight slices through naked tree branches, and odd-looking shadows dance over the frozen soil. They remind me of that cheesy 90s movie with Patrick Swayze and Demi Moore, the one where the dude dies, but his soul can't move to the afterlife because his love's life is in danger. In the film, the shadows come for the ones destined to go to hell. Pretty ironic, huh?

*Hell.*
*Purgatory.*
*Hell.*
*Purgatory.*

It's all I can think about. I don't believe the demon lied when it said there's a special place for hunters in hell. Geez, I can't even begin to imagine what sick pain these creatures will inflict on Alex's soul. Maggots chewing on his eyeballs, vipers and reptiles slithering over his tortured body—those are the less cruel scenarios flickering across my mind. But purgatory? From what I've heard, it's ten times worse than hell. Created for creatures who abused their power—evil witches, demons, and every other supernatural being dumb enough to consort with malevolent forces during their lifetime. I can still see the terror in Isobelle's eyes when she spoke about the place where the bokor had trapped her soul. And the kid had been in purgatory for what—a day? Whereas I'd spend an eternity there if I accept the demon's offer.

*I'm screwed.*

Bonnie has her family. They'd protect each other. What about Melinda and Leandro? There's no doubt my sister would die trying to keep Leandro safe. She loves him more than she loves her own life.

Doesn't matter what she did, or how many times she slammed the door in my face pretending I don't exist, she's still my sister. More importantly, I, too, would rather give my life than see anything happen to Leandro. He's innocent. Never asked to be born into a screwed-up witch family. Never had a fucking choice in the matter.

*Damn it!*

My palm burns. I look at the sigil. It glows like burning coal. When I first examined it, I didn't immediately recognize it but was sure I'd seen it before. Now I know where. It was carved into Mister Sinister, the guy Alex thought I'd killed. I didn't. But I'm pretty sure I know who did. *The thing.*

I'd never needed a vision to confirm Anna isn't the one. Never needed the demon to tell me. Sure, the girl is sweet, and I have no doubt she fell head over heels for Alex. But he doesn't love her. Accepting the demon's offer would save him.

I'm selfish and reckless. I don't care about anyone but myself. Yet, I'm sitting here contemplating an eternity in purgatory and for what? A—

There's a faint knock on the door. "Manda?"

*Alex. Awesome. Thank you so much, God. You're too fuckin' kind today.*

I shove my burned palm between my knees and straighten. "Yeah?"

The door cracks open, and he shoves his head in. "You up?"

"No, Alex. You're talking to my spirit."

He walks over to the window. "Ever since we left Bay's, you've been acting weird." He doesn't sound pissed or anything. Just worried.

I can't tell him the truth. He'd kill me before he let me trade my soul for his. Neither can I lie to him. He'd smell my bullshit instantly.

"Hey." He scoops two fingers under my chin, forcing my head in his direction so we're eye to eye. "Talk to me." He tries to bribe me with puppy eyes. "Please?"

There's nothing to talk about. Nothing will change the reality tossed at my feet, and the longer I look into his eyes, the harder truth hits. I am selfish enough to let him live with the fact I traded my soul for his. I am reckless enough to strike a deal with a demon, consequences be damned. And yes, I do only care about myself. So much so, I don't give a shit about how anyone feels as long as I won't lose them.

"Alex?"

He smiles. "Hm?"

I shift closer, soaking in his scent. "You remember what you said in that closet at Amelia's?"

He squints. "I said a lot of things."

I suck in some air, getting ready to jog his memory. "About how you want to spend the last night of your life?"

A deep understanding flickers across his gaze. "Manda, you're freaking me—"

"Shh," I say, curling my fingers around the nape of his neck and pulling him down. "No more talking." I stare into his sparkling eyes, drowning in them. "Okay?"

His lips part, but I claim them before a single word can leave his delicious mouth. I find his tongue, and he roars like a hungry panther. Every time I've been near him, I held back. Persuaded myself what we had was wrong. But when the world around you goes up in flames, what difference does another scorch mark make?

He slips a hand under my shirt.

"Don't stop," I order when he stills just under my bra.

He doesn't. He traces my left nipple, causing all sorts of explosions in my belly.

We kiss, more passionate than ever. Our tongues explore each other as if it's the first time they met. It's then I realize he wasn't kidding when he said this is the way he would want to spend the last night of his life. I know, because it's exactly how I want to spend mine.

My mouth leaves his. "Alex?" I whimper, breathless.

He presses his forehead against mine. "Amanda?"

My head flies back as he pinches my nipple, and for a fraction of a second, I forget what I'm so desperate to say. "You know," he whispers with that smoky-as-hell voice of his. "I'm not sure what caused *this*, but I think I like it."

My heart freezes. He wouldn't like it. He'd hate me more than he already does. I run my fingers through his wild hair. And then I remember what I need him to hear. What I so urgently need to say. "Getting in that car with you and your brother was the biggest mistake of my life." His eyes go wide, and he tries to pull back, but I hold him hostage. "But I'd do it again, Alex. In a heartbeat."

An emotion I can't quite read passes through his beautiful eyes. An emotion he doesn't give me enough time to decipher, 'cause all of a sudden, he lifts me from the windowsill and carries me to the bed.

He climbs on top of me. And when he kisses me again, the roughness and need change into a soft longing. I don't think I've ever been kissed like that. Like I'm precious and worthy. Like I'm being loved for who I am rather than what I look like.

The hardest part of him presses against the softest part of me. Clothes come off until our damp flesh melts against each other.

"Fuck," he moans into my mouth, his hand trembling as he traces my wetness. "There's nothing like it." He pauses and his eyes lock with mine. "There's nothing like you."

Consumed by him, my noggin hits the headboard as I enjoy the delight his fingers cause between my legs. Bonnie kept saying I needed to stop comparing every guy to Alex. How could I? If your life has been touched by magic, you can't go back to pretending it doesn't exist.

What comes next is nothing like last night. He gently dives inside me. No hate between us. No fury or rage. The world around us freezes in a moment of unspoken emotion. There isn't a part of me he doesn't touch with his lips. Not a part of him I don't explore with my hands. Our hands stay locked as we move to the rhythm of our in-sync hearts.

*Love is for children.*

But sometimes even Amanda Bishop luxuriates in child's play.

## Chapter 36

I park JJ's car—the one I hot-wired last night with the help of wikiHow—in my sister's driveway and rest my head against the steering wheel. I'm exhausted. Need a minute to gather the last resources of energy. After Alex and I spent most of the night worshipping each other, he fell asleep in my arms. For a while, I just lay next to him, watching him. Then I did something I never thought I'd do—I took a strand of his hair and performed the soulmate ritual Melinda had given us. It took everything I had to go through with it, but I had to be certain accepting the demon's offer was my only shot. I mean, who would voluntarily go to purgatory without testing every possibility? The result was exactly what I'd expected—the smoke stayed as black as night. My last hope to get out of this mess went up in flames, and I did the only thing I could; I wrote Alex a quick note, saying something like *Sorry, but you were right. I do only care about myself.* Then I switched my phone off, got in the car, and drove to Salem, because before I surrender my soul, I have to warn my sister of the Malleus Maleficarum Order.

I yank the door open, get out of the car, and walk to the porch. I don't fear my sister's reaction. Fear is newly defined when you're about to be shipped to purgatory.

Melinda opens the door before I can ring the bell.

Her eyes are red and swollen. She looks like she's been up all night crying. I've never seen her like this. Between the two of us, she'd always been the one who had a tight lid on her emotions. Geez, she didn't even sob as ugly when her husband of a day was slaughtered. "You've done some crazy things, Amanda," she croaks. "But *this*...it's suicide."

Spirits can be real fucking snitches. I manage a half-hearted smile. "All right, Miss *Long Island Medium*. Who told you?" Melinda is probably the closest thing there is to a real *Ghost Whisperer*. She has a direct line to the other side, and, apparently, the dead are just as engaged in gossip as the living.

"You have to ask?" she murmurs, choking back a fresh burst of tears.

*Thanks, Grams.*

A silent moment passes. I glare at the wind chime above the door, the swing on the porch—anything to keep my gaze off her.

Melinda moves toward me. I half expect her to slap or kick me. Instead, she does something that scares the living shit outta me. She fucking hugs me. And not like she has to, to keep up the picture-prefect family façade. Nope, she pulls me into a real sisterly embrace.

"You're suffocating me," I grumble, barely able to breathe.

"I'm sorry," she whispers, tears spilling down her cheeks.

Okay, that's enough. I wiggle out of her grip and stare at her. Her messy red hair cascades down over her shoulders. She wears yoga pants, and don't even get me started on the old UMass football shirt. "Who are you? Dr. Jekyll and Mrs. fuckin' Hyde?"

She raises her brows. "Language, Amanda."

*Nope. Still good old Melinda.*

She takes my hand and pulls me inside. "Bonnie called," Melinda informs me as we reach the living room.

My heart flutters. "Did you...did you tell her?"

Her gaze drops to her faux fur, mid-calf snow boots. "I wanted to, but I couldn't."

A rock lifts off my chest. Bonnie would raise hell if she knew my plan. Worse, she'd tell Alex, and he...well, I think he'd decapitate the demon and me.

"You have to call her, Amanda. She's worried sick."

I bet she is, and I will call her. *Just not now.*

I feel something soft under my foot. It's the plush tiger cup I'd sent Leandro last Christmas. "Where is he?" I ask, picking it up.

A lukewarm smile tugs at her lips. "Upstairs. It's nap time."

"Good," I murmur. I don't think I have the heart to see him.

Melinda pivots. "I'll get us some coffee and then you tell me everything, okay?"

Coffee? Since when does she have coffee in the house? I'd ask, but she's already gone. I had plenty of time to play this out in my mind. Me showing up here, Melinda being all disappointed and giving me one of her "you're a disgrace to our family" speeches, but never in my wildest dreams did I anticipate her being so freaking nice to me. I swear it gives me the fucking willies.

Pacing up and down the living room, I stop at the only picture of myself in this house. It was taken by my dad, just months before he fell down the stairs after he'd killed three whiskey bottles. The funny thing is, high-functioning alcoholics don't usually have balance issues. At least, my dad never had any. Then again there's a first for everything.

I trace the silver frame and study the photo. Melinda and me on the porch, holding each other's hands. Back then we were inseparable. Everyone called us the Bishop twins. Melinda was two years older, but that didn't stop us from doing everything together. Hard to believe if you look at us today.

"Do you still take sugar?" she asks, putting a tray with fresh brewed coffee on the table.

I grab a cup. "Just black."

She takes a seat, gracefully crossing her legs. "Tell me everything," she orders.

Of course, I don't tell her everything. She'd have a fucking stroke if I did. I focus on the part about the hunter Order and only mention the demon briefly.

Her face turns red, then green and eventually loses all its color. "M-Malleus Maleficarum?" she stammers. "Are you sure?"

I lean against the wall and cock a brow. "You've heard of them?"

She barely manages to nod. "They killed the Kansas coven last year."

"Yeah. Yeah, they did."

The cup in her hand trembles. "And you're certain they're hunting you?"

"One hundred percent. Which is why"—can't believe I'm going to say this—"you need to take Leandro and stay at Mom's place."

Her eyes go wide and the porcelain cup slips

through her fingers, shattering on the hardwood floor. "You want me to go to Mom?" She doesn't pay attention to the spilled coffee, which means she's on the brink of a nervous breakdown. Even Melinda knows what a bitch our mother is.

I bite on my lip. "Look, I hate to say it, but you'll be safer at Mom's." Mother Dearest might be the worst kind of parent, but she's a damn powerful witch. Like me, she isn't just blessed with one gift. The woman has many talents, including making her kids' lives living hell.

More tears wet her cheeks. "That's why you're doing it, isn't it? Not just for Alex, but for—"

"Stop," I snap, holding my hand up. "I'm not a hero, M. I have my own selfish reasons to strike a deal with the thing. Don't get confused about me looking out for anyone else but myself, okay?"

Melinda rubs her temples. "Do you have any idea what happens to witches who sell their souls?" she asks, shoulders sinking, eyes hooded.

I flash her a smile. "I'd say they get hotter, but I doubt I'd be legal if that was the case."

"Amanda." The softness in her voice is gone. Raw anger takes over. "This isn't a game. Grams said there is no way out if you accept the offer."

"Did she?" I wonder what else Grams told her.

"There must be another way," she says, more to herself than me. "Together, we'd stand a chance against the Malleus Maleficarum Order."

*Maybe, but Alex would still go to hell.*

"Amanda?" She squeezes my arm. "Please think about this. You know what Mom saw before you were born."

357

How could I ever forget? She reminded me daily. "I guess it's about time I live up to my reputation as Satan's bride."

We stare at each other in uncomfortable silence.

After some time, she rises to her feet. "I know you want to save Alexander, but—"

I stop her. "Don't. I've made up my mind, and there's—"

"Nothing that can stop you," she finishes. "I know that. Grams was very clear about that last night. But what about Leandro?"

A bitter taste crawls up my throat. Of course, she'd play her only good card. I didn't expect anything less of her. Melinda and I might be as different as the sun and the moon, but in situations like this, it's obvious we share the same blood. "What about him?" I say.

Melinda frowns. "What happens when he grows up and learns the truth?"

Tears burn the back of my eyelids. I blink them away. Plunking down on the couch, I rest my head against a soft pillow. "I'm not here to hear you preach to me, M. Just thought I should give you a heads-up on that hunter club." Okay, I also need the "To Summon a Knight of Hell" spell from the grimoire.

Her eyes narrow into two slits. "You've always been stubborn, Amanda."

"Damn right," I yawn, as lack of sleep finally catches up with me.

**** 

Four Hours To Hell.

I almost have a heart attack when I open my eyes. It's a little after eight p.m. Four hours to midnight. Four hours to purgatory. Fuck. How long did I sleep, and why didn't Melinda wake me? I can't do the ritual before midnight, but still.

I get on wobbly feet. The house smells like apple and cinnamon, and the sweetest sound echoes off the walls—laughter. Child's laughter. My heart does a somersault.

Hypnotized, I stroll to the kitchen. A dozen apple pies are lined up on the counter, and Leandro sits on a high chair next to them. The second he lays eyes on me, he smiles like the Cheshire cat and stretches his tiny hands toward me. "Dadada…Mam…Mam…Ma."

Melinda looks over her shoulder and smiles. "You should be honored," she says, wiping flour off her face. "He never smiles when it's bedtime."

I came in here to yell at Melinda 'cause she didn't wake me. The second I saw Leandro, I forgot all about it. I let him grab my hand. "Hey," I say, staring at him in amazement. "You grew so big." The last time I saw him, he'd been a toddler, barely the size of a watermelon.

Melinda snickers. She hasn't snickered since…I can't even remember the last time she did. Shouldn't surprise me. Being a mother changes people. "He loves spinach," she explains, pointing to a glass of green baby food.

Running my hand over his soft, dark-brown hair, I smile. "I'm sure he does."

Leandro's big shamrock-colored eyes lock with mine. God, he looks so much like his dad, it's scary. Same eyes. Same smile. Even the same lips. I just hope he didn't inherit the same wit.

Baby boy plays with my fingers, inspecting each one with great care. Then he moves on to my rings.

"You dig jewelry, huh?"

Melinda raises her brows. "Actually, he loves everything shiny and sparkling. If I didn't know better, I'd say he's a fairy in disguise."

He laughs and pounds his tiny hands against the high chair. The delightful sound pierces my heart. I always thought I'd leave this world without regret, but when I look at him, I see something I will never have—unconditional love. Not to be melodramatic or anything, but it feels a bit like drowning in a green ocean of missed chances.

As if he can sense my pain, he looks at me with those big eyes and tilts his head to the side. "Nana...Dada...Ma...."

"He's very sensitive," Melinda says, seeing the surprised expression on my face.

I force a smile. "Yeah, well, I wonder where he gets that from."

An alarm goes off, and Melinda rushes to the oven to rescue yet another pie. "Hey," she says, pulling it out. "Can you take him upstairs?" She eyes Leandro, and uses a baby voice. "It's way past his bedtime."

Leandro giggles at the sound. Melinda might be a rotten sister, but she's a good mother to him.

"I don't know." I wipe my sweaty palms on my jeans. "I'm not exactly the lullaby type." I don't think I even know one.

Melinda waves the comment off. "Never mind. He's more of a Metallica kid."

A proud smile crosses my lips. "You've got taste, baby boy."

Melinda rolls her eyes. "I wonder where he gets that from," she says, throwing my own words back at me.

I face Leandro. "Definitely not your father."

Leandro throws his head back and laughs as if he truly understood the meaning of those words.

"C'mon." Melinda puts the pie next to the others. "Take him up."

Part of me wants to say no. Then he smiles at me, and even a wicked witch like me can't escape his magic. "Let's go," I say, lifting his petite body out of the chair. "I'm gonna introduce you to some real music, little man."

Once we're in his room, I take a seat on the rocking chair in the corner and hum "Renegade." His big eyes grow heavy with sleep, and by the end of the song, he's drifted into the land of dreams.

I sit there for a while, rocking back and forth, watching him sleep peacefully in my arms. There's a weird energy around him. Something strong and fierce. The aura of a fighter.

Running the palm of my hand over his rosy cheeks, I bend over him. "You won't remember this," I whisper, careful not to wake him. "But I still need you to hear it."

He shifts in my arms, snuggling against me.

"I know you never asked to be born a witch, baby boy. But no matter what anyone says, don't ever let them make you feel less worthy because of what you are." I curl my fingers around his. "You hear me? You're not defined by magic. You *are* magic."

I kiss him on the forehead, and twenty minutes later, I put him in his crib and stroll to Gram's library.

Grabbing pen and paper, I fling myself in the armchair next to the large front window. I suck at writing letters, but this one needs written and at some point read.

"Is he asleep?" Melinda asks when I walk back into the kitchen.

I nod and pull myself up on the counter, shoving the envelope under her nose. "Hey," I murmur. "Can you give this to Alex?"

She says nothing, takes the letter, and puts it in Gram's favorite drawer.

"You expecting guests?" I ask, pointing to the pies.

She sighs. "I just needed some distraction."

I glare at the clock above the door. It's only quarter past nine. "Need some help?" I, too, could use a little distraction.

She throws a towel my way. "The dishes won't dry themselves."

Chapter 37

*Thirty minutes to hell*

I stand in front of the Old Burying Point Cemetery, the piece of paper with the summoning ritual held against my chest, and glare at the large sign behind the spiked iron fence. It reads: The Burying Point 1637. The Oldest Burying Ground in the City of Salem. Six names of people who had been buried here are written under the heading. Amongst them is no other than the famous John Hathorne, one of the ruthless judges in the Salem witch trials. I could have gone to any cemetery with a crossroad, but I figured, why not piss off the spirit of a man who not only harshly questioned my great-great-great-great-grandmother Bridget Bishop, but had also been responsible for her execution? Hathorne and others had been convinced Bridget consorted with the devil. She hadn't. Her only crime had been her fun-loving, independence-seeking nature. She was executed on Gallows Hill. It's fitting that over three hundred years later, a Bishop witch will consort with a demon right next to the asshole's grave, and there's nothing he can do about it.

*Karma, baby. Karma.*

I hum "Renegade," pull my phone out of my jacket, and switch it on. Half an hour to midnight. More than enough time to prepare the ritual and give Bonnie a buzz. I'm not sure what to say to her, but I need to call her. She's been by my side for as long as I can remember. The least I can do—now that I'm about to be shipped to purgatory—is say goodbye.

Dialing her number, I try to even out my breath. Each time I inhale, it feels like I'm drawing in fire.

Bonnie picks up on the first ring. "Amanda!" she shouts into the phone.

"Is that her?" Alex barks in the background.

"Shut up," Bonnie hisses to him. "Where the fuck are you? Have you gone mad? How can you just disappear like that? Oh my God, are you okay? Is this about the hunters on your tail? Did they find you? Are you…are you hurt?" She talks fast, throwing question after question at me.

"I'm okay," I assure her as she pauses to take a breath.

"You're *o-kay*?" She sounds like she's about to reach through the phone to strangle me. "Is that all you have to say? Do you have the slightest idea what's happening here? Alex is coughing up blood, Jesse is close to a nervous breakdown and I've been worried sick."

Digging my nails into the cell, I sigh deeply. "Listen, B, I know you're mad at me for leaving, but I *really* don't want to fight with you right now."

She falls silent. I think she stopped breathing altogether.

"What's she saying?" Alex inquires. He sounds less than happy. "Bonnie, what is going on?"

Hearing his voice only hurts, so I say, "I'm just calling to let you know I'm all right."

"Amanda," she whispers. "You're freaking me

out." The edge in her voice is gone. Anger turns into deep-rooted concern.

I could tell her the truth. They'd never make it here in time, but I don't have it in me. "Where are you?"

She doesn't answer right away. "At Anna's. I'm about to perform the ritual. Alex isn't well." She pauses. "Where are *you*?"

*In front of a freaking cemetery, about to trade my soul.* "Here and there and everywhere."

"Stop it," she yells, frustrated. "I'm not in the mood for games. You took off in the middle of the night, stole a hunter's car, switched off your goddamn phone, and now you're giving me cryptic answers?"

"I'm annoying like that," I say, a smile on my face. "Only reason I'm calling, B, is to tell you I'm okay, and to let JJ know she gets her car back *ASAP*."

"Who cares about some stupid car? Just tell me what's going on!"

"Give me the damn phone," Alex shouts. "Amanda?" His voice vibrates through my brain.

I'm tempted to hang up, but I can't. "Alex," I say as calmly as possible.

"Where are you?" He's fury incarnated.

"None of your business."

"Are you fucking serious?" He blows out a long breath. "You run off after...after we..."

"Slept with each other?" I offer. He clearly can't say the words.

He's quiet for a moment, gasping for air. "Why are you doing this?"

*I can't let you or anyone else die, that's why.* "Because I'm selfish, Alex. Don't act as if that comes as a surprise. I'll always put myself ahead of others."

"You're lying," he snaps. "Why would you put your new life on hold to help me, only to walk away after...after..."

Not being able to articulate we had sex seems to have become an ugly habit of his. "After we shared a bed? After we screwed each other like we had so many times before? After what, Alex? You think because we spent two more lousy nights together, I'll change my ways?" I laugh bitterly. "God, and here I thought you had a freaking brain."

"I know what you're doing," he says, much calmer than before. "It's not working, Amanda. I won't let you walk away like last time."

I laugh harder. "Oh my gosh, you're clearly out of your fuckin' mind, Alex. I mean, dude, you're at that Anna chick's place, hoping she's your soulmate, yet you're telling me you won't let me walk away?" I exhale sharply. "See the mistake?"

"Manda," he says in a hushed tone. "I'm here because you are gone. I'm here because you didn't give me a chance to ask for your blood. I'm here because you walked away before I could find out if we're—"

"We're not, Alex."

"Amanda, please."

This is going nowhere. If anything, it hurts, and since my soul will be tortured enough in purgatory, I will not put more pain on myself. "I gotta go, Alex. I'm sorry if I mislead you, but I always figured you didn't believe in fairytales."

He mutters something. I end the call and switch off my phone. Enough has been said. It's time for action.

A shadow of my former self, I walk to the iron gate, thinking of the nightmares that tormented me for weeks. *Abandon all hope, ye who enter here, huh?* It's not hard to leave the bitch called hope behind.

The wind rattles dead leaves as my old Gringo boots toil through the wiry, grassed-over burial ground. Pale moonlight sheds light on gravestones ranging round the edges like a row of watchful gray figures. Bonnie and I used to make fun of chicks in horror flicks dumb enough to walk right into such a trap. Guess the joke's on me.

Clinging to the ritual in my hand like a drowning man holds onto his life jacket, I walk deeper into the land of the dead. Fear and despair bite through my skin as I gasp for air. God, I'm pathetic.

A pair of watchful orange eyes looks down on me. The nocturnal creature doesn't move, but its hoot echoes through the night, a harbinger of death.

I quicken my pace, moving straight for the center of the cemetery. Once I get to the crossroad, I put the paper on the ground and go to work. Starting with the salt and juniper circle, I follow the instructions precisely. Lighting twelve black candles and one red? Check. Tracing the sigil burned into my palm with a knife? Check. Drawing the same sigil into the ground at the center of the circle with my blood? Check.

All I gotta do now is focus on the demon and say the spell. Easy-peasy.

I kneel, concentrate all my energy on that thing, and start the chant. "In this night and in this hour, I call upon the darkest power. Come to me, I summon thee. Come to me, I set you free." I'm about to repeat the incantation, but there's no need.

"Hello, love." The familiar creepy voice says.

It takes a few moments before I find the lady-balls

to turn around, but when I do, I stand taller than ever. "What's with you and that love shit? You British or something?"

The demon looks less like a thing and more like a Calvin Klein model—amber eyes, a body like Matthew Noszka, and a face so striking, there's no one I can compare it to. It grins. "Let's just say I have a thing for the island."

"Whatever," I grumble. "That your real face?"

It winks. "Just a vessel, love. Do you like it?"

"The vessel? Sure. You? Not so much."

The demon smiles. "I assume you finally came to your senses?" it says, brimming with confidence.

All I wanna do is use the knife in my hand and drive it through the thing's black heart. Instead, I cross my arms and curl my lips. "How about we just cut the crap?"

The demon pivots around me. "Why in such a hurry, love? We have an eternity ahead of us." I flinch at the prospect of an eternity with this bastard. "I must admit," the demon goes on. "I didn't think you'd really come. You are, after all, the most selfish of all the Bishop witches."

A demon calling me selfish? That's a contradiction at best. Having had enough of the thing, I ball my fists. "Destroy Alex's contract, and I will sign mine."

A mischievous smile tugs at the bastard's lips. "I'm afraid, love, that's not quite how this will work."

I'm about to go to purgatory; the thing really shouldn't fuck with me right now. "Then how will it work?"

Devilish laughter echoes through the night. "Before you can sign, I'm required to make sure you understand the terms of this bargain."

I cock a brow. "Why, is hell scared I'll sue them?"

"What can I say? The boss is very accurate when it comes to deals."

Great. "Satan is a lawyer?"

He grins. "Would that surprise you?"

"Hm…let's see. Manipulative, deceptive, and arrogant?" I shrug. "Nah, not really."

It reaches into its jacket and pulls out something. It kinda looks like…skin? Oh my gosh, it *is* skin, and there's writing on it. I stumble back.

The demon smiles at my shocked expression. "I'm trying real hard to get the boss to use iPads instead of these"—he holds the skin up in the air—"old-fashioned human remains."

I wish I had a snarky comment on the tip of my tongue, but I'm too busy wondering what the fuck I'm doing here.

The bastard glares at the skin. "So," it says. "You're here to trade your soul for Alexander Remington's. That right, love?" It gives me a look. "Please answer with yes or no."

I roll my eyes. "Yes." The second the word leaves my lips, a spot on the skin ignites. Only lasts a few seconds, then the sparks are gone.

"Very good." The demon nods approvingly. "Moving on. Are you, Amanda Caroline Bishop, fully aware that your soul, hereafter, will be mine and mine only?"

I suck in air, already pissed as hell. "Yes."

More sparks fly over the skin. The demon keeps babbling on about how I can never share these terms and conditions with anyone, how the contract would be void if I fail to keep my end of the bargain, and so on.

Had I known how dry selling your soul was, I would have brought aspirin and Uno. Having no other choice, I keep saying yes to everything he throws my way.

The demon flashes me a brilliant smile. "Good girl. Moving on to the most important condition."

I raise my brows. "Never try to seduce the boss?" I shouldn't joke, but it's either that or screaming.

It gives me a sinister look. "No, love. In order to trade places with Alex, you must give up your right to be reclaimed."

My jaw drops. "What? Are you insane? That must be against every freakin' law between heaven and hell."

It taps his foot impatiently. "Not if you voluntarily agree to it."

I shake my head. "No way."

The thing turns around. "Well then, I should be going. I do after all have a soul to claim."

It walks away and takes with him every rational thought I ever had. "Wait," I shout. "I'll do it."

It turns around and grins. "That's what I thought." The demon runs its hand through its shiny black hair and announces the last terms. They're pretty much a mixture of you will do as I say and never question me, and in exchange Alex and everyone you love will be safe. I agree to all of them.

"Very good, Amanda. Step out of the circle."

*Fuck.* I do.

The Knight of Hell hands me an athame. "Sign here," it says, pointing to the only free spot on the skin.

I close my eyes. Melinda was right. I've done a lot of stupid-ass things, but this tops them all. I slice my finger open and let the blood drop onto the contract. The second the crimson liquid connects with the skin, it *puffs* into flames.

"Welcome to the family," the demon says as I glare at my burning future.

My belly cramps, and I can hardly breathe. "How long do I have?"

It narrows its eyes. "What do you mean?"

Everyone knows that a deal with a demon comes with a time stamp. Some get years before they rot in hell (or like in my case, purgatory), others only months. "How much time do I have before I die?"

"Die?" It laughs. "You think you will die?"

*What the hell is so funny?* "Dude, are you on crack?"

"Not now, no." It swallows the laughter. "Don't tell me you didn't know?"

My heart beats faster than it should, and I'm close to a cardiac arrest. "What don't I know?"

The demon is close enough, its sulfur breath beats against my cheeks. "Witches who make deals don't die, Amanda." It steps back. "They become our whores, bound to do hell's bidding."

My heart fails me. "What?" I scream, more terrified than I've ever been.

The demon winks. "Sorry, love, did I not mention that?" The thing strokes my temple. "Don't worry. I already have the prefect job for you."

As I stand there, gazing into the demon's fiery amber eyes I realize two things. One: my mother had been right all along. I am about to become a dark queen. Two: I'd sign that damn deal all over again if it meant Alex lives a happy, hell-free life.

Nadine Nightingale

## A word about the author…

A passionate reader and writer, addicted to the dark side of the craft, Nadine grew up with Marvel heroes and horror films. She loves stories that challenge gender stereotypes, religious beliefs, and tackle topics such as racism and cultural differences in an entertaining way. Nadine has a BA in Comparative Religions and studied Creative Writing at the University of Oxford. If she isn't traveling the world, she's reading, writing, or watching movies.

Thank you for purchasing
this publication of The Wild Rose Press, Inc.

If you enjoyed the story, we would appreciate your
letting others know by leaving a review.

For other wonderful stories,
please visit our on-line bookstore at
www.thewildrosepress.com.

For questions or more information
contact us at
info@thewildrosepress.com.

The Wild Rose Press, Inc.
www.thewildrosepress.com

Stay current with The Wild Rose Press, Inc.

Like us on Facebook

https://www.facebook.com/TheWildRosePress

And Follow us on Twitter
https://twitter.com/WildRosePress